Copyright 2022 Cal Clement
All Rights Reserved

The characters and events portrayed within are fictitious. Any similarities to real persons, alive or dead, is coincidental and not intended by the author.

No part of this book may be reproduced or stored in a retrieval system or transmitted in any form or by any means, electronic, mechanical, photocopying, recording or otherwise without express written permission of the author.

ISBN-978-1-7376655-3-3

Cover Artist: Juan Padron
Printed in the United States of America

This book is dedicated to my daughter, Cerena Johnson. Never lose the fire in your heart.

"Damnation seize my soul if I give quarter to you, or take any for myself."
-Captain Edward 'Blackbeard' Teach

RESURRECTING THE MAIDEN

by Cal Clement

PART ONE
"THE SEAS RUN HIGH"

Chapter 1

Pirate Cove
18 Apr 1809

Lilith awoke with her head cradled in the lap of a young Spanish woman. Pain rolled over her in waves as warm blood seeped from a laceration that extended from the edge of her scalp, over her eye, and across her cheek to her jawline. The rain intensified, driving big droplets through a heavy wind until they impacted with a slap. Smoke mixed with the rain mist over the surface of the cove. Her head and neck throbbed. She fought to keep her eyes open, grasping for consciousness like the handle of a knife just out of reach. A woman's voice spoke over her. It was the girl holding her head. Lilith couldn't understand her at first. She fought her eyes open. The eyes that looked down at her were big and beautiful, deep brown and framed in lashes that seemed almost as long as her eyelids.

Her jaw was prominent and strong looking, and Lilith was in awe of her high cheekbones. The girl spoke again, but in Lilith's pounding head, all she could make out were deep muffled tones and a high ringing. She looked up at the girl and their eyes met. Confusion and fear crossed her expression. The girl gently pulled her thighs from beneath Lilith's head and eased it to the ground. Confused and afraid herself, Lilith fought through her pain to crane her neck to keep the girl in her sight. She watched her stand, raising her hands in front of her shoulders in a surrendering gesture. A shiver crept through Lilith's body, quaking from the chilly wind and driving rain. She wondered who this girl was surrendering to. Lilith rolled her head onto its side, pulling her chin downward towards her chest. Blood occluded her vision, stinging her eyes. Lilith lifted an arm to her face and attempted a clumsy wipe to clear the blood from her sight. Sand stuck to her everywhere. Her eyes burned and her neck ached. The throbbing in her head made her feel ill, and she fought back the urge to retch as she lifted her head from the sand.

Walking up the beach with a sword in hand was Chibs. His eyes were wide with a bewildered look. His off arm was tucked against his belly. She could see the forearm had several wounds that were dripping dark blood. Lilith felt her chill replaced by a warm rush as her vision blurred with tears. Chibs remained focused behind her, his sword hand raised and pointed over Lilith's shoulder.

Confusion swept over her again. The ringing faded in her ears. Lilith could feel Chibs speak as much as hear him.

"Who are you? Why are you here?" His face was twisted in a menacing grimace. Lilith turned, twisting her torso to look at the girl who had been cradling her head moments ago.

"My name is Emilia. I came to this cove because the man who murdered my father came to us after escaping from that ship." The girl pointed over to the mouth of the cove where the hulks of both the H.M.S Valor and H.M.S Destiny were being battered against the rocky shore.

Chibs raised an eyebrow and looked down at Lilith, then back up to Emilia. "Why come here?"

Emilia's voice was unwavering. "I came to find the crew who failed at killing him the first time. I thought I could help you finish your work. From the looks of it, I was wrong."

A bolt of admiration lit through Lilith's veins. She looked at Chibs, who turned over his shoulder to throw a glance at the Drowned Maiden as her hull slipped further beneath the cove's surface. "She's not wrong, Chibs. We must be a sorry sight."

Chibs lowered his sword a little. "Aye Cap'n, I suppose she has a point."

"If she meant me any harm, she would have let me drown in the cove, Chibs. She didn't. As far as I'm concerned, if she wants to give herself to the Maiden, let her."

Emilia stepped around Lilith's shoulder. "You're the Captain?" Her eyes were wide in shock.

"I am…" Lilith replied, as Emilia knelt next to her again.

"Your eye." Emilia extended her hands toward Lilith. Lilith could tell she didn't want to say what she was thinking.

"Is it still there? I can't see out of it." Lilith asked, realizing for the first time that her field of vision had been cut in half.

"It is there. But there is a cut through it." Emilia tore a strip of white cloth from the bottom of her shirt. "Let me bandage it." She carefully wrapped Lilith's head with the strip, covering a portion of her forehead along with her wounded eye.

"Chibs." Lilith called for the old sea dog's attention, while Emilia tended to her wound.

"Yes Cap'n?" Chibs stood with sword still in hand, scanning over the cove.

"Trina?" Lilith could barely speak the name.

Chibs' gaze fell back onto Lilith. His shoulders gave way and his head slumped toward his chest. "The last I saw, she leapt from the mast as it was going over. I didn't see her again."

Emilia tied the strip of cloth together behind Lilith's neck. "The woman who jumped from the mast was struck by it. I watched the surface. She did not come back up." Her voice was flat. "There are others who swam from the wreckage. We should go, gather your survivors and get them inland in case that ship sends a landing party to search out survivors."

Lilith pulled away. "Trina…"

"Is dead." Emilia interrupted. "We need to keep the rest of your crew from suffering the same fate."

Lilith felt a chill creep through her bones and a spark of resentment light in her belly. She looked at Chibs, hoping he would refute the girl's advice. "She's right, Cap'n. Trina is gone, but that warship is not. If they send a landing party, we'll be fish in a barrel here on the beach. Let's gather who we can and get ourselves inland."

Chibs sheathed his sword and extended a hand to Lilith. She took it and he pulled her to her feet. "Is it too late for the Maiden Chibs?"

Chibs grimaced and looked back to their ship. She was listing to one side, her keel was bare to the world as the stern heeled toward the cove's sandy bottom. "Too soon to tell Cap'n. But she may well be too far gone. I suppose we could see if any of her is salvageable once the damned Navy leaves."

The winds began to slack as Lilith, Emilia, and Chibs made their way around the cove's beach. Along their trek, Chibs stopped several times to help crew members that had made it to shore. Lilith noticed that Chibs' off hand was mangled in deep cuts, contorting his fingers into unnatural positions. Blood dripped from the hand and large forearm above it. She wondered if Chibs would have been spared the wound had he not taken the time to heave her from the deck of Drowned Maiden before the cannon fire had decimated her.

"Chibs. Your arm..." Lilith raised her concern.

"Not to worry, my dear. It's just a few scratches and splinters. Old Chibsy will heal up." The old sailor interrupted. On the beach ahead of them, several of the surviving crew members huddled around in a group. "I'm sure there are others in more dire condition than I am."

As Lilith, Chibs, and Emilia approached the group, a woman's voice cried out in an agonized wail. Chibs' stride quickened. Lilith could see Dr. LeMeux in the center of the gathering, kneeling in the wet sands of the beach. Chibs pushed his way past the first line of crewmen standing in the group and disappeared from Lilith's sight for a moment. Lilith followed and was struck by the sight of Dr. LeMeux and Jilhal kneeling next to the lifeless body of one of the freed slave women that had come aboard the Maiden from the Gazelle, the same ship they had been freed from. Dr. LeMeux held two fingers to the victim's neck. He looked up and found Lilith's gaze locking with his own. The doctor slowly shook his head from side to side. Jilhal cried harder, cradling the dead woman's hand in her lap.

Lilith fought the tears welling in her eyes as she rose her voice over the crowd. "We have to go." Every eye in the group turned to her. "That warship will send their small boats to search for and kill survivors. We can't be here when they make landfall. We must go. Now."

Chibs led the way with Emilia hot on his heels.

The crew began to file in behind them, leaving Lilith, Dr. LeMeux and Jilhal. Dr. LeMeux began to reach his arms beneath the dead woman's body. Lilith stopped him with a hand on his shoulder. "There is no time, Doctor." A look of defeat crossed Dr. LeMeux's face. His eyes were watery and red.

"How many more must die, Lilith?" The doctor's voice dripped with disdain.

Lilith felt a pang of guilt, followed by a slow rise of irritation. She had never been fond of the doctor and he knew it. "As few of ours as I can manage, doctor. And as many of theirs as it takes." Her voice grew colder with each syllable. "Into the tree line, now, before they send landing parties and we add even more to our count."

The group of them left the beach and ducked into thick growth beneath an overarching canopy where the white sands met lush vegetation. Ahead of them the forest seemed an impenetrable maze of branches, bushes and vines. Lilith pressed into the darkened woods with only thin fingers of daylight already softened by the storm clouds above to light the way. The air was thick. Lilith's head pounded and ached. She could feel a sting under the bandages covering her wounded eye with each movement of her head. The jungle felt like a wall surrounding her. She had lost sight of Chibs.

"Lilith!" The voice came through the screen of leaves and branches. It was hushed, but unmistakable.

"Chibs?" Lilith replied. The brush in front of her

exploded in movement.

"Gaaa... This infernal forest. I can't see a foot in front of my damned face. Men aren't built to live this way!" Chibs' graveled voice announced his presence as a swath of broad leaves was hacked away, revealing the barrel-chested sailor. A look of relief and recognition splashed across Chibs' face as he met the sight of his captain. "There you are." He turned and gestured over his shoulder. "That girl, Emilia. She has a little camp cut out of the undergrowth just ahead. We can catch our breath and make a plan, Cap'n."

Lilith's pounding headache brought on a wave of dizzying nausea. "For now. If they start combing the forest, we'll move further inland."

"Aye, Cap'n. Follow me." Chibs said, gesturing for Lilith, Jilhal and the doctor to follow. He led them further into the trees and the dense foliage.

The brush opened around Lilith, revealing a small clearing surrounded by thick vegetation on three sides and a sheer rock face on the other. A carpet of leaves lined the ground everywhere she looked and a small ring of rocks contained the remnants of a campfire long burned out. Along the rock wall were branches covered by a thick layer of leaves and grass. Lilith looked through the camp, searching for any signs of other inhabitants.

"It's just me. If that's what you were wondering." Emelia said, helping one of the wounded crew members to lie down on the leaf lined floor of the camp. "I've no other companions, no friends, no family left."

"And you've been camped here?" Lilith asked as she peered into the lean-to with a cautious hand on her sword's grip.

"For weeks." Emilia replied, she walked around the small fire ring and stood close to Lilith. "I was ready to wait for months if it came to it. I have no other place. I wanted to find you and your crew. I want to sail away from here and I want to avenge my father's death."

Lilith's head split in an ache that started behind her wounded eye and radiated out, through her skull and down into her neck and shoulders. She felt a sudden ill in her stomach. Her legs became unstable. She leaned an arm out onto the rock face and lowered herself down to sit.

"Cap'n, are you alright?" Chibs asked through the patter of rain on the leafy canopy above.

Lilith nodded. "I'll manage. My head is spinning and splitting at the same time, but I'll live." She caught Chibs exchanging a look with Dr. LeMeux. "I'll be fine Chibs. Gather whatever you can of the crew, the Maiden has truly drowned this time, but that doesn't stop her captain. Nor her crew."

"Aye Cap'n. I'll get right about it." Chibs said disappearing back into the thick brush. She couldn't see him any longer, but his profanities regarding land life lingered long after he was out of sight.

'North Wind'
18 Apr 1809
19 Degrees 34' N, 73 Degrees 0' W

Driving rain pelted Will's back. The cold drops stung as they soaked into his shredded blouse and burned as they ran down his wounds. Clouds of gun smoke drifted away with the stout wind. They ebbed and swirled, washing over the cove and intermingling with smoke from the burning hulk of the Drowned Maiden. Will's head was still spinning from his sudden retrieval from below decks. He had been forced up to the weather deck and pushed to his knees before larboard bulwark. Volley after volley careened over the stormy chop and eviscerated Lilith's ship. Will looked on helplessly as timbers had shattered and masts toppled and splashed down into the waters of the cove. The decks of North Wind erupted in cheers when the last volley had landed and sent a final spray of debris shattering away from their target. Order restored quickly. Admiral Torren stood like a stone sculpture against the inclement weather. Rain dripped from his heavy boat cloak as his eyes remained locked on the dying ship across the expanse of sea separating them.

"Your companions have tasted the king's justice." The admiral didn't even spare a look at Will as he spoke. "You shall have your taste as well. In Kingston." The admiral tapped his cane as he finished speaking and gave a nod to the pair of marine sentries that had ushered Will from his cell up to the weather deck. The marines snapped to and quickly moved to hoist Will to his feet.

"You think you have rid yourself of this menace?" Will snarled through pangs of burning pain that shot through his back and abdomen as the marines wrestled him to his feet.

Admiral Torren turned on his heels, cane in hand. "Did you not just witness?"

"She was but a symptom of the plague at your doorstep, admiral." Will sputtered through the rain washing over his face. He cringed as one of the marines tugged at his arm. "You will see the beast rear its ugly head. When you do, you will know you have been chasing the wrong enemy and you will have already hung the wrong man."

"Traitor's words, Sir." The marine said as he gave Will's arm another tug to coax his feet to move. "We'll have him locked back below straight away."

Admiral Torren lifted his cane and touched the sentry's shoulder. "Hold fast a minute there, young man." He looked at Will with his steely gray eyes. His face was a picture of sullen reserve. "You know nothing you can say to me will change the fact that when we arrive in Kingston, you will be hanged for murder and treason."

"I do Sir." Will replied as rivulets of rainwater continued running over his face, invading his eyes and mouth. "All the same. The threat to Britain did not die here today."

Admiral Torren looked down his nose at Will. A glimmer of disdain flickered through his eyes. He paused with a breath behind his lips, as if he had something to say. The moment lingered until a petty officer shouted an order across the deck in a voice rasped by long years of abuse. Rain drizzled from the brim of Admiral Torren's bicorne. He pursed his lips and looked up to the sentries holding Will by his arms. A curt nod set them back to pulling Will across the deck. Too pain stricken to resist, Will went along as the marines toted him, dragging his bare feet across the rain-soaked deck and down the narrow stairwell. Below deck was an echo chamber of cacophony. Men shouted back and forth as they went about their final reload of the cannons. Past three decks of guns the marines urged Will on with little empathy for his wounds, jabbing him in the ribs around each turn of the stairs and jostling his arms down the flights and up the corridor. A lone sentry snapped to attention as they approached the ship's set of four cells. Lantern light hung dim and yellow in the depths of the ship, gleaming off of the marines' brass coat buttons and the metal fixtures of their rifles. Will's heart seemed to sink lower than the lowest drag of keel as the sentry standing guard jangled his keys and opened the heavy door to his cell. Inside, the matted straw that made up his bed was rotten and soiled from weeks of weeping bulkheads and sentries neglecting to empty his waste bucket. The smell was horrendous, though Will hardly noticed anymore. As the door slammed shut behind him, the only light that entered his cell was buffeted by a set of three iron bars that intersected the cell door's small window. The lantern light continuously danced with every flicker of the flame and each movement of the ship.

"A special case you are indeed, being brought up to witness the full might of his majesty's royal navy. Pray tell, what was the old man's target today?" The voice sneered with a thick accent from the American south. Tim Sladen loved to taunt the only other prisoner aboard the admiral's grand flagship. Will ignored his comments. The marines did not.

"He sunk that bloody pirate. We. We sunk that bloody pirate." One of the marines snapped at Tim's cell door, "And now it's off to Kingston. You two have an appointment with the gallows."

"Hang a man without a trial?" Tim drawled back through the cell window at the sentries. "How very British of you. Have you boys ever heard of a little place called Boston? I suppose we didn't learn our lesson the first time."

One of the marines slammed a kick against Tim's cell door. "You'll shut your mouth before I open this door and give you something to howl about."

"Easy, now. I meant no offense. It was all in jest, I swear it. Even that bit about hanging a man without a trial. I am sure your admiral has already selected a jury to render a guilty verdict." Tim's voice was dripping with sarcasm.

"Are your ears full of shit?" the marine shouted, "I said, shut your mouth." He kicked the cell door again for added measure.

Tim's voice faded. Inside the dark of his cell, Will struggled to find a comfortable position where he could avoid rubbing his raw wounds on the soiled bed of straw. He eventually surrendered to just laying in the filthy pile, wounds be damned. Low chatter from the sentries filtered its way through the cell door and kept Will attuned to straining his ears for what bits of information he could hear. That too eventually ceased as the two marines who had so abruptly escorted him up on deck took their leave and left the lone sentry to stand watch over the two cells.

Will edged in and out of a fleeting dreamless slumber as the big flagship pitched and rolled with the motion of heavy seas. The storm outside seemed not to be letting up. Timbers wept seawater and soon his cell was almost as wet as the weather deck had been. Exhaustion won out though and Will's mind was soon drifting just as freely as a wind tossed ship with no rudder.

"Your friends are so obtuse. Nothing like you." Tim's voice sounded muffled through both cell doors and the passageway. "Have you ever given thought that you are not amongst a company of equals?"

The marine standing guard muttered something Will could not hear. He then raised his voice. "That's enough out of you. Quiet."

"I take back what I said. Perhaps you are surrounded by intelligence of your own standing. But has it ever occurred to you, that perhaps you are indeed a cut above these others?" Tim's voice was slithery smooth. Will rolled his eyes and took in a deep breath. His ribs were still lit with pangs of fiery pain with every movement. Blood and pus collected in the straw beneath him. Tim's voice was hardly a comfort. "Perhaps it is just ingrained in you Brits. Kneel, nod, yes sir and all that. But you strike me as a more independent thinker."

"What of it?" the sentry groaned. "If I were to agree with you, would that shut you up?"

"Not likely. But we needn't carry on about it, it was just an observation I thought to share. Nothing more." Tim said after a long pause. "Perhaps it doesn't trouble you that your own admiral is on a course dangerously close to treason himself. But, what of it? The crown wouldn't punish a man for the crimes of his commander. Would it?"

"What in the name of Mary are you talking about?" the sentry asked.

Will could almost hear Tim smile through the cell doors. The American's voice came through louder, like he had stood up to speak directly through the bars in his cell door. "I am telling you information that could get me hung by my own right in America. After a due trial of course, but nonetheless. Your admiral is conspiring against the crown, against parliament. He is in league with a confederation of British and French nobles that

Resurrecting the Maiden

aims to continue profiting from the illegal transport of slaves to America."

"Bah." The sentry laughed, "You're mad. That's exactly what this bugger said about you!"

"And wouldn't you believe it? He happens to be a traitor himself." Tim's voice lowered as if he were conveying some closely held secret. "Why do you think your admiral is so hell bent on our execution? Your dear lieutenant must be hung in order for the admiral's true plans to remain hidden from the crown. Look beyond what you've been told man, use your reason. You will see it is true."

Will could barely believe his ears. The web this American was spinning was so thick and twisted he could barely separate one lie from the next. The sentry remained quiet for a long while after Tim spoke, the only sound that echoed through the narrow corridor between cells being the swaying lantern that creaked with each pitch and roll of North Wind.

"Hey. You there." The sentry called. Will heard a knock on the thick slab door of his cell. "You hear this? Pretty serious accusations from this one. What say you to it? Were you involved in smuggling slaves?"

Will writhed on the soggy straw. His anger welled inside of him. "Does a royal marine give more credit to a prisoner than his own commander?"

"Well, no." The sentry replied in a thick voice, "But you didn't answer my question. Was you smuggling slaves or not?"

Will let out an exhausted sigh and pulled himself up to his feet. The deck swayed beneath him, but he managed to stand at the cell door and look out between the iron bars. "Are you supposed to be carrying on with your prisoners, marine? He is obviously a madman. The admiral is an honorable man executing the king's justice as he sees it."

"Lies won't un-stretch your neck." Tim retorted through his cell door.

Will could see the guard was contemplating everything he had been told. He stood at his cell door in a mixed state of agony and shock, knowing exactly what this American was trying to accomplish. "There is a conspiracy to smuggle slaves, though I was not involved. For my part, I tried to end it, as it were."

"See there, he admits it. Though not in full." Tim interrupted.

The sentry looked at Will through the iron bars, lantern light swaying through the corridor behind him. "If you weren't involved, why were you with pirates?"

"Those pirates were trying seizing ships smuggling slaves." Will replied without giving it a thought.

"Right." The sentry looked back over at Tim's cell. "so if they were trying to stop the smugglers, then why would the admiral engage their ship?"

"See! There it is!" Tim's voice rose in accusation. "Your admiral is in league with these smugglers.

Even a blind man could see it!"

Will's jaw gritted hard while his ribs and back burned in a fresh wave of pain. He inhaled and began to speak until the sentry cocked his eyebrow. "Perhaps this is all a bunch of hogwash. We'll see."

"Seek reason amongst your peers, man. You might find that they come to a similar conclusion." Tim's voice was muffled again, like he had withdrawn deeper into his cell.

"My relief should have been here by now." The sentry darted a look up the corridor. "I'm going to find out what is delaying him. You two keep quiet."

The marine plodded through the walkway of the dark hold, taking the lantern with him. Will was left in the dark with only his thoughts and the voice of Tim in the cell across from him.

"Well done, sailor. Well done. By morning, half the crew aboard this monstrosity will be grumbling and doubting their commander's true intentions." Tim called from his cell. "Well done indeed."

Will slunk back down onto the straw and huffed as he settled into his miserable state. "The king's sailors aren't so easily swayed." Even as he said it, images from the Valor and the Endurance played through his mind. He himself had been mutinied on by the king's sailors, twice.

"We will see." Tim said from the depths of his cell. "We will see."

'LeFouet'
18 Apr 1809
19 Degrees 57' N, 65 Degrees 58' W

"Haul away on the main!" Gaspar Bouttit shouted through his hands cupped around the corners of his mouth. A stout wind had risen and the watch officer's orders required an adjustment of sail. Gaspar, an experienced sailor, was the first mate aboard LeFouet. Crewmen pulled the line taut and began heeling the weight of the sail upward hand over hand as the winds continued to batter the fabric. The order was wrong, Gaspar knew it. The watch officer should have ordered a slight variation in course and nothing more. Instead, they were making a sail change for what would likely be a temporary change in the wind. It was a common mistake for young men unaccustomed to command and seafaring. But Gaspar had already tasted the wrath of this particular officer. He chose instead to follow his orders and let the consequences play out as they may from the captain.

"Sail on the horizon!" a voice carried down from the lookouts high aloft.

With men still hauling at line to reef the main sail, Gaspar looked to the watch officer for what his command would be. The young man shifted on his feet, visibly uncomfortable with a sudden change of conditions. The crew pulled their lines the last few hauls and top men scurried across the main yard to begin the work of tying off the sail for quick deployment later. Gaspar again looked at the watch officer. It appeared that his feet were glued to the deck, where he stood just behind and to the side of the helmsman. With a grumble, Gaspar approached the young officer.

"Sir. Should we have a look for this vessel?" Gaspar asked with a nod.

The young man stood rigid, his uniform coat collar clasped tight at his neck. He didn't even spare a look in Gaspar's direction. "What vessel?"

"The lookouts called out a sail spotted on the horizon, sir. Did you not hear?" Gaspar asked, trying to lower his voice to not embarrass the fresh-faced man.

The watch officer snorted. "If he did call out, it wasn't loud enough. Are you sure?"

"Yes, Sir. Would you like for me to point it out for you?" Gaspar asked, extending his hand out toward the side of LeFouet.

"No. I am quite capable of spotting a white sail. Carry on about your business." The officer snapped. He shot a look at Gaspar as he spoke then resumed a distant gaze out over the deck of LeFouet.

"Aye. Capable." Gaspar grumbled and turned back to making the sail adjustments. It was a frivolous exercise and one that would be undone in less than an hour if Gaspar was correct. Efficiency was not a priority for the young officer who desired above all to constantly remind Gaspar of his authority over him. It was maddening, but Gaspar had seen it before. The young officer would folly, he would make mistakes and draw the ire of the captain. Once the captain grew weary of his foolhardy blunders, he would be set ashore in some remote port of call and LeFouet would sail away without the encumbrance. The captain was a hard man, the son of French nobility and a sailor who learned his trade during the American revolution when France sent her fleets across the world to engage the British and give the fledgling rebels a fighting chance against their king's might. Captain Henri Callais was a barrel-chested behemoth that hailed from eastern France, where his family's name still caused heads to turn when it was uttered along the streets. The Callais family could trace their lineage back for centuries to the court of Charlemagne, where an ancestor of theirs served the great king as a knight. Or so they claimed. Gaspar himself put little stock in that sort of business. He preferred to focus on the here and now, and here on LeFouet. They were about to have a problem.

The sighting of a sail at sea can be a tricky thing. Sailors on watch with little to do can be deceived by a rolling whitecap, or a bit of cloud. At night, the combination of darkness and fatigue can cause a man to see things that are not actually there at all. Gaspar himself had been awoken in the dead of night on many occasions for what a crewman swore they saw. More often than not he would grumble his way back to his hammock and grudgingly fall back asleep. This was different. A sighting in fair weather by an experienced hand was not something to scoff at, especially in these waters. A sail on the horizon could mean anything. The days of pirate marauders terrorizing vessels peaked decades ago, they were more of a rarity than anything, and usually short lived. But that didn't mean there weren't still pirates on the high seas. Every now and then in port Gaspar would hear tales of a crew flying a black banner. Most recently while they made port in Tortuga he had been inundated by a barkeep telling tales of the newest scourge to plague the Caribbean. The Drowned Maiden had made a name for herself in a remarkably short time. Rumors had it she was an East India ship that was taken by a crew of mutineers. Gaspar continued his work with an uneasy feeling in the back of his mind. Pirates were one thing, but the waters of the Caribbean were often prowled by another enemy flying the British union jack.

It was late in the afternoon when the captain's cabin door swung open. Captain Henri Callais stepped into the glory of sunshine on the wooden deck and a stout wind whipping over them. He was a broad-shouldered man with a square jaw and long hair as black as coal. His eyes were bright as gems and as blue as the sea itself. The captain left his door swinging on its hinges as he stepped onto the quarterdeck and looked over the helmsman, it took only a moment for him to notice things were out of sorts. He looked over his lieutenant with a scowl.

"Why are we flying jibs and not square-rigged. I said we need to be sailing with haste. Do you know what that means?" The captain taunted the younger officer.

His lieutenant replied. "A shift in the wind, Sir. I thought it best…"

Henri interrupted him, "That was your folly. Thinking. I told you to run us square rigged. LeFouet sails quickest under square rig sails." The captain shook his head in disgust and started his way up a short set of stairs to the aft castle. Gaspar nearly held his breath. He knew what was coming next.

"Lieutenant!" the captain shouted.

"Yes, Sir!" the lieutenant snapped and started his way up the stairs.

"How is it that I come on deck and spot a sail? Why was I not informed of this?" The captain shouted.

The Lieutenant stumbled on his words for a second, the folly was his last. Captain Callais braced his arms on the stair railings to either side of him and extended his leg in a savage kick that landed on the young man's chest. "Either you are derelict of your duties on watch or you mean to give us over to the enemy." The captain seethed through clenched teeth. He followed the young officer down to the deck while the young man toppled over and fell onto all fours. Captain Callais wasted no time in grabbing the young officer's uniform coat and hauling him to his feet. In an unceremonious jerk, the captain ripped the uniform coat off of the young man's shoulders and smacked away his ornamented bicorn hat. "If you want to play at being a seaman, then have at the sea boy!" The young lieutenant stood in a state of shock while Captain Callais' rage continued. The captain advanced toward him after throwing the uniform coat onto the deck and as the lieutenant began to back pedal he stopped abruptly at the larboard rail with nowhere to go. Captain Callais lifted his tree trunk leg again and delivered another shoving kick to the lieutenant's chest, toppling the young man over the side of the ship with a vicious splash.

Gaspar yelled across the deck, "Toss a line!"

Captain Callais held up a hand and yelled back, "Belay that. The boy wants to play at seamanship, let him drink of the deep. We have more pressing matters easterly."

Gaspar's feet came to a halt on the grainy wooden deck. "Aye captain."

"First mate, you have the ship. See us eat without delay. Square rigs, or you will be swimming with the lieutenant." Captain Callais ordered as he smoothed at the loose sleeves of his shirt. "I mean to have a look at this ship."

Pirate Cove
18 Apr 1809

Lilith leaned against the cold metal blade of the cutlass. The point dug into soft soil between her knees as she sat on a large rock. The roaring pain from her eye had receded to a dull ache, but warm blood still oozed from beneath the bandage wrapped around her head. Chibs had managed to gather the surviving members of the Maiden's crew. As rain trickled down from the canopy, she looked over the lot of them. Her once fearsome crew of over eighty was whittled down to less than a quarter of that and many among those, including herself, were wounded. Chibs himself had taken a wound on his arm, though he refused to let Dr. LeMeux have a look at it. The old sailor had just shaken his head and growled, "I'll be fine, tend to the others." He was a stubborn old sea dog. Their host had disappeared into the thick vegetation surrounding her little makeshift camp. Lilith liked the girl. She was about her own age, and fiery. Jilhal sat near Lilith's feet with her back leaned against the large rock. Omibwe had come in with the last group of survivors Chibs had brought in. He had hobbled into camp, missing the crude prosthetic his friend Dr. LeMeux had made for him. The sight of the one-legged African boy had lit the doctor's face with joy. "My friend, I thought you were dead!" The two embraced and the doctor immediately began to fuss over the young man as if he were his mother. As for his mother, Lilith could find no truer companion than Jilhal. She was as loyal as Chibs and just as protective of her captain. A dozen more sailors shuffled into camp, some led by Chibs himself, some simply staggered in through the dense vegetation after being directed there by the salty quartermaster. There was broad shouldered Damriq, he had been with them since they pillaged the Gazelle and had a penchant for using a length of chain in a fight rather than a sword or ax. Renly was one of the British marines that had come aboard with Lieutenant William Pike, he was the only one of the Brits who survived the sinking Maiden. Renly had taken to pirate life, Lilith knew it had become a concern for some of the other Brits who had joined her ranks. He was as zealous for Lilith as he had been for king and country. A few more Africans from the Boston Autumn, freed slaves. They were new to her ranks and still green to the ways of sailing ships and loading guns. So few she had.

"Cap'n." Chibs popped his head through a patch of broad leaves, "Begging your pardon cap'n, but you're going to want to see this." Chibs waved her over toward the trees with his meaty, rope calloused hand.

Lilith slid off of her seat on the rock and sheathed her cutlass. "More bad news? Are they coming ashore, Chibs?"

Chibs beamed a broad smile and shook his head. "No. They make for calmer seas."

Lilith radiated as they wove their way through the thick vegetation. Her options had been bleak if the Royal Navy had decided to send a shore party out. She hadn't the numbers to stand and fight, and those she had would not make a quick retreat. Daylight was failing behind dark storm clouds as they broke out of the thick of the forest. The sand of the beach was thick with rain and clung to Lilith's feet as she walked down to the waterfront with Chibs at her shoulder. The flank of his shirt was stained with blood from his wounded arm, it was darkest close to his ribs where he had been holding it but the constant soaking of rain had run the stain downward edging it out to a light pink at the bottom of the fabric.

"See there?" Chibs pointed with his good hand, "They make for calmer seas. We will live to fight another day cap'n."

Lilith looked out over the water. It was thick with chopping waves driven by a stout wind out of the south. Little caps of white toppled as each wave rose to meet the next. The surf inside the cove was the strongest Lilith had ever seen it inside the tucked away shelter, strong enough to make waves collapse along the sandy shore and stretch high up along the beach. Outside of the cove, the massive warship had donned her sails.

"She was facing east when they fired on us." Lilith noted to Chibs.

Chibs, wheezing a little, summoned a breath to answer his captain. "Aye, she was. They made a turn with the wind. Running broad reach for the west, in a hurry too. It's odd that they wouldn't send a shore party out. They must have pressing business somewhere west of here."

"It makes no difference. We are locked ashore without the Maiden." Lilith put a hand on Chibs' big shoulder, "Our first order is to tend our wounded, then perhaps our best hope is to steal a vessel from a port here in Haiti." Chibs' shoulder faltered beneath her hand. She turned and looked at her quartermaster. Behind his burling salt and pepper beard his face was ghostly pale. "Chibs?"

"She's not lost cap'n, not by a long shot…" Chibs uttered, his voice growing weaker with every word. His legs wobbled, like he was on the deck of a ship being pitched about in a violent storm. Except even on deck, in the worst of storms, Chibs never lost his footing. "Cap'n, … I don't feel well…" Chibs collapsed to his knees in the sand at Lilith's feet.

"Chibs?" Lilith cried. She tried to stop his fall, but her slight frame was no match for the old sailor's falling weight. Chibs fell over onto his side, his wounded arm clutching against his ribs. Blood trickled freely from the wounds on his forearm and the dark red stain down the side of his shirt had only grown. Lilith pulled at the fabric opening a small tear further to reveal a gaping gash just below Chibs' lowest rib. The wound extended along his side and wrapped its way upward in a crescent disappearing around his back where the sand he lay on met his flesh. "Chibs!" Lilith cried. Her hands shook with terror. She wrapped her arms around his massive chest, "Oh god, not you too! Chibs! Don't leave me." Lilith rose to her knees and frantically pulled in air, "Help!" she screamed so loud she thought her voice would give out. "Help me!"

Lilith looked down on the burly sailor. His skin was so pale, she had never seen him look that ghostly, like the years he had spent under the sun on the deck of a ship had all been stripped away. His chest rose in shallow breaths so faint Lilith could barely see. Blood collected beneath him giving the wet sand an even darker stain. "Help me! Chibs is dying!" Lilith screamed again. The winds howled, driving rain into her face. Her vision blurred with rain and tears. Chibs became a smear of white and red and pale skin. "Somebody help!" Lilith's voice broke as she cried, she held a hand onto the side of Chibs' jaw and pleaded. "Please, Chibs. I'm begging you, don't leave me. Trina is gone. James is dead. I've lost so many, don't leave."

"Aye." Chibs' voice huffed in a groggy croak.

"Chibs!" Lilith choked out a cry of relief in between sobs, "Oh god Chibs, just hold on. I will get the doctor."

"Don't let that Frenchman lay a finger on me. I'm right fit to sail." Chibs growled after drawing a wheezing breath.

"He will look you over, Chibs." Lilith replied,

"Your captain commands it."

Chibs' eyes cracked open, he looked around without focus before shutting them again. "Aye cap'n."

Behind her Lilith could hear Jilhal calling for her. "Captain? Captain Lilith, what is it? What is wrong?"

Lilith turned and called back to her. "Get Renly and Damriq, and the doctor too, it's Chibs, he's wounded worse than I thought."

Jilhal's eyes shot wide. She turned and disappeared back into the forest. Lilith waited as the chopping surf crashed onto the sandy shores. The sound of the waves and the wind dominated everything around her. She felt like a spec of sand on the beach, lost in the enormity of the world, at the mercy of the wind and waves.

"Captain. What happened?" Dr. LeMeux's voice cut through the wind as he knelt next to Lilith in the sand.

Lilith lifted the torn fragment of Chibs' shirt. "His wound, doctor, it's much worse than he let on."

Dr. LeMeux grimaced as he looked over both Chibs' wounds on his arm and on his side. He pulled a small leather case from a soaked coat pocket and removed a pair of spectacles. In a swift motion, the doctor unfolded the glasses and perched them on his nose. He gingerly pulled the shirt flap away and looked closer at Chibs' side.

"A deep laceration. I can see bare bone on two of

his ribs." He let the cloth down gently and eased Chibs' arm into his lap. "The arm wound is severe as well. See the fragments of wood here?" Dr. LeMeux motioned his hand over the torn forearm flesh and looked up at Lilith, "It appears he also has a fracture of the ulna."

"Doctor. Can you help him?" Lilith's voice betrayed her loss of patience.

Dr. LeMeux looked up at her over the top of his spectacles. "I can, Captain Lilith, but the consequences for him may be dire. Even if I am able to save his life, the outcomes may be quite undesirable."

"What does that mean?" Lilith snapped, her eyes narrowed at the doctor as she spoke.

Dr. LeMeux pulled his glasses off and folded them in one hand. "Captain. I am afraid his arm will fester, given the amount of foreign material in the wound. There's no way of knowing for an absolute certainty that all of the material is removed, unless..." the doctor's voice trailed off. He looked down at the unconscious quartermaster and then back up at Lilith. "I'm going to have to amputate his arm."

"Now?" Lilith asked as a roiling wave of shock swept over her.

Dr. LeMeux shook his head instantly, "Oh no, he has already lost far too much blood. If I did the operation now, it might kill him."

"Then what can you do?" Lilith asked as Renly and Damriq arrived.

The doctor looked over Chibs' wounds again with a careful eye. "We will try to stop or slow his blood loss as much as possible. Once his bleeding is under control, I will have a better idea if I can save his life."

"Whatever you need, you will have." Lilith replied. She looked up at Damriq and Renly, their eyes were both wide, faces long. "Whatever the doctor commands, do it. He holds Chibs' life in his hands now."

"Sit him up so I can bandage the wound on his side." The doctor ordered. He looked around for anything he could use to staunch the flow of blood. At a loss, the doctor stripped off his own shirt and began tearing strips of material to use as bandages. Lilith watched with her hand resting on the hilt of her sword while the doctor tied each strip of material around Chibs' torso. He motioned to Renly and Damriq, "Alright. Let's get him up to the camp." He looked at Lilith, "I'm going to need a fire, a flat piece of metal, some very strong cordage and a sharp knife."

"You intend to take his arm?" Lilith cocked a brow at his change of heart.

The doctor looked down at the sand, "I fear if we don't, in his weakened state, if infection does set in it will kill him."

Lilith's fingers wrapped around the handle of her cutlass. "I don't envy you doctor."

"And why is that captain?"

Lilith looked at him with her one good eye, her

fingers squeezed against the grip of her sword. "Because if Chibs lives, he will likely kill you for taking his arm." She paused and watched as Renly and Damriq carried Chibs toward the camp. "But if he dies, I will do it for him."

The doctor went a shade paler than he already was. "Guess I'd better not fail, best to take my chances against a one-armed man."

Lilith turned toward the camp and offered over her shoulder. "Better not fail then doctor."

Chapter 2

'North Wind'
20 Apr 1809
19 Degrees 14' N, 73 Degrees 42' W

"Is it true?" The guard whispered in the dim swaying light. "Is it because of what you know that the admiral has you locked up like this?"

Will's stomach wrenched as he awoke to the sharp whispers outside of his cell. The many cuts on his stomach had begun to scab and heal, though a near constant ooze of blood and pus told him he had a long way to go and an infection to fight off as well.

"I suppose it may be." Tim's voice answered the inquiring guard. "But how do I know you weren't sent by the admiral himself? Suppose I tell you and then he pops around the corner with a couple of your friends and hangs me to guarantee my silence. What would I gain from that?"

"No. Honest to god, I'm just curious. There was

talk about it after the watch change. That's all." The guard continued to whisper. "They say the admiral is involved in something. Some kind of financial dealing with the Americans or France."

"But that would be treason. Wouldn't it?" Tim's voice replied with the slippery pointed question. Will shook his head in the dark of his cell. He knew better than to try and intercede. This American had North Wind's crew by the ear and any objections he raised only wound up working in Tim's favor. His tongue was made of pure silver and his wits were far sharper than Will's. Days had passed since he had been dragged up into the rain and wind to watch as the Drowned Maiden was pummeled by volley after volley from the admiral's batteries. His wounds were a constant torture, some reopened with even the slightest provocation. A twist, a slight movement, anything it seemed would open them and re-start the near constant ooze of blood.

"But what are we to do?" the guard whispered lower. Will knew he feared the wrong ears would hear. Collaborating with a prisoner could bear serious consequences. If his neck didn't feel it, his back most certainly would. Will's back still throbbed with sharp pain from the kiss of a cat of nine tails. The whip had torn deep. Deeper even than the razor-sharp barnacles under North Wind's hull. He had dreams about it more nights than not. The slow progression from hanging by his bleeding wrists and ankles next to the ship's rail down into the frothing wash of seawater. It invaded his nose, choked his breath from his throat with its briny tang and blurred the vision from his eyes. He would be battered against the hard wood of the hull over and over while being tugged along unmercifully by a crew of strong backs on the deck above. Just when Will felt like he could bear no more and he would surely die the surface would break around him and he would cough out a lung of seawater, just to endure the same torture in the opposite direction. Sometimes he would wake in a cold sweat, sometimes it continued on until his nightmare induced writhing would painfully open one of his wounds. Other times he dreamed of the day he had witness Tim Sladen fire a pistol shot into Admiral Sharpe's chest. The cloud of gray smoke, the blood. His dreams were so vivid. It was like experiencing it all over again. Will longed for the days when his dreams were of home. A farm house in the English countryside or a green-eyed girl with dark hair.

"I say. I am no expert in British justice, but, if the admiral is involved in some plot against the crown, wouldn't you be spared?" Tim asked with a false naivety in his voice. "They wouldn't label you all as traitors, would they?"

"Well, I don't know." The guard was hesitant, his voice betrayed cogs turning within his mind. "But a treason is a treason. Whether it's unknowing or not I suppose."

"Then I would suppose you must do something." Tim replied. His voice curdled Will's blood. Every syllable was a patronizing falsehood. Each of the sentries he had spoken to in the past few days seemed to bite onto the hook faster than the last.

"I suppose you're right. But, what's to be done? The admiral commands all the same." The guard whispered back.

Tim's voice grew louder. Will knew the American had pulled his face up close to the iron bars to emphasize his point. "Well, that is up to you." He paused. Will knew the words that were coming next. "But I know what I would do if I were you."

"And what's that?" the marine's voice was thick with intrigue.

"Take the ship." Tim's whisper was low, so faint Will almost couldn't make out what he was saying. "You must take the ship and arrest the rogue admiral. Only then could you all present him to your king and explain what he has done."

"That would be mutiny." The guard remarked with a sigh.

"It would, unless the king happened to see for himself what is truly going on." Tim whispered, "Then, well, you would all be heroes. The saviors of your country."

Will could hear all the workings in the silence that followed. The naive guard was actually considering what he had been told by this American prisoner. North Wind pitched with a wave and the decks beneath them rolled, the sound of seawater slipping by her hull played through thick timbers.

"Silence is your watchword my friend. You mustn't trust the wrong fellow or you're likely to wind up in a cell right next to mine. Or worse…" Tim continued spinning his web. "Talk to that fellow you relieved off of watch earlier. He has his wits about him."

Barely. Will thought to himself. Pale yellow lantern light danced over the inside of his cell. The lantern creaked with each movement of the ship. Will wondered how far these vile lies would circulate among the crew. Sailors talked, it was inevitable. Usually farfetched stories of mermaids or kraken would grow some experienced old hand's legend the further from shore a ship ventured. Hands would recount tales of great battles they had or hadn't been in while working high aloft in the rigging. Sailors would talk about beautiful girls in far flung ports while scrubbing deck boards. Marines would exchange tales of their grizzliest engagements or recount a particularly remarkable shot they had landed while storm tossed high in the tops. But there were a few subjects that could get a man dragged from his post and clapped in irons, mutiny being the foremost among them.

The roll of North Wind softened. Above him, Will could hear gun crews rolling cannons into firing position. Rumbling and creaking were interspersed by shouts among the crew. Gun drills. A drum rattled out its repetitive beat and the cannons all rolled back out of firing position. No thunderclap sounded, just the arduous labor of wooden wheels groaning against the wooden deck. They were doing dry fire drills. Will closed his eyes and remembered the glorious cheer of a gun battery that had just made their goal time. Brows glistening with sweat from the back breaking work and mad rush of trying to hammer out every step as quickly as possible. Will had always loved leading gun drills, especially in the evening just before dinner. The crew would work up a hearty appetite moving the massive guns and working through reloading steps. Gun drills were always most satisfying when live firing the cannons, but it seemed the admiral preferred to conserve his shot and powder. *Probably spent most of his stores sinking the Maiden,* Will thought to himself. Though he had no idea what the ship's magazine actually held. North Wind was an enormity. A first-class ship of the line, she was at one time Admiral Nelson's flagship. Her cabins were grand in both size and furnishing. Her hull was ornate and her lady on the prow almost obscene. Will lamented in his cell, a ship like he had always dreamed of serving aboard, perhaps even commanding someday and he was locked away deep in the hold as a prisoner.

"About time you showed up." The sentry outside growled. Will presumed he was bellyaching at his replacement.

Another voice answered, "They're doing gun drill up there. All three damned decks. It was all I could do to get past them."

"It would be a wonder if you ever showed up on time. I'd probably want to check you for fever." The sentry replied. "Say, did you happen to see Thomas on your way down? I need to speak with him."

Will's heart skipped a beat. This could tell him just how far Tim's web had spread. "Yes, in fact, I was just talking with him up by the bow."

"Really?" the sentry replied, "About what?"

"I think you know exactly what. And there's more of us wondering the same thing. All on larboard watch though, not sure about the others." The voice of the relieving sentry answered. "A few of us are going to talk to the sergeant about it. Thomas said he heard the sergeant and a midshipman say the same thing."

Will's heart fell, his stomach twisted into knots harder than he thought possible. This was how it happened. Rumors flew amongst the crew, getting embellished and twisted at every step. If they did not die immediately the ship was at risk of mutiny. He thought about the admiral. As hard a man as he was, as much as Will had suffered at his orders, he still did not wish a mutiny against him. As advanced in age as he was, Admiral Torren wasn't like to survive an uprising on ship, even less so incarceration in the hold. The marine sergeant and a midshipman being in on the notion was alarming as well. Midshipmen spoke with quite a bit more freedom than the regular seamen, if one of them had bought into the notion, it was likely they all had. Will tried to push himself into a sitting position only to find the pain too excruciating to bear.

"I think he's right. And what's more, I think the admiral is rushing to Kingston to cover all this business up before his royal majesty catches wind of it." The first sentry remarked, "Why else would we have fired on that ship and not gone to check for survivors?" His voice lowered, "Have you ever heard of such a thing?"

"No. I can't say I have." The relieving sentry answered. "But what's more is the gold involved. You know how much gold the Spanish have been pouring into old Bony's coffers?"

Will marveled inside of his cell. How wild had the tale turned? Now Napoleon himself had a part to play in this farce of a scandal.

"You mean the old man has been collaborating with the French?" the first sentry almost gasped as he spoke.

"Why else would he risk so much?" the relieving man added, "And what's more is when we were in Nassau, while you were guarding that turncoat pirate over there, I heard some of the officers talking to a merchant sailor. He said there's a French fleet prowling about the Caribbean. Now why else would they be all the way over here when Bony has his share of war going on in Europe?"

Will's head spun. The list of coincidences was astounding. They just happened to all play nicely into Tim's tapestry of lies. The sentries continued talking outside in the passageway. Their voices remained hushed, barely audible once the gun crews on the deck above started moving their cannons again. *Back at it? Must not have made their reload time.* Will thought to himself as harsh whispering continued to cut and hiss outside of his cell. The groaning of timbers and wheels stopped and the sentries' whispers became audible again.

The relieving man spoke, "If we can get to the old man, it's all over."

Pirate Cove
18 Apr 1809

Rain pattered on broad green leaves overhead. The canopy broke the strength of the rain so that as it reached Lilith and her crew it had degraded into a fine mist. Afternoon had long faded into late evening and the setting sun had been prematurely choked away by the storm clouds that the British navy seemed to have cast upon them. The steady mist soaked everything in sight and combined with an intermittent gust of wind that made its way in land and through the dense foliage and into the camp to bring them all a skin tingling chill. At the center of the camp clearing Dr. LeMeux labored over an unconscious Chibs next to a small fire as Lilith and Jilhal looked on.

The doctor looked up at Lilith, his eyes bulged over the top of his spectacles. "Whatever flat metal we have, I will need it heated red hot in the fire."

Lilith walked over to the fire and drew out her cutlass. "Chibs won't be the first man burned by this blade doctor. And I promise you, if you fail, he won't be the last." She placed the blade into a bed of orange hot coals.

"Your threats won't help your friend my dear. Do you not have anything broader? It would be best to cauterize the wound all at once." Dr. LeMeux retorted with another glare over the top of his glasses.

Jilhal answered before Lilith could speak, "That is the captain you are talking to. Not some fish wife in port."

The doctor hesitated for a moment and then turned to his patient. Lilith watched as he peeled Chibs' shirt sleeve away from his forearm and extended the limb outward from his torso. A leather belt had been provided by Renly for Chibs' tourniquet and the doctor slid the strip of leather up over the bicep of the wounded arm.

"I will need someone to hold him down, if he is to wake while I am cutting, it could kill him if he struggles to much." The doctor's request was met with a flurry of the crew looking amongst each other. No one wanted to be in the precarious position of trying to control Chibs' rage if he should wake and discover his arm was being amputated.

A reluctant Renly finally approached with a huff, "I'll do it." He looked around the gathering of crew, "Sorry bunch of cowards you all are. He's halfway bled to death already. How bad could he be if he comes to?" As much bravado as he was trying to show, Lilith could see an edge of fear in him.

After the scolding, Damriq came up to help. His eyes were wide with apprehension as he and Renly knelt down to keep a hold on Chibs' good arm. Dr. LeMeux cinched the leather strap down as tight as he could, he heaved two more pulls when Lilith thought he'd had all the slack he could get out of the belt and wrapped it around in the opposite direction. "Here Renly, hold tight onto that." He extended the leather into Renly's hand. "If he does come to, ahh... Just. Well, just keep him as still as you can."

Dr. LeMeux took up a razor-sharp knife Emilia had provided to him and made a deep cut just above Chibs' elbow. Bright red blood oozed from the wound and dripped from the knife blade. Lilith's skin crawled as she watched the doctor saw the knife back and forth through Chibs' meaty arm. The wet sound of the blade working apart muscle fibers and tendons seemed to drown out the patter of raindrops on the canopy above them. As the doctor continued his blade bit into bone and a horrible grinding scrape filled Lilith's ears. She gritted her jaw, clamping her teeth harder with every merciless rasp of Dr. LeMeux's blade. Light from the fire glistened off of the blood that dripped freely from Chibs' arm. Little rivulets traced a spider web down the wounded limb and traced off of the wrist and fingers. The doctor's face was flushed, firelight glinted off of his glasses as he continued his work. Finally, just as Lilith felt like she could not stand the sound of another pass of the knife blade through Chibs' arm bone, the offending limb fell free.

Dr. LeMeux pointed to Lilith's sword. "Hurry now. We must cauterize his arm to stop the bleeding and prevent any subsequent infection."

Lilith withdrew the blade and held it up to Chibs' bloodied stump. She shook her head as Dr. LeMeux reached to take the weapon from her. "I will do it doctor." She paused for a heartbeat and looked at Chibs' drawn face. He looked so pale. Holding the blade as steady as she could Lilith pressed it against the bleeding end of Chibs' upper arm. Blood sizzled off the orange hot metal smoking and burning. The air filled with a horrid stench of burning flesh and Lilith slowly passed the hot metal blade over the rest of Chibs' wound.

"Gaaaah!" Chibs cried out, suddenly awake to the pain. "What are you doing? Ahhh… Son of a mother's…" He wrenched against Renly and Damriq with his good arm. It was all the two men could do to keep him contained beneath their full body weight. "Cap'n! What in blazes?"

Lilith withdrew her sword and held it out away from where Chibs lay on the ground. "Your wounds Chibs. The doctor had to remove your arm to save your life." Renly and Damriq braced for what they knew would be a struggle.

"Where is he? I'm going to wrap his neck with the arm I have left!" Chibs bellowed with a strength that shocked everyone in camp.

"He did so on my orders Chibs." Lilith said as she handed her sword off to Jilhal. "You have a wound on your side as well. The doctor will see to that one, and you will let him."

"He won't put another bloody damned finger on me if he knows what's good for him." Chibs screamed, "You hear me Frenchman? You better start running now, when I get my hands on you…"

"Erm… Hand actually." Dr. LeMeux corrected him as he lifted his glasses from the bridge of his nose.

"You son of a…" Chibs howled and heaved his good arm lifting both Damriq and Renly.

"Oh my." Dr. LeMeux stuttered as he backpedaled away from the campfire.

"Doctor." Lilith said, with her eyes locked onto Chibs as he writhed beneath Renly and Damriq fighting with everything they had.

Dr. LeMeux stumbled to his feet. "Yes captain?"

"Run." Lilith uttered as she watched Damriq fall over backwards slamming his shoulder onto the large rock she had been sitting on earlier. In a flurry of stuttering feet and swatting foliage leaves the doctor beat a hasty retreat out into the darkness of the evening while Renly struggled over his last grip on Chibs' arm.

"Come back you slimy little snake!" Chibs

bellowed as he struggled to his feet. Renly and Damriq had all but given up on holding him down.

"Chibs!" Lilith's shout brought everyone in camp to a halt. "It was your limb or your life. I ordered the doctor to do whatever he must to save you." She stood next to the campfire, it's orange glow felt warm against her exposed skin. "We have lost too many, and there are too many of us left who are wounded. Stop. Rest. We need to decide what we are to do next."

Chibs' face went slack. He stooped back down and plunked himself onto the ground next to the campfire, looking over the fresh wound where his arm used to be. "Aye, cap'n. At least I still have my sword arm."

Lilith looked around at the camp, she commanded all of their attention, their eyes were fixed on her. "If the Maiden is lost to us, so be it. We will move on. There are ports in Haiti where we could commandeer ourselves a ship. The Maiden is gone, but her crew must carry forward."

"Begging your pardon cap'n." Chibs interrupted, "Before I fell ill I was trying to tell you, she's not too far gone to raise."

"What do you mean?" Lilith asked, her face flushed at the possibility.

Chibs' hulking frame leaned back, and he looked skyward rubbing his beard with his remaining hand. "I've seen ships brought up from shallows before. Some were further gone than the Maiden is now. It will be difficult, but it could be done."

Lilith's head spun, the eyes of everyone in camp seemed locked onto her, awaiting what she would say next. "How?"

Chibs head was slouching again, the effects of his shock and rage were wearing away. "It's a matter of leverage to get her far enough ashore. Once we beach the ship, we could repair damages and replace anything that cannot be repaired. Her prow line remains exposed and part of her starboard side, if we can drag her up out of the cove we could probably repair her." His words began to drift, his voice grew weaker the longer he spoke.

"What do we need?" Lilith asked, she stepped over to Chibs and knelt next to him on the matted leaves where he sat.

"Tools cap'n. We're going to need a lot of tools, near a mile of line, block and tackle, hammers, saws, chisels..." His voice faded and his head slumped onto his chest, with a snort he sat up abruptly. "We'll need more crew as well, we've not even a third of what it will take."

Lilith sat down and lowered Chibs to lie on his back. "First, quartermaster, we will take the watch while you rest. If we are to do anything beyond squander for the rest of our days ashore, I will need you by my side."

"Aye, cap'n. Rest." Chibs replied while looking up at her. Firelight danced on his eyes and lit his face with a red orange glow.

"Leave getting tools and crew to me. Once you are rested you can bring the Maiden back from the grave." Lilith brushed Chibs' beard with the back of her fingers and watched him close his eyes to sleep.

"I can help." A voice came from behind Lilith. It was Emilia. She had watched Chibs' ordeal from the edge of the camp. "My father worked wood for a shipwright. His tools may still be at the home I left."

Lilith looked at Jilhal and then back to Emilia, she rose to her feet and stood between Emilia and the campfire. "How far is it to this home you've abandoned?"

"A day on foot, maybe less of we hurry and cut through some of the cane fields between here and there. I avoided them on my way here to stay well away from the field bosses and cutting crews." Emilia moved closer to Lilith and Jilhal as she answered. Lilith could see it in her eyes, she wanted to help, she wanted to join them.

"Cane fields you say?" Lilith held her sword up to the firelight and shot a look at Jilhal with the eyebrow over her good eye raised.

"Yes. Since the revolt, many of the landowners have taken to snatching anyone who wanders their properties and forcing them to labor with their field hands. My father always warned me to stay well away from cane fields when I would walk in the woods behind our home." Emilia looked confused, her eyes shifting back and forth between Lilith and Jilhal. "If we started out at first light we could get there by sundown."

Lilith flicked her wrist and swung her saber in a wide arc letting it drift back down to its original position pointing into the firelight. She watched the orange hues work up and down the blade. Her eye socket ached and she could feel the wound throbbing slow with dull pain. "We won't be going around any cane fields."

Emilia lifted her hands, her palms facing upwards. "But the way is separated by cane farms, there is no way to get there without at least going close to one."

"You misunderstand." Lilith said as she sheathed her sword. She extended a hand toward Jilhal and lifted her faithful companion to her feet. "We will be going right through them."

'North Wind'
20 Apr 1809
18 Degrees 46' N, 75 Degrees 13' W

A slight foam washed along ridges of gray green seawater, North Wind was sailing westerly and judging by her pitch and sway she was making almost seven knots. Admiral Torren stood watching the ripples of wave collide and melt away into the sea's natural swells through an array of ornate glass windows in his cabin. The glass was of the finest grade but his view of the waves below was still slightly distorted. The cabin, kept piping hot by a wood stove in the corner, was furnished with every manner of comfort including a feather bed and a massive dark hardwood desk. He had spent the evening examining charts until his eyes were sore of looking at them. A problem sat on the admiral's mind, and no manner of experience or seamanship seemed to be helping.

Watching the waters swirl and collide beneath him Admiral Torren poured over the events that had led him into his present standing. His fleet was but a skeleton of the one he had departed England with. He had lost one ship to a formidable American frigate that represented a threat to Britain's sea superiority before he had even ventured into the Caribbean. Upon his arrival in Nassau, he had discovered a web of plots surrounding a treasonous lieutenant that had claimed the lives of two colonial governors and three of his fleet's ships. The admiral had already crossed personal boundaries to glean information out of his prisoner, yet he still felt like there was something missing. With the Caribbean fleet rumored to be lost and his own a hollow shell of the strength he had intended to bring, he faced a perilous problem. In waters often prowled by both French and Spanish warships, a flagship without the strength of a fleet would be a target too sweet to pass. North Wind was a fine vessel, one of the finest in all the king's navy, but without the ability to command subordinate ships and amass fire against an enemy its only hope to decisively win in an engagement was to maintain fire superiority. The sheer volume of ammunition he had already used to sink a pirate vessel had been a mistake.

"I had them dead to rights. It was folly to use that much shot and powder." The admiral scolded himself out loud as he looked through the fantail windows. "Folly, Alistair. Use your better judgment next time." A knock at the door sounded. Admiral Torren answered without moving his gaze, "Enter."

"Pardon, Sir. I've brought your supper." Lieutenant Thatcher's voice answered. He was a naive young officer and ignorant to much of life at sea in the naval service. "Salt beef, Sir. With the spiced mustard you like so much."

"Well done lad, leave it on the desk for me and take a seat." The Admiral turned and sat into a padded chair behind the ornate desk. "I have a few questions to ask you."

"Is everything quite alright Sir? Lieutenant Thatcher deposited the admiral's plate and took a seat in a much smaller chair on the opposite side of the desk.

Admiral Torren smiled and looked over his dinner. "That is what I wish to discuss with you lad. Is everything quite alright?" He paused and cut into the meat on his plate, separating a healthy bite and dabbing it into the spiced mustard. "My walk on deck this morning was complete solitude, apart from your interruption, not another soul aboard spoke to me. I didn't think much of it at the time, but once I returned to my cabin I contemplated further. It has been days since any of the sailors spoke a word to me, apart from their customary greetings of course. But if a man only renders a 'good day' to keep from being flogged, there is a reason behind it." The admiral forked a bite of beef into his mouth and chewed for a moment. "Moreover, the crew weren't even conversing amongst each other. Which is odd. Has there been some talk you have heard? Any griping about the old man, this or that?"

Lieutenant Thatcher looked puzzled. His eyes wandered over the desktop between the admiral and himself. "No, sir. I don't think I've heard any such grumblings. None at all."

"Curious thing. Usually when a man gets flogged the crew will be rigid tense for a few days. It wears away in due time of course, but there are always a few days where you can slice it out of the air with your sword. Tension. Like an awkward fear mixed with a mutual and silent understanding that it needn't happen again." Admiral Torren swallowed his bite and took a sip of wine from a plain cup the lieutenant had delivered with his dinner. "I reckon it all stems from keelhauling that Lieutenant Pike. They probably thought me too cruel on the lad." Admiral Torren paused to watch for Lieutenant Thatcher's reaction.

Hesitation passed over the young officer's face. He opened his mouth for a moment before forming words. "The crew knows the law admiral. They know the articles of war, I believe they are with you to a man."

Admiral Torren scoffed. "Hardly. If you believed that it wouldn't have taken you until the second coming to figure out how to say it. What have you heard?"

Lieutenant Thatcher went a shade paler than he normally was. "I... I haven't heard much of anything sir. There was talk about the keelhauling for the first few days. After we sank the pirates, I'm afraid I haven't heard much at all."

Admiral Torren nodded his head and took another bite of his dinner. "Aye. Therein lies the problem. Sailors talk lad. Whether it be tales of war or women, pining over dreams of home or their next port abroad. Sailors rarely carry about their day in silence." He paused to drink a sip of wine and held the cup in front of him for a moment after he'd drunk. "Have you spoken with the officers much? The ship's lieutenants or midshipmen?"

"They rarely speak to me outside the course of their duties sir. I'm afraid my lack of experience at sea makes me a bit of a pariah amongst their company." Lieutenant Thatcher's face flushed. His eyes dropped to the desktop again and the admiral could see his embarrassment. "I have heard some of the mids refer to me as Landsman Thatcher."

"Good god man, are you serious? Did you challenge them on it?" Admiral Torren set his cup down with a thud causing some wine to slop over the brim and spill down onto his hand.

"No sir. I believe to do that would be to invite further distrust amongst them." Lieutenant

Thatcher answered sheepishly.

Admiral Torren let out a deep sigh. He'd known when they set off from England that his aide would experience some growing pains at sea. He'd never imagined it would take this long to adjust and fit in with the crew. "You're still taking the watch occasionally as I've instructed, are you not?"

"Yes sir. I take midnight to four bells every other day." Thatcher's chest inflated a little as he answered.

The admiral grinned as he saw the display of pride. "Well, are you taking your meals in the mess with them? It's hard to make friends with a man who won't even break bread with you."

Lieutenant Thatcher shook his head. "No sir. Most often I eat while your dinner is being prepared. If you remember sir, you insisted that every man aboard be fed before you received your dinner."

Admiral Torren nodded with a knowing smile. "Yes lad, and an important lesson is in there for you if you will find it. But my intention was to ensure every man aboard ship eats, not that you would eat whilst watching the cook prepare my dinner."

"Yes sir. I will start taking my meals in the officer's mess." Lieutenant Thatcher answered with a nod.

Admiral Torren cut away another piece of beef and swabbed it through spiced mustard, he longed for green beans or an ear of fresh corn to go with his meat, but England was far too long ago in their wake and Nassau had only meager stocks for replenishment. "Tell me, Lieutenant, have you ever heard of a mutiny aboard a king's ship?"

The Lieutenant's eyes widened at the question. "Well, none specifically sir. No, I don't suppose I have."

The admiral chewed at his beef and took a sip from his cup. "By design really. The navy keeps news of mutinies as quiet as possible." He took his last bite of dinner and put his fork onto the plate before pushing it away from him on the desk. "Crews will talk. Word travels in ports. Before you know it every ship that set to sea would be up in arms against their command. It's strong discipline that keeps the lads in line. Strong discipline and a good leader. Men want to know their leader has their common best interests at heart, along with king and country." Admiral Torren stood up from behind his desk and stepped away from the padded chair. He turned and looked back out the fantail window array, arms folded behind his back. "Knowing a crew's morale is an important aspect of leadership son. To do that, you need to talk with them, the sailors and officers alike."

"Would you like for me to summon someone to your cabin, sir?" The lieutenant stood out of his seat stepping toward the cabin door.

Admiral Torren's head slumped forward. He rubbed the bridge of his nose with his thumb and forefinger. "No lad. I don't mean for you to tote someone in here for an inquisition. Speak with the men, get to know them. Honestly, this far along in our voyage I should think it would be second nature to you by now." He turned to find the lieutenant sheepishly holding his hat in both hands. "You should be dining with them, standing watch with them, making yourself as much a part of the crew as possible. It is what it is for now. Work on it."

"I will sir."

"Silence among the crew can mean several things, none of them bode well for us or our task here in the Caribbean." The admiral's voice lowered as he spoke. "For now we will have them carry on as they are. Kingston is not long off our bow, four days, maybe three if this wind holds. Is the crew adequately provisioned with food and fresh water?"

"Yes sir. We are stocked for several weeks at full rations, longer if need be." The lieutenant answered.

Admiral Torren shook his head, "No need for rationing. Best not to make a tense situation even worse."

"A t-t-tense situation sir?" the lieutenant stammered.

Admiral Torren paused. He let out a deep sigh, "Yes lad. As I was saying, silence from the crew can mean several things and none of them are good. It would be best for us to tread lightly and keep our ears open. Hence, you being as involved with the crew as you possibly can. I'd rather not be caught unaware should our situation turn drastic. We must conduct our affairs as if there isn't any problem while keeping mind that there quite possibly could be."

"You really think there could be a mutiny sir? Aboard a flagship?" Lieutenant Thatcher's face suddenly drew tight as a drum with apprehension.

"It could happen aboard any vessel lad. No matter her class. In fact, with a larger crew comes a larger risk of things developing into a situation we cannot control." Admiral Torren brushed his fingertips along the polished desktop and gave Lieutenant Thatcher a hard look. "But I can assure you son, if it does get to that point it will be the most hellish experience of your short life. I can think of fewer fights that can get as savage as a crew trying to take or retake a vessel from within."

"Right, sir. I will do my best to visit with as many of the crew as I can and report back to you." Lieutenant Thatcher said as he rendered a salute and opened the cabin door to leave.

"Lieutenant." Admiral Torren said holding up a finger, "One more thing."

"Yes sir?"

"Have the marines post a watch at my door. Around the clock." Admiral Torren instructed in a soft voice. "Best start that tonight as well."

'LeFouet'
18 Apr 1809
19 Degrees 57' N, 65 Degrees 58' W

Gaspar grit his teeth as he approached his commander. The stream of obscenities that poured from the captain were enough to make the seasoned sailors aboard pause to consider. His temper had not cooled any since the sighting of the vessel and his subsequent ejection of the young officer over the side of the ship. In fact, Captain Callais' fervor was escalating into a full-blown rage. He paced the deck of the bow from rail to rail cursing and kicking the hard wood railing and bowsprit. The hands on deck went about their tasks without making eye contact and avoiding getting too close to the French officer, but as the two ships closed range Gaspar knew he would have to get his captain's orders.

"Captain." Gaspar called as Captain Callais grabbed the curled iron stand of a brazier and hurled it overboard. Gaspar took a deep breath and raised his voice as much as he dared, "Captain Callais!"

"What? What could you possibly want right now?" The captain snarled and took a step toward him.

"The ship is closing. Do you have orders?" Gaspar asked as he fought the urge to run for cover below deck.

Captain Callais smoothed back his long dark hair

and tugged his buttoned vest back into its place. The flush that had risen into his face shone beet red under the afternoon sun. For a moment he looked around, scanning the horizon as if he had lost where the ship was in relation to his own. As his eyes caught sight of the sails bearing down on them he cursed out loud and then looked to Gaspar. "A telescope. Do you have a telescope? Mine is in my cabin."

Gaspar nodded and pulled his small telescope from a pocket inside of his vest. It was a humble instrument in comparison with many of the collapsing scopes that officers possessed, but for what Gaspar had needed it served him just fine. Captain Callais took the scope and held it up to his eye, aiming it toward the ship that was now drawing close to cannon range. Wind whipped at the Captain's jet-black hair blowing strands around tugging on his loose linen sleeves. The long awkward pause stretched on for what seemed like hours, Gaspar shifted his stare out onto the sea where he tried to define any useful detail with his naked eyes. She was a decent sized ship, comparable to LeFouet or even slightly larger. A chill gripped Gaspar's ribs despite the warm Caribbean sun. The silence from the captain was excruciating, Gaspar almost wished he would begin cursing again.

"Captain? Do you have orders for the crew?" Gaspar asked, shifting his gaze between the approaching ship and his captain and then back again.

"She is an American, a frigate by her look. Slack sheets and come up on the wind. Have the crew prepare to render honors." Captain Callais gently plopped Gaspar's scope against his chest. "Thank you for letting me borrow this, but you should get a better one next time we are in port."

Gaspar gave his captain a squint, "Yes sir. Next time we are in port. A nice collapsing scope and maybe even a hat with some fancy stitching."

Captain Callais ignored his sarcasm. His eyes locked out onto the approaching ship.

Gaspar turned to have the crew prepare for the Americans. "Slack those sheets and come about larboard. Prepare to fire all cannons." He turned to a pair of sailors standing nearby. "Where is the drummer?"

"Below deck." One of them answered.

"Go and fetch him. Captain wants us to render honors to the Americans as they approach." He spat over the side. "We'll probably be boarded too."

The sailor hurried below to find the ship's drummer while Gaspar watched the crew make their maneuver and loosen the lines holding their sails taut. LeFouet handled like a dream in winds like these, if the captain so desired he could have flown a pair of auxiliary sails and left the Americans chasing after them until darkness fell over the sea. Then a curt maneuver and they would be lost to them forever. Gaspar studied the

American ship as she drew close. She was about their size, but she outclassed LeFouet in gun count by at least ten, just by counting gun ports. She had a heavy hulled look about her, but the way the water broke at her bow as she slid closer told Gaspar of a speed nearing ten knots. It seemed odd to him and gave him a sort of morbid curiosity to see her closer.

"Guns ready." A sailor called out from below deck.

Gaspar looked up to the bow where Captain Callais remained with his eyes locked onto the American vessel. "Captain, guns are ready."

"Fire all." Captain Callais replied without breaking his gaze at the frigate bearing down on them. LeFouet had made her turn and her guns all faced harmlessly over open water. Gaspar relayed the captain's order and a near simultaneous firing of all LeFouet's cannons followed. The drummer came on deck as gun smoke drifted over the ship. He fiddled with a strap around his neck and dropped his drumsticks as he did.

"Get up to the bow by the captain and rattle out a beat when he says to. Be quick about it, he's already sent one for a swim today." Gaspar growled and pointed toward the bow.

Gaspar grabbed a hold of a stay line and lifted himself up to stand along the larboard rail. The Americans had not returned the gesture of firing their cannons to show that they carried no ill will. They were slacking their sails however and were on course to pull right alongside LeFouet. An officer in a deep blue colored coat stood high on the bow of the ship with a cone made of dull metal.

"French vessel, this is the U.S.S. Chesapeake. Slack your lines and prepare to be boarded." The American officer called across the distance.

Gaspar looked over the crew of LeFouet. There was an uneasy stirring. Many of them looked to the captain, who was only staring at the incoming vessel. Questions floated among the sailors.

"Why would they be boarding us?" one asked.

Another asked in a louder voice, "We fired our guns, won't they do the same?"

A grizzled sailor with a weathered face retorted, "Probably right into our hull. Send us all down to pay the lieutenant a visit in his new home."

"We'll be having none of that." Gaspar shouted, "The captain has given his orders. Now turn to your tasks and pipe down with it."

The deck of the American frigate was alive with activity. Her rail was lined with marines and as the two ships drew nearer, the clacking noise of gun ports slamming open one by one echoed over the water.

"You see that! They mean to blow us away!" a sailor cried out in terror.

Gaspar held a hand out to hush the sailor. "No. It's a show of force. The captain knows what he is doing, now pipe down all of you. Keep your mouths shut when they come aboard."

The men aboard Chesapeake tossed lines as they

drew near LeFouet and together, the two crews pulled their ships alongside one another. A broad gang plank was dropped across the gap allowing the Chesapeake to send a boarding party across. A dozen marines filed over the plank two by two they fanned out around LeFouet's deck space carrying muskets. A pair of finely dressed officers followed them. One was older, with an immaculate uniform coat that displayed several rows of medals on his chest. The other officer followed a pace behind the first, he was younger and wore a more plain uniform.

Captain Callais met them at the gangplank. "What is the meaning of this intrusion? We rendered honors to show we have no hostile intentions here. Why are we being forcibly boarded."

The younger officer spoke up, "You are being detained by Captain Stephen Decatur of the U.S.S Chesapeake, it is our intention to search your holds and check your ranks for men unlawfully pressed into service from ships of the United States Navy and any merchant vessels bearing our colors. It would be most unwise for you to resist."

The older officer gave a look over his shoulder. "Evan. I can speak for myself." He looked up at the crew of Frenchmen on LeFouet's deck, his eyes settled on Captain Callais. "As the young man said, I am Captain Decatur. I have been ordered to enforce our nations tariffs at sea and ensure that my countrymen are not being forced into the service of European powers unduly. In addition to this, I am also here to ensure that a message be delivered to the captain of this vessel. Is he present?"

Captain Callais looked around at his crew, his eyes met with Gaspar's for a fleeting moment. "I am the captain of this vessel. We have no trade goods bound for any American port, nor do we hold any Americans aboard."

Captain Decatur nodded, a smile spread across his face. "LeFouet isn't it? You must be Captain Callais."

Captain Callais nodded, his brow scrunched into a deep frown. "How do you know this? How did you know we would be sailing these waters?"

"Mutual associations captain." Captain Decatur took a step toward the stern of LeFouet and motioned for Callais to do the same. "If we could speak somewhere privately, what I have to tell you is of a, well, a sensitive nature."

Captain Callais gestured toward Gaspar, "I would have my first mate accompany us."

"No." Captain Decatur shook his head, "No, this message is for your ears alone captain. I trust that your crew remains oblivious to your mission here in the Caribbean?"

Captain Callais stopped walking for a moment, he faced the American officer with a hard scowl on his features. "How do you know our tasking? I was commissioned by the French Navy…"

"To sink a very particular group of vessels? Am I

correct? They were bearing the stars and stripes if I am not mistaken Captain Callais." The American captain lowered his voice, something followed that Gaspar could not hear. His back was facing Gaspar. Captain Callais stood facing the man, his frown melted into the picture of defeat. He nodded and shot a look over the American's shoulder to Gaspar.

Captain Callais responded to something the American asked him, "The fleet parted ways off of the coast of Jamaica. There are several ships bound for Kingston. This ship and another have been tasked with finding a particular vessel."

The American turned and Gaspar could hear his response, "Ah, yes, the infamous girl captain. I'm told she is a Negro. If you could believe such a thing." He motioned back toward his ship, summoning a pair of sailors carrying a small chest. The American captain leaned in very close to Captain Callais and spoke something Gaspar could not hear.

Gaspar watched his captain's face, the expressions changed it seemed with almost every exchange. He had never seen Captain Callais act so humbled as he was in the face of the American though he had every reason to be. There was an armed host aboard his own ship, a full crew on the decks of the Chesapeake and the guns facing LeFouet were all run out. This American had only to lift a hand in signal and the entire crew aboard LeFouet would be cut down into ribbons, holes blown into her hull and fires set in her hold. Though the American Captain seemed to be friendly enough, the look of dread that spread across Captain Callais' face told Gaspar a very different story.

Their conversation continued in hushed tones that failed to reach Gaspar's ears. Captain Decatur reached his hand up and clamped it onto Callais shoulder, he gave the French Captain a smile and a nod. Captain Decatur patted Callais' shoulder and turned to give the crew on deck one last glance.

"As a representative of the United States Navy, I trust Captain Callais on his honor that he holds no contraband nor any pressed men. Be forewarned that any hostile action against a ship bearing the colors of my country will invoke a much different response next time our sails are spotted." Captain Decatur announced loud enough for everyone on deck to hear. He turned to Captain Callais, "You might want to have a word with your sailors on watch. We've been stalking you for the better part of a day."

With that the American Captain nodded to the younger officer with him and together they departed back to their ship. The American marines filed across the plank behind them and lines were promptly cast off. A flurry of orders flew from the American sailors and their ship began making way in moments.

"What did they want sir?" Gaspar asked his captain ad Callais stood at the rail watching the

Americans depart.

"It makes no difference. Gaspar, have that chest moved into my cabin at once." Captain Callais growled under his breath, "We have a new heading. Make sail for Haiti. Port-Au-Prince."

Chapter 3

Haitian Interior
22 Apr 1809

Muggy heat pressed in while Lilith and her crew moved through the densely planted cane field. Lilith could feel the kiss of the sun as it sliced in between the cane and landed on her skin. The air was thick and the cane almost impossible to navigate through. To make matters more complicated, Lilith had discovered that the loss of vision in one eye had affected her far more than she had first thought. Depth perception was more of a challenge, her field of view was hindered terribly, and the focus of her good eye seemed to suffer as well. She pressed on though, weaving her way in between the stall stands of sugar cane with the soft soil under her feet. The morning sun had risen to a midday high, and the temperatures climbed with it. Working through the sugar cane grew more arduous as the heat intensified until Lilith and her crew were drenched and dripping with sweat. Sugar cane dominated everything, Lilith could only see a few steps ahead or behind where she walked. Jilhal remained close with Renly following right after and Damriq only a few paces behind him. Just ahead of Lilith, Emilia wove her way gracefully through the clumps of cane and looked back to Lilith to urge her on every few minutes.

"Not much further captain, the field will open up to a road soon."

Lilith didn't like the idea of being caught out in the open on a road. "Keep to the cane field."

Emilia stopped and faced the young pirate captain, "If we are caught by the cane crews, they press you into their service captain."

Lilith shook her head, "No girl. We do not fear slavers. Slavers fear us. Keep to the cane field, you will see."

Emilia seemed taken back for a second. Her eyes widened at Lilith before she turned to continue winding their way through the can fields. Lilith watched her movement. The girl moved deftly, weaving in between stalks of cane with ease while Lilith and the rest lumbered their way through half choked by the dense air and lack of wind. It was a claustrophobic feeling for Lilith and she began to understand Chibs' lament about being on land. She longed for the feeling of wooden deck board beneath her feet. The grain worn down to a smooth finish that shined with a depth beauty that reminded her of the sea itself when water soaked into its surface. The motion beneath her as her ship crested a rolling wave out on the open sea. The wind kissing her face with droplets of saltwater as the Maiden would plow ahead breaking through chop and cutting a path through glistening blue waters. Lilith longed for a night sky laden with millions of stars and an evening breeze that filled her ships sails and propelled her toward a glowing sunset with high arcs of wispy cloud painted orange and gold. The suffocating cane field was her newest idea of hell. Lilith's thoughts shifted to her mother. How many days had she spent laboring over cane in fields like this? Her mother had never known the exhilaration of tacking over the wind or feeling the roll of a ship from high up in the tops. She had never sailed for an empty horizon to see what could appear on it after days of vast openness. Lilith's heart sank, her good eye began to well with tears. Her mother hadn't, but she had. Lilith had come to love all of those things and so much more. The smell of a cooked meal at the end of a long day, the adrenaline of a cannon roaring, the intricate dance of a fencing lesson.

Emilia halted. She turned to face Lilith with her hand over her mouth, her eyes wide with fear.

"What is it?" Lilith asked. She tried to look beyond Emilia through the maze of cane but could only see the greenish tan-colored stalks of cane. They were surrounded in it, a sea of cane.

Emilia removed her hand from her mouth just long enough to say, "I hear voices. Can't you hear them?"

Lilith held up her hand to bring her crew to a stop behind them. The air was still. It felt like the very breath they exhaled was recycled back into their lungs. Lilith strained to hear, focusing everything she had on her ears. Her heartbeat, the soft exhale of Jilhal behind her, Renly's feet moving as he adjusted to the stillness. She could hear no other sound. Emilia's eyes went wider, and she pointed ahead of the group into the dense cane.

"It's coming from over there. Don't you hear it?" Emilia asked.

Lilith held up a hand to silence their guide and turned her head to expose her ear to the direction Emilia had pointed. For a moment Lilith could hear nothing but the soft sounds around her. She squinted her good eye and looked at Emilia with a flicker of doubt rising inside her. Was she hearing anything? Then it met her ears. It was so faint Lilith barely detected it at first. A sharp noise, like a hammer being rapped against a chisel. Lilith closed her eye and tried to concentrate on the sound. The sharp clacking was joined by another. Like a pair of carpenters working at fixing damage aboard a ship. But they were too far inland for it to be the sounds of crew repairing a ship.

"I can hear it." Jilhal whispered through the muggy heat. "Hacking. Cutting. They are cutting the cane."

Lilith nodded. She reached out a hand over Jilhal's shoulder and motioned for Renly and

Damriq to fan out behind them. "When we reach the edge of the field, kill the field bosses. We may have found our first recruits."

With the group moving in a line parallel to each other then continued through the rows and bunches of sugar cane. It was slow progress, but Lilith remained focused on the echoing noise of blades hacking against the cane stalks. Voices drifted through the dense foliage. Lilith could hear slaves speaking to one another.

"Hurry up! The wagons will be back soon. If they have to wait on you to haul this to the road none of you are getting any water for the rest of the day!" A voice growled out the threat. Lilith felt a chill run through her arms and into her fingertips despite the oppressive heat that surrounded her. Her heart started to beat faster. They continued working their way forward, step by step through the dense cane. In between the shafts of cane, daylight began to appear. A bright blue sky was visible just a few paces ahead of them.

The sound of blades hacking against cane filled the air. Lilith could see the shapes of slaves pulling down the tall canes and bundling them together. Dark skinned faces covered in sweat leaned over the base of the sugar cane plants, their expressions were drawn with fear and exertion. Lilith stopped between two large clumps of sugar cane with a single row separating her from the labor of the slaves. A warm breeze filtered through from the opening in front of her. It did little to quell the stifling heat clustered within the packed stands of sugar cane. For a long moment Lilith and the others watched while the workers diligently cut into the base of cane stalks. When the tall stalks fell to the ground others would close in around them and begin cutting the tall stalks into smaller sections. They then bundled the stalks together and hauled the bundles away. There was a crest of hill that sloped downward, as the slaves carried away bundles of sugar cane they disappeared from view while walking down the gradual slope.

Just a few feet away from Lilith a young woman stooped over with a curved knife in her hand. She swung the small blade and stuck it into the base of a cane stalk. The young woman worked the blade back and forth sawing it deeper into the greenish tan cane stalk until the blade was nearly cut through. Her eyes wandered deeper into the shadows of the thick growth. Lilith could see her freeze as her eyes recognized the shape of Lilith's feet. Her gaze lifted until she was staring into Lilith's face. Confusion crossed the young woman's face, confusion and then terror. Lilith lifted a finger to her pursed lips hoping the girl would remain quiet. Their stares remained locked for a moment. Lilith knew she probably was a horrifying sight with the ragged bloodstained bandanna covering one eye and clothes all in tatters from the battle that sunk her ship. Lilith held her hands up, with her palms facing the young slave. She held her finger in front of pursed lips and motioned for her companions to step forward into the light of day. As they emerged from the shadows of tall cane stalks the blades ceased their hacking. A glaring silence covered the opening where the slaves had been toiling away at harvesting sugar cane.

Lilith drew her cutlass and held it low while the eyes of everyone gathered on her. "I am Captain Lilith of the Drowned Maiden." She hoisted her sword and pointed it at the curved knife the young woman near her held. "They give you knives to cut cane. If you would rather use your blades to claim your freedom, follow me." As Lilith stepped past the wide eyes and wondering looks of the slaves Renly and Damriq drew their swords. Jilhal drew hers next and extended a hand to a young man who was still bent down from cutting cane stalks. Lilith smiled as she heard her loyal companion encouraging the slaves to join them.

"Your freedom is in front of you for the taking. Join us and we will cut down anyone who would stand in your way!"

The line of slaves began to filter away from the front of tall cane. They followed Lilith and her small band toward the crest of the hill. Lilith looked over each shoulder. There was close to twenty of them. Some followed, some hesitated and then began to follow along as she came near the crest of the gradual slope downward. The hill gave way in a gentle sweep down to a muddy rutted road where a band of men were gathered under the shade of a line of tall trees with a thick overhanging canopy. At first the men appeared to be reveling together, laughing and talking. Lilith stopped at the top of the slope. She looked over the hillside dotted with cut cane stalks. Many of them were jagged and sharp looking, a few were stained by blood. Lilith pulled in a deep breath. The men and women had been traversing this slope with heavy bundles of sugar cane strapped to their backs. They've had to navigate the gauntlet of sharp stumps to haul their load down to the road. The men by the road hadn't taken notice of her yet, no doubt they were absorbed by some bawdy tale or recollection of past glory. The shade they had gathered under was just over a hundred yards distant. She could challenge them from afar and draw them up the hill. Lilith knew the climb would discourage their assault. The sharp stumps where cane had been cut may even slow them further. But sitting on top of a hill and shouting a challenge would not do. The men and women she had just rallied deserved better. They deserved to slay their captors, to watch their eyes fill with fear and see hope abandon their spirits as their company was cut to ribbons. Lilith counted eight men standing beneath the shade of forest canopy. She pulled out a pistol that was tucked into her belt and began walking down the slope.

'North Wind,'
24 Apr 1809
18 Degrees 05' N, 74 Degrees 56' W

"Steady lads. All together now, heave!" The shout came from a grizzled petty officer that stood watching over a line crew as they hoisted a new spar for the topsail on North Wind's main mast. The old spar had cracked and given way during the maneuver off the coast of Haiti. Admiral Torren had just emerged from his cabin to begin his daily ritual of walking laps around the ship. The admiral hadn't missed a single day of his daily walks, inclement weather, cold nor heat had kept him from it. He told Lieutenant Thatcher that his walks served to keep his lungs full of fresh air. They certainly served that purpose, but Admiral Torren had begun to pay special attention to the crew on deck as he made his daily walks. He had noticed of late an odd quiet from a crew that had been high in spirits and zeal for duty just a matter of weeks before. The admiral had his suspicions as to what caused the change of temperament.

Far below the main deck, in a pair of cells within North Wind's hold were two prisoners. Both men were a drain on the crew's morale. One because he was accused of killing a highly respected admiral, the other was a traitor against the crown. King's men loathed treason, and the crew aboard North Wind were truly king's men. Admiral Torren watched as the top men and line crew worked together to accomplish their task. They were a first-rate crew, not some bandy group of pressed men sniveling for home. These were seasoned sailors, some of England's finest. The spar was lifted high above the deck and men crawled along the top mast yard to attach the sail to the wooden spar. When it was ties off securely the line crew on deck eased away the tension they had held for the better part of an hour and let the sail unfurl in the wind. A cheer went up as the canvas snapped taut and the new spar held the sail's shape.

"Alright you dogs. Let's have the sheets tightened before we go to patting each other on the arse. The job isn't finished until it's finished!" The petty officer snarled over the sailor's hearty claps and laughter.

Admiral Torren smiled to himself. The task had been well handled. He hoisted his cane and began to walk the deck. The early morning breeze was cool coming off of the sea, but not quite so cool as to require a cloak. The admiral had shunned wearing the heavy garment weeks ago, except during the deluge that ensued while they had fired on the pirate ship. The days since had been blessed by steady firm winds and plenty of sunshine. The seas rolled a bit higher than normal for the Caribbean but nothing Admiral Torren had not seen before. Fresh air and sunshine lifted the admiral's spirits as his heels clunked along across the wooden deck. He had made almost a complete circuit at his normal brisk pace when he noticed the deck hands were going quiet as he passed. They averted their eyes and avoided making any invitation to contact with him.

"And there it is again." He uttered beneath his breath. "Lurking just beneath the surface like an unmarked shoal."

Admiral Torren slowed his walk. He began to take notice of the individual tasks going on around him. Sailors coiled line into neat formations after they made their adjustments and tied off, the coils lay flat on the deck so as not to pose a tripping hazard. A pair of young-looking seamen were scrubbing at the deck midship, their eyes were locked onto their work as he passed. At the stern a lieutenant was leading a class for the midshipmen, teaching them the finer points of the sextant and reckoning latitude. Admiral Torren came to a halt beside the small gathering and listened in.

"Now take your sextant and aim the instrument toward the horizon." The lieutenant instructed while demonstrating for the junior officers, he paused and held his sextant away from his eye and focused on a young man that had taken more interest in watching a pair of dolphins leaping from the sea behind the wake of North Wind. "Young man, if you do not master this you cannot hope to pass your lieutenant exam. It is critical for you to take an accurate reading so your calculations will bear true." He lowered his sextant and focused on the young midshipman. "Do you know the dangers of being wrong?"

The midshipman shifted his weight in between his feet and stared back at the stern-faced lieutenant. "A ship could run aground?"

Admiral Torren clenched his jaw at the exchange. He watched and listened intently for the lieutenant's response.

"Running aground is a danger. Shoals and reefs require precise navigation and yield terrible consequences for even a small miscalculation. The greatest danger though is quite simply being lost at sea. His majesty's navy has lost more than a few crews to starvation or dehydration because they lacked the necessary skills in navigation. If you make a miscalculation, you could plot your course too far out from land to see a necessary landmark. If a ship were to sail by their landmark, they could mistake one spit of land for another, or make their course correction at an inappropriate time. Imagine a ship sailing for weeks, their supplies dwindling as time passes, without so much a sighting of land and not even a foggy notion of where they are." The lieutenant took a deep breath and looked over his charges. He softened his tone, "Much rests on your ability to navigate properly. Our king and our great nation expect us to be the masters of the seas and by God we will be." He raised his sextant again, "Now, pick up your sextant and aim for the horizon." The Lieutenant went through the exercise as well. "Adjust your index arm along the graduated arc until you get an orb from the sun." He went through the step himself as he instructed, gently adjusting the delicate brass fixtures of his own instrument. "When you have the orb adjusted down so that it is touching the horizon line, tighten the drum and we take an arc minute reading." The lieutenant twisted a small screw near the bottom of his sextant and looked at the gauge. He examined the instruments held by the midshipmen around him. "Good, good. Now that we have that piece, what do we need next?"

One of the midshipmen spoke up, a young man Admiral Torren recognized as Midshipman Elliot Brant. "We need a time on deck lieutenant. And a compass azimuth toward the sun."

"Very good, Midshipman Brant. Well done." The lieutenant faced the quarterdeck and called down. "Can I get the time on deck?"

A sailor standing next to a set of hanging hourglasses cupped a hand around the side of his mouth. "Two turns past eight bells, sir."

"Eight twenty in the morning. And now for our azimuth." He handed Midshipman Brant a brass compass covered in patina. "Midshipman Brant, would you be so kind as to attain our azimuth to the sun?"

Admiral Torren watched while the young officer made his reading. Midshipman Brant called it out for the rest of the class and the midshipmen standing around all wrote down the recording on a small card of paper.

"Alright then lads. We will take our readings and apply the formula, be sure to use your sun chart and Mr. Brant's azimuth reading as well. You have ten minutes to calculate our latitude and longitude to within five nautical miles." The lieutenant announced, he turned around and came face to face with Admiral Torren. "Oh, sir. My apologies sir, I did not know you were observing my informal class."

Admiral Torren gave the lieutenant a nod. "A job well done lieutenant. Well done indeed. Is this their first time calculating longitude and latitude?"

"No, sir. No, we have been working on the sextant and compass azimuth since we departed Nassau. Only when we are not occupied by pursuit or combat, sir." The lieutenant replied with a hurried cadence.

Admiral Torren lifted a brow. The young officer seemed terribly frightened for some reason. "Of course, of course. I do appreciate you expounding the consequences of poor navigation skills to the lads. So much of what we do aboard ship becomes a series of life-or-death choices. Wouldn't you agree lieutenant?"

The lieutenant went a shade of pale. He fumbled with his brass sextant, nearly dropping it to the deck. "Y-y-yes sir. Yes life or death."

"Indeed lieutenant. It's of the utmost import these young men understand the consequences of their actions. Especially when it is so easy to veer off course. So easy in fact, one might not even realize he is sailing in dangerous waters until it is too late." Admiral Torren watched the lieutenant's face carefully as the younger officer reacted to his reply. "It would be good to teach the lads the importance of the chain of command, or readdress it rather. They can always come to their lieutenant with a question. Clarity is the twelve pounder we use to fight against mistakes before they happen."

"Yes sir. Absolutely, I will do that, sir." The lieutenant blurted and shrugged one shoulder.

Admiral Torren narrowed his eyes and leaned forward. "Do you have anything you wish to ask me lieutenant?"

The lieutenant fumbled with his sextant again. He shrugged his shoulders and allowed his gaze to sink down to the wooden deck of North Wind. "No sir. No, nothing."

"Good. Well, if something arises, you have my leave to call on me in my quarters. Day or night." Admiral Torren looked over the group of midshipmen, "That goes for all of you as well. If you have a question, or a concern. You may call on me in my quarters, or while I am out on deck. I don't want to deprive any of you the benefit of my decades at sea. There are very few situations I have not experienced at sea, those I have not experienced I have either learned about through reading detailed reports or conversations with officers who have a firsthand account."

The midshipmen all looked back at the admiral with blank stares. He tapped his cane on deck and turned to continue his walk. He reached the foremast before Lieutenant Thatcher came out on deck and hurried to his side. In the shadow of sail, with a slight mist washing up from the windward side of the ship the admiral could feel a chill. His bones ached as it sank deeper into his flesh. The chill took deep root as he heard a sailor across the deck grumble. "There he is, and with his pet too."

The admiral tapped his cane onto the wooden deck and continued his walk without breaking gait. His jaw clenched tighter as the sailor's words burned into the back of his mind. They were at the very edge of challenging, though not outright enough to warrant a reaction.

"Sir. If I may have a word?" Lieutenant Thatcher requested as the admiral continued his hurried stride.

Without looking over his shoulder Admiral Torren replied, "What is it?"

"If I may sir, privately?" Lieutenant Thatcher's voice was strained. The admiral knew that his young aide was well aware how urgent a matter must be for him to abandon his ritual walk.

He turned and faced Lieutenant Thatcher, "What is it? Have you heard something? Something from the crew? The officers?"

Lieutenant Thatcher's face flushed red. He nodded and affirmative answer and looked over each shoulder. "Some of the marines sir. They have been talking about the prisoner, Lieutenant Pike."

"And? Out with it son. What have they said?" The admiral pressed in a hushed tone.

Lieutenant Thatcher stepped closer and leaned

toward Admiral Torren's ear. "I heard one of them say there is a mutiny afoot."

Cold finger cemented the chill in Admiral Torren's bones. He felt the blood leave his face. His hand gripped onto the pommel of his cane, digging the ornate brass handle into the flesh of his fingers. He looked at his aide for a long moment and then shifted his gaze over the deck of North Wind and finally let it rest out on the sea horizon. "Alright lad. Pay very close attention to everything from here on. And do exactly as I tell you."

"Yes sir." Lieutenant Thatcher quickly replied.

Admiral Torren's eyes remained locked on the horizon where a blue green sea met with the pale blue sky. Thin wisps of cloud stretched in striations over the horizon fading into nothing as the sky turned into a fierce deep blue high overhead. "Have the watch officer sound the alarm to quarters. He is to have the crew run through dry fire gun drills until he is instructed otherwise. Once they begin I want the master at arms to report to my cabin with two of the sergeants from our marine contingent. Lively now, every moment works against us."

Pirate Cove
20 Apr 1809

A layer of perspiration covered Chibs' bald head and face. Great drops of sweat ran down through bushy eyebrows and dripped from his beard. He laid under the shade cover of the forest canopy struggling for every breath through stabbing pains. His ribs were on fire. The wound there had been far more serious than he first noticed. Once he had noticed it though, he had tried to hide it from the captain and the crew. No use getting everyone frightened over nothing. But it hadn't been nothing. His arm ached worse than his ribs, every few minutes there was a dull pounding sensation followed by prickly needle pokes that danced up the limb and drove Chibs mad. As he drifted in and out of sleep there were times Chibs could almost feel the fingertips that were now gone. He awoke and drifted his eyes back to the wounded arm only to find a bandaged stump with blood seeping through the fabric. His eyes couldn't focus on anything for long, he felt seasick but without the sea.

"Seasick. That'll be the day." He coughed and sputtered. "More like sick for the sea." He dragged his head around to scan the little camp. "Cap'n?"

"No captain here. Only me." Dr. LeMeux replied with a smile.

Chibs jolted where he lay. He sat upright and faltered as his head spun from the sudden movement. "Who said that?" He growled, reaching for his saber with his good hand. "Show yourself you son of a…"

"I am right here Chibs." LeMeux replied in a soft voice, he put a hand on Chibs' shoulder. "You should be resting."

Chibs found the pommel of his sword and laced his fingers around the grip. "You! I told you to run."

"And be glad I came back, you have lost a lot of blood Chibs, you really should rest." LeMeux looked directly into Chibs eyes. He turned to face someone else, Chibs tried to follow where he looked but his head spun too much. The world shifted and pitched beneath him like a drunk at sea in high rollers. He could see doubles of the doctor, then triples. The whole world seemed to be oozing in and out, colliding with itself and then separating back into threes and fours. Chibs let out a groan as his arm radiated another wave of pain. He felt hot all of the sudden, blinding suffocating heat that would not let up, it radiated from his arm.

"Rum, doctor. Get me rum." Chibs slurred, barely able to form the words with his thick tongue that didn't want to obey his brain's commands.

"I'm afraid that isn't a good idea either." Dr. LeMeux answered, "You are too weak…"

Chibs shot his hand from the grip of his sword to one of the floating heads of Dr. LeMeux that danced in his vision. He must have picked the correct one because his fingers found the soft flesh of the French doctor's throat. He squeezed, "I don't give a shit if you have to sell my rotten arm to get some. Get me rum or I will pop your head right off of your damned little neck!"

Dr. LeMeux's voice ground and hissed through his squeezed throat, "Let go, please…"

A familiar voice cried, "Chibs, let go, you're going to kill him!"

Chibs released his grip and looked for Omibwe. The young African boy whose mother had stolen his heart aboard ship. "He'll be fine lad. I was just expressing my thanks, for cutting off my arm. Thank you doctor, don't know what I would do without you."

"You would be dead sir." Dr. LeMeux's voice squealed as he sucked in a deep breath.

"Maybe so, but I'd be dead with both of my damned hands. Do you know how important a sailor's hands are? I'll never climb the rigging again, you barnacle sucking land lubber. If it weren't for the boy I'd draw my steel and run you through right now." Chibs roared as fever sweat continued to run down his face and soak into his shirt. "Get me some rum doctor. Before I get up and get it my damned self."

The doctor leaned away and smoothed the front of his shirt. Chibs almost laughed at how ridiculous it was, everyone's clothes were dirty and stained with mud and blood. The doctor wanted to make sure he still looked presentable. The Frenchman stood and disappeared from Chibs' sight leaving him with Omibwe.

The young African boy stared at Chibs for a long moment, looking at his bandaged arm and his sweat covered forehead. "I lost my leg and I can still be on the crew."

A sharp pang went through Chibs, it struck him

all the way to his core. In his anguish and pain he had forgotten how brave the young man was. Here he was blubbering about his arm when this boy had been missing his leg since before the two had met. Omibwe still made for a damn fine helmsman, and his smile was as bright as any sunrise Chibs had seen in his many years at sea. "Ah. Damn. You're right lad. I'll quit my bellyaching." He paused and looked over the young boy as another flash of heat overcame him. "I suppose it's this fever that's robbed me of my sense."

"Did you mean what you said? By the fire? Could we really save the Maiden?" Omibwe's eyes went wide as he asked.

Chibs' heart swelled. He caught a glimmer of the hope the young man felt and it gave him a new course to tack. "Well, yes." He relaxed back onto the pile of green leaves Captain Lilith had bundled under his head. "It won't be easy mind you. And I'm going to need a lot of help. But, together, I think we just might be able to salvage her." Chibs coughed and shuddered as a wave of fever heat seemed to sweep over his body. He took a slow breath and focused back onto Omibwe. "The first thing to do is to winch her as far ashore as we can. We'll have to get ropes set on her hull wherever possible, strong timbers that won't give. If we can brace the lines against large tree, two or three per line if we can, then we may be able to heel her into shore far enough to make repairs."

"What about the cannons? There were guns that

took direct hits, Chibs." Omibwe squatted next to Chibs and leaned his chin onto the knee of his goon leg. "How do we replace those?"

Chibs nodded his head back and closed his eyes. The world seemed to spin with he and the boy at the very center of it. "Replacing the guns could be tricky. But once we get her fit to sail we can worry about that later. There's plenty of armed merchant vessels that frequent these waters. Maybe we can find one filled with cowards that will give them up without too much of a fight."

Dr. LeMeux's voice cut in, "And just how do you suppose we are going to repair the Maiden? She was blown open from the waterline to the railings on her starboard side. Her hull must be completely full of seawater, it will be impossible to bring her on shore."

Chibs opened and eye and saw a blurry figure resembling the French doctor. "Old sailor's tricks, doctor. Leverage and such. I said it is possible, I didn't say it would be easy, or quick."

"I found a half bottle of wine in Emilia's things. If you want it." Dr. LeMeux's voice dripped with disdain, "Although I can't say I would recommend you drink anything but water at this point, you lost a lot of blood, and your body is fighting off infection."

Chibs closed his eye and reached out with his good hand. "I asked for a drink doctor, not your opinions. This isn't the first time I've been wounded in a fight neither. I've chased away fever with drink before, it worked just fine." The cool glass bottle slapped into the palm of Chibs' hand, and he cocked a half smile. "Cheer up doctor. If you want to toast my health, I'll save you a sip."

"I will abstain, thank you."

Chibs raised the bottle to his lips and found a wooden cork, he bit into the soft wood and spit the cork away toward the long smoldered out campfire. The glass touched his lips and cool sweet wine washed over his tongue and down his parched throat. He swallowed a big mouthful of wine and wiped his beard with the crook of his good arm. "I have to save her doctor. I've been with her for too long to just give up on her."

"I'm sure the captain will understand if you cannot raise the dead Chibs…" Dr. LeMeux began to reply.

"Not the captain you dolt. The ship. I have to save the ship." Chibs snapped in an annoyed growl. The wine was already working on his frayed nerves, soothing his ragged mind and numbing the pain radiating from his ribs and arm. "I've been at sea with the Maiden since before Captain Lilith. Before Captain James even. She was the King's Maiden then, pride of the fleet wherever we sailed. We were ordered to escort East India ships around Good Hope and to the Caribbean. But the fleet master had other ideas, he stopped along the African coast to load more goods. Ivory he told us, load and loads of it. But when we came into that little bay there were no stocks of ivory. So he crammed every nook and cranny of the fleet with living, breathing Africans and we all made sail for the Caribbean." Chibs lifted the bottle again and drew in a big gulp of the dark wine, purple dribbles left the corner of his mouth and trickled into his beard. It smelled sweet. It tasted even sweeter. The world seemed warmer, he started to feel like his sea legs were coming back. "As we crossed the Atlantic we came upon a storm like something out of a song. Winds howled so hard I thought they would pluck the masts right through the deck and tear us all to pieces. The Maiden shuddered, god her decks groaned that night. We set off from Africa with seven ships, after the storm there were only three. It was like looking into the face of god while he set his vengeful ways down right on top of us. I've never seen a storm so bad. I hope I never see one like that again. Seasoned hands were washed right off deck, stay lines snapping and whipping about. We had a cannon come loose, it near punched a hole right in the Maiden's belly. That would've been the end of us, but we got her under control." Chibs opened his eyes and looked right at the doctor. "But when the storm was over. That's when the real nightmare began."

"How is that?" Dr. LeMeux lowered himself to sit next to Omibwe, his brows furrowed as he asked. "The storm wasn't the worst part?"

"Aye." Chibs tipped the wine bottle up and finished the last deep drink it offered. "The storm

Resurrecting the Maiden

was over, but it had blown us so far off course we had no idea where we were. To make matters worse, the officers couldn't get a handle on their navigation. They argued back and forth about our position and which course to set. Every time they came to a conclusion we would sail for a few days and fail to spot land." Chibs set the bottle onto the leafy ground of the campsite and propped himself up onto his good elbow. "You know what happens first when a ship is lost at sea?"

"No. I can't say I do." LeMeux replied with a shrug.

"The officers got real testy. They argued with each other behind closed doors at first but eventually it boiled over and they wound up on deck bickering and snapping like a bunch of dogs fighting over meat. Soon enough they got the notion in their heads that the crew was to blame. They'd flog a man for the slightest misdeed. Then the water ran out." Chibs took a breath and spat toward the rising ashes of the dead campfire. "Too many mouths to feed, too many souls needing fresh water. Our good captain decided it was time to lose unnecessary cargo…"

"He started to throw the slaves overboard." LeMeux finished Chibs' sentence.

Chibs nodded, "Aye, he did. And it pains me to say, he managed to toss a few of them over before we stopped him."

"How did you do that?" LeMeux asked, exchanging a glance with Omibwe.

Chibs looked the doctor right in his eyes, "We mutinied. I ran him through with his own sword and then pushed him over to sink to the depths." Chibs leaned back onto the stack of foliage beneath him with a grin spreading across his face, "And I would do it all again doctor."

'North Wind'
24 Apr 1809
18 Degrees 05' N, 74 Degrees 56' W

The sound of water rushing and trickling past North Wind's thick wooden hull was a constant melody deep in the recesses of her hold. Will's cell seemed to grow darker and colder with every day of progress they made toward Kingston. A small square of yellow light from the sentry's lantern in the passageway danced up and down, back and forth with the movement of the ship. The metal handle of the lantern creaked at each pitch of the ship to punctuate the sound of water sloshing and rushing past the outside of the hull. There were times when seawater would collect at the bottom of his cell and make lying down unbearable. Will thought back to the first time he had met Admiral Torren in London, that roasting office in the august afternoon heat with a fire crackling away in the fireplace. Will shifted on the damp straw beneath him. He imagined the admiral in his cabin, dry, comfortable, with an aide to fetch his meals and light his fires. He tried to think of something else, anything else. His cell was a cold, wet, miserable hell that smelled of putrid waste and rotten straw. The sentries rarely emptied his waste bucket and when North Wind was moving through high seas or foul wind he was forced to either hold the bucket in place or let it spill all over the floor of his cell. Eventually Will figured out if he lay on the piled straw at an angle and braced the bucket with his bare feet he could lie down and avoid letting the waste pour over everything, though some would still slop over the wooden brim and get on his feet.

Every waking hour was an excruciating torture. The cold. The smell. The constant damp misery of his cell made sleep near impossible. His wounds were far from healed. Will was sure that he could smell infection oozing from the deeper gouges in his belly. His face was still so swollen it pained him to open his mouth when the guards pushed a tin cup filled with food through his window. He had no reference for time. Only the changing of watch outside of his door. It wasn't long until Will had gotten the watch order confused and he could no longer tell what time of day it was by looking to see who was out in the passageway either. He could feel his sanity slipping away with each creak of the lantern, every smart quip by the sentries outside and every time his waste bucket toppled over and spilled on his cell floor. He was surely losing his mind.

He wasn't sure what time it was, or even if it had

been real when he heard the sentry outside speaking to the other prisoner. At first he dismissed it as the squeak of the lantern or maybe a rat out in the passageway. It started in low hisses and wisps. A moment would pass and then more hisses met his ear. A quiet mumble replied to the whispering and then the passageway went silent. Will tried to decipher what he was hearing, or if he was really hearing anything at all. North Wind groaned and shifted beneath him. The ship's rhythm changed. Or perhaps his mind was playing more tricks on him. Will opened his eyes and tried to lift himself off of the matted straw. His chest and belly burned with pangs of pain. He lifted one of his hands and braced it against the bulkhead. His wrists were still raw from iron shackles biting and grinding the flesh away while he had been keelhauled, twice. He managed to get onto his feet but still had to steady himself against the wall, his knees were so shaky he felt they would give out from under him at any moment.

"It's going to happen tonight, after the watch changes." A voice drifted in through his window. "We have more than half the ship, including both of the marine sergeants." A long pause followed. Will shifted his feet as quietly as he could to get closer to his cell window. "Once it is over, we'll come down and release you. When we make port in Kingston you will be free to go."

Will was sure of the voice now. It was the same sentry that had been exchanging conversation with

Tim for days. He peered through the square window frame and spied the back of a royal marine's red uniform coat. The marine was leaned up against the door to speak into Tim's cell.

"And what of the other prisoner? Surely you will see to it that he doesn't escape justice. Won't you?" Tim's voice asked. "Will he stand trial?"

The sentry leaned back from the wooden cell door "I suppose he must. I don't know."

"He cannot be allowed to go free. That much you must understand. He is in league with some very powerful people. If he is allowed to go free he will be a threat to your nation, perhaps even the king himself!" Tim's voice grew more tense with each word.

Will grit his teeth, despite hot pains shooting through his jaw and into his skull when he did it. The American had managed to corrupt this crew against their commander. He wanted to yell out the window, to talk some sense into this dull sentry. But every time he had argued through his cell window with these two men he had played right into Tim's hands and cemented what the slippery American had been trying to accomplish.

"Once we have control of the helm and roust the old man from his cabin we'll lock him down here in one of these cells. He can plead his case before the monarch." The sentries words were rushed, like he half expected someone to pop out of the shadows and seize him at any moment.

"You mean to return to England then?" Tim

asked.

"After we take on supplies in Kingston. Yes." The sentry replied after letting out a deep sigh, "The admiral will be delivered to London to answer for his crimes against the crown and we will all move on from this whole affair."

"I'm sure." Tim's voice oozed through the passageway and slithered into Will's ears.

The sudden rattle of drums beat through the timber decks and reverberated down into the ship's hold. Within moments the clacking of gun ports being wrenched open echoed down and the deck above them creaked and groaned under the load of cannons being heaved into their firing positions.

"Quarters?" the sentry asked out loud. His voice sounded confused. The noises came to a stop and there was a moment of silence before the gun carriage wheels started back across the deck again. "No, not quarters. Gun drills. I haven't seen gun drills this early in the day for years."

Will bit his lip. He hoped it was a good sign, a sign that the owly old admiral had caught a whiff of what was festering amongst his crew. He could keep the large majority of them occupied with gun drills and a few sail changes while he sorted through the mess of conspiring crewmen. Will had heard tales of senior officers using this tactic when they suspected a mutiny was imminent. Captain Grimes had even told him of such an occurrence when he had been a fresh lieutenant. His commander had ordered the helm to come into the wind and tack over close reach every fifteen minutes. At the same time he initiated gun drills below decks and ordered a double guard put onto his cabin. A list of suspected conspirators was called in for questioning one by one until the truth of the matter was laid bare. By the time it was all finished, three sailors and one officer swung by their necks from the yard and the rest of the crew was so fatigued that any fight on deck would have been put down by the marine detachment with ease. Will dared a half smile in the darkness of his cell, the old man knew exactly what he was doing. The smile faded after an instant as he remembered that several of the conspirators were a part of the ship's marine detachment. Slinking his back against the coarse bulkhead behind him Will sank down to sit at the base of the wooden cell door. Will could feel ragged pains shooting through his flesh and railing along his ribs as the rough wood bit at his wounds but he didn't care. The admiral was about to blunder into an ambush.

Chapter 4

'Le Fouet'
24 Apr 1809
17 Degrees 48' N, 69 Degrees 52' W

Long tails of wispy pink clouds stretched high into the majesty of deep purple skies punctuated by a hundred thousand stars that twinkled away their last light before giving way to the stronger light of dawn. Gaspar loved the dawn of a clear morning at sea. Chilled fresh air coming off of the water, a tame breeze and the promise of sunshine ahead made for an intoxicating greeting to the day. This particular morning had been lost on Gaspar, though the majesty that played out overhead was no less spectacular, his mind was centered on his captain. Gaspar knew the proud commander had not slept in days. The meals he had brought to his cabin remained untouched until Gaspar had need of the plate to bring the next meal. Since their run in with the American frigate Captain Callais carried on more like a man under hostage than the commander of a storied French privateer vessel. Most of the captain's time was spent at the base of the bowsprit, staring off into the horizon. When he hadn't stationed himself on the bow, the captain would retire to his cabin and bar the door. He neglected to answer any calls, even when Gaspar attempted to deliver his meals, the door remained barred and plate sat just outside the wooden door on a barrel until it was time for the next to be delivered.

Under the pink and red hues that invaded the last inky spots of night sky Captain Callais remained stationed on the bow of LeFouet. He wore a cloak and tricorn hat against the chill, and hadn't shifted his eyes away from the horizon for hours. The seas slapped LeFouet's hull in a rhythmic repetition as she plowed her way forward through low choppy waves Her sails filled with a cool morning breeze that propelled them toward the Haitian coast that lay somewhere over the golden pink horizon. Gaspar had been putting off the conversation he needed to have with his captain for days. The events that had transpired aboard LeFouet had left the crew shaken and unsteady. The captain's sudden and violent removal of his newest lieutenant followed shortly by the oddest encounter with a foreign ship Gaspar had ever witnessed.

It was common knowledge in any port that the newly formed nation was growing weary of British overreach and the abuse of ships bearing her colors was common practice among several European powers, France included. Until recent years the Americans lacked sea power. Their ships had been old relics of the days of its colonial era. But a new age was coming and the balance of power on the Atlantic was at stake. The shipyards in Boston were producing heavy hulled frigates that could meet or exceed the speed and maneuvering capability of just about anything afloat. To raise the stakes even higher, the Americans had armed their new class of ships to the teeth often exceeding the gun count and weight of a British ship of comparable size. Rumors in the Martinique pubs had it that the U.S.S Constitution had already engaged a British fleet, sinking one of their vessels under the cover of night only to watch the Royal Navy tuck tail and run when the sun rose on a flotilla of debris. Gaspar had chuckled when he heard the telling by a couple of French merchant sailors over a table full of ale mugs and plates of food. He had not found the idea of cocksure Americans prowling about the seas in a ship of superior design and armament nearly as comical when the U.S.S Chesapeake had been bearing down on them. Once they had been boarded he realized just how drastically the balance of power was about to shift.

The Chesapeake was unlike any man of war Gaspar had seen in his years at sea. She was sleek and quick with tall masts and four huge sets of sails on three masts. Her hull looked to be white oak, widely sought after for its strength and density but rare in England or France. But what set her apart was her armament. She was armed to the teeth, the Americans had marine sharpshooters high in the top rigging when they had come aboard and more cannons bristling from their gun ports than Gaspar would have expected to see on a ship of her size. And she wasn't alone. In addition to the Chesapeake, the Americans had built and launched the U.S.S Constitution, the U.S.S United States and the U.S.S Essex. There were more, Gaspar was sure of it, he had spoken with a sailor that had come from the Boston shipyards in a pub in Brest, France before LeFouet had last set off for the Caribbean. The Americans were not to be counted out on the world stage of sea powers any longer.

"Are you on watch for something in particular captain?" Gaspar asked as he approached the brooding officer on the bow.

Captain Callais broke his gaze from the horizon to look over Gaspar for a scant moment before returning to his constant search. "Yes I am Gaspar." The captain's eyes narrowed as beams of sunlight began to crest over the horizon.

"Something I can tell our lookouts to be on watch for?" Gaspar pressed the captain, watching the side of his face. His expression remained stony, unchanging.

"The Haitian coast for one. I expect our first sighting of land should be the far northwestern finger of the island. From there we will patrol the coastline in search of a ship." Captain Callais answered in a monotone grumble. He looked down onto LeFouet's deck for a moment and lifted a foot up on to the bow railing.

"Right. A ship..." Gaspar looked out to match his captain's stare at the shining horizon, "A specific ship sir?"

Captain Callais remained silent and nodded, the early beams of morning lit his face with their brilliant glow. He hadn't shaved in days, his eyes were lined by dark circles and his cheeks looked drawn and hollow in contrast to his broad, square jaw. "We are in search of a vessel flying pirate colors, first mate."

"We're hunting pirates sir?" Gaspar's face shriveled into a deep frown.

Captain Callais shot him a long glance before turning back out to sea, "Yes Gaspar. We are hunting for a pirate vessel. That was always our task, I thought it best to keep that to myself for the time being."

"Captain, the crew is already unsettled from being boarded at gunpoint by the Americans. They aren't going to like hearing this." Gaspar braced himself for Captain Callais to snap in a vehement show of anger. The captain only turned to him with a sorrowful glare.

"It is difficult enough for me, first mate. See to it the crew is kept unaware as long as possible. This is our tasking, we will see it through, to whatever end." Captain Callais mumbled and shot a look over the deck of LeFouet as her crew continued the work of sailing. "It is bad enough that I have had not been afforded the opportunity to sail under contract for the French navy, now I have been heeled and redirected by a nation of upstarts and brigands."

Gaspar twisted his mouth and frowned. He looked down at the deck beneath his feet and scratched his head. "I don't understand, sir. We're doing the American's bidding now?" He shifted a glance back toward the cabin at the rear of the ship. "Does this have anything to do with the chest they brought aboard?"

Captain Callais snapped his head around and glared at Gaspar. There was the anger he had feared. "That is not your concern Gaspar. Your job is to make sure the crew performs their tasks as instructed. The contents of that chest are of no concern to you. When you need to know what is in it, I will inform you."

A chill gripped Gaspar in his belly. Icy fingers of fear laced their way around his spine. He could feel the captain's glare as much as see it. "Yes, sir."

A snap of canvas sounded and drew both men's attention to the sails above LeFouet. A shift in the wind had not been corrected for at the helm and LeFouet's main and topsail on the main mast were spilling precious speed with every guttering flap of canvas.

"It appears you have some things to attend to Gaspar. We will speak again later." Captain Callais coldly turned back toward the sea without so much as a dismissing gesture to the first mate.

Gaspar looked at the captain from the corner of his eyes. "I will have it handled, sir." He left the captain staring off into the sunrise. In a strange way, Gaspar felt even more troubled than before his visit with the captain. *Why had he reacted so suddenly when I mentioned the chest? What business were they conducting that an American vessel could redirect them?* Gaspar's head spun as he considered the possibilities. It wasn't unheard of for a privateer vessel to accept commissions from a foreign nation, but they were currently sailing at the behest of the French investors. He knew Captain Callais was from a family of repute. Could he possibly be trying to levy his position into favor with the Americans?

Slack hands at the ship's wheel jolted Gaspar's mind back to the task at hand. He narrowed his eyes at the man's loose grip and sagging eyelids. "Hold onto the damned wheel boy, or you'll wind up swimming to shore."

"The wind shifts, I adjust and then it shifts back again." The sailor complained, "I am trying to hold a middle ground so we don't lose our course."

Gaspar shook his head, "Never mind that. If we make a course change we will adjust sail, a point to either side won't break our navigation but it could mean an extra knot or even two, keep the sails taut." Gaspar reached up and adjusted the ship's wheel with the sailor's hand still on it. He looked aloft and watched at the fluttering edge of sail caught and went tight. He looked back to the sailor manning the helm. "If you make small adjustments and the sail still flutters like that, it means we've lost a sheet or one has gone slack. Look to the lines holding her corners taut." Gaspar pointed to the four corners of the main sail, "If you keep the wind in her sails and the sheets are all adjusted tight LeFouet can make twelve knots with a fair wind. That means the captain expects twelve knots no matter the conditions." Gaspar looked up into the rigging again and continued, "He is a good man, but that temper of his... You don't want to rouse it. Keep her sails full boy."

The shout came down from high in the rigging. One voice at first, a younger sailor who could barely get the words out without tripping on his tongue. Other sailors echoed his call, passing the word down to the deck of LeFouet where Gaspar stood by the helm looking high up with his eyes squinted and a hand cupped around one ear.

"What in hell is he saying?" Gaspar shouted up in frustration as the men in the rigging all tried to shout over each other. *They're on edge, the captain is on deck and they can feel something is off, none of them want to catch his ire after he tossed that poor lieutenant.*

"He called out a sail on the horizon. He says it is a red sail, flying a red flag!" a sailor shouted down to Gaspar once the chorus of voices waned enough for him to be understood.

Gaspar's eyes shot wide. "Which direction?"

The sailor lifted an arm to point south. Gaspar

raced to the starboard rail of LeFouet, nearly toppling overboard as he came to halt with his hands arresting his momentum. He could see nothing but the bare horizon of dark blue ocean meeting the lightened blue skies of early morning. He looked back to the sailor that had called down. "Are you sure? A red sail and a red flag?"

The sailor looked to one of his mates along the yard and nodded calling back down to Gaspar. "Two-masted brigantine by the look of her. Red sail. Red flag."

Gaspar's stomach turned. A queasy wave washed up and took hold of him like he was a green landsman taking the Atlantic rollers for the first time. He swallowed a sour taste that rose into his throat. His heart fluttered. Everything seemed to grind to a halt. Scouring the horizon with his naked eyes he patted over his vest looking for the round shape of his telescope. He cursed himself when he remembered he had placed it in his trunk of belongings far forward in the hold. The captain's disparaging remarks had left him embarrassed but now he felt naked without it. A glimmer of a red shape caught his eye. Gaspar turned and cupped his hands around his mouth. "All hands prepare to run out auxiliary sail." He looked to the helmsman, "Four points to larboard and stay ready on the helm."

The sailor at the helm replied, "Four points to larboard and ready for maneuvers."

Captain Callais footsteps clomped along the

deck. His eyes flitted between the red spec at sea and Gaspar. "Belay that. Come about and make your course south for that ship?"

Gaspar's jaw dropped wide, "Captain, you can't mean…"

"I do Gaspar." The captain snapped, "That is our pirate."

Haitian Inland
20 Apr 1809

Sword met flesh in a jarring impact. Lilith's arm trembled under the force of it. She pulled at the handle of her cutlass and wrenched the blade free, hauling back for a vicious lunge that impaled her opponent just above his waist. His eyes gleamed over with fear and shock. A guttural breath escaped his lips. His grip released on the sword in his hand. A shout caught Lilith's attention and she raised the pistol in her other hand and fired at another of the field bosses collapsing him where he stood. To her other side Jilhal was locked in a fight with two men. Her sword was a blur of fury and precision as she parried and countered keeping both of her opponents at bay. Lilith stepped toward Jilhal to lend her sword to the fight when her friend lunged a powerful kick at one of the men toppling him over backwards. Jilhal parried and spun at the next strike from the other man and drove her sword across his throat in a graceful whirl. As blood poured from the deep incision Jilhal shoved the dying man to the ground and drove her sword through the eye of the first man while he was struggling to get to his feet. The slaves flooded around them giving chase to the remaining field bosses as they fled the onslaught. Cheers rose in the narrow valley as the last of the fleeing men fell to the blades of the workers.

Lilith raised her voice to a shout, "You are free now. Free to go where you want. Leave, if that is what suits you." She paused and licked her lips with a dry tongue, "But if you wish, you may come with us. Long days and hard struggles lie ahead for us. But the rewards will be many, and those who join us will have their share as free men and women." She looked around at the eyes of the laborers as her words took root. Most of them were dressed in rags, torn and stained from their days laboring under the constant glare of Haiti's sun. They looked ragged. Tired. They looked how Lilith felt. A few filtered away, trying not to be noticed while the rest gathered around Lilith and the companions she had brought inland.

Lilith focused on Jilhal, "That was well fought my friend."

Jilhal gave Lilith a nod, "You and Trina trained me."

The revelation brought a sinking feeling into Lilith's chest. She fought back a tingling in her nose and throat, barely keeping tears at bay as she was reminded of her dear mentor recently lost. "She has done well by us both." She looked to Emilia. "The tools you have. How far from here are they?"

Emilia shielded her eyes from the sun and looked down the rutted muddy road. "Not far. A few hours walking."

Lilith nodded to Jilhal, "Go with her. Whatever you need to do to get the tools to Chibs, do it. Take some of the new faces to help."

"And the rest of us, Captain?" Damriq's baritone voice boomed over the carnage site.

Lilith sheathed her cutlass and nodded toward the road. "Renly and I will continue on toward Tortuga. Damriq, I want you to see our new crew back to the cove. I'm sure Chibs and the doctor could use the help, if they haven't killed each other by now."

Damriq's smile spread wide. "I'm not worried about Chibs. Even with one hand…"

Lilith returned his smile and patted the broad man on his shoulder. "Best head back. Emilia and Jilhal won't be far behind you once they get the tools Chibs needs."

"And where are you going, captain?" Damriq asked.

Lilith smiled. "Renly and I are going to Tortuga."

Damriq's eyes widened, "Captain, you will need more men. There could be a city watch, soldiers, what if you…"

Lilith interrupted, "I will be quite fine Damriq. I'll have Renly with me. And we will need more men, more crew and supplies. That is precisely what I'm going to Tortuga for. We'll be back at the cove in a few days."

"Aye captain. We'll look for you then." Damriq waved to the gathering of Lilith's newest crew and trudged up the cane stump spotted hill. Lilith watched as they all filtered away disappearing into the thickness of tall sugar cane.

"Tortuga captain?" Renly asked over her shoulder as the last of the freed slaves were out of sight.

"Yes. Tortuga. There is a harbor." Lilith answered with her gaze still locked onto the tall cane that swayed slightly as Damriq led them through the field.

"Aye captain. The harbor in Tortuga is one of the busiest in the Caribbean."

Lilith turned and faced Renly, "And there will be ships there, right?"

"Many ships captain. But also a city watch, soldiers, maybe even navy ships." Renly toed the mud and looked down as he answered.

"The ships in harbor, some of them will be loaded with goods we could use. Won't they?" Lilith narrowed her eyes at the tall dark-haired Brit who was now one of her most loyal and lethal crew members.

Renly nodded and scratched the whiskers at his jaw, "Yes captain, many of the ships there will be loaded with all manner of trade goods."

"And if we can find one that is readying to make sail, they will have loaded food and fresh water aboard, yes?" Lilith started walking up the road.

"Yes captain. But the two of us sailing a ship won't do." Renly began to object.

Lilith gave him another squinted look as they walked. "Well, we will have to find more crew. Especially since we will have two ships once we bring up the Maiden. Do you know where we could find more crew in a town that size?"

Renly smiled, "I don't know if I should be honored or insulted captain. Before you took me aboard your ship I was a right honorable man of his majesty's royal marines. I didn't spend time in taverns of ill repute or bawdy houses. I don't have a clue where to even begin."

Lilith laughed, "You never drank away your pay in port? Lieutenant Pike told it differently, he said that royal marines were worth their weight in gold in a fight and usually spent that every time they visited a tavern!"

Renly averted his gaze away from his captain as Lilith looked over toward him. "I may have visited a tavern or two, when the fleet made harbor, but I didn't make it my business to go looking for pirates."

"Well, that is the business we have at hand now Renly. We need more hands, and capable ones, preferably." Lilith answered as they came to a slight bend in the road. Trees now towered over them, looming over both sides of the rutty track at their feet. Daylight filtered down in little golden spots between broad green leaves that danced in the breeze. "I've no gold, nor silver. In fact, any men we win to our crew will have to help me steal a ship." Her brow furrowed and caused her wounded eye to ache. "I don't think a tavern is the place to look."

Renly was silent for a long moment. "The men and women you've had have served you well captain. Why would we go looking in a tavern? That's not where we've found the others."

A gentle hill rose in front of them, Lilith could see clear blue skies peeking through the trees where the road crested. "I don't understand."

Renly quickened his pace to keep up with Lilith as she climbed the incline, her strides were purposeful. "Perhaps a tavern won't do at all. We can't just plop down at a table and announce that we are pirates looking for able hands willing to steal a ship." He took a deep breath as they continued up the slope, "The men and women we have serve the Maiden because you have set them free from bondage captain. They all, we all are more loyal to you than any crew I have ever seen. We won't find that sort in a tavern."

Lilith's head throbbed. She wished an answer would present itself. "Renly. If we don't want to sail a rowboat into the cove three weeks from now, with no food and no water, we need to find a crew. A crew that can help us sail a larger vessel, loaded with supplies, back to our ship."

The brightness of daylight unfiltered by the thick canopy overhead stung Lilith's eyes. They approached the top of the hill where tree lines gave way to an open field and a long downward slope. The ocean lie ahead in the far distance. Blue and bold against the pale sky. Along the shores was a cluster of buildings with smoke rising out of chimney pipes and horses, cart and people all traversing the roads in between. The pair stopped where the shadows gave way to open daylight and looked down toward the coast and the town that hugged onto the banks of Haiti's shores.

"There she is captain. Tortuga. Baking under the sun. I'm sure it smells worse than the hold of a four-hundred-man warship." Renly huffed and turned toward Lilith, "It may be wise to wait until nightfall before we go to wandering the streets captain. The look of us, we're sure to draw attention."

Lilith nodded. Her head ached from the back of her wounded eye down through her neck. "Aye. We'll get closer and wait until dark before we head in."

The road stretched out in front of them and Lilith felt an instant rush of warmth as they passed from the shadows of tree canopy into the direct rays of the Caribbean sun. A gentle slope descended beneath their feet until Tortuga disappeared behind tall trees ahead of them with a thick leafy canopy that danced and fluttered in the steady breeze coming off of the sea. Sweat collected on Lilith's forehead, it beaded and soaked into the bandanna covering her wounded eye and the neck of her stained and tattered shirt. Her pants were tattered and torn at the knees, the shoes she had worn for nearly a year were gone and her feet felt every step of their journey. They were certainly a sight that would draw attention, maybe even after night had come. Lilith tried to imagine how the townspeople would react to her in her rags of clothes.

The road drew closer to the rushing waves of the coast until all that separated them was a sloping hill of tall grass and a few trees. The sun was scorching. It beat down on them mercilessly until even the gusts of wind off of the water failed to cool either of them. Lilith listened to the waves as they came rushing in, toppling over themselves as they slammed into rocks and gravel or stretches of sand. Little caps of white crowned each wave as they rolled in and then collapsed and stretched up the shore beneath a constant barrage of squawking from gulls high above. Tortuga was ahead in the distance, obscured by trees, but Lilith could already smell an array of fragrances emanating from the town. Smoke from wood fires, cooking meat, spices and the flowery sweet smell of fruits in the market would all dance before her nose, tingling her palette before suddenly vanishing beneath a blanket of the briny smell of the ocean breeze. As the pair drew nearer, one particular odor grew strong enough to stamp out even the lingering surf beside the road. It was a pungent smell, sweet almost but earthy as well and somehow mixed with smoke. It was a smell Lilith knew only too well.

Her heart fluttered as the scent grew stronger and stronger. She could almost taste it in the back of her throat.

A bend in the road snaked around toward a rocky stretch of shoreline and plunged beneath an overhang of tall trees with fluttering thick green leaves and tangles of undergrowth beneath them. As they made their way around the bend Tortuga stood out in front of them, bold and smoky and filled with commotion. But Lilith didn't focus on the town. Her eyes found a long single story wooden building that was set back from the road. Not quite on the edge of town, the building had a wooden shake roof with chimney pipes sticking up every dozen feet. Windows with open shutters billowed steam and smoke out in great churning clouds. Behind the extensive building were a series of three large structures with grass roofs. A line with laundry hanging to dry stretched between two of them. Lilith had never been here, but she knew exactly what she was looking at.

"Renly." Lilith stopped walking and grasped at his sleeve.

"Yes captain?" Renly replied with a concerned look. "We can probably get a little closer if we wish."

Lilith shook her head. "Do you see that building there?" She pointed to the long wooden one with the open shudders belching out thick clouds.

"Aye. It looks to be on fire miss." Renly nodded like he wanted to keep walking up the road.

Lilith remained still, her feet planted and her eyes locked onto the wooden building. "Do you know what that is?"

Renly squinted at the structure and then looked back to Lilith. "Not sure, but I don't think it'll be standing much longer. Looks like it's burning to me."

Lilith smiled and slowly continued after Renly. "There are fires in there. But they're in ovens beneath huge vats. That's a boiling house."

"For sugar?" Renly asked with a cocked eyebrow.

"Yes. They're processing sugar out of sugar cane. It's miserable, hot and dangerous. More than a few slaves have been burned alive in houses just like that one."

Renly looked hard at the boiling house and then back at Lilith. "And those huts behind it?"

"Slave quarters." Lilith replied with an edge icy enough to freeze the waves rolling into shore.

"I see." Renly continued walking as they both stared hard at the compound between them and Tortuga.

Lilith let her hand rest on the hilt of her cutlass. "I think you were right Renly. The tavern is no place for us to find a crew." She looked up at him with a devilish squint in her good eye. "I have a much better idea."

'North Wind'
24 Apr 1809
18 Degrees 02' N, 74 Degrees 58' W

"Come in here lad. There's something afoul with this crew and I mean to get to the bottom of it before supper." Admiral Torren gestured with a wave for the young midshipman standing in his cabin doorway to come inside. "Close the hatch behind you and have a seat lad." The young man looked hesitant but did as he was beckoned to. He clutched his hat in both hands, fingers nervously rubbing at the texture of the fabric. Admiral Torren sat behind the great desk in his cabin, carefully watching every move and change of affect the young officer displayed.

"Begging your pardon sir, I am the officer for the larboard battery. Shouldn't I be down with my gun crews?" the midshipman managed a mumbling feeble plea.

"I think not lad. I summoned you here for a reason." Admiral Torren shifted in his seat and leaned pressure against one foot. Pangs of pain were coursing from his gout and arthritis afflicted feet. White hot aches that radiated misery and forced the admiral to do anything he could to ease the constant throb. Normally he would grimace or bite his lip when the pain flared beyond what he could tolerate, but while he was looking at a junior officer face to face he dared not show any sign of weakness. For the moment, the admiral settled on pressing the aching foot against the floor which somehow made the pain seem more bearable. He motioned to a glass bottle on his desk. "Would you care for a drink son?"

"No, sir. I'm afraid I don't partake." The midshipman answered with an earnest wide-eyed look on his face.

He was a young man. One the admiral recognized right away. He had caught the officer dozing on a coil of line at one point during their long voyage across the Atlantic. Admiral Torren had chosen to display restraint that day, he hoped his gesture had purchased some rapport with the young man now. The midshipman was Mr. Elliot Brant, the only son of Captain Brant commander of H.M.S Bayonet. The young man had been named for Elliot Sharpe, the Royal Navy's last admiral in command of the Caribbean fleet.

"Why do you think you are up here in my cabin instead of below deck leading your battery son?" the admiral asked with a raised brow. He watched the young midshipman's face scrunch as he tried to formulate an answer. "No need for formalities midshipman, out with it. I'll have my answer."

Midshipman Brant's finger closed tight around the brim of his hat. "If it is about my performance, sir, I can assure you I have been giving every effort to improving my calculations and asked for help with the sextant several times."

Admiral Torren waived a hand in front of his face, "Your performance is not in question young man. Reckoning can be taught, it can be learned and it can always be improved. I have a more grave matter in mind and I must insist that we dispense with this game. You must be aware of some foul work amongst the crew." The admiral paused to watch Midshipman Brant's reaction. The boy hardly flinched. "You dine with the other officers, you sleep in the officer berthing. You are quite often visiting with sailors on watch. If there is something that I need to be made aware of son, now is the time to tell it and tell it true."

Midshipman Brant's face was pale, his features stretched in a look of hesitation until Admiral Torren thought his jaw would surely hit the floor. "I have heard some of the other midshipmen grumbling sir."

Admiral Torren eased himself forward and pressed his fingertips onto the desktop. "What kind of grumblings lad?"

The midshipman's head drooped while he chewed at his lower lip for a moment. "I'm not sure exactly where it started sir. Where they got the idea. But, I have heard some of them discussing the possibility that you are somehow involved with slave smugglers, that you want to hang Lieutenant Pike in order to keep him silent and that we sunk the pirate vessel that had been interfering in the transport of slaves."

Admiral Torren's face flushed as he listened to the younger officer's explanation. Silence enveloped the two men as they sat across the desk from each other. The admiral stared hard into Midshipman Brant's eyes, which flitted between making contact with his own and looking at the cabin deck below their feet. The rumble of gun carriage wheels continued to creak and groan through the ship echoing their way into the admiral's grand cabin. "That is absurd. I was dispatched to the Caribbean to investigate the disappearance of our fleet, including the ship under your own father's command. The ridiculous things sailors come up with…" He clamped jaw before continuing, gritting his teeth until an ache crept into the muscles right below his earlobes. "If I were involved, lad, don't you think I would have already hung the lieutenant? Would I have stopped in Nassau to quell the unrest there? Would we be making our way toward Kingston this very moment to…" Admiral Torren's voice trailed as his mind began to work with a full wind behind it. If the midshipmen aboard his flagship were coming to these conclusions, there was undoubtedly similar feelings amongst the crew itself. He narrowed his eyes and pursed his lips while staring at the young officer. He expected a nervous look, a squirm or a tic. If the midshipman knew more or was holding back some information there would be something. The young man sat across from him, face sagging like he had just relieved himself from a great burden. "You've done well by telling me this." The admiral reached for the brandy bottle on his desk and poured some into a cup. He raised his drink and motioned toward the midshipman, "This conversation needs to stay between you and I for the time being lad. It's a touchy situation."

"Y-yes, sir." Midshipman Brant stuttered in reply.

"If you hear anything more serious than grumblings, you are to report right here to me. Directly. Whatever time of day or night. Do you understand?" The admiral drained his cup in one large gulp.

"Yes sir. I will."

"Good. Now off with you, go lead your battery. I imagine you will all be at gun drills for quite a while." Admiral Torren gave the midshipman a forced grin as the young man headed for the cabin door. "See to it that Lieutenant Thatcher finds his way here, will you?"

"Aye sir." Midshipman Brant pulled the heavy wooden door shut.

Admiral Torren was left alone in his cabin with only his thoughts to keep vigil. The roaring fire in his wood stove had tempered to a mild crackle, and a chill had begun to sneak into his bones. He considered the young officer's answers carefully while he awaited his aide. The midshipman had been painfully hesitant to offer any information. And while giving his answers, the young man had almost seemed to suffer from some plague of guilt. A pang of pain shot through Admiral Torren's left foot causing his leg to twitch. He looked under the desk as if to scold the offending appendage. *Age.*

He thought. *My body mutinies me while my command attempts to do the same.* A long moment of silence was broken by the rumbling wheels of cannon carriages below deck. A muffled cry erupted through the timbers and the rumbling stopped. Another muffled cry followed, and the rumbling continued. North Wind's decks shifted as her sailing master ordered another unnecessary tack across the wind. Admiral Torren smiled to himself. He shot a glance at his belt hanging by a hook on the wall next to his desk. The hilt of his sword caught a glimmer of lantern light that danced across the metal.

The last time he had used a sword in the course of his duties had been purely ceremonial, and the time before that as well. He narrowed his eyes and shifted in his seat, gazing on the ornate scabbard and sword hilt. The last time he had used a sword for its natural purpose in combat had been decades ago. He remembered the day clearly. He had been a senior captain, eagerly awaiting his next promotion after a grueling campaign against the American rebels. A privateer ship had caught them unaware under a thick layer of late evening fog and hit them with a series of raking shots that had rendered his ship nearly useless. When they had come alongside, he stripped off his officer's coat and drew sword and pistol. Admiral Torren smiled as he recalled, he had rallied his crew with a shout of "For England!" They met the enemy at the ship's rail and held their ground in a bloody fight. When it was finished, he could not even count the dead that lay strewn across the decks of both vessels. Covered in blood and still clutching both his sword and spent pistol his crew had to carry him to his quarters. It took days to recover from the fight, but when they had he ordered his ship to set sail for home while Elliot Sharpe followed in their newly taken prize. It was the fight that had launched him into the realm of flag rank, and the wounds still haunted his body. He closed his eyes and pictured Elliot Sharpe. The joy on his face when he received his captain's orders. They had been the talk of London upon their return home, a moment of sunshine and glory rarely seen in the service to the king's navy. It faded almost as quickly as it had come. News of General Cornwallis surrendering in America soon eclipsed their brief moment of glory and after a few days it seemed almost as if it had never happened at all. The payment from the crown's prize agent frittered away all too quickly and before long even the mention of their captured rebel ship only brought looks of confusion. But the wounds he sustained that day continued to plague him.

The admiral shook his head at the recollection, he muttered under his breath, "For England indeed." A pain throbbed through his ankle and up his shin prompting him to sit taller in his chair. Scanning over his desk he found his notes and a chart. The admiral looked over the position he had plotted hours ago and began to work his estimation of their arrival in Kingston. His leg twitched again and he grit his teeth while pain flared through the limb. A knock sounded on his cabin door.

"Enter." He replied through his clamped jaw.

Lieutenant Thatcher opened the door with a rush of noises from out on deck flooding in behind him. The lieutenant hurriedly closed the door behind him and made his way into the cabin. "Reporting as ordered sir."

Admiral Torren inhaled a sharp breath through his nose as his ankle throbbed with increased intensity. He had not felt this level of discomfort in a long time. "It is exactly as I feared lieutenant. Rumors are circulating amongst the crew that I am somehow involved in this slave smuggling conspiracy."

"Preposterous." The lieutenant scrunched his face, "Why on earth would a man of your standing and reputation…"

"It makes no difference lieutenant. These are the same men who pass on stories about giant sea monsters and mermaids and the sort. Reason means little to the mind dulled by mundane tasks day in and day out. When something comes along to spark interest, the more fantastic it is the more likely it will take hold." Admiral Torren's voice was just short of an angry snap. The pain from his ankle was crawling its way to his knee.

Lieutenant Thatcher nodded his understanding, "Yes sir."

Admiral Torren braced both of his hands onto

the close edge of his desk. "The crew is to continue conducting gun drills until the midnight watch change." He paused for a moment and drew a slow, deliberate breath before exhaling slowly. "When the watch changes I want a double watch on the helm, the arms locker and this cabin. It will remain in place until we have made port in Kingston. Is that understood?"

Lieutenant Thatcher nodded with each order. "Yes sir. I will see to it personally."

Pirate Cove
22 Apr 1809

Hot sand burned against his feet as Omibwe followed Dr. LeMeux around the sheltered cove. The sands were glaring white where the water didn't touch and a deeper ivory shade where the water had just receded. Over his shoulder Dr. LeMeux was trying to support as much of Chibs weight as he could, but the old sailor wasn't making it any easier on him. Chibs cussed him most of the way around the edge of the cove saying horrible things about the doctor's mother and father. He threatened to do terrible violent acts to the doctor in retribution for stealing away his hand. Finally when they reached the waterline closest to the Maiden, Dr. LeMeux eased Chibs down and helped him sit on a large rock just out of reach from the wet sands. The old sailor sat and stared out into the cove. Omibwe almost thought he saw tears forming in the salty old man's eyes.

Waters of crystal blues and emerald greens gently lapped against the white sandy shore inside the cove as the sun's brilliant rays kissed the water's surface and made it glitter like a million diamonds were bobbling along the gentle ripples. The flow of the outgoing tide lapped away from pale sands and slipped around the protruding prow of the Drowned Maiden. She was a bramble of cracked and twisted timbers, broken railing and line floated on the surface next to the bow that was too proud to surrender to the sea. The wind blew high over the cove, Omibwe could see the forest canopy dancing and swaying but down at water level they could only feel a slight breeze. The sun was warm and the heat creeping up through his deck toughened feet felt good.

Chibs huffed for a moment and stared over the water. "We need line. Thick line, and a lot of it." Chibs voice sounded as ragged as he looked. "We'll need blocks too. Lots of them."

"Where exactly do you plan to procure these things?" Dr. LeMeux asked. He stood a few feet away from Chibs and gave Omibwe a puzzled look. "We barely have food to survive the week. I'm afraid if the captain does not return soon we will have to set out over land and try to find a town or something."

Chibs sneered, "You think I'm leaving here doctor?"

Dr. LeMeux shook his head, "No. You are in no

condition to be traveling anywhere. It would have to be me. I could go and find us some help."

Chibs chuckled. The chuckle grew to a laugh that started in his belly. He laughed louder until his voice echoed off of the rock face at the mouth of the cove. The laugh turned into a cough and he grumbled for a moment before toppling off of his seat on the big rock. "You?" Chibs bellowed between fits of laughter and coughs, he grimaced at his ribs for a moment and swatted his stumped arm at the doctor as the Frenchman tried to reach in and help him up. "You think you're just going to go for a stroll in the countryside and come back with a gaggle of people lined up to help a crew of shipwrecked pirates?" Chibs pushed off of the sand with his good arm and sat himself up, "That'll be the day. No, we need to start work on raising this old girl. The captain will be back with crewmen and tools. I don't mean for her to get here and find nothing has been done in her absence."

Dr. LeMeux went rigid as Chibs laughed and hacked at him with rasping breaths. He stood in between Chibs and the waterline and gestured toward the Maiden. "And how, may I ask, do you plan on procuring the line and blocks from the ship? It is sunk!"

Chibs lifted an eyebrow at the doctor in a bewildered look. "I'll swim my arse out there and fetch it. That's how!" He struggled onto his knees with his one good hand beneath him for support.

"Absolutely not! You are in no fit state to be

walking, let alone swimming. You'll run short of breath and drown before you reach the Maiden's exposed hull."

The two men continued their argument, getting in close to each other's faces at one point. Omibwe thought for sure the big sailor was about to hit the doctor. He winced at their shouts as they echoed around the peaceful cove. The waters were pristine clear, with shades of blue and green taking hold away from the shore as the bottom plunged deeper out toward the hulk of the Maiden. Doctor LeMeux shouted something at Chibs. Chibs shouted back and poked the lanky dark haired French doctor in his chest.

"I will go." Omibwe interrupted their argument.

The two men ceased their shouting and cast a look of shared confusion on him. "No, lad. It's too dangerous. I wouldn't forgive myself if you drowned trying to finish my errand."

"I won't." Omibwe answered in a stern voice.

Dr. LeMeux's face scrunched into a deep frown. "You know how to swim?"

Omibwe clamped his jaw and nodded. "I am from the coast doctor. I can swim. I can dive. I learned from my father, he was the best diver in our village. He could stay under so long that everyone else had to go up for air twice. I'm the best person to go out there and do this."

"With one leg?" Chibs challenged, "No, if you drowned your mother will be devastated. She'll kill me and the doctor for good measure. I'll go."

Omibwe squatted himself down onto the sandy beach. "You have one hand and a hole in your side. You can't go. I will go out and find something that floats, I'll put as much on it as I can and then pull it back to shore."

Chibs and the doctor looked at each other. There was a long moment where only the breeze rustling foliage and the gentle lap of water could be heard in the cove. Chibs' eyes narrowed, and he looked at Omibwe. "If you can swim out there to the hull, and then dive along the deck, you may be able to free one of her longboats." Chibs wrapped his fingers around the long whiskers of his beard beneath his chin. "The clasps are brass, hook and lever type. If you can undo those, there might be an air pocket enough still in the boat to float it to the surface."

Dr. LeMeux gave Omibwe a softened look. He knelt into the sand and raised his eyebrows, he looked at Omibwe as if he were looking over the top of his glasses even though they were not on his nose. "Are you sure Omi?"

Omibwe looked the doctor in the eye and motioned at the prosthetic he had fashioned for him. "Help me take this off. I'm going."

Dr. LeMeux fumbled with the leather strap that held Omibwe's wooden leg in place against his thigh. As the doctor pulled the prosthetic away Omibwe let what remained of his leg rest against the warm sand, the heat felt good. The doctor stood and offered a hand out to Omibwe to help him stand.

"I'll help you down into the surf. But I'm afraid I am not a swimmer myself, once I get you in, you will be on your own."

Omibwe stood with the doctor's help and together they made their way down into the cool water of the cove. Omibwe could feel Dr. LeMeux get tense as the waterline came up above his waist. "This is far enough. I'll swim from here doctor."

"Be careful Omi!" the doctor uttered as Omibwe thrust his body out into the lapping waves. He shot his hands forward beneath the surface and brought them down to his sides in a wide arc. Water covered his face for a moment. It felt cool against his skin which had been in the sun all morning. Omibwe turned his head slightly to the side and sucked in a quick breath, the air had the salty tang of the sea in it. As Omibwe stroked again with his arms he buckled his leg and snapped it together with what was left of his other leg. The push he got from a kick wasn't nearly as powerful as it had been, but it still managed to keep him moving. He stroked again with his arms and opened his eyes beneath the water's surface. For a moment all he could see was a blur of blue and green, he blinked away the blur and let his eyes adjust. Columns of daylight penetrated the cove and lit the sandy sea floor. He could see rocks and bits of coral, a sword, planks of wood and strings of rope littering the sand beneath him. He pulled at the sea, surging himself forward with every stroke. The hull of the

Maiden sat at an angle, her stern planted firmly into the sandy bottom. Two gaping holes marked her hull beneath the surface. Inside of them was a dark void where the sparkling rays of sunshine filtering down from the surface could not penetrate. Omibwe turned his head for another breath, when his eyes focused again he could see a fish dart away as his shadow passed by against the sandy bottom of the cove. The hull of the Maiden loomed larger and larger in front of him until his fingertips touched against the coarse wood grains of her timbers.

Omibwe raised his head out of the water and paddled big circles around himself to keep his face above the surface. The exposed bow cast a shadow that shaded him from the direct sun. The coolness felt good and Omibwe relished the sensation of the seawater against his skin. Walking had become difficult since he had lost his leg, running was out of the question, but in the water he felt like he could fly.

"Way to go Omibwe!" Chibs voice echoed out from the shore, "The boats will be attached to her deck, around the side of her rail there, to your left!"

Omibwe waved a hand out of the water. His face sunk below the surface far enough to cover his nose and he quickly pulled his hand back into a circular pattern. He took a few deep breaths and looked over the Maiden. From where he was treading water she towered over him. Keeping his face just above the surface Omibwe extended one arm and pulled at the water with a cupped hand. He glided along next to the Maiden's hull causing little rippling waves to radiate off of his stroke and lap against the side of the timber hull. As he passed the ship's railing and turned toward her deck he crossed back into the sunshine. The warmth kissed the skin of his face and shone down against the submerged deck in a bright column. Omibwe dipped his face down into the water and opened his eyes. For an instant the deck was a blurred smudge of brown against hues of dark blue in the deeper waters of the cove, as his eyes adjusted he caught a glimmer from the sun. A brass fixture below him glimmered in the rays of sunlight that bent and shimmered beneath the sea surface. The longboat came into focus in Omibwe's eyes no more than two dozen feet below him in the water.

Sweet air met his lungs when Omibwe pulled himself up by a rope hanging from the bow. The sun warmed his skin as he took several deep breaths and looked around on the surface of the water. The breeze was warm and brought little ripples to the cove. With a final deep breath, he let the rope go and dipped beneath the water. Omibwe pulled himself deeper with cupped hands edging deeper and deeper with each stroke. The familiar pressure began to build in his ears and he could feel the sea pressing in around him, squeezing his ribs and belly. As he crept deeper and deeper Omibwe focused on the closest brass latch holding the Drowned Maiden's longboat onto her deck. The brass gleamed under the wavering light that flicked and fluttered through ripples on the water's surface. He could almost reach the metal fixture. Omibwe stretched his arm out through the cool sea, stretching his fingers to reach the clasp and release it. His fingertip brushed against the smooth metal. It felt strangely cool. Another sensation grabbed Omibwe's attention, but it wasn't from the brass latch. A rope tickled against his leg as he kicked deeper to grab a hold on the brass in front of him. Omibwe kicked his leg to push the rope away and pulled at the water with his hands, for a moment it felt like the rope had drifted away from him. Omibwe's hand clasped onto the handle of the brass fitting. His lungs ached with the pressure of depth and he began to let a slow dribble of air escape in a stream of bubbles that raced along the side of his face and danced over his shoulder toward the surface. With a pull against the latch handle, Omibwe freed the first of the latches holding the longboat onto the larger vessel. Looking deeper, Omibwe found the next latch that he must open to free the small rowboat. He gripped the wooden lip of the boat in his hands and began to pull himself deeper to reach the latch. A bolt of shock ran through his blood. His ankle burned with a rough sensation that pulled against his effort. Omibwe twisted his body to look up towards his legs. An icy chill ran through his blood when he found that the rope had become cinched around his ankle.

Chapter 5

Haitian Inland
20 Apr 1809

The brilliant hues of evening had climbed high, ambers and pinks faded toward a deep purple as the sun light faded from view. When the last light of sunset had finally given way to inky dark skies the heavens came alive with stars. Lilith loved stargazing. It reminded her of an evening on the deck of the Maiden when Captain James had serenaded her to sleep recounting the tales of myth and legend behind the constellations large and small. She later had learned how to navigate by them from Chibs. Lilith often lingered on deck long after nightfall to take in the majesty of starlight. The stars were out in full force above the Tortuga skyline. Lantern's and fires from town did little to pollute their brilliance. Lilith noted a series of shooting stars, one after another they would streak for a short distance through the dark night before being lost to her sight. The moon hadn't risen yet and Tortuga's glow barely penetrated the darkness surrounding it. The boiling house was lit by lamps within its walls and by a pair flanking the front entrance. Smoke and steam continued billowing out of the parted shudders as the pots and fires were tended by slaves. To the side of the long building a group worked by the light of a small fire processing lengths of cane into smaller pieces to be boiled. The grass roofed huts behind the boiling house were alive with the light of cooking fires. Lilith let her gaze fall from the stars to watch the compound. The sound of a child laughing carried through the night in between the clinking noise of blades on cane.

"You see any guards yet?" Renly asked in a low voice as they both looked on to the compound.

Lilith chewed at her lip and shook her head. "No."

"Maybe it's our lucky night, captain. Maybe the guards are all off in town falling down drunk." He suggested with a smile.

Lilith wasn't sure, but she wasn't about to let her guard down. "Someone profits, so someone else will be standing guard." They had chosen a thicket of trees and brush a few hundred yards from the compound to wait for the cover of night. Lilith crouched low to the ground and held the pommel of her cutlass in a tight grip. "Our luck will be that the guards will all be watching the slaves do their work. Hopefully we can cut their throats before they even see us coming."

"How many of them do you think there are? The slaves I mean…" Renly asked as he squinted at the firelight they were using to process cane.

"Probably a hundred. Maybe more." Lilith answered, "Whenever my mother was loaned to work in the boiling houses outside of Port-Au-Prince I went with her. We stayed in huts just like the ones over there." Lilith stood from her crouch and started to pull away boughs of leaves obscuring her view. "I thought the labor camp was Port-Au-Prince when I was a little girl. There were so many people and so many of them looked like me. When I was young, I thought it was a happy place. Other slaves had sons or daughters and we could play. When I was nine one of the workers got the attention of a pair of guards. They accused him of taking extra food or something, I never knew quite what happened. But I saw him after they had thrown him into a kettle. My mother said they threw him in and hit his hands with clubs when he tried to pull himself out."

"Barbaric." Renly growled in the back of his throat.

"When they brought him out of the boiling house my mother tried to cover my eyes. I peeked through her fingers. His skin was covered in broken blisters. His face was so swollen nobody could recognize it." Lilith gave Renly a long look before turning back toward the firelight. "Have you been to Tortuga before?"

Renly shook his head in the darkness, "No captain. Never visited Tortuga. I've sailed past here, seen it on the horizon. But I know nothing of the town really."

Lilith let out a sigh. "Do you know if there is a garrison here?"

"Oh, I'm sure of it. A town this size in the Caribbean, they will absolutely have a garrison of soldiers. Likely a town watch as well." Renly replied. Lilith could feel his gaze along the side of her face. He drew breath as if to speak but only let a slow sigh escape.

"We will need to free the boiling house workers and make our way to the harbor. Any of those who decide to come with us can help us make sail." Lilith hefted her pistol from out of a thick leather belt around her waist. "We will find a ship making ready to sail and take it. Then onward to Chibs and the rest."

"Aye captain." Renly replied emerging from the brush at her shoulder.

"If we strike fast, we may even be able to get away before the alarm is raised." Lilith began walking toward the boiling house. "I'll go into the camp, you take the boiling house. Keep your wits about you. We may not see them now, but there will be guards."

Grass pulled and slid along Lilith's legs as she walked toward the small fire lighting the outside of the compound. The echo of blades hitting against cane rang through the darkness in a constant chatter. Lilith emerged from the night at the edge of the firelight with her sword and pistol in hand. She stood for a moment, taking in the workers as they toiled over cutting the large cane sections into pieces that would fit into the kettles. She counted seven men, three were scurrying around picking up pieces as the other four made quick work of each cane length with machetes. For a while they continued their work, so wrapped in their task that they didn't notice the armed woman watching them from the edge of their fire's glow. A piece of cane fell after one of the workers struck a long section with his machete. It rolled across the ground and rested a few steps in front of Lilith's feet. Lilith watched as one of the slaves hurried over to pick up the stray piece of cane. He knelt down and retrieved the section as the fire crackled and spurt a stream of sparks into the night sky. The fire flared and hissed, it grew brighter for a moment and the crouching slave froze. His eyes traced up Lilith's feet to her legs. He continued to slowly pan his head upward until Lilith could see the wide whites of his eyes stark against the dark of night and the orange glow from the fire behind him. She raised her cutlass and let the firelight glint off of the steel. The slave rose to his feet, he left the small chunk of sugar cane to sit on the matted grass beneath them and raised his hands in surrender.

"I am not here to hurt you love." Lilith told the frightened man, "I am here to free you." She motioned with her head toward the rest of his group working by the firelight. "Come with me. I need your help." The man followed Lilith as she stepped further into the ring of warm orange firelight that danced and flitted with the licking flames. A hush fell over the group of men, their blades stopped the steady crack and split against sugarcane while their eyes gathered on her with confused looks of bewilderment. Lilith looked around the group for a long moment as the fire crackled and blazed away. "I've come to lead you to your freedom. When it is finished, you can leave with me or on your own course. My name is Lilith and I am the captain of the Drowned Maiden." She lifted her sword towards the light of the fire and let the steel glimmer with flashes of orange and yellow light. "How many men guard the boiling house?"

The men exchanged looks between each other. Lilith couldn't tell if they were confused or if she had somehow amused them. One of the machete wielder's stepped forward, "How are you going to free us? Have you ever used that?" He pointed to the sword in her hand with the tip of his machete.

"What is going on over there?" an angry voice cut through the night air. "Why don't I hear cane being cut?" He was a big man, broad in shoulder with a thick beard and even thicker chop sideburns. The orange glow shone on his white linen shirt and Lilith could see as he emerged from the darkness between them and the boiling house that the angry man was carrying a short whip with a long handle. Without a sound, Lilith slipped behind the man who had first noticed her and darted around to the far side of the campfire. The angry man cursed and kicked at the matted grass. "Get back to work you worthless piles. I'll beat you all bloody if you stop again. If they run short for the next batch it'll be your necks!" He swung the long handle of his whip around and raised it as if he would strike. The orange light of the fire flickered on his balding head. Lilith circled the fire at the edge of its light, moving into position to pounce on her prey. The angry man shouted and cursed at the slaves again while they all exchanged an awkward glance with each other. "Didn't you hear me? Or are you too stupid to understand? Cut the cane! It's too big to fit in the kettles!"

He didn't hear Lilith until it was too late. The angry man turned with his whip held high and received the point of her cutlass straight into the apple of his throat. The whip fell from his hands as he tried to clasp at the blade. Blood oozed down the steel edge and dripped onto the ground while firelight danced glimmers across the blade. Lilith pulled against her sword and thrust a kick into the man's belly while he choked on his own blood in between hissing gasps for breath. She turned to the slave who had pointed at her cutlass with his machete. "I can wield my blade. Can you? Or is cutting cane all you can manage?" Her challenge was met with widened eyes. Lilith crouched and wiped the blade of her sword against the chest of the man she had just killed. "How many more of them?"

"Two were out by us. There are four more inside." The man pointed with his machete toward the boiling house, "The instant you go inside they will cut you down."

Lilith looked around cautiously at the shadows that fell away from the ring of light surrounding them. "You said there were two out here. Where is the other?"

A voice carried out from the shadows, "Kill her! Kill her now or you will wish to God you had!"

The group of men faced Lilith. For a moment she could see conflict pass through the face of the man nearest her. He flexed his fingers around the handle of his machete. Lilith stood up from her crouch, sword in hand.

"Damn you all. I said kill her, now cut her down or it will be no meals for a week for all of you!" the voice shouted. Lilith shot her eyes where she thought he was. A flash gleamed. The brilliant shine of orange firelight hitting steel. Just beyond the reach of her eye she could hear a grunt. A guttural gasp brought goosebumps up on Lilith's arms followed by the sound of a body dropping to the ground. Renly stepped into the light with a broad smile.

"I thought it might be a good idea to keep an eye on you captain. Turns out I was right." He nodded to one of the slaves holding a machete. "So? Is that big damn blade just for cane?"

The broad-shouldered African man held his

machete up to the light of the fire. He looked at his companions and then up to Captain Lilith. "We'll go with you."

Lilith smiled at him and gave Renly a squinted look with her good eye. "Good. Onto the boiling house." She looked at the man who had first spotted her. "Go to the camp houses, tell them who I am. If they wish for freedom, now is the time."

'LeFouet'
24 Apr 1809
17 Degrees 48' N, 69 Degrees 52' W

Tension rose on the deck of LeFouet as it drew closer to the ship over the course of several hours. She was a two-masted brigantine with taut, wind filled sails that were dyed a deep crimson red as if they had been soaked in the blood of their victims. Her sides told the story of many engagements at sea with battered hull timbers and recently replaced deck rails. Her bow was ornate, a carved figure with the body of a woman and the head of a lion was displayed high under her bowsprit. Above her stern floated a banner, a pair of crossed swords sat on a field of red as dark as the sails, the swords were flanked on one side by an hourglass and on the other by a trio of crude looking skulls. Gaspar had never seen the banner before. But he had heard tales of the ship flying it. The tension on deck soaked through him, knotting his gut and seizing his breath in his throat. The closer they drew the worse he felt. Dread grabbed his limbs and paralyzed his voice. He had tried to summon the courage to talk to Captain Callais and warn him off of this fool's errand. Each time he had worked up enough gumption to speak with his commander the words would not formulate as he opened his mouth. When the red sailed vessel came about her course and angled their bow toward LeFouet it was too late to turn and run. Gaspar grit his jaw and watched from the bow as the two ships drew closer and closer while terror wrung his insides with iron hands.

When the two ships were only separated by a quarter mile Captain Callais shouted from the quarterdeck. "Fire all cannons and strike the colors!"

The roar of cannons made Gaspar tremble, a shiver that started in his bones like he had been dumped overboard in the far north. His hands quaked uncontrollably even through the blazing Caribbean sun. The blood-red sails and banner was all he could see. When the two ships began to pass one another Captain Callais called out another order to spill the wind and reef all sails. Gaspar watched in a helpless state of shock while the crew carried out his directive. *He is surrendering the ship! How could he do this? Why?* The sails were not even completely gathered when a series of lines with grapples were tossed over LeFouet's rail. The pirates heaved the lines taut and dropped a gangplank between ships. After that, it was a matter of seconds until LeFouet's decks were flooded by a gang of thieves. Rough-looking men, even by a sailor's standard. They came across wielding pistols and swords, pointing them at each of LeFouet's crewmen until there wasn't a soul who would dare resist. Gaspar stood, a helpless observer while one man held a blade to his throat and another aimed a cocked pistol at his chest.

The last of the pirates to cross onto LeFouet's crowded deck looked very different from the rest of the crew. He was a head taller than any man that had come over, curly black hair fell past his shoulders onto a fine linen shirt of bright red. He was broad shouldered and his chest seemed almost the size of a barrel. His face looked as if it had seen a fresh shave that very morning. Scars criss crossed his jaw and cheeks and lined the backs of his hands and his forearms. Covering one of his eyes was a black leather patch embroidered around its edge in crimson stitch work. As the man stepped off of the gangplank and onto LeFouet's railing he grabbed a stay line and drew a cutlass from his belt.

"I am Captain Laurent Fontaine of the Batard De Mer. You were wise to strike your colors, perhaps you will die quickly. Or perhaps not." He waved the point of his sword around and aimed it toward the captain's cabin. "Where is your commander?" Gaspar looked around with a desperate fear. The red shirted pirate captain stepped down onto the deck and approached him. "You there. Where is your captain? Did he abandon you all to your fate?"

Gaspar tried to wet his lips, but his tongue was like sun dried leather. His voice refused to work as he opened his mouth. Captain Callais interrupted the exchange, "I am the Captain."

Fontaine turned his head and locked his one bright blue eye across the deck where Captain Callais stood. "And what sort of captain are you? Running your ship directly into my clutches. Have you not heard of the dreaded crimson sails?"

Captain Callais looked over the pirate crew with a disdainful glare before answering. "I have heard of Batard De Mer and its feared captain and crew. That is why I have sailed here, looking for you."

Gaspar watched as Captain Fontaine narrowed his eye in a glare that sent a chill running through him. The pirate raised his sword point to Captain Callais chest and let the edge of his blade rest on his breastbone. "And why would you do something so stupid?"

"I have in my cabin a pardon for you and your crew as well as a considerable payment in gold. I am here to offer you and your crew payment and redemption in exchange for a service." Captain Callais voice was strong and clear. Gaspar couldn't believe what he was hearing. Was this what the Americans had spoken with him about? Why would they be relaying a message to the captain? His head spun. He almost didn't notice when Captain Fontaine held a hand up and waved it over his shoulder. The pirates all lowered their weapons.

"Why would we be interested in a pardon? Suppose I take your payment and sink your ship? What could you do about it?" Captain Fontaine sneered before looking around to his crew. "I thought you said you knew who we are?" His sneer was met with a round of laughter and cheers.

Captain Callais voice cut through the laughter of the pirates. "The payment I hold on board is just that, a payment. The first of many, should you prove successful. In addition to a pardon for your crimes, and those of your crew, there is also a letter of marque authorizing you to engage any ship bearing the colors of the British empire."

Captain Fontaine lowered his sword and drew his face close to Captain Callais "And what would be required of us? What task is so distasteful to Napoleon that he would send us, a crew of thieves and cutthroats, instead of his own great navy?"

"It is a sensitive matter, captain." Callais voice lowered. His eyes shifted to Gaspar for a moment before settling back onto the pirate captain.

"Out with it. I don't have time for games of cloak and dagger!" Fontaine snarled.

Gaspar watched Captain Callais carefully weigh his words. He shot Gaspar another look, this one seemed almost apologetic. "There is a pirate vessel sailing the Caribbean captained by an escaped slave woman. Your first payment is half the bounty for sinking her and bringing forth proof of her death."

"You speak of the Drowned Maiden." Fontaine growled under his breath, barely loud enough for Gaspar to hear. "I've heard her captain is a beauty to behold." He looked around the crew and settled his one eye back on Captain Callais, "What interest is it of Napoleon's? I've heard she sunk a British man of war, he should be looking to give her a medal!"

Captain Callais voice remained low and steady, almost inaudible over the steady wind. "She is interfering in a delicate matter."

"He wishes for the smuggling of slaves to continue, is that it?" Fontaine gestured toward two of his men standing nearby. "Go with the good captain and fetch our payment and papers. Let's see if it is all he claims."

Gaspar looked on intently while his guts knotted with tension. The pirate captain paced to LeFouet's railing and stared out over the sea for a long moment until his men returned carrying the chest Captain Callais had received from the U.S.S Chesapeake. The chest dropped onto the deck with a heavy wooden thunk and Captain Fontaine watched while his men unlatched the lid and propped it open. He dipped a hand into the chest and seized a fistful of golden coins. "Will you be joining us on the hunt then captain?"

"We will lead the search, Captain Fontaine. Part of our fleet is searching the southern coast of Haiti, part of them are patrolling the eastern shores of Jamaica. Once we locate the pirates…"

Captain Fontaine's face flushed red with rage, he held his saber up to Captain Callais throat, "You may join us on the hunt, captain. But do not presume to lead me anywhere. The Batard De Mur sails where she will." His gaze shifted around the deck and landed on Gaspar. "There is another matter which we must attend before casting off." Gaspar's blood ran cold. The pirate captain's eye was locked onto him. His lips curled into an angry grimace. He shifted his sword around and pointed it toward Gaspar's chest. "We have boarded your vessel. Blood must be shed."

"What? Why?" Captain Callais shouted in objection.

"It is our way." Captain Fontaine stepped in front of Gaspar, "Think of it as sealing our agreement in blood captain."

In a swift, violent lunge Captain Fontaine thrust his sword deep into Gaspar's chest just to the side of his breastbone. It felt cold and sharp as the blade entered his flesh. He struggled to breath, but he could not draw anything into his lungs. A stream of blood began to pour around the blade. Gaspar could feel his heart race and flutter for an instant. Then cold. Cold overtook him as his life slipped through his fingers. The pirate captain lifted a boot and kicked it into Gaspar's blood covered chest while wrenching his sword back out of the wound. Gaspar fell backwards, the wooden deck rushed up and slammed against his head. It felt like all of his warmth was draining away as blood gathered around him in a pool on the deck.

"Cross me captain," Fontaine threatened, "And I will kill every last one of you."

Pirate Cove
22 Apr 1809

The sun felt hot on Chibs weathered face but a chill grabbed him from within all the same. A breeze flowed through the cove whipping ripples along its surface. Omibwe had disappeared around the corner of the Maiden's rail and had not been seen in what felt like hours. Chibs shifted his feet nervously in the sand, he'd been grinding the wet granules beneath them back and forth until there were two-foot size trenches beneath where he sat on a large rock. He looked at Dr. LeMeux and then back to the portion of the Maiden's bow that still protruded stubbornly out of the water.

"He's been over there a long while doctor." Chibs growled, "Don't you think we should check on him?"

Dr. LeMeux gave Chibs a glance over his nose as if he were still wearing his glasses, which he was not. "I told you both, I cannot swim. If he has drowned, there will be very little we can do for him by the time we got out there anyway."

Chibs watched over the water that separated them from the Maiden while gentle ripples slid up the sandy shore and stretched toward them before retreating. Part of the foremast floated on the surface, it bobbled with the gentle motion of the cove while being held in place by a web of lines. He couldn't stand it any longer and fought to rise up from his seat. "Suppose he got tangled in those lines doctor. I need to go out there."

Dr. LeMeux stepped in front of him. "In your condition, you would only create another body that must be recovered. Chibs, give him a few more minutes. I have seen that young man overcome some terrible odds before, don't consign him for lost just yet."

Chibs raised his voice, he could feel his face flushing. "I'm not consigning him anywhere doctor. I only mean that he may need some help!" He used his good arm to push the doctor's shoulder, "Now get out of my way before I drag you in with me." Chibs took a purposeful stride toward the water's edge. He could feel his head beginning to swim. He'd stood up too fast, that was all, he would feel just fine after the water cooled him. The sand beneath him seemed to pitch like he was on the deck of a ship. Chibs halted his stride for a moment to let the world catch up to him. The edge of water meeting sand seemed to shift in front of him, it bobbled and yawed in his eyes moving in about before splitting and becoming a double image. Chibs cursed under his breath and squinted to stop the illusion. His heart was thundering in his chest, beating hard and fast like he had never felt outside of battle. The sand rushed up toward him and slammed him to his knees. "Gaah!" He cursed his wobbling legs. "Too much time ashore. I'm not used to it doctor, that is all."

Dr. LeMeux walked in front of Chibs again and offered him a hand up. "Too much time ashore, and perhaps the blood you lost." He motioned back toward the rock Chibs had been seated on. "Let's get you up quartermaster, we wouldn't want the captain to see you like this if she happened back this way."

Chibs rubbed his hand on his beard and nodded. "Aye, I suppose you're right doctor. I did lose quite a bit of blood." He took the doctor's hand in his own and heaved himself back to his feet.

Dr. LeMeux wrapped his arm beneath Chibs shoulders and started to help him back toward his seat. "Be patient Chibs, the boy will be paddling his way back around the Maiden's rail any minute now."

Chibs grumbled as he plunked himself back onto the weathered rock. He felt his heartbeat slowing back to a normal rhythm, the sand and the trees were in their normal place with only one image of each in his sight. "Aye, you're right. The boy is probably fine."

Chibs slouched in forward with his hand on his knee, he looked down at the drying sand beneath his feet. Little flecks covered the bottom of his calloused soles. His head was awash with thoughts he could not quite grasp. His eyes felt heavy.

"I'll be damned." Dr. LeMeux mumbled.

Chibs grimaced at a spike of throbbing pain from

his side, "What's that doctor? Did you find yourself a book?" He would have smiled at his own jest but in the moment the pain was too much.

"Omibwe." Dr. LeMeux gave Chibs' tattered shirt a tug at the shoulder. "He freed the row boat!"

Chibs raised his head and saw the wooden bow of a rowboat plowing its way through the cove. Omibwe's triumphant grin beamed across the gap of water as he pushed at the oars. Chibs gave Dr. LeMeux a grinning look and growled, "I told you he'd be fine doctor. Now don't you feel like a horse's ass." The doctor narrowed his eyes and shook his head. He drew a breath to begin to correct Chibs. "It was a jest, doctor. No need, no need."

Dr. LeMeux straightened his back and paced toward the water's edge. When the wooden boat slid its way into the sandy beach he helped the young man up over the side.

"A line wrapped my leg Chibs, I nearly drowned." Omibwe's voice carried up from the water's edge.

Chibs' nose and forehead scrunched into a frown, "How did you free yourself?"

Omibwe shook his head and shrugged his shoulders. "I didn't."

Chibs exchanged a confused look with the doctor. "Then how are you here and not fish food?"

"A woman. Like from the tales you told me doctor, one of the sea creatures." Omibwe replied as he hobbled and hopped his way toward Chibs with Dr. LeMeux at his shoulder giving aid.

"A mermaid?" The doctor asked recoiling his head. His face flushed when he looked up and saw Chibs scorn.

"No, not really. I mean, she didn't look like I would have thought. She had no fish tail, and her skin wasn't white like the story you told me. She looked like me." Omibwe's voice was charged with excitement. "She pulled slack into the rope around my ankle and unlatched the boat for me. When I woke up, I was in the boat on the surface and she was nowhere to be seen."

Chibs coiled his fingers around his beard and looked hard at the young African. "You mean she looked like you. Like she was one of the crew?" He shifted his feet in the sand and darted a look out to the exposed bow of the Maiden. "Trina?"

Dr. LeMeux rolled his eyes at both of them, "He's delirious Chibs. Trina died in the battle and there certainly was no mermaid."

"You shut your mouth!" Omibwe pushed the doctor away and hopped to balance on his one leg. "I saw what I saw."

Holding up his good hand Chibs shouted, "Okay, easy now. Both of you." He took a ragged breath and dared another look back out over the water. "Whatever happened, you got the boat. Now. Did you see line? Was there any block that you might be able to get to?"

Omibwe's eyes widened at Chibs, he nodded with a big smile. "There's lines and blocks. She even has one of her deck cannons still tied in place."

Chibs recoiled his hand back to his beard and tugged at the thick of it. "That's good. We'll have no use for a cannon until she's raised, but that is a good thing." He looked back down at the small rowboat at the water's edge. "Do you think you could go for another dive Omi?"

Omibwe looked out at the proud wooden bow of the Maiden, refusing to surrender to the cove lapping all around its sides. "Yes. I can dive all day and all night."

"Now hold on," Dr. LeMeux cut in front of Omibwe again, "Don't you think you should rest first? If you came so close to drowning that you were seeing things, you shouldn't go right back out there."

Omibwe's face was cold as stone. He clenched his jaw and stared at the doctor with a look that made Chibs blood run colder. "I can't run. I can barely walk. But I can sail, and I can dive."

Chibs cackled a big laugh that came from deep in his belly. "Well doctor, I think you have your answer." He turned and looked at Omibwe with a grin. "I'll go out in the boat with you. You can fish up lines and I'll help you haul them into the boat. What do you say?"

Omibwe nodded and smiled. "Yes. So we're ready when Captain Lilith comes back."

"Aye, we'll be closer than we would if Lubber LeMeux were in charge." Chibs cackled and shot the doctor a look, "The one-armed sea dog is going with the one-legged boy. We've been on land too long. Do landsmen things while we're gone and find some food would you? I'm starved."

Haitian Inland
21 Apr 1809

Flames engulfed the wooden boiling house as Lilith stood outside watching the structure being consumed. Blood dripped from the edge of her cutlass as sweat dripped from her brow. The newly freed slaves gathered around to watch as their former constraints evaporated into the night sky in a thick column of dark smoke that blotted out the stars. The guards inside had tried in vain to fight them off. They had killed one of the workers inside. Watching the young woman die had been like a spark to a powder keg deep inside Lilith. The guards had stirred a storm inside of her and the rage that followed was far from quenched. The guard hadn't hesitated, as soon as Renly had kicked open the wooden door and Lilith walked through he had grabbed the slave closest to him and held a dagger to the poor woman's throat. Without a word, the guard cut his blade deep into the woman's throat opening a gushing wound that poured down the front of her chest. As his blade finished its work, the guard attempted to haul a pistol out from his belt. It had been too little too late to save him. Lilith lunged with her cutlass as soon as he had opened the woman's throat, the point of her blade plunged deep into his chest and drove him into one of the boiling kettles. The rest was a bloody blur in Lilith's recollections as she watched the flames wrap around the wooden shake roof like fingers curling into a fist.

All around her the slaves were watching as the inside of the building turned into an orange ball of flame hotter than a forge. The breeze flowed in through the open shudders and fed the inferno fresh air, the flames stoked like they had been hit with a blast from a bellow. Soon the fiery fingers cast a bright glow all around them. Lilith smiled at the destruction she had wrought with her newly recruited crew until the hollow sound of a bell tolling rang out from within Tortuga.

"The fire! They've spotted it from town!" Renly grasped at Lilith's ragged sleeve as the peal of town bells began to fill the night. "Captain, soldiers. The town garrison will turn out for this. We'll never make it to the harbor if they pin us in a fight."

Lilith's heart skipped as she heard voices echo from Tortuga. In the distance she could see lanterns moving with the gait of running men. She had to think quickly. She had to be bold. For a fleeting moment she thought of a story Chibs had told her about Captain James and the Drowned Maiden. She narrowed her good eye and squeezed the grip of her sword. "Into the brush all of you!" She shouted while waving her arms for the freed men and women to get low in the grass and bushes that surrounded the far side of the road. "When I give the signal, show them no mercy, they will give you none."

Renly followed Lilith as she scurried for the high grasses across the road that led to Tortuga. The swinging lanterns were drawing closer and sound of shouts and footfalls carried through the air between crackles and pops from the fire. "Captain, perhaps we should make for the countryside."

Lilith dropped into the weeds and brush and pulled Renly down alongside her. "We'll take them by surprise. By the time they figure out what is happening it will be too late."

"We have no guns captain. The soldiers will be armed with muskets and swords and bayonets." Renly objected in a hushed tone.

Lilith gave him a hard look through her squinted eye. "Then we had better make sure they don't get the chance to fire their guns or fix their bayonets." She craned her neck upward, pushing up with her arms to sneak a look at the road. "As soon as it looks like their attention is focused on the flames, we charge with everything we have." She looked back at Renly. His lips were drawn in a tight grimace.

"Damn it all then." He grumbled, "I hadn't really expected to die of old age anyway."

Footsteps crunched on the road. Muffled shouts between the soldiers echoed into the night.

"It's a lost cause. The building is beyond saving." A voice shouted in between ragged panting breaths.

Another voice asked, "What do you think happened, sir?"

"What do you mean? It was a boiling house. I'm sure one of the fires inside got out of hand." The first voice answered in an irritated rebuke.

"Do you think anyone escaped?" the second voice continued his questions.

"If only I had a fresh recruit to send into the camp to find out." The first voice snapped. A pause passed. "I'm talking about you! Go find out if there are survivors in the huts behind the burning building. Be quick about it!"

Lilith crept her knees up underneath her torso and edged her face over the top of the tall grass to have a look. Silhouettes of soldiers lined the road between her and the burning boiling house. Most were carrying guns, others were holding wooden buckets. Lilith silently counted the figures on the road. She stopped when she reached twenty, though there were more soldiers still to count.

"More than twenty of them." She whispered over her shoulder to Renly.

He was silent, "It will be a glorious fight captain."

Lilith nodded and gripped the handle of her sword. She cocked the hammer of her pistol and drew a long deep breath. "Are you with me Renly?" She peered over her shoulder at Renly's drawn face.

"Right behind you captain." Renly whispered.

Lilith looked around the gathering of soldiers one more time. She picked one that was standing closest to where she hid in the tall grass. Silently, Lilith rose to her feet and took several paces forward. The soldiers were all enamored by the spectacle of the blaze eating away what remained of the boiling house. Lilith Leveled her pistol at the soldier she had picked out. "Now!" She shouted and fired the pistol. A ball of sparks and flame exploded from the barrel of her pistol. The soldier buckled to the ground.

Behind her, Lilith could feel the rush of her new crew rallying behind her. At the edge of the light from the roaring flames they ran through tall grass and brush. The soldiers barely managed to turn in time for their attack to land. Lilith swung her cutlass and felt its edge bite into the side of a soldier's neck. They hadn't had time to react to the charge. It was a slaughter. Machetes hacked and stabbed at the soldiers who were stumbling over themselves trying to retreat. Lilith's crew had been outnumbered by four when she had stopped counting, the odds were quickly evened within the first few seconds of their attack. One soldier managed to raise his rifle and fire it, he was quickly cut down by a flurry of swinging machetes. Lilith ran another soldier through with her cutlass as he tried to aim his rifle to fire. The crew she had just freed gathered dropped weapons. Soon they were all wielding a weapon while the remaining soldiers were cut down to a man.

Shouts and cheers rose from the crew as the last soldier fell while one man swung the stock of a spent rifle and the other hacked at his throat with a machete. The road had become a scene of carnage. The bodies of soldiers lay scattered in various positions of agony. Smoke from the burning building drifted across the road and created a red haze. Renly stood in front of Lilith. His shirt was as blood soaked from the engagement as his blade.

"Captain. You were right." Renly managed through heavy breaths, "We've won!"

The cheers of the crew lifted high into the night air as the boiling house finally gave way and collapsed in on itself. A flurry of smoke and sparks lifted with their cheers and rose high into sky, thousands of little embers drifted away and extinguished like dying stars. Lilith looked over her victorious band. Their faces shone in the orange hues given off by the fire. In the distance, bells continued to ring. Lilith gazed up the road toward Tortuga. It would be hours until daylight broke the horizon and revealed the destruction she had caused. It was a small victory, but after having her ship blown full of holes and sunk in a cove, Lilith felt like she had regained her wind.

"Onward! Tortuga awaits!" Lilith shouted lifting her sword high overhead. The crew gave another loud cheer and followed their captain as she started walking toward Tortuga. Lanterns hung in the streets, giving off small circles of warm yellow glow about every dozen feet. The air was warm and charged with possibilities. Lilith felt the tingle of adrenaline still playing at her fingers as she trudged on. She could see people fleeing the streets ahead of them. The tangy smell of blood still hung in her nose, mixed with a tinge of smoke. Behind her, Lilith could hear the footfalls of her newly recruited following. Tortuga rose in front of them as they drew near. Windows that had been lit from within when the bells first sounded were now dark inside.

"They think they know what's coming." Lilith said as she scanned over the town.

Renly kept his pace just behind her right shoulder. He leaned forward to speak, "What is coming, captain?"

"Everything they fear, and worse." Lilith said through clenched teeth. She stepped onto a wooden walkway and seized a lantern from its sconce on a pillar. A few more steps found her in front of a tall glass windowpane that looked in on a dark room. Lilith swung the lantern in a wide arc from its metal handle and slung it through the window showering broken glass and flames into the building. She looked over her shoulder to the crew as they filtered into town from the beaten path of the road as flames grew inside the building behind her. "If you can't steal it or kill it, burn it. We work our way to the harbor from here and set sail at dawn!"

PART TWO
"MUTINY"

Chapter 6

Pirate Cove
24 Apr 1809

Trails of bubbles streamed to the surface. They came in bursts, trickling their way up from the depths where Omibwe was plying his skill as a diver to fetch every manner of useful items from the belly of the Drowned Maiden. Chibs sat in the rowboat leaning as far over the side as he dared. Every time the bubbles disappeared for more than a minute his heart would do flips inside of his chest while he wondered about the wellbeing of the young African man in the water below him. It was Omibwe's fourth dive since they had rowed the small craft out next to the wreckage of their pirate ship. Chibs had started by fishing in all the lines they could reach from the surface. It made for a healthy coil sitting in the stern of the rowboat. The first three dives had yielded heavy lines. Omibwe clung to the side of the boat while Chibs had pulled them in and coiled them into neat piles. The third dive saw Omibwe return to the surface with a large pulley. After a brief argument, Omibwe went for another dive at his own insistence while Chibs nervously looked down from the rowboat. He could tell the young man was straining himself. Whether it was because he had found a meaningful way to contribute to the cause that aligned so well with his skills, or whether he was trying to prove something, Chibs did not know. The deep blues and greens of the cove obscured his view and after Omibwe crossed deeper than twelve feet it was nearly impossible for Chibs to spot him working his way along the deck of the Maiden.

The bubbles had stopped. And Omibwe had not returned to the surface. Chibs ran his hand over his beard repetitively. He squinted and tried to focus on the dark shapes beneath the surface, searching for any sign that his young friend was in distress. For a moment, Chibs held his focus on where he thought Omibwe had entered the Maiden's hull. The differing shades of dark and light where empty voids of seawater were interspersed by the hull or the deck danced in lazy circles as the surface moved in little rippling waves. Chibs pulled in a deep breath and held it. He thought of how long Omibwe had been under as his lungs ached for relief. What felt like forever had only been half a minute when Chibs finally released his breath. He stared down, hoping to see any sign of the stubborn diver. Half dazed from holding his breath, Chibs sat up in the rowboat. He looked toward the shore to see if Dr. LeMeux was still pacing through the white sands. The Frenchman had gone. Chibs gritted his teeth and cursed the doctor. He shifted around to rest his knee in the boat while he contemplated plunging into the cove to find his friend. As he leaned over again to look beneath the surface A shadowy figure boiled up from the deep and exploded the calm water in a great splash.

"Omi! You scared me half to death!" Chibs growled and seized the young man's shoulder. "Don't stay down that long again. Do you hear me? I thought you were crab food! I was about to go in after you!"

Omibwe brushed droplets of water away from his eyes and twisted his face at the furious sailor. "I was down longer the first time Chibs."

Chibs searched for a sharp response, but found nothing. Omibwe's face was broad with a smile. He couldn't be mad for long. He softened his voice and heaved to pull Omibwe into the rowboat. "What did you find?"

"Another pulley and more of the heavy line." Omibwe answered as he scrambled his one good leg inside of the boat and squirmed on a big coil of line to sit up. "But that isn't all. I went inside the hull this time, below deck. Her guns Chibs, most of her guns are still on board."

Chibs coughed for a moment, a dry hacking

cough that made him long for his pipe. He cleared his throat and nodded, "That is good. I imagine once we get her up out of the water we'll be able to give those guns a good cleaning and oiling. They'll be fit to fight in no time." He reached for the rope Omibwe still gripped in one hand and began taking turns hauling in the thick line. "Powder will be another matter entirely. We'll have no dry powder, and the damned stuff takes forever to dry out once it's been soaked through." He clamped a foot down into the wooden rowboat and heaved in another pull after Omibwe had made a pull with each hand. "Even drying it out, it's not the same afterward. The kiss of the sea is spoiled on gunpowder. Damn stuff doesn't appreciate the finer things in life I guess. We'll be better off getting fresh gunpowder from somewhere."

Omibwe grunted as he hauled at the line again. "Where will we get it though? We can't set sail without working guns."

Chibs shook his head and pulled his turn at the line, it was heavier this time, far heavier and he noticed Omibwe was struggling with it also. "Well that is one of the questions we will have to answer. I'm hoping we may chance ourselves on a merchantman. But there's no telling. Captain Lilith has probably already thought of a plan, clever as she is."

"Clever. And pretty." Omibwe smiled his broad grin and pulled another heave of line into the boat.

"Aye. Pretty too." Chibs grinned back, "The line

is damned heavy. Are you sure it isn't snagged up below?"

Omibwe nodded. "I tied it to something."

Chibs frowned and clamped his hand on top of his head. "We can't haul her up that way, lad. We'd sooner haul ourselves down to the bottom."

Omibwe laughed and shook his head. "Not the ship. Something smaller."

Chibs gave the young man a suspicious look. "What did you find?"

"You will see Chibs." Omibwe smiled and continued to haul on the line.

The murky blue and green hues of the depths gave away no secrets as Omibwe continued hauling the rope in hand over hand. Sunlight gleamed off of the water's surface and the breeze had died away, Chibs could feel a layer of sweat forming on his brow and running down the sides of his neck. The water looked cool and inviting and the little droplets that dripped off of the rope Omibwe hauled in felt good as they fell onto Chibs' legs. He thought for a moment about lunging himself off of the small boat for a cooling soak, but as he leaned over the side to see what it was Omibwe had tied the rope to, his ribs ached again with an awful throb. In the depths below them, Chibs began to see a familiar shape take form.

"A chest?" Chibs guessed while squinting through the glare of the water. "You found a chest?"

"More than that Chibs. I found many things.

Many things that I put into the chest." Omibwe replied through a strained voice. The line was almost all the way in, and Chibs reached out with his good arm to help haul the loot his friend had gathered aboard. Sunlight gleamed off of brass banding that reinforced the corners and lid of the chest and seawater spilled from the opening as the two friends hefted it into the boat. Omibwe hurried to unlatch a brass buckle on the front of the box and pulled the lid open. A pair of mallets, a chisel and a sextant all caught Chibs eye right away. He reached in and fished the tools out, praising Omibwe for each find. Next there was a pistol that leaked a sludge of water-soaked gunpowder out of the barrel as Chibs pulled it from the chest. He found a knife and a small leather pouch at the bottom of the chest.

"What is this?" Chibs motioned at the bundle of leather.

Omibwe smiled and nodded his head toward the chest. "Look and see Chibs. Open it."

Chibs pulled the leather pouch out of the chest and unwrapped opened it. His eyes were blurry with tears. His pipe and a water-logged wad of tobacco were contained withing the folds of leather. "You found it! How did you find this Omi?"

"It was on the bottom, near the stern." Omibwe beamed a proud smile.

Chibs eyes shot wide. His blood seemed to thicken and his chest went tight. "You can get all the way to the floor of the cove? That's near forty feet!"

Omibwe nodded, "It takes a while. But this time I found an air pocket inside the Maiden's hold. I can go there if I need a breath of air."

Chibs grinned. "You sly shit. I thought you were holding your damn breath the whole time you were down there!"

Omibwe leaned back onto a coil of thick rope and folded his hands behind his head, satisfied with himself. "YOu have your tricks Chibs. I have mine."

Chibs laughed and looked back down into the leather pouch his friend had retrieved off of the bottom. The tobacco could be dried and the pipe was no worse for the wear. "Thank you friend. I thought I'd lost it." He pulled the wooden pipe stem out and blew on it sending a sprinkle of seawater over the both of them. Omibwe laughed. Chibs bellowed a thunderous laugh that shook his whole body until he toppled backwards onto a coil of line.

"Chibs!" the irritating voice of Dr. LeMeux drifted over the water and interrupted the joyous moment. "Chibs, look!"

Chibs sat up, growling at the pain in his ribs. The doctor held out a hand and pointed uphill. "Can't see anything doctor. Too many trees in the way." Chibs shouted back at the panicking doctor. "What is it?"

Dr. LeMeux looked as if he was dancing a thin line between answering Chibs question or running away. He cupped his hands and called back over the water. "There's people coming!"

Chibs slumped back onto the coil of rope behind him. His ribs ached and throbbed, but he would not waste the opportunity to jab at the French doctor. "Hopefully it is a tribe of natives here to rid us of your annoyed looks and rolling eyes. We'll all be the safer for it too. Everyone can rest more peacefully knowing they will still have their hands and feet when they awake."

Chibs chuckled as the doctor threw his hands up in dismay and then called back. "I thought perhaps you would come to shore and let me row out with you." He looked over his shoulder for a moment and then called again, "Until we know it is safe."

Omibwe's face was long, he tugged on the front of Chibs mangled shirt. "Shouldn't we go get him?"

"What? And miss the show he is putting on?" Chibs laughed again until a pain shot through his ribs. He nodded, "Alright. We can go and fetch him. But if it is native cannibals, I'm offering him up as a sacrifice."

Omibwe shook his head. "He is our friend Chibs."

Chibs growled, "Tell that to your missing leg, and my bloody stump of an arm!" He motioned around with what remained of his left arm. "Look at us though. Rowing and diving and hauling in barrels of treasure! That damned Frenchman couldn't stop us!" Chibs shited around and took and oar in his right hand. Omibwe grabbed the opposite oar with both and together they started rowing toward their very panicked scholar.

"Hurry! They're getting closer!" Dr. LeMeux urged from the sandy shore.

Chibs turned around in between rowing strokes to have a look for himself. Out of the thick underbrush a tall, broad shouldered African man emerged from a thicket of leaves and branches. Chibs grumbled under his breath for Omibwe to hear, "That dumb bastard. It's only Damriq. You would think he could recognize a man he's been at sea with for months."

'Havana's Mistress'
22 Apr 1809
20 Degrees 15' N, 73 Degrees 17' W

The flames of Tortuga raged. Early morning revealed a scene of bedlam and slaughter. Pink and orange rays lit the heavens and reflected along the buildings as columns of smoke rose to muddle their glory. Lilith sat on the deck of her new ship, breathing in the sea air and nursing a wound just above her hip. The water was calm as they made way out of the harbor. They had struck a good fortune of finding a merchant galley, Havana's Mistress. Lilith didn't particularly care for the name, but she was a stout two masted ship with plenty of freshly loaded hull space. To her delight, Renly reported that her hold was full of barrels of fresh water, fruits from the market in Tortuga, crates of salted pork, casks of rum and wine and an assortment of other supplies her crew would find useful in the coming weeks.

Lilith had not intended to take Tortuga by storm. She had imagined slipping in and stealing away on a ship under the cover of night. Burning the boiling house had been an unintentional side effect of freeing the slaves held there. The soldiers who came running to the flames were the first salvo in what proved to be a battle that lasted through the night. Lilith and her crew had managed to remain relatively unscathed for the most part. A couple of her newest members fell to a volley of fire from soldiers who had formed a firing line in the street next to Tortuga's abandoned marketplace. The crew rallied after the cloud of gun smoke drifted back over the line of soldiers. The soldiers broke ranks and ran. Lilith was impressed by the bravery and resolve of her newly recruited crew. They were ferocious in a fight.

"They have a long way to go before we can stand toe to toe with another ship. But I think Chibs will be able to make sailors of this lot." Renly said leaning against the rail next to where Lilith was slouched onto the deck.

"How many?" Lilith asked as she lifted the bandage off of her wound to check the bleeding.

"My last count was thirty-two. The dockworkers that joined us could make quite a difference. They know their way around a ship at least."

Lilith grimaced as she looked at the cloth bandage, dark red blood still oozed from a deep gash she had gotten just below her hip. The captain of Havana's Mistress had not been of a mind to give up his ship without a fight. Lilith had faced him sword to sword in what had been the most trying struggle she had ever encountered. The same lunge that resulted in her wound had opened her opponent's guard long enough that Lilith managed to land a fatal strike against the side of his throat. Swords and pistols quickly encouraged the rest of the merchant crew to make sail out of the harbor with all haste. The morning tide was beginning to slack and a favorable wind caught their sails and ferried them out into the open sea.

"What of the ship's crew? The merchantmen?" Lilith asked, holding the bandage back against her wound.

Renly shrugged and offered Lilith a grim nod, "We could offer them a place with us. If they so choose. But if they do not, once we arrive in the cove we will have no choice captain. They either join or die. We cannot leave loose tongues to tell the tale of a girl captain and her pirate crew resurrecting their ship from the depths. At least not until the Maiden is seaworthy again."

Havana's Mistress made a turn westward with the sun shining bright on the back of her wind filled sails. The deck started to pitch in the growing roll of waves further out from the Haitian coast. Lilith grimaced with the movement. She was used to being at sea, the pitch and rock of the ship no longer bothered her, but with each movement her wound throbbed a little harder. She gave Renly a wincing smile as her hip bled through the cloth bandage she was holding tight onto it. "Would you mind giving me a hand up Renly? Let's see if the former captain at least had a decent cabin."

Renly nodded and tucked and arm under Lilith's, "Aye, captain. We'll get you set up." He lifted her to her feet with a gentle pull. "Don't you worry about the crew. I'll see to it the merchantman sailors keep us on course."

Lilith gave a feeble nod. "It's nothing. I just need some rest Renly. I'll be back at it by tomorrow." The blood seeping from her hip told a different story.

"Captain. If you don't mind me saying. I've been in more than my fair share of fights. I served with Captain Grimes aboard the Valor when Lieutenant Pike was still a damned midshipman off doing God knows what, maybe before he was even in the royal navy. That wound will need tending."

Lilith felt her head bobble as she made her way toward the cabin hatch. "You will tend my wound?"

Renly gave an awkward smile. "I've helped patch up a few. I think I could help get the bleeding stopped, depending on how bad it is. But we'll need to do something for you or it could get infected."

"Dr. LeMeux…" Lilith's voice trailed away as her

head began to spin.

Renly put more of her weight onto his shoulder and continued toward the cabin. "Aye the old French sawbones. Hopefully we can get you fixed up before he gets his claws on you. That bastard will want to cut off your leg, maybe both."

Lilith laughed despite the weakness she felt. The doctor had gotten himself a bit of a sour reputation with the crew even though he had saved Chibs' life. "It's low on my hip Renly. Don't blush too hard when I take down my pants."

Renly chuckled and shook his head as he pulled the cabin door open. "Not to worry Captain. I'll be looking at your wound anyways."

The cabin was dark, but it was warm and mostly kept out the wind. A few of the window panes along the fantail array were cracked and missing some of their glass. The bed had a straw stuffed mattress and there was a wood stove situated in one corner of the cabin. As Renly helped Lilith lay down she could feel the blood immediately start to collect in the fabric and straw below the wound. "I thought it would slow after a while, but I feel like it has gotten worse." She lifted the makeshift bandage and pulled the waist of her trousers below the wound.

Renly grimaced. "Press that cloth back onto it. Hold it there as tight as you can."

"Can you mend it?" Lilith asked with a fading voice. Her head was swimming now, it took twice as long as it should for her to form her words.

Renly snapped to the wood stove and began shuffling through a pail of kindling. "It's a cut, a deep one. But I think I can get you patched up captain. If it were a stab, well, I don't know. Those are harder." Renly continued shuffling through the pail and suddenly stood. He darted to the cabin door and pulled it open to shout out to the crew. "I need a wick with a flame, a lantern, something. Hurry!"

Lilith held the bandage against her hip as tight as she could. The warm wetness of blood crept through the fibers and covered her fingers and palm. She could feel the warmth invading the mattress below her and creep up her side until the wet blood cooled. It gave her a bit of a chill to think of how much blood she may have already lost. She was vaguely aware of Renly now. He was working furiously to stoke a fire in the stove, cursing the whole time.

"This isn't going to be pleasant captain. I'm afraid it will leave a scar too. One that will put the scar on your face to shame." Renly uttered. Lilith could feel warmth returning to the cabin. Her eyes were closed, she felt exhausted, drained and cold all at once.

"Do what you need to. I'm not scared of scars." Lilith's tongue felt thick, and she had to fight for each word. "Not like suitors are lining up for me anyway."

She thought of Captain James. His big beautiful eyes and those powerful shoulders. His beard. The crisscrossing scars across his powerful chest. Scars were not so ugly on men. But James was gone. Slain by an onslaught of sailors aboard H.M.S Endurance over a year ago. Lilith could still remember the pitched fight, the smoke, the screams.

A clang of metal snapped her back into the present. Lilith pried her eyes open and searched the cabin for Renly. He was squatted in front of the wood stove, a bright orange glow washed from the stove's chamber illuminating his chest and face. "I am sorry for this captain."

Lilith felt a streak of confusion in her head. She watched Renly pull an iron rod out of the stove. It glowed so hot the orange red metal had an almost white sheen to it. Lilith summoned what strength she could and grit her teeth. "Do it. If it will stop the bleeding. Do it." Lilith turned her head away and lifted the bandage away from her wound. Renly's footsteps crossed the small cabin and she could hear the hissing metal as he pulled it close to her. The heat radiated off of the metal, she could feel as he brought it close.

"Ready?" Renly asked.

"Just do it!" Lilith snapped, gritting her teeth again.

The pain that came was unlike anything she had ever felt. At first it felt hot, and then for a moment there was nothing. The sizzling noise filled her ears while the pungent smell of burned flesh invaded her nostrils. The numbness left and pain came in waves. Lilith clamped her teeth together until she felt like they would crumble from the pressure. Renly withdrew the searing hot metal.

"Forgive me captain. I know that hurt." He mumbled, "But it's done. Your wound is cauterized."

Lilith forced out a deep shot of breath from her nostrils. Her hip ached and throbbed, the wound felt like it was on fire. She held her fists clamped to her temples. "Renly." She growled through her teeth.

"Yes captain?" He answered.

"I thank you for your service. See yourself out." Lilith drew in a breath, "If I should appear on deck with sword in hand. Run."

'North Wind'
24 Apr 1809
18 Degrees 02' N, 74 Degrees 58' W

"Reload!" the raspy shout floated its way down through deck planking. It was followed by the drolling rumble of cannon carriages being rolled into position. Feet clambered on the decks as sailors went through the motions of reloading their guns. Will had been listening from the cramped misery of his cell as the gun crews above him went through another iteration of their gun drills. At first the drills had been lively. Sailors threw their whole strength into the arduous labor of moving the guns and even through layers of deck timbers Will could hear their urgency. That had been hours ago though and now each order was followed by a pause longer than the previous. The gun crews were tiring. If the admiral planned to wear them down and discourage illusions of mutinous grandeur, it seemed to be working.

It had been weeks since Will had endured the ordeal of being keelhauled. His wounds continued to agonize him, the deep gouges on his back smelled of infection. The cuts on his hands and belly would open every time he moved within his cramped cell. Deep in the belly of Admiral Torren's flagship, Will's cell was constantly in a varying state of flooding. When North Wind listed to her starboard side with a turn or the force of her sails all of the water that collected in her hull would come washing across the deck and build up within Will's cell. At its worst, the flooding would come up above Will's ankles, sometimes even mid-calf. When the ship was listing to her larboard, or in a turn that favored that side the collection of constant seepage would drift to the other side of the hold and Will would enjoy relative dryness while listening to the aggravated complaints of Tim Sladen occupying a cell across the passageway. On rare occasion, the crew would work their bilge pump until there was hardly any water within the hold. While the gun drills were being conducted on the decks above him, a group of sailors had been working the bilges with diligent fervor. Though North Wind was making near constant sail and course adjustments, after a while the hold was as dry as it had been since Will had been locked into his cell. For hours the pattern continued. The muffle of a shouted command would creep through the decks as North Wind pitched and rolled with the sea. Following the command the decks would come alive with rumbling as cannon carriages were heaved into place. A symphony of creaks and groans from the deck planks was interspersed with footfalls and the occasional hot-tempered reprise from an officer or petty officer. When all the guns were in place a shout would send them back into their full fury. It went on like this for hours.

Outside in the passageway a pair of voices conversing signaled to Will that the watch was changing. He relished the thought for a moment. If the watch was changing, they may cease their gun drills. With a dry hold, an almost dry cell and without the serenade of gun drill commencing above him, he may actually be able to get some restful sleep. Hunger pains gnawed at his insides, but Will ignored them. He sprawled on the damp straw and relished not having several inches of putrid water sloshing around him.

"I thought you'd never get here." The sentry outside of Will's cell barked at his replacement.

"I wouldn't get too excited. The old man has ordered double watch. You'll be at his cabin door for the rest of the night." The replacement grumbled, "All the same anyway, nobody will sleep tonight as long as they continue doing gun drills."

Will could hear the irritation in their voices. "He knows something is coming. I've seen this before." The first man said. Will strained his ears. He didn't want to climb to his feet, but his curiosity was too strong to resist.

"Aye, he may think he knows. But there's naught he can do about it." The voice of the second man rang through the passageway and crept into Will's cell. "He can wear out the crew all he likes. When the time comes, it will be us that takes the ship. Mark my words."

Will's stomach wrenched into knots. They had a plan. The admiral was playing into their hand and there was nothing he could do to stop it. Another mutiny. Will's soul was weary of the word. He had watched from the deck of H.M.S Endurance as Cobb had mutinied against Captain Grimes on H.M.S Valor, helpless to stop it. He had later been mutinied against by the sailors of the Endurance. Now he was confined to a stinking cell, in the belly of a ship that was about to commit another act of treachery. He was marked for death, wounded and weak, and yet again unable to intervene.

A pause in the gun carriages rumbling their rough wheels across the deck above him lasted longer than normal. Will's breath caught in his throat. He waited for the rumbling to return, for a coarse voice to shout out and resume the repetitive rolling and shouting and footfalls that had been driving him half mad only minutes ago. Deck boards creaked, and the ship groaned with a shift of direction, but the gun carriages remained silent. *Is it happening?* Will didn't know how he was supposed to feel about another mutiny. He despised the fact that Tim Sladen had stoked the entire notion with his poisonous lies and sly deceits. But Admiral Torren had been the one to order Will run under the keel, twice. The wounds still weakened him. His every movement was plagued with agonizing pangs of pain. Every few days he would suffer another fever from the infections his body was battling. His treatment since the keelhauling hadn't been any better. There were days Will wished that he had succumbed to the seawater or the wounds he had sustained, but somehow he lingered.

Footsteps out in the hall caught Will's attention. They were rushed. One man in a hurry to traverse the passageway. Will kept his eyes glued to the barred window in the top half of his cell door. Warm yellow light from a lantern washed through, swaying with the ever-present motion of the ship.

"Now is the time. Open the cells." A voice commanded the sentry standing just outside of Will's door.

Will held his breath for a moment. *Why would they let me out? Are they going to kill me and be done with it?* The sentry stepped away from the lantern light and Will could hear a metallic jangle of keys.

"You want both of them out?" the sentry asked.

"Aye. We will settle this all tonight. In front of the entire crew." The other man replied. "Once we have the old man out of his cabin, we will get to the truth of it."

The sharp rattle of keys echoed in Will's cell. His cell door burst open letting in a flood of warm light from the lantern hanging out in the passageway.

"Alright you. Get off your arse and come along with us. We're all going to have a meeting with the admiral. If you're lucky, we might even feed you a proper meal when we're all done. The sentry barked and kicked at the wet straw in Will's cell, "Come on now, get going!"

Will's heartbeat rang through his ears. He stumbled against the rough wooden wall as he stepped towards the sentry. His feet ached with pains from bearing his weight. His back throbbed where the hull of North Wind had flayed him open. The light of the lantern seemed overwhelming. It blinded him at first, but as his eyes began to focus he could see that the two marines outside of his cell were about to make good on their mutiny plan.

There can't be just two of them. That would be madness.

One of the marines threaded a hand beneath Will's left arm and started to march him up the passageway toward the stairs. The jangle of keys sounded again and Will could hear another cell door opening.

The marine pulling Will along by his arm tensed as Will tried to turn his head and look. "Mind yourself there lieutenant. You are still our prisoner."

Will couldn't believe what was going on. "Why are you taking us out of our cells?"

The sentry lifted his grip high under Will's arm which caused a bolt of pain to rack through his ribs. "We have a few questions we'd like to settle with the old man."

"At the point of a sword?" Will asked as the sentry led him up the first leg of the stairs. "I can tell you how this ends. Every one of you that tries to overthrow the admiral will hang."

"Might be." The sentry replied, "Or it might be that if we continue along with him, we'll see that same fate."

Will bit his lower lip, the sentry was not hearing reason. The stairs were a struggle and Will could feel the wounds on his lower back stretch and open with each step. "Has anyone approached the admiral with these questions already?"

The sentry scoffed and gave Will a push, "What? Pardon me sir, but we were wondering if you've betrayed the crown to smuggle slaves into the Americas? You think we would get an honest answer?" The sentry grabbed Will's shredded rag of a shirt and gave it a tug. "Why do you care anyways. He had you flogged and keelhauled. He plans to hang you. Why would you give a rats arse what happens to him?"

On the deck above, Will heard a shot sound. Voices rose in shouts and cries followed by another shot. It was happening. They were taking the ship even as they marched Will up toward the admiral's cabin. A scream cut through the noise as Will and the sentry made their way up from the hold to the first gun deck. The battery crews were 1gathered around a sailor with a wound in his stomach.

"What happened here?" the sentry pulling Will along with him asked a group of marines that had formed a line across the deck near the stairs.

"We ordered them to stay back. That one was trying to grab my rifle." A marine replied. Will could see that the marine's rifle was fixed with a blood-stained bayonet.

Will's sentry nodded. "Alright then. Keep them below deck."

The marine with the blooded bayonet nodded and replied, "Aye, sergeant!"

A tinge of shock laced Will's nerves. The ship's marine detachment were the ones committing this mutiny. The very men employed to ensure that the ship's command remained secure. A sour taste spread through Will's mouth. His stomach heaved. He felt like retching. The marine sentry urged him on with another painful prod.

"Come on, up you go. Off for our meeting with the old man!" the sentry half sneered as he said it. "We'll get to the bottom of the matter. Though I'm sure you know, we wouldn't have gone this far if there were any doubts."

Will made his way around the landing on the gun deck and began another painful ascent up the stairs. "What the American has told you are lies. I witnessed him murder Admiral Sharpe. Can't you see what he is doing? He's sown chaos among you to further his own ends." Will hissed with what little breath he could muster. His legs ached from cramps forming in his thighs. Sitting in that cell had withered him considerably and his wounds made him all the more weak.

"Shut up!" The sergeant barked, "You will answer for your crimes as well. Right next to your dear old admiral. I can't see why you want to protect the old man, after everything he has done to you."

Will stumbled on one of the stairs. The sergeant jerked his arm and hoisted him to his feet. A knife of pain ran along his spine as they continued up the steps. "The admiral is doing his duty with the knowledge he has. He has no grounds to believe what I have told him, just as you shouldn't be listening to that American."

The marine sergeant swung a backhand that caught Will alongside his jaw. The force of the blow rocked his head back and forced him to stutter step backwards. Before Will toppled headfirst down the steep stairs to the gun deck below the marine sergeant clamped onto a fistful of Will's tattered shirt and began to drag him up the remaining stairs. When they reached the weather deck, the sergeant pulled Will to his feet and motioned for the two sentries guarding Admiral Torren's cabin to stand aside. The sergeant drew his sword from out of its scabbard at his waist and used the hilt to knock on the cabin door. "Admiral," He called through the thick wooden hatch, "Open the door. We have some questions we would like to ask you."

'Batard De Mur'
24 Apr 1809
18 Degrees 14' N, 67 Degrees 47' W

A fair wind was filling the crimson sails of Batard De Mur as she clipped along on a south easterly route. Captain Laurent Fontaine stood high on the aft castle watching while his crew continued the work of pushing the ship as hard as she would go. The sun was hot, Laurent could feel its kiss on his skin, but the winds pushing them on their course kept him from breaking into a sweat. Off of his stern and a quarter toward starboard the French privateer ship shadowed his course. Laurent knew if he ordered his stunsels to be put out he would leave LeFouet and her sulking captain in his wake. Far ahead of him, the south-western coast of Haiti approached. Laurent had a decision to make, bear off southeast and leave the wretched privateers or keep his course north of the small peninsula extending from Haiti's western coast. He had a chest of gold in his cabin and a letter of marque. It would be months before word traveled back to France of his treachery if he decided to split with the privateer. But Captain Fontaine knew where the gold had come from. He knew the network that was pulling strings in the Caribbean. As he looked across the expanse of sea separating Batard De Mur from LeFouet a chill gripped his spine. He recalled the encounter that had turned him from his original course in life.

Four years ago Laurent had been a successful merchant captain. His last voyage between Brest, France and Martinique had gained him enough profit that his collective savings would be enough for him to purchase a ship. He had written a letter to one of his childhood friends and taken it to the next ship bound for home. The letter detailed Laurent's plan to purchase a vessel of his very own, what would be the beginnings of his very own trading company. His friend, a Doctor Laurent had known all of his life, would make an excellent addition to his crew. Excited for the next chapter of his life to begin, and anxious to hear of his friend's response, Laurent had decided to celebrate. He left the letter with the captain of a ship hauling back a cargo of molasses to France and departed the harbor in search of a pub. His crew was most likely well into their cups by then and Laurent had every intention of doing the same.

The pub was crowded, noisy and smelly. A small building close to the dockyards, it emanated a warm yellow glow out into the night while cheerful music spilled through open windows and doors. Laurent had managed to get a bottle of wine from the barkeep and was making his way to a table in the back of the sweltering room. Just before he reached the only empty table in the establishment he was interrupted by a tap on his lower forearm.

"I've got room here for another, and drink of my own. Care to sit with me and share the evening?" The man had a scar along the side of his face and spoke with an accent from the American south. He smiled and gestured toward an empty seat across the table from his own.

Laurent shrugged and pulled the chair out with his free hand. "I wouldn't mind the company. Tonight, I am celebrating."

The American smiled and raised his mug. "Then I will celebrate with you. What is the cause of this merriment?"

Laurent returned the smile. "I have finally raised enough money for the purchase of a vessel of my very own. One big enough to haul trade goods with money left over to fill its hold. I intend to start my very own trading company."

The American took a deep drink. "It just so happens, I am looking for merchant vessels for hire!"

"Truly?" Laurent could not believe the good fortune, "Perhaps fate made our paths cross this night." He extended his hand. "Captain Laurent Fontaine, sir. It is a pleasure to meet you."

The American wiped at the corner of his mouth with the back of his sleeve and set his mug down. He took Laurent's hand, "Tim. Tim Sladen. The pleasure is all mine captain. I have been asking about town for willing crews to take on a risky, but very profitable venture. I was beginning to lose hope."

The pub seemed to quiet around them as Tim shook Laurent's hand. "What kind of cargo do you seek good sir?"

Tim pulled another hearty drink from his cup and shook his head. He swallowed and wiped his mouth again. "We can discuss particulars later my friend. What I need from you now is your silence. This is a sensitive affair Laurent. One which the British would like to see undone altogether."

Laurent scrunched his face into a frown. "Tim, I think you have mistaken me. I do not mean to sail as a privateer. I intend to haul merchant freight, spices, silks, tobacco, tea, that sort of thing."

The American nodded and held his cup high while motioning to a serving girl. "No, I understood you sir. I don't intend that you should be a fighting vessel at all." A serving girl with a brilliant broad smile and full-figured bosoms placed a pair of mugs on their table and ferried away Tim's empty. Tim leaned forward, "I'm suggesting that you should use your new vessel to help smuggle goods to the Americas."

Laurent's spine tingled with a chill in the sweltering pub. Smuggling? He would never. He shook his head in protest. "I don't think I am the man you need…"

Tim interrupted, "You could earn yourself enough to buy a second ship in less than a year. Maybe even two ships."

Laurent's thoughts seized like a hull hitting a reef. If he could purchase two more ships, he would be able to vault himself from the humble status of his family into wealth and luxury. In time, he might even be able to purchase property with the proceeds from his fleet. For a moment Laurent's fears of illegal pursuits and ill repute faded. He looked the American in the eye. "You said it could be dangerous." He paused and pulled a sip of ale from the mug in front of him. "How dangerous?"

"Oh, you've nothing to fear. There will be an escort most all the way. You will only have to slip into American waters on your own. With a false cargo and a decent story, you can't fail." Tim raised his mug in a gesture towards Laurent. "What do you say Frenchman? Are you in?"

Laurent paused to think for a moment, but the growing smile on Tim's face grew infectious, and the possibility of becoming rich was too tempting to pass. He raised his mug and let it clunk together with the American's, "I'm in."

That fateful evening had haunted Laurent since. The American had left out so many details. Laurent had believed he would be transporting some sort of trade goods. It was only when he had made his rendezvous off the ivory coast of Africa did he learn exactly what the American had intended for him to be smuggling. Surrounded by armed vessels, Laurent's opportunity to decline the endeavor had long past. In addition to a hold full of African captives, Laurent's ship also played host to a band of men that had been responsible for hunting and abducting them from the African mainland. That trip across the Atlantic was the longest of his life. Every day he feared for the men who had signed his ledger to partake in lawful trade sailing. His greed had made criminals of them all.

Their arrival back to the Caribbean saw their armed escorts peel away and slip over the horizon, off to make port and resupply for the next trip to Africa. As for Laurent and his crew, they plotted their course and aimed the bow of his new ship Son of the Sea toward the American Carolinas. With a hold full of captive slaves and hearts full of fear and shame they pushed through navigating the tricky waters of the northern Caribbean. Laurent had been careful to avoid any major towns and kept to less traveled seas in an effort to avoid the American navy entirely. It had all been in vain. As they drew within a day of sighting the Carolina coast they were beset upon by two American ships.

Laurent had weighed his options carefully. His new vessel was stout and could haul its fair share of cargo, she had been a Spanish trade galleon before being sold in Martinique. But she wasn't fast enough to escape two warships that had the advantage of the wind on her. Laurent ordered his crew to spill the wind from their sails and allow themselves to be boarded. It was his last act as a smuggler. As the Americans boarded, Laurent went to his cabin to find the false paperwork he had been given in an effort to throw the navy men off from discovering the true nature of his cargo. When he returned, an American naval officer was kneeling on the deck of his ship with a sword shoved through his chest. The mercenaries he had been forced to take aboard took up the battle with the Americans and forced them back to the deck of their ship. In what seemed like a landslide blur of events to him now, Laurent could barely piece together how his ship had come out of the engagement with hardly any damage at all. The mercenaries fired the few cannons he had and blew a hole in the first warship below the water line. The second ship fired a few shots, shadowed them for a while and then altered their course and sailed north.

"Captain! Land ahead!" One of Laurent's crew snapped his mind back into the present.

He looked out over Batard De Mur's stern and narrowed his eyes on the ship following behind them. "SO it would seem. How far off?"

"On the horizon, four hours maybe." The pirate answered as he shot a glance over the captain's shoulder at LeFouet.

"Keep our course for now, I haven't made up my mind yet." Laurent growled while shifting his gaze between LeFouet and the eastern horizon where Haiti's coast was barely a shadow against the open sea. Most of Batard De Mur's crew had been with him since his days as an honest trade sailor. The events that followed their engagement with the

Americans only served to solidify their course as outlaws. After emptying his hold full of slaves in Charleston, Laurent had been invited to the home of a wealthy southern landowner. The company had been a strange motley of men from America, Britain and France. Mr. Clyde Ritten regaled them all with promises of fortune beyond imagining, but Laurent had heard enough of that song for one lifetime.

"I am afraid, Mr. Ritten, That this will be my only voyage under contract from you. I do not wish to invite any more confrontation with the American navy." Laurent had said when asked about the time frame for their next trip to Africa and back. "I do appreciate that you have an arranged demand, and many pieces in place to see it fulfilled. But I find smuggling slaves distasteful, and I did not set out to become a smuggler, only an honest merchantman."

Clyde's welcoming demeanor had faded into a scowl, "It appears that you don't quite understand captain. You have committed to us."

Laurent shook his head. "I agreed to one haul, sir. Mr. Sladen said nothing about a further commitment."

Clyde stood from his seat at the long dining table abruptly, screeching the chair legs along the wooden floor. "You cannot walk away from us. It is simply not an option. We have organized investors from America, Great Britain and France. I assure you, this incident with the navy will be taken care of. It won't be a problem."

Laurent felt a hot flush of red rush into his face. He felt the eyes of every man in the room on him. "I am sorry, sir. But that is not what Tim Sladen described when I agreed to make a single trip to smuggle cargo. I was not told I would be taking abducted Africans from their home and delivering them to bondage."

Clyde waved his hand and sat back into his dining chair. "Fool. You aren't hearing what I am telling you." He extended his arm and forcefully planted his index finger on the dining table in front of him. "If you make sail from Charleston to part company with us, it will be your last voyage."

Laurent's blood had run cold at the threat. He opened his mouth to respond but fell short of forming words.

Clyde filled the silence for him. "If it isn't the American navy that gets you, then it will be the British. If they cannot do it, then the French will. You will be branded a pirate and hunted to the very ends of the earth. Your chance to decline passed when you decided to agree to Mr. Sladen's offer."

Chapter 7

Pirate Cove
24 Apr 1809

Beneath the surface, everything was calm, quiet, slower. Pale shafts of light from the sun penetrated the cove and formed brilliant columns in the blue-green hues that shifted and shimmered as the lens of sea surface rippled and waved above him. Omibwe had been diving since he was a young boy. One of his earliest memories is sitting in a roughhewn canoe with another boy from his village and looking toward the depths while their fathers plied their trade. The men were superior divers, both of them, though Omibwe felt his father was the best from their village. They would return with netting bags full of clams, oysters, crabs and spears laden with fish. The men would spend a few minutes recovering at the side of the canoe while Omibwe and his friend unloaded their bags and pulled the fish from their spears. They would heave a few breaths in and out in rapid fashion and then draw a long deep breath before returning to the world beneath the waves. Young Omibwe would look on in awe, yearning for the day when he would be able to join his father and dive into the depths by his side. The events that transpired aboard the ship that had stolen them away from Africa ended that particular dream. But while Omibwe pulled his way through the cool crystal waters of the Haitian cove, he could feel a closeness with his father. Omibwe had been a talented diver, from an early age he could stay beneath the surface nearly as long as the most experienced men from his tribal village. He loved the sleek feeling of pulling himself along beneath the water, the rush of discovering something new and exciting while his lungs burned for fresh air. Losing his leg to a slaver's musket ball had been crushing to the young man, but when he took to water, he felt like he could do anything. It was like flying.

Hidden within the wreckage of the Drowned Maiden, Omibwe had discovered a few pockets of air tucked away in the nooks of her hull. The first he could reach through a narrow gap in the hull that had been blasted by a cannon ball. Omibwe had to be careful, the edges were sharp with jagged splinters of wood sticking out like hungry fingers waiting to pierce his flesh, but without too much effort he could wriggle himself in between the wooden spines and into the dark recess of the Maiden's hull. Once inside, Omibwe would swim upward for a few feet until he got close to the forward bulkhead of the gun deck. There was a large air pocket there, big enough that he could get most of his upper body out of the water and rest on a gun carriage. Light drifted from the columns of sun that penetrated the surface and found one of the holes the big navy ship had blown in the Maiden's hull. From his air pocket near the bow the light looked like brilliant green splotches beneath him, shifting and shimmering as the disturbed surface lapped against his waist. From this large air pocket, Omibwe had access to the entirety of Drowned Maiden's gun deck and hold, he could swim down her passageway and retrieve items from the captain's cabin or the galley and even make it to the ship's magazine. The next air pocket he discovered was much smaller, it was astern of the galley, below deck from where Captain Lilith had her cabin. This pocket of air was much smaller, Omibwe could only get his head and shoulders above the water line. It was difficult to breathe in much air with the majority of his torso still in the water it felt like he was being squeezed beneath his arms. There was no light that penetrated this part of the wreckage, Omibwe had found the air pocket by pure chance while looking for anything he could retrieve from the Maiden's galley. The last and deepest air pocket was smaller still, Omibwe found it when he had gone into the deepest portion of Drowned Maiden's hold. A deep blue glow penetrated the dark space inside the Maiden's lowest space and Omibwe found the cannon blast which had forced the ship to succumb to the cove. It was broad. Wide enough that even Chibs could get through with his big broad shoulders and stout belly. When Omibwe had first found it, he swam through the opening and found the sandy bottom was only a few feet away. From here he could see the Maiden's shattered rudder. When he looked up, the surface seemed like a hazy border to another world, and miles away. Just inside of the large breech in the hull, the air pocket was only large enough for him to stick his head into. Omibwe was wary of this small spot. It was too far from the surface for him to make it without another breath of air and the space between the opening of the hull and the sandy bottom seemed to vary with the tide. The first time he had discovered the spot, he was able to swim through without even touching the sand. The next time, when he had discovered Chibs' pipe and loaded it into a chest to be hoisted to the surface, he had to bend at the waist and in order to get his legs through the opening. All it would take is a slight shift and the Maiden could come crashing in to pinch him between the unforgiving timbers of her hull and the sandy floor of the cove.

Omibwe was staring down into the water from the gun carriage perch. Outside, the sun was beating down directly on the cove and beams of light pierced through the pristine waters shining their brilliance below the surface and illuminating the inside of Drowned Maiden as much as Omibwe had seen. Chibs was on shore, organizing an effort to secure lines to large trees and rocks. Dr. LeMeux was somewhere above in the small rowboat, offering whatever support and encouragement he could in between Omibwe's ventures into the depths. Omibwe was on a very specific mission. He had retrieved as much line and blocks as he could find, Chibs seemed to think it would be enough. The next step was to find strong places to secure the line before the rest of the crew could begin heaving her closer to shore. The main mast was an option. It had been shattered by cannon fire and most of it had broken away and tipped into the cove, but there was still a twelve-foot portion of the massive wooden beam affixed to the Maiden. The upper portion had not broken away clean though, and on the dive to his large air pocket Omibwe could see that part of the mast would be in the way of the line Chibs would use to haul the ship in. After taking a break to look around the gun deck from his gun carriage perch Omibwe took a few sharp breaths in the same manner his father had taught him followed by a long big breath. He pushed himself back below the surface and swam down to the small breach in the hull. After wiggling his way through, Omibwe scoured the outside of Drowned Maiden's hull for somewhere to attach a line. Chibs had told him it would take several. He'd found a spot on the bowsprit that looked sturdy enough while they had been rowing out to the wreckage. The Maiden's bow was still defiantly protruding from the sea, unwilling to give in to the watery clutches beneath her. Working his way along the deck, Omibwe continued downward while searching for another place to secure a line. The tide was running out of the cove and Chibs was set on getting lines secured to the wreckage in order to use the incoming tide to aide in their efforts. As Omibwe reached the lowest portion of railing, he could on the Maiden's stern he could feel his lungs burning for fresh air. Not wanting to venture beneath the hull and risk the narrow entry into the lowest air pocket, he decided to try and make the surface without it. A sensation on his shoulder alerted Omibwe. It was a tickle, barely there, like a fragment of seaweed or a fish had brushed against his skin. Omibwe looked around. At that depth, the light penetrating from above cast faint bluish glow that enhanced the shadows all around him. It was difficult to make out anything besides the figure of the ship. An urge from his chest told Omibwe the time for him to start back toward the surface had already passed. He grabbed the stern railing and pulled himself deeper, working his way around to the deepest of the holes in the Maiden hull. The sandy bottom stretched out ahead of him and Omibwe pulled his arms through the water, fighting the panic in his mind. His lungs ached and began to pull inside of his chest. If he could not get through, he may not even be able to make it back to the other air pockets.

Omibwe eased the tension in his lungs by letting a little bit of air go, dribbling away from his lips in a slow string of bubbles. He continued along the side of the hull until he felt the ragged edges of split timber. The gap between the hull and the sand had shrunk even further. Omibwe had just enough room to squeeze through the narrow passage between sand and hull. He pulled himself into the dark inner workings of the Maiden and found his air pocket. As his face broke free of the water, Omibwe pushed what remained from his lungs and heaved in new breath. The pocket was small. He could see nothing from where it was located. Only darkness. As he sucked in another breath, Omibwe felt another sensation on his shoulder. This time it was not slight. It was a hand. He felt a tug against his arm. An urgent gesture that nearly pulled his head back beneath the surface. His blood seemed to cool, prickles stood on his arms and back. "Hello?" Omibwe spoke into the darkness. He waited for a response, hoping and fearing that he would meet one of the mermaids Dr. LeMeux had first told him about but no longer seemed to believe in. "Hello?" He called again. No answer came. Only silence and the echo of Omibwe's breathing in the narrow corner of the ship that held his small pocket of air. He wiped his face with a hand and strained his eyes to find anything perceptible in the darkness. Nothing. Omibwe started his routine of taking a few sharp breaths before pulling in a lungful of air. On his last deep breath in the Maiden began to groan. Her timbers shuddered and the air pocket he was breathing in began to shrink even further. Panic laced his nerves. He rushed as big a breath as he could muster before diving back below the waterline and clawing his way toward the hull breach. He could feel the Maiden shudder. Her timbers groaned in the darkness. As Omibwe pulled himself through the open hole in Maiden's hull he realized the ship had shifted. When he entered there had been over a foot of space between the wooden hull and the sandy bottom. As Omibwe extended an arm through the opening he was shocked again as it almost immediately dove into soft sand. His heart began to beat faster. There was no way he would be able to squeeze himself through the gap now, even if he could the Maiden's trembling, shifting hulk could come down onto him at any moment crushing his body between the hull and the sand. Pale blue light fluttered outside of the hull breach, filtering down from the surface far above him. Omibwe could feel the tension of his lungs already beginning to build. A shadow passed. The blue glow disappeared for half a heartbeat. A tremble of fear rose inside of Omibwe. For a moment panic engulfed his thoughts. Had the ship shifted and occluded his only way out of the hold? His head spun. His lungs were already aching for fresh air. Omibwe stretched his arm back through the opening. He expected to feel the grit of sand at his fingertips almost immediately but was shocked to find that his hand did not tough into sand. He stretched his arm further, nothing. There would be enough space, but he had to move quickly. Omibwe took hold of the jagged edge of the hull and launched himself through. A groan sounded. He could feel the ship tremble and shake. Clawing at sand and wood he tore his way out from beneath the Maiden's hull just before the hulking mass of the ship shifted over to come crashing down. A cloud of sand obscured everything around him. In desperation Omibwe pushed off of the sandy bottom with his one good leg and launched himself toward the surface. He clawed at the water swimming harder than he had ever before. To ease the tension in his lungs, Omibwe let a trickle of air out as he tore his way toward the surface. He could feel his head spinning. His thoughts came in jumbles. The light above him was all he could focus on. Through the seawater in the cove Omibwe could hear the Maiden groaning as her hull shifted. The surface was just out of reach, just a few more strokes and he would make it. A cracking noise sliced through the dense depths reverberated in the cove. Omibwe could feel it in his bones. His hands broke through the surface first, he clawed and pulled at water until his face broke free from its grasp. Sweet air hit his lungs in a massive gasp. He had drifted inward, between where Dr. LeMeux was waiting in the rowboat and Chibs on the shore.

    With everything he could muster, Omibwe screamed with his first breath. "Chibs! She's shifting, her hull is moving!"

Chibs stopped what he was doing and ran to the water's edge. "Are you sure?"

"Yes. She's moving, I could hear the hull cracking and groaning. I was almost crushed beneath her." Omibwe cried back in answer.

Chibs looked around to the crew gathered on the sandy beach. He cupped his remaining hand around his mouth and called back to Omibwe, "We have to hurry then. We have to get lines on her and haul her in now! Before she drifts further out on us."

'North Wind'
24 Apr 1809
18 Degrees 02' N, 74 Degrees 58' W

"Steady now lads." Admiral Torren gruffed as the pounding knocks sounded at his cabin door. "Steady. Now is the time to show your courage and keep your wits."

A muffled voice carried through the thick wooden hatch, "Open this door admiral. We don't want to have to batter it down."

Admiral Torren looked around his grand cabin at the small number of trustworthy men he had gathered. His aide, Lieutenant Thatcher, stood near his desk. The lieutenant's face was drawn with anxiety, pale as a ghost. Admiral Torren could hardly fault the young officer, though he had grown weary of his aide's ineptitude with all things pertaining to life at sea as well as combat. An unfortunate side effect of spending the majority of his young career in London and not out with the fleet. Midshipman Brant was at the front edge of his desk, his officer's sword gripped tight in hand and a pistol in the other. By the door was Lieutenant Spears, the North Wind's master at arms, he had brought with him two of his marines and given the admiral the stoutest assurance that no matter how widespread the mutinous sentiments had gotten, they would remain loyal lads. *Six men crammed into my cabin against the rest of the crew. Damn the luck.* Admiral Torren stood from his seat behind the desk and stepped to the sidewall of his cabin. His arms belt was hanging from an ornamented row of hooks along the wall beneath a framed painting of the North Wind sailing in her prime glory. He pulled the belt from its hook and wrapped it around his waist.

"If they want to take the ship, they will have to batter down that door and kill me first. Prepare yourselves lads, it's going to be a long night." Admiral Torren growled as he fastened the buckle of his arms belt. He looked over his small band of officers and marines as the door shuddered with another series of pounding. "Gentlemen. If tonight be our last." He paused and gave each man a glance, trying to express his gratefulness. "It has been my honor to serve with you. Don't judge me too harshly for my failings, I will extend to you the same courtesy."

The men returned Admiral Torren's glance, the marines nodded, Lieutenant Thatcher gave a weak grin. Midshipman Brant shook his head. "Sir. If they mean to take the ship, they have it already." The midshipman spoke softly.

Admiral Torren cocked his head and furrowed his brow. "What do you mean son?"

Brant shrugged his shoulders, his face was flushing red from the attention of everyone in the cabin. "I mean sir, they don't need this cabin. If they want to take over the ship and make course for somewhere other than our intended destination, they could do it now if they have the majority of the crew."

"You don't believe they do?" The admiral inquired with a deeper frown. He could see the midshipman's red hue beginning to take root. "Speak your mind lad. I'm listening."

"The only reason they would need you sir is to sway the rest of the crew. Otherwise they would have just locked you down in a cell and taken command for themselves." The midshipman looked around at the rest of the room and then back to Admiral Torren. "They are wanting to get you out on deck in front of the crew sir. Why? Why would they do that unless they needed to gain the support of more of them somehow."

"Well done young man. Well done indeed." The admiral gave a solemn nod and drifted his gaze out into the darkness beyond the cabin's array of fantail windows. "I should say lads. If that is the case, then our cause is not lost. Should we still have the loyalties of some of the crew out there, there is still hope for the fools left in this cabin." Admiral Torren tensed his abdomen as a writhe of pain crawled up his ankles and into his knees. He grimaced as the pain spiked to an intolerable level while facing outboard to hide his break of composure.

"What shall we do then sir?" Lieutenant Thatcher leaned over the side of the admiral's desk as he inquired. "Even if there are men among the crew who would join us, we are trapped in here and unable to rally them."

Admiral Torren choked down a gasp and took a breath as the pain in his legs subsided. He turned toward Lieutenant Thatcher and gave him a grim half smile. "We will meet them in battle lad. The surest way to rouse the fight in the crew is to demonstrate our unbending resolve. If we should perish, so be it."

The pounding and shouting at the cabin door relented. Lieutenant Spears withdrew a pistol from his belt and cocked the flint hammer back. "I doubt that means they have given up gentlemen. We should prepare ourselves."

Midshipman Brant withdrew his sword from its scabbard. The marines locked the hammers of their rifles into place and positioned themselves in front of the cabin door. With a deep breath Admiral Torren turned to face the room and slowly withdrew his sword from its scabbard at his waist.

Muffled voices continued outside of the cabin door. Footfalls could be heard clamoring across the deck. The admiral gave Lieutenant Thatcher a glance before focusing back onto the wooden door separating them from their mutinous shipmates. "Draw your steel lad. You don't want them to think you a coward."

The raspy noise of Lieutenant Thatcher pulling his sword from its scabbard was interrupted by a loud crash against the stout wooden planks of the cabin door. A moment of silence followed. Voices shouted out on deck. Another slamming crash sounded. A voice followed, "You had your chance old man. Now we will drag you from your cabin and have this out in front of the crew with you on your knees!"

Admiral Torren looked at Midshipman Brant and gave the young officer a nod. A rush of pride swelled inside of his chest as another impact slammed against the wooden hatch. The sound of timbers cracking split through the cabin's interior and sent a chill into Admiral Torren's bones. He clamped his jaw and flexed the grip of his sword hand. Outside of the cabin door voices shouted threats and curses while the battering continued. The wooden beam that barred the door was cracking. The admiral knew it would only be a few more hits before it finally gave out and they would come face to face with a rush of assailants.

"Fire your rifles and pistols first lads. Then we will have to hold them at the door with edged weapons. Whatever you do, hold the line at the door. We cannot permit them to breach this cabin or we will be overwhelmed." The Admiral hefted his pistol from out of his arms belt. "Hold your fire until I let fly."

The men in the cabin replied in unison, "Aye sir."

Another slam against the cabin door seemed to shake the wooden deck boards beneath their feet. Cracking pierced into Admiral Torren's ears. The wooden door flew open. Outside the threshold of the door a pair of red coat clad marines were holding a section of spare yard as a battering ram. Over their shoulders were more of the ship's marine compliment. A crowd of them were gathered on deck, some holding lanterns or torches, others were wielding weapons. Admiral Torren leveled his pistol at the first marine he laid eyes on and pulled the trigger. The hammer fixture slammed home sending a shower of sparks into the small pan beneath it, the pistol roared in his hand sending a cloud of gun smoke pouring from its muzzle. The marines inside the cabin fired their rifles, Lieutenant Spears and Midshipman Brant fired their pistols. The cabin became a choking cloud of gun smoke. Through the haze Admiral Torren watched the first two lines of men outside of the threshold fall. They dropped their improvised battering ram, and all collapsed to the deck. A scream erupted as the section of spar thudded down onto the deck. "My leg! Oh god, my leg!"

A rush of men came forward stumbling and stepping over the fallen mutineers as they made their way to the cabin door way. Lieutenant Spears and his trusted pair of marines intercepted the first two men right at the threshold of the door. The marines' bayonets pierced flesh while Lieutenant Spears stabbed at the attackers with his sword. Midshipman Brant added his sword to the fray, stabbing at the oncoming mutineers over the shoulders of the steadfast marines guarding the entrance with their bayonets. Screams and shouts filled the night air and Admiral Torren stood close behind, watching as the fight continued. Limbs and sword flailed. Blood fell onto the deck at the threshold of his cabin door. One of the marines let out a cry and stumbled backward, he quickly regained his footing and drove the point of his bayonet into an attacker's throat. It was a scene of violent bedlam, but his loyal men were holding the line right at the threshold of the cabin.

Through the chaos and smoke, Admiral Torren caught a glimpse of a man outside of the cabin. Light flashed up on the man's face as a lantern swung nearby. He seemed a hollow shell with sunken eyes and a scraggly unkempt growth of patchy beard along his jaw. The man's shirt was a ragged threadbare mess of stains and cuts. Admiral Torren felt his temper flare up into his throat. *Lieutenant Pike. I should have known.* The insolent, treacherous, murderer had orchestrated this. The admiral clenched his jaw until he noticed something off about his observation. Pike was wearing irons. A pair of metal shackles bound the man's wrists, his chains hanging in front of his waist. Admiral Torren watched him closely as chaos continued in between them at the cabin door. The lieutenant looked around on deck, for a moment it looked like he was about to make a break for the rail and jump ship. To Admiral Torren's shock, Lieutenant Pike swung the chains that bound him over the head and across the throat of one of the men assaulting the admiral's cabin. He pulled the marine back and wrenched on the chain until both men fell over backwards. While Midshipman Brant thrust his sword at an advancing sailor, one of the North Wind's young officers, Admiral Torren saw Lieutenant Pike emerge from behind the chaos with a sword in his shackled hands. *What in God's name is going on?* Lieutenant Pike ran across the deck and disappeared from view. Admiral Torren puzzled over what he had witnessed for an instant before one of the marines holding back the onslaught let out a cry and fell to his knees.

In an instant, Admiral Torren added his sword to the fight. He stepped next to Lieutenant Spears and thrust his blade at the attacker who had just wounded one of his marines. His legs were throbbing with pain, every movement was tortured. A shot fired. Lieutenant Spears collapsed into the admiral's shoulder. The weight was too much for Admiral Torren to bear, it pushed him against the bulkhead and took his balance as one of the mutineers attacked with a thrust aimed at his chest. Admiral Torren's parry deflected the thrust, but it landed in Lieutenant Spears throat sending a rush of blood down the admiral's arm and covering part of his uniform coat. The mutineers rushed forward storming the cabin doorway and pushing past Lieutenant Thatcher and Midshipman Brant. Admiral Torren fell to his knees under the weight of the master at arms with his sword in hand. He slashed a wild blow at an attacker's leg opening a deep gash and sending a spurt of blood onto the already gore soaked deck. As the mutineers flooded into the cabin Admiral Torren's heart sank down into his stomach. He felt bile in the back of his mouth. Successful mutinies rarely end well for the deposed officers.

A roar of voices erupted below deck. At first, Admiral Torren thought it was cries of victory from the mutineers. But when he saw the men that had stormed his cabin react, he knew there was something else afoot. A shout came from the stairs leading below deck. "Go lads! Go defend your commander! For England!" The reply was thunderous, "For England!" Footfalls followed the battle cry and a rush of sailors stormed up the stairs and onto the deck. Admiral Torren looked out as the attacking mutineers rushed from his cabin to get back onto the weather deck. Lieutenant Pike was at the head of a group of sailors with a sword in his hand. He looked ragged and weak, but when the first of the mutineers came within striking distance the lieutenant parried an attack and drove his sword right through the man's chest.

'Batard De Mur
26 Apr 1809
18 Degrees 48' N, 74 Degrees 18' W

"Bear off to the north! We will search the western coast first. Most of the tales I have heard of this girl captain originated on these western shores." Captain Fontaine called down to his helmsman. The privateer ship was shadowing his course, drawing closer with each hour. He mumbled under his breath, "I ought to run out stuns'l and leave you wondering where your gold went off to. Or turn about and loose a full broadside." The fallen merchant sailor clasped a hand around the pommel of his sword. He had already turned on The Order once before, the results had been disastrous. From London to Washington and Paris to the Vatican, The Order's fingers had managed to grapple the world's powers into a stranglehold. Captain Fontaine stared out at LeFouet as she made a slight course correction. The tri-color banner of France trailed off of her stern lines in the stout breeze, furling and flapping as the ship's angle changed. Captain Fontaine was facing a critical dilemma. If he caved to The Order, he would never be free of their clutches again. It would be easy enough. The ship they had sent to deliver their message was no match for his own. He could outmaneuver them even without the wind at his advantage. His gunnery, built up from years of plundering smaller British warships and merchantmen, was nearly double their firepower. But the threat of what would surely follow. Captain Fontaine knew the resources The Order could wield, he knew how far their corruption had stretched. The utterings he had heard from Captain Callais aboard LeFouet had not been the first he had heard of this girl pirate and her crew of rebel slaves. As far away as St. Kitts and Barbados the taverns were full of stories about some sighting or encounter. Reports varied. Some men said she had sunk the entirety of the Brit's Caribbean fleet. Some claimed she had raided every plantation within fifty miles of Port-Au-Prince. But the tales of the Drowned Maiden and her crew of ex-slaves all relayed one detail. She was targeting the slave trade and anyone who profited from it. Captain Fontaine looked over his crew as they worked his ship onto the course he had ordered. His crimson red sails fluttered for a heartbeat as they adjusted and then snapped full and proud, propelling them along on an easterly course just inside the finger of land that extended from Haiti's western coast. Port-Au-Prince would appear along his starboard side just before sunrise. Until then, he had miles of sand beaches and shoals to navigate. The last fingers of sunshine played along the tops of his crimson sails. Laurent looked high up into the rigging where his banner flew on display for all the world to see. He had chosen red instead of black. A red field means no quarter. He would give no quarter to an enemy ever again. He had sworn it after his last dealings with The Order. Captain Fontaine lifted a hand to the leather covering over his right eye. He wondered if he had the mettle to live out the oath he had sworn to himself. He looked back on LeFouet and remembered those early days when he still thought he would somehow be able to make his way as a legitimate sailor someday.

The months following his meeting with Mr.Clyde Ritten at his estate outside of Charleston had been filled by voyages around the Caribbean. He and his crew had been reduced to being Mr. Tim Sladen's personal escort as he went about the business of moving payments and recruiting new ships and captains. The voyages hadn't been without their rewards. Every time Captain Fontaine turned around it seemed there was more gold being brought aboard his ship, and every time he and his crew were given a share of it. They visited ports spanning all across the Caribbean. In each locale, Tim Sladen would spend time visiting with the local governing authority before prowling through the pubs and dockyards looking to recruit captains and crewmen looking for work. In St.Kitts, Tim had nearly been locked away by the garrison commander when he made his proposition to the local governor. Captain Fontaine and his crew found themselves branded as outlaw pirates by the local authority after they successfully rescued Mr. Sladen.

In Martinique, Mr. Sladen paid a handsome sum to the commodore of a squadron of French navy warships. In Nassau, he had managed to strike a deal with governor, Captain Fontaine and his ship and crew were guaranteed safe passage and harbor there, as well as a number of other ships which would be making their way through to the American coast. In Port-Au-Prince Mr.Sladen met with local landowners. In Nevis he arranged for a ship to ferry payment from the Caribbean to a destination in Europe which Laurent never did figure out. Everything was relayed in an ambiguous cloud of vague detail. It would have continued if that was Laurent's only complaint.

The last trip he had sailed for The Order, Mr. Sladen had them convinced they were searching for a merchant ship that had gone missing. Searching for a ship of lost sailors seemed to be about as noble a cause as any in Laurent's mind. He was all too glad to be tasked with something besides ferrying the American around so he could better smuggle his abducted slaves. For weeks they scanned shorelines and visited ports in search of the missing vessel. Tim Sladen told him they were looking for a French brigantine that bore the name Nouveau Monde.

It was early in the morning, just after sunrise, with a thick layer of fog covering gentle sea swells.

The northern coast of the British colony of Jamaica lay just a few miles off of their larboard rail. Captain Fontaine had been anxious to sail that close to the coast in poor visibility but his Tim had insisted. Tim Sladen had stayed on the bow of Captain Fontaine's ship all through the night scanning the horizons and visiting with the men. Captain Fontaine had been the first to spot her. A dark silhouette against the gray haze that surrounded them. She was a two-masted ship, and about the same size as the vessel they had been searching for.

"Fire on her!" Tim had demanded. "Send her to the bottom!"

Captain Fontaine objected, "We've been searching for her for weeks! You've wanted to sink her this whole time?"

The look on Tim's face had been something Captain Fontaine had never seen before, something he wished never to see again. Visceral hatred. Instant and overwhelming rage. "I am ordering you to fire on that ship. Now do it! Or I will have you removed and I'll do it my damned self!"

Captain Fontaine gave the orders to his crew. They ran out the guns. A small adjustment of course ran them alongside the vessel they had spotted. As they drew nearer, Captain Fontaine could clearly see the French colors flying from her stern. The crew rapidly ran them down and replaced them with a solid white sheet. They had surrendered. Through a telescoping looking glass,

Captain Fontaine spied her stern carefully. Nouveau Monde was carved in intricate design across her fantail. She had precious few gun ports, and even fewer armaments on deck. They never stood a chance. As Captain Fontaine continued looking over the ship he could hear Tim Sladen's bellowing scream. "Fire!"

The cannon fire was thunderous. It shook Captain Fontaine right into his bones. Smoke plumed from the snouts of his guns, a short whistle later the shots impacted with devastating effect. Nouveau Monde became an instant scene of carnage as wooden shrapnel sliced into the sailors on her decks. Cries and pleas for mercy floated in the air after the first volley. Cries that haunted Captain Fontaine every day since. The next volley came within two minutes. It blew a hole low along the French merchant ship's hull. More screams sounded from inside the sinking ship. It might as well have been a coffin.

"Why?" Captain Fontaine had demanded as Tim Sladen made his way back to the helm. "Why would we scour the Caribbean to find this ship? Just for you to sink it?"

Tim had only smiled, "No, captain. Just for you to sink it."

"I don't understand. Why? Why did you want it sunk?" Fontaine demanded.

Tim had straightened his jacket and ran a hand over his dark hair. "They failed to deliver a shipment of slaves procured for us. One of my informants had information that led me to believe they were delivering them to Jamaica."

Captain Fontaine's guts twisted into knots. His heart had crawled into his throat and threatened to choke away his breath. "That ship had a hold full of slaves?"

"It certainly did." Tim replied, the smile had faded from his face. "This is what happens, when someone defies us."

Pirate Cove
25 Apr 1809

"He has exhausted himself, Chibs. He needs rest!" Dr. LeMeux's voice floated over the water of the cove.

Chibs clamped his jaw and rubbed at his beard. He longed for his pipe. It helped him concentrate. "Doctor, if we don't get her in now, she could roll to one side and submerge completely. She'll be lost to us forever!"

"There are more ships in the world Chibs." Dr. LeMeux called back.

Chibs swung his hand away from his face. Frustration consumed his guts, gnarling them into knots. He cupped his good hand back around the side of his mouth. "Omibwe. What do you say? Can you get a pair of lines fixed to her masts?" He squinted and shielded the sun out of his eyes. The young African boy was hanging on the side of the rowboat Dr. LeMeux was occupying out amongst the wreckage of the Drowned Maiden. Chibs held his breath as he waited for the diver's response.

"Yes. I can do it!" Omibwe's voice floated back in to the beach.

Chibs smiled. It wasn't just that his young friend had made the French doctor look like an ass, that was a double ration, but the young man had proved himself to be more than valuable to the shipwrecked crew. If they had any hope of resurrecting the Maiden, it rested in young Omibwe's hands. "Yes! Good! Take the thick lines from the row boat. Doctor, when he gets them attached you need to row into shore so we can thread them through the blocks. Everything on shore is ready!"

Omibwe waved his arm high above the water. Chibs waved back with a chuckle. There seemed to be an exchange between Dr. LeMeux in the small rowboat and Omibwe in the water below him. The doctor put his hand up in a frustrated gesture and pulled a coil of thick rope towards himself in the boat. Chibs watched as he fed the line overboard and Omibwe disappeared beneath the water's surface.

"You think he can do it?" Damriq's voice asked over Chibs' shoulder.

Chibs gave Damriq a quick glance before looking back out to the cove. "I sure damn hope so. He's the best chance we have."

"Do we have enough to pull it in?" Damriq pressed further with his booming deep voice.

Chibs winced at the sunlight and then looked back up the beach where he had gathered the crew they had. "I don't know. Maybe. It's a lot of weight. But if there are air pockets in her like Omibwe says, we might be able to get it closer." He looked back out toward the cove and found Omibwe had resurfaced. "We need to get her beached high enough that she's out of the water once the tide goes out. Then, we'll be able to figure which timbers need replacing to make her seaworthy again."

"And the masts?" Damriq continued.

"Aye, the masts will need replaced as well. But I've already found a pair of tall trees with stout trunks as true as we're like to find. Once the captain returns with more tools, we'll have our masts. But we need to get her afloat before we worry about that mess."

Dr. LeMeux waved an arm at Chibs before cupping his hands around his mouth and shouting, "He's got one attached to the main!"

Chibs nodded and shouted back, "Good! Now put one on the bowsprit and get those lines run into shore!"

"Even with everyone we have pulling those lines Chibs. She's a lot to drag out of the water." Damriq continued speaking after Chibs shouted his instructions.

Chibs kept his gaze out on the prow of the Maiden. "Aye, she is. But I don't plan to drag her completely up out of the water. The plan is to drag her as high as we can while the tide is rising. We will drag her along using her buoyancy to our advantage. Once the tide recedes we will have a window of time to work on her every day until she's seaworthy again."

"And how long do you think that will take?" Damriq continued. "Wouldn't it be better to sneak into a harbor and steal ourselves another ship?"

Chibs gave Damriq an insulted look over his shoulder. "No. It wouldn't be better. She's the Drowned Maiden for Christ's sake. If I lose her, God, I can't even fathom it."

Out on the cove, Omibwe had climbed from the water into the rowboat. It took only a few minutes for Dr. LeMeux to row them both over to the protruding prow of the ship. Omibwe scaled the short climb and was on top of the bowsprit faster than Chibs would have guessed. *That little shit is just full of surprises. I wonder what he will amaze me with next?* After a few minutes, and many failed attempts by Dr. LeMeux to throw the end of the thick rope up to Omibwe, he finally managed to muster a toss that sent the end of the line careening over the top of the bowsprit. Omibwe huddled over the line, wrapping it and counter wrapping before he sealed a thick knot just beneath the base of the wooden structure. As soon as the knot was secured, the young African boy wriggled himself off of the bow and plopped into the water of the cove.

Chibs cupped his hand around his mouth. "Well

doctor! We're waiting on you! Get those lines in to shore so we can get to work!"

The rowboat moved at pace that had Chibs in a fury by the time the doctor pulled the last stroke. The wooden keel slid into wet sand and ground to a halt. Chibs and Damriq hauled the heavy lines out of the boat and began pulling the ends up the beach toward a set of blocks. One block was secured to a clump of trees, the other was anchored to a massive rock that sat a dozen yards from the trees. Both pulleys were at a narrow angle between each other and the mostly sunken hulk of the Maiden. Once the heavy ropes were thread through their respective pulleys Chibs called for every available hand to haul tension on the lines.

"Pull with everything you've got! The tide is coming in!" Chibs bellowed out while reefing against the thick braided rope with his one good hand. "Keep the pressure on! When the water level rises she'll make her way further in!"

The sun was riding low in the evening sky when the water level began to rise again. The Drowned Maiden had shifted only a fraction of what Chibs had hoped to gain. Her decks were groaning and creaking from the force being applied against them. At first it started as low, soft sounds, but as the line crews continued to pull against their ropes the sounds amplified. They were making small progress, but it was enough that the prow of the Maiden had changed direction and now faced further in toward the spot on the beach where the two crews toiled away for every inch of line they could gain. Pink and orange hues lit the heavens and reflected their glory down onto gentle rolling swells as they washed up to the soft sands inside the cove. A soft breeze blew in from the sea. Dr. LeMeux was working on lighting a fire on the beach to cook some fish Omibwe had managed to obtain on one of his earlier dives with a crudely made spear.

"She's not buoyant enough." Chibs growled to himself while the crews strained at pulling on the lines nearby. "We've dragged her into the sand but we won't get any further. We need lift as well as pull. Damn it."

"How can we lift something that big?" Omibwe asked Chibs, startling him as he appeared at his side.

The salted old sailor held up the stub of his amputated arm to point out toward the ship. "Well, I was hoping the air pockets you talked about may be enough to float her in as the tide rose." He looked at his stump of an arm and shook his head replacing it with his good hand. *I'll never be used to this.* "See how the water has risen along her prow? It means the water is rising around her, she isn't coming up with it at all. Which bodes ill for us lad. We need her to come up with the tide, if only a little, to get her high enough so that she's beached when the water subsides."

Omibwe stared into the cove as daylight slipped away in the heavens. "If the air pockets will help, but they aren't big enough, make them bigger."

Chibs smiled at his young friend. "I only wish it were that easy lad. But it isn't a simple matter of pumping out the water. Her hull is breached low, we could pump until time ends and never make a dent." He fidgeted with his good hand, searching for the leather pouch Omibwe had recovered. The tobacco hadn't dried well enough yet to smoke, but he enjoyed clamping his teeth around the pipe stem. It made him feel more settled.

"If we can't pump water out, couldn't we pump air in?" Omibwe looked up at Chibs with an inquisitive squint. "If her hull is holding in the air that's in there now, wouldn't it hold some more? Would that be enough?"

Chibs clamped his teeth around the wooden pipe stem. He squinted hard at the dark shape of the Maiden's bowsprit protruding out of the cove. "Aye. That would work. It would help us, that's for sure. But we would need a special pump for air. A huge one."

"Like the bilge pump?" Omibwe asked, "We already brought in the hose."

Chibs shook his head and squinted harder. "No, the bilge pump wouldn't move near enough. It would take us ten years. What we need is a bellows. A damned big one." He gave Omibwe a look through the corner of his eyes, "Every time I turn around you surprise me lad. You really are something."

Omibwe beamed a broad smile. "What do we

need to build your damn big bellows?"

Chibs looked over his shoulder as the doctor finally managed to coax his fire to life. He grumbled for a moment, "About damn time you got that thing going. I suppose it's not quite like hacking off a limb though."

Dr. LeMeux shot to his feet, "Will you ever relent? I saved your life." He pointed toward Omibwe, "And his!"

Chibs shrugged and looked back at Omibwe. "Sailcloth. We'll need sailcloth for the permeable material to make the skin of the bellows. We can make a frame and nozzle from wood. I'll need some leather to make a flapper valve. We'll want to let air in one way and only give it one direction to go." He looked up toward the beginning flicker of the evening's first appearing stars as the oranges and pinks blended with deeper violets and faded to the inky sheet of night. "We'll need something to treat the sailcloth too. Oil or wax or some such."

"Maybe the doctor can help." Omibwe added, giving Chibs a jabbing look.

Chibs smiled and nodded, "Aye, maybe he can. We need to make sure he's busy, else we'll wake up with less of ourselves than we already have." He turned back toward the crews pulling against their ropes. "We should keep pressure on these lines though. Hopefully we can get her further in before we try to float her up."

Chapter 8

Pirate Cove
27 Apr 1809

The oars slipped quietly in and out of the cove's waters. Omibwe pulled long strokes under the warmth of the sun while Chibs and Dr. LeMeux fiddled with their contraption. It had taken them most of the night to put together. In that time the tide had come into to its full height and then receded again. The hulking mass of the Maiden threatened to shift further into the depths with every minute that passed. The lines that held her secure had become too much for the crews to hold steady, at one point during the night The crew holding tension on the line attached to the Maiden's main mast had collectively lost their footing as she shifted, the lost tension caused the ship to heave further onto one side. Omibwe had not seen bubbles escaping from the ship after the shift, but Chibs insisted that Omibwe could return to find his air pocket gone. The only way they would know for sure was for him to return to the Maiden's hold and find out.

When they arrived near the wreckage Omibwe pulled the oars into the small row boat. With Chibs newly built bellows, there was hardly room for the three of them. The device was so big that Chibs had to steady it with his good hand while balancing it on one side of the boat as Omibwe rowed them out.

"Alright lad," Chibs pulled the bellows across to sit on both sidewalls of the wooden rowboat. "I'll attach the hosepipe and we'll be ready." The plan was for Omibwe to snake the other end of the hose into the Maiden's hold and put the end of it into the air pocket he had discovered near the bow. Chibs seemed to think that if they could use his new bellows to pump enough air into the pocket, the Maiden would float higher and they could possibly get her further into shore. Omibwe didn't mind going, he enjoyed diving and he was happy that something he was good at was so helpful to the crew. He eased himself over the transom of the rowboat and into the cove. The tide was still on its way out and Omibwe could feel the water shifting beneath him. It pulled and wisped around his foot, tickling his leg as he held onto the back of the small boat. Chibs was fidgeting with the hosepipe connection with his one good hand. Omibwe watched while the salty old sailor got more and more frustrated until he finally looked up at Dr. LeMeux.

"Care to give me a hand here doctor? Or are you only in the business of taking them?" Chibs scorned.

Dr. LeMeux had been staring off at the sharp edge of the hills surrounding the cove. His attention snapped to their task when Chibs had started in at him. "I saved your life Chibs. I don't know how many times I must tell you that before it sinks in."

Chibs glowered at him, "Aye, you did mention it Doctor. I suppose I should be thanking you then?"

Dr. LeMeux looked shocked. "It couldn't hurt. Honestly Chibs, I took no pleasure in what I did. It was to save your life."

Chibs scoffed and finished attaching the hose to their bellows. He looked down at Omibwe and gave him a smile. "If you can get the end of the hose down into that air pocket, we might have a chance at floating her. If we get her to float high enough, we can pull her into shore far enough that when the tide goes out we'll be able to make repairs." He looked over his shoulder at the doctor, and then back to Omibwe, "Once you get the hose down there, you don't need to stay. Come back up. You can dive down there again after we pump the bellows for a while to see if it's working."

Omibwe nodded and took the thin line that was attached to the end of the hose and slung it around his shoulder. "I will stay down there until there's air coming through the hose."

"Don't be too long Omi, you've been diving for

days now. It takes a toll on you, friend." Dr. LeMeux interjected, "You need to rest, it's not good for you to keep pushing yourself so hard."

Omibwe smiled. His friend had always looked out for him, but Omibwe was starting to believe the doctor viewed him as a child. "I will be fine doctor." He smiled up at the two men in the rowboat, "You just worry about getting along and pumping the bellows." The duo exchanged a look between themselves and then both looked back down at him. Omibwe took two rapid breaths, followed by a long slow inhale before he pulled himself beneath the surface.

Below the waterline the cove was serene. Sun beams flickered and glinted off of the waves above and shimmered in the depths below. Omibwe pulled at the water with his hands while kicking his leg the way he imagined how a mermaid would. The opening in the hull he needed to get through had shifted around, Omibwe needed to swim just a little further to get inside of her hold. As he pulled himself through the opening and looked toward the bow Omibwe felt the hose attached to the line tremble. The line he had wrapped around his shoulder vibrated. Chibs and the doctor had begun pumping their bellows. Omibwe pulled himself further toward the bow. He could see where the water had formed around the pocket of air he had used before. It was smaller than the last time he had seen it. Much smaller. Omibwe pulled himself toward the surface of the water inside the Maiden's hull. His head found the air pocket, he could fit his head and shoulders in the narrow gap of air, but no more. Before the Maiden had shifted, Omibwe had been able to pull his entire upper body out of the seawater.

The hose gurgled and shook while Omibwe wrestled it around in front of his chest. He wasn't sure if the end needed to be out of the water for the plan to work. He pulled the hose end up, seawater gurgled and splattered in the small space. For a moment, Omibwe panicked. Had he done something wrong? He forced himself to keep the end of the hose up in the small pocket of air. It gurgled and splattered seawater, moving rushes of water in groaning coughs and sputters. Omibwe tried to quell the panic building in his guts. Each rush of water that spilled from the hose brought forward more questions he didn't have the answer to. Was there a break somewhere in the line? Was the plan Chibs had come up with going to work? Would their pump be able to move any air down into the belly of the wounded ship? Just as Omibwe was about to give up hope a rush of foamy water spewed out of the hose followed by the wheezing sound of air. It was working. Another cough of air came through. Omibwe found a spot to attach the thin rope he had used to drag the hose into the ship to the bulkhead. The hose hissed with long surges of air moving through it. Omibwe could feel pressure building in his ears almost immediately. He stayed in the air bubble and waited while the

Resurrecting the Maiden

bellows continued to pump air. The Maiden groaned and Omibwe could feel her timbers shudder. He looked around in the darkness, only the reflection of sunlight from below served to illuminate the inside of the hull. Another shudder from the Maiden sent a chill into his blood. He did not want to be inside if the ship rolled any further over. Taking a few rapid breaths and then one long slow one, Omibwe pulled himself below the surface and swam for the breach in her hull. Even the water seemed to be charged with energy as he pulled himself through the dark depths and out into the cove. It was like the ship was coming back to life.

Omibwe pulled his arms in broad strokes toward the surface. He could hear the Maiden's timbers groaning and creaking from strain, the sounds echoed through the cove's sheltered waters and reverberated through his body. Pale columns of blue green light surrounded him as he ascended to the surface. Omibwe's face broke through the water and he inhaled clean, fresh air. The sunlight was warm on his head and shoulders. He wiped the sea away from his eyes and looked up to the rowboat. Chibs was pumping at the bellows with his good arm while Dr. LeMeux sat against a coiled rope looking exhausted.

"It's working Chibs. The hose has air coming through into the belly of the Maiden" Omibwe said in between breaths. "I was worried for a moment when nothing but seawater came out of the hose, but it's working now!"

"Good!" Chibs huffed as he reefed on a wooden handle to drive the top half of the bellows down and compress the air inside. "Now we'll only need to pump on this day and night until the old girl starts to float free of the bottom."

Omibwe scrunched his face and looked at Dr. LeMeux, "Are you going to help pump the bellows doctor?"

Dr. LeMeux gave Omibwe a distressed look, "I took the first turn my friend. I'm afraid I do not possess the stout constitution of the good quartermaster here." He made a vague gesture toward Chibs who was pouring sweat while heaving against the bellows.

Chibs gave the doctor a sideways glare and nodded his head, "Enjoy basking in the sun doctor, your next turn is coming."

Omibwe pulled his arms through the cool water until he could grab a hold of the row boat's transom. Chibs was pulling down on the handle of the bellows and giving each effort a groan. Omibwe could see that it took all of the old sailor's strength and weight to move the contraption and each pump looked to strain Chibs harder than the last. "I'll help," Omibwe offered as he pulled his upper body out of the water and leaned into the boat.

Chibs shook his head, "I'd love the help Omi. But I'm not sure if you are big enough to move this cumbersome bastard." He nodded at the French doctor reclined against a coil of rope in the bow of the little boat. "The doctor can handle another turn. It won't kill him to break a sweat this time."

Omibwe smiled at Chibs and peered at Dr. LeMeux over the top edge of the bellows. "If he can force the bellows shut, so can I."

Chibs beamed a broad grin, "Somehow I knew you were going to say that. Alright, we might as well try before I'm too spent to take another turn." Chibs pulled one last heave down on the handle and shuffled aside for Omibwe to try. Omibwe wrapped his hands around the rough wooden shaft of the bellows handle and pulled at it with all of his strength. Chibs hadn't lied, the pump was stiff, and it took every ounce of strength Omibwe had to force the top of the structure down toward the bottom. When it did finally reach as far down as Omibwe had seen Chibs pull it he forced the handle back up, pushing with his arms and his leg. The frame of the bellows creaked and the small leather flap Chibs had installed along the frame to allow air in hissed as it opened just enough for a stream of air to make its way into the accordion structure of oiled canvas framed in wood. As the top reached its high point, Omibwe shifted to pulling and leaned his body weight on the handle until the top frame of the bellows began to sink back down forcing a whoosh of air through the hosepipe leading down into the belly of the Maiden. This continued. Omibwe got into a rhythm. He pulled the handle down and leaned his weight as hard as he could to sink the top of the bellows until it was only a few inches from the bottom. Then he would push with all his strength forcing the bellows open again allowing air to fill the accordion structure. Sweat poured from his head and shoulders. The sun was relentless, it kissed his skin with warmth and soaked into his muscles. Omibwe continued putting everything he had into each stroke until a loud groan sounded through the cove. Chibs bolted upright from where he had been leaned back to rest.

"What was that?" Dr. LeMeux asked.

Chibs held up his hand and looked down into the cove. Another groan sounded, this one louder than before. "That's the ship doctor." Chibs motioned toward the portion of the bow still protruding out of the water's surface. There was half a foot more showing than when Omibwe had first climbed aboard the rowboat to take his turn at the bellows. "It's working."

'North Wind'
24 Apr 1809
18 Degrees 02' N, 74 Degrees 58' W

The rush of combat steeled Will's aching nerves against the pain that coursed through his limbs with every movement. Shouts echoed up from the gun deck below his feet. The crew was not about to give up their ship. At the first sound of a struggle from the decks below, Will seized the sword of a marine who had kept his attention focused on the sergeant knocking on Admiral Torren's cabin door. The first moment had been the most painful. Will's abdomen wounds stretched and burned with searing pain as the scabbed tissues cracked and opened. The marine whose sword Will had taken was met with a quick slash across his throat. A gun shot sounded below deck. Screams followed. In a moment the screams and shouts were drowned away in the sound of a hundred sailor taking up the fight to regain control of their ship. Before the body of the first marine had hit the deck Will moved to engage another. His shoulders were ablaze with every movement, pain wracked through them and radiated into his torso. One of the marines who had mercilessly dragged him on deck lunged at his thin frame with a sword. Will deflected the blow and expertly swung his weapon around catching the marine across his face with the edge. One of the sailors below deck shouted out a battle cry that echoed up from the stairs leading below deck, "Go lads! Defend your commander! For England!" A fleeting moment of time elapsed before the next marine moved toward him and Will looked through the ragged edges of Admiral Torren's battered cabin door frame. The Admiral stood just a few paces inside of the cabin with his saber in hand and a look of bewilderment on his face. *I am as shocked as you are, sir.* Will deflected another driving blow from one of the marines and danced his sword blade up in a sweeping cut through the attacker's midsection. For a moment the marines gathered on deck faced Will. Their faces displayed varying degrees of hatred. A collective shout from the crew below deck broke their focus. "For England!" The marine sergeant drew his sword from a scabbard at his waist and faced the admiral's cabin. Will turned to one of the mutineers and drove his sword through the man's chest all the way to the weapon's hilt. Shots rang out. The acrid taste of gunpowder filled the air. More shots sounded as a rolling thunder of footfalls came rumbling up the stairwell from below deck.

The first man to emerge from below was one of the ship's marine contingent. He was in full retreat with several of his fellow mutineers right behind him. They made their way out onto the deck just ahead of a flood of sailors. Will stood his ground midship on deck with a trio of the mutineers surrounding him while the struggle at Admiral Torren's cabin door continued. Shots echoed through the night in between the steel clash of swords. Will shuffled his bare feet on the wooden deck, turning himself in a slow circle. The mutineers were holding around him just out of reach. They were spread around him at just a wide enough angle that he could only see two at one time. Chaos embroiled the quarterdeck as sailors from below emerged into the fight. Will's focus remained locked on the three mutineers gathered around him. Light from the lanterns on deck cascaded around them, it was cut intermittently by shadows as the fight at Admiral Torren's cabin door intensified. Will's hand grew tired as he strained to keep his grasp locked onto his sword. One of the men surrounding him stepped forward, Will shifted his feet and raised his guard. The attacker only smiled and withdrew himself to a safe distance. Will knew in the back of his mind that the fight on deck would only press the attack of the men surrounding him. If they thought the fight was turning against their favor, they would surely try to dispatch him in favor of loaning their effort to the broader struggle. Another of the mutineers lunged toward Will, this one committed to the attack with an overhand slash. Will stepped into the attack and glanced away the blow with a sweeping parry. He turned to the attacker and whipped the pommel of his sword into the man's jaw. As Will followed his defense with the strike he caught a movement out of the corner of his eye. Another of the mutineers came in for an attack. Will wheeled his sword hand and raised his steel just in time to catch a sideways slash. The attacker withdrew his blade and quickly followed with a low thrust. Will's feet didn't move as quickly as they once did, nor did his arms. He moved to evade the lunge but was too slow. His ribs felt the cold kiss of steel as the attacker's sword penetrated his flesh. The sword withdrew immediately, and the attacker smiled at his success. Will could feel blood oozing from the wound. With his off hand,

Will reached up to the wound. It was small, no more than an inch across. His attacker had only scored a shallow stab, but it was bleeding nonetheless. *No matter. I've been slowly bleeding for weeks.* Will tightened his grip on his sword. Pain coursed through his entire body. He could feel his strength waning with every passing moment. He had to put an end to this fight.

The first man to attack him had recovered from the hilt strike against his jaw. He stood holding a sword in one hand and his jaw in the other. "Kill him!" He shouted as he stepped forward with a wild overhand slash. Will sidestepped. The slash missed him so closely he could feel the wind being separated by his attacker's blade. In his quick evasion of the slash, Will had sacrificed his balance. As the sword blade sliced through the air next to him Will began to raise his lade in a countering attack. When he felt his left leg tremble under strain, he quickly reverted the movement downward and put the point of his sword into the wooden deck beneath his feet. As Will's left leg buckled under the strain of sudden exertion after weeks of neglect, he tried to hold his weight upright by leaning against his sword. Another swinging slash came, and Will was forced to drop onto his knee. He freed the sword point from the deck and wielded the blade in a block that clattered his steel against his attacker's with a loud crash. Another swing came and Will could barely wield his sword quickly enough to defend himself. As he knelt on the the deck, two of the mutineers stood over him, raining blows one after another. Will could feel his arms and shoulder aching with fatigue. Each strike took more effort to defend than the last. The sharp twang of steel swords ringing together beat out against the clatter of battle on the ship's deck until Will felt like it was the only sound in the world. Crashing impacts reverberated through the blade and up Will's arm. Each bone jarring hit seemed stronger than the last. It was all Will could do to maintain his grip and continue fending off the hacking swings of his attackers. Each clash of steel on steel drew the next blow closer and closer until Will could only maintain his sword mere inches above his head. He had no time to mount a counterattack. He couldn't entertain the thought of battling back to his feet, it was all Will could do to keep his sword in front of the next attacking blow. Will glanced his blade off of each attack, each defense coming slower and slower. Will could feel the strength leaving his arms. His back and shoulders were ablaze with searing pains that sapped his resolve and stole away the skillful swordsmanship he knew he was capable of. Through the dim yellow light on deck the shadows of his attackers loomed large above him. They closed in around him and continued pummeling his sword with slash after slash, each one stealing a little more of his strength than the last. Will knew it wouldn't be long. He would feel the piercing kiss in his chest or his back at any moment. One of the attackers would manage to slip a blade past his defense and impale him or slice open his neck. One of the mutineers landed a high arcing swing that collided with Will's sword. The steel rang in his hand and reverberated so hard it stung his fingers. Instead of withdrawing the blade, the attacker pressed forward forcing Will's sword down toward his own head. Will could feel the man's off hand grip his sword arm. *Here it comes. This will be my end.*

Will's eyes found focus on his attacker's face. The eyes were balls of fury, wide with rage and hatred, burning with the conviction of a man who knew he was about to win. Will's arm trembled. He felt the muscles beginning to fail as the attacker pressed down with all of his weight. A shot sounded. It was louder than any gunshot Will had ever heard. His ears rang with a piercing whine. Smoke clouded his vision. The attacker who had been pressing his blade against Will's suddenly collapsed to the deck. In a flurry of movement Will watched as a sword blade plunged into the chest of one of the mutineers standing over him.

"For the North Wind! And for England!" the voice was familiar, but stronger than Will had remembered. A wave of sailors engulfed him. Hands and arms tore the last of the mutineers away from Will as they rushed across the deck. With a flurry of footfalls all around him, Will dug the point of his sword into the deck and put his weight on it. He lifted himself on unsteady knees. The voice returned, "I am not above admitting a mistake lieutenant. Perhaps I should have listened to what you had to say all along."

Will looked up to find the stony expression of Admiral Torren staring at him. "How could you have known sir?" Will replied, "I wouldn't have believed me either."

Haitian Inland
27 Apr 1809

Heat settled over the Haitian inland while Emilia and Jilhal made slow progress behind a horse pulled cart. There was no room to sit up on the roughhewn boards of the cart where Emilia had stacked every tool of her father's that she could fit. A two man saw for taking down large trees extended over the length of the cart and flopped up and down with each little rut the wheels overcame. A box of assorted hammers, smaller saws and wood planes took up the front of the cart. A pair of heavy splitting axes and a box full of smaller tools sat in the rear of the cart. As the sun beat down on them mercilessly, the duo walked alongside the old horse. The cartwheels creaked and groaned as they made their over dried ruts and bumps in the parched pathway. The sky was piercing blue even as the sun dipped lower toward the west. The small path they had chosen was lined on both sides by tall sugar cane. The towering stalks served to hide their movement from any onlookers that would come asking questions, but it also choked away the breeze coming from the coast. Occasionally a whisper of wind would follow along the narrow road and cut away the day's heat for a moment, but for the most part Emilia and Jilhal suffered the relentless sweltering with little to comfort them.

As the day wore on, Emilia knew they were nearing the coast when the salty tang of sea air began to slowly replace the smell of the thick vegetation surrounding them. Her companion, Jilhal, had been mostly silent on their foray to Emilia's childhood home. The two women walked on through the heat of the day with precious little respite from the sun a dwindling prospect of finding any.

In the early hours of the morning a column of smoke could be seen towering to the north. Emilia told Jilhal that it was coming from Tortuga. The two women briefly discussed the chances that Lilith had something to do with the sudden appearance of the smoke. Emilia wondered just how dangerous this girl captain really was. She got the feeling from Jilhal that whatever had transpired in Tortuga, Lilith was most likely the one who would emerge victorious.

"If that is her work, I feel sorry for that town. Those soldiers won't stand a chance." Jilhal had remarked when they saw the black plume stretching up into the morning sky.

"How can you be sure it is Lilith who came out on top?" Emilia asked with a frown of concern spreading across her forehead. "Maybe she has been taken captive? Maybe we should go to make sure she is okay?"

Jilhal only shook her head and looked at the dark tower of smoke, "No, girl. She is fine. The captain could fight off a hundred soldiers. Two hundred if she had Chibs with her."

Emilia looped a lock of her curly hair behind one ear and gave the horse's lead a tug, "That one armed man?"

Jilhal smiled, "Yes. The one-armed man. He is the quartermaster of the Maiden. I promise you this, losing his arm won't slow him down. He is probably making jokes about it already."

"But he wanted to kill that doctor." Emilia gave Jilhal a confused look.

Jilhal smiled and laughed, "His blood runs hot, like mine."

Emilia noticed Jilhal's smile lingered for quite a while despite the insufferable heat, "You like him don't you?"

Jilhal averted her eyes back toward the skyline, "He is kind and brave. He is loyal to the captain and treats my son like he were his own."

"I know all of that," Emilia pressed, "But, you really like him. You are interested in him?"

Jilhal gave Emilia a flat look. For a moment Emilia questioned if she had pried too far, but the smile returned to Jilhal's face. "He is mine."

Emilia could not help but return Jilhal's broad smile, "I am happy for you-"

Jilhal froze in her steps. She held a hand out in front of Emilia, motioning for her to stop. At first Emilia was confused, she didn't understand Jilhal's sudden alarm. Emilia stopped the old horse by holding the lead tight and pulling downward. "Did you hear that?" Jihal whispered low with an edge of urgency in her voice.

Emilia strained her ears. Wind rustled the tops of sugar cane. Cicadas chirped in a repetitive chorus. Birds sang their songs off in the distance. For a heartbeat Emilia wondered if Jilhal confused the sound of the sugar cane with someone moving close by. She listened harder, holding her breath to avoid drowning out even the tiniest of sounds. There was a voice out in the sugar cane. It was a deep voice, but the words were indistinguishable.

"Someone is out there," Jilhal slowly drew her curved sword. "If they find us, we cannot let them live to spread word of us."

Emilia's throat went dry. She wondered if the voice belonged to a soldier or to a field hand. Whoever it was, Jilhal didn't plan to let them live long enough to tell the tale of the two women they met out in the middle of the Haitian cane fields. She lowered her voice to barely a whisper, "If there is more than one, we must abandon the wagon and run."

Jilhal looked back at Emilia and held her sword up near her shoulder, "I am not running from anyone. Wait here." Jilhal darted quickly into the thickets of sugarcane and disappeared from

Emilia's sight. Emilia suddenly felt exposed on the road by herself. *How many are there? Where did Jilhal go? Did she abandon me to my fate? Why would I trust these pirates?*

A rustle of sugarcane gave way to two burly men that emerged from the thick vegetation just a few yards up the road. Both men appeared disheveled and rushed. Their clothes were a mess of tears and bulging masses where items were stuffed into them. Emilia watched as they both stumbled out onto the road. The bigger of the two had a thick mustache and carried a scabbarded sword at his waist. The other man was tall but thinner than the mustachioed man and had a clean shaved look to him. Both men were wearing soldier uniforms and appeared to be in quite a hurry.

"There is no way we were followed, not through that mess of sugarcane!" the thinner man said as the two burst out of the cane field.

The other soldier leaned his weight forward and put his hands on his knees to catch his breath, "I'm not chancing it. Port-Au-Prince is a three-day journey on foot. If those brigands…"

The big mustached soldier's voice trailed away. He looked up the road. Emilia's heart fluttered as the two soldiers turned to face her. She could feel her palms tingling as the big soldier stood up straight and let a hand rest on the pommel of his sword. His shirt was half undone revealing a broad chest and a big belly, inside of his shirt was stuffed with an assortment of goods.

"What do we have here? A little mouse all by herself?" The thinner soldier sneered with a half grin, "Where are you going all by yourself?"

Emilia searched for a response. She still had her father's sword at her waist, but there were two of them and one of her. *Where did Jilhal go?* "I'm taking tools west to a cove. There is a ship there that my father is working on."

The soldiers exchanged a look between themselves and then focused back onto Emilia. "What kind of ship makes repairs in a cove when there is a perfectly good shipwright in port just a few days sail from them?" The big soldier lifted one hand to his mustache and ran his thumb and forefinger over it, "Curious thing, why do they have a girl like you bringing their tools to them?"

Emilia's eyes darted toward the cart for a moment and then landed back on the bigger of the soldiers, "I don't know anything about them. I'm bringing the tools for my father. He works for the shipwright in Tortuga."

"Does he always send you to fetch his tools by yourself?" The thin soldier challenged, "It's dangerous out here in the countryside. Especially for a beautiful girl like you."

Emilia felt a rush of blood running to her face. The soldier looked her over with a crooked smile. For a moment, Emilia forgot her fear. Her arms lit with the fire of rage she had felt since the day she had watched Tim Sladen murder her father. Her right hand let go of the horse's lead and drew her father's sword from her waist in a flash, "Come closer and I will gut you both!" She held the blade out in front of her.

The thin soldier held his hands up in a surrendering gesture, "Relax little girl. We aren't here to hurt you. See, we're soldiers." He pointed to his uniform and gave Emilia a broad smile, "It's our job to protect innocent little things like you all alone out on the road. Don't you know that there are bandits? In fact, a band of them just hit Tortuga last night. Put the town to the torch and stole everything they could get their grubby little hands on."

Emilia stepped backward as the thin soldier took a slow advancing stride, "That's far enough." Her hands were shaking even though she was trying with all of her might to hold her sword steady.

"It's too dangerous for you to be out here all alone." The thin soldier took another gliding stride and put himself in between Emilia and the horse. "We can keep you safe, for a price-"

A shadow moved between the thickets of sugarcane. It was fast, so fast Emilia barely caught the motion out of the corner of her eyes. Like a predatory cat, Jilhal lunged out of the thick growth into a towering leap over the big soldier with the mustache. She held her sword in a reverse grip in both hands and plunged the blade point down into the big soldiers back. He loosed a guttural breath at first, trying to reach his hands behind his back and gain a hold of his attacker, but Jilhal was too fast. In one swift motion she drove the hulking soldier down to the hard ground and heaved her sword out of his back. His lungs echoed a gurgling noise while he clawed at the dried mud around him, blood gushed from his mouth and surged from the wound high on his back.

"What the-" the thin soldier spun to see the source of the commotion. Before he could react, before he could raise his hands in a helpless effort to defend himself, Jilhal descended on him with a vicious overhand swing of her sword. Her blade sliced across the front of the soldier's uniform, butting deep into his chest. Without hesitation, Jilhal followed her first attack with a plunging stab into the soldier's chest. The attack drove him from his feet and Jilhal withdrew her blade and followed with another slicing swing of her blade that cut the thin soldier's throat almost clean through his neck.

Emilia stood in a state of shock. Her trembling hands lowered the point of her father's sword down to the ground while she looked over the scene of carnage Jilhal had just created.

"I thought you left me." Emilia managed to speak through a breathless gasp.

Jilhal smiled while she stooped down and wiped the blade of her sword clean on the thin soldier's uniform coat, "You saved the captain. You are one of us now."

Emilia suddenly saw the African woman she was sharing the road with in a different light. She was beautiful, her features and her complexion. Dark and angled and beautiful. But she was fierce. When the soldiers had seemed to pose a threat she had killed them both in savage fashion without a whisper of hesitation. Emilia suddenly envied her. She wanted to be fierce and dangerous like her new friends. She wanted to be the woman who could dispatch two soldiers without even a thought. Not a girl who missed with her pistol shot while her eyes were full of tears. She wanted to be like Lilith and Jilhal.

"Jilhal. Where did you learn to fight like this?" Emilia asked as Jilhal grabbed their horse's lead and started to move up the road again.

Jilhal gave Emilia a sideways glance and a sort of half smile. "The same person who taught Captain Lilith. Her name was Trina."

Emilia remembered Lilith speaking about Trina the day she had met her in the cove. Trina was the one who had gone into the water and never came out. "Could you teach me?" she asked.

Jilhal smiled a broader smile than Emilia had ever seen her make, "Yes, girl. I will teach you."

Pirate Cove
27 Apr 1809

Wooden groans echoed through the cove as the hulk of the Drowned Maiden protested her forceful exhumation from the depths. Chibs stood on a coiled rope in the small rowboat while Omibwe and Dr. LeMeux took their turns working the bellows contraption they had devised. Their plan was working. Not only was it working, it was more successful than any of them had dared to hope it would. The Maiden had risen considerably, her hull protruded higher up out of the water with every hour that passed. Chibs watched with his pipe clamped into his teeth while the air was forced into the sunken ship's hull. She was rising.

The problem was to get the Maiden far enough ashore that the remaining water inside of her could be drained and repairs made. Chibs' mind worked at the problem furiously, every moment that passed was another moment separating him from life out on the open waves. The thick ropes that were attached to the Maiden thrummed with tension. Every inch that was taken in by the crews manning them ashore brought the Maiden that much further toward the beach. By Chibs figuring, at the rate they were bringing her in, the Maiden would be beached enough to make repairs around the time dawn broke over the cove. The bellows was working to push air into the hulking hull, but it wasn't enough. Chibs could see that the hull was floating higher, but as the crew continued to pull the wreck further ashore the bottom would get shallower and shallower. The last time he asked Omibwe to dive beneath the surface and report back how much space they had between the Maiden's keel and the soft sandy bottom he had reported back to the surface in a splash, gasping for air that there was four feet of space where before there had been mere inches. That was before the line crews had hauled in nearly a dozen feet of their ropes and moved the Maiden a considerable distance toward the beach. Progress had slowed to a crawl though, and by Chibs reckoning they were not only hauling at the weight of the water filled hull, but they were fighting the hull through mucky soft sand. She must float higher. Chibs knew the portions of hull that had been breached. If he sent someone aboard the Maiden to bilge out the water that had invaded her, they would be pumping water out into the cove only for it to leak its way back into the gaps of broken timbers where cannon fire had breached her hull. Pumping more air into the Maiden would help, but only to an extent. He needed to somehow seal the holes in her hull and work some of the water out while at the same time moving air in.

Sunset came and went, while the sky faded from her piercing daytime blue to hues of orange and violet and then finally surrendered to the milky black of night dotted by a million gleaming stars. Chibs pondered over his problem while chewing at the smokeless pipe stem between his teeth.

"We've got to patch her hull…" he muttered while Omibwe took his turn heaving his slight frame against the handle of the bellows.

"What?" Dr. LeMeux asked with a squint from the back of the rowboat.

Chibs turned and looked over the French doctor who was recovering from his last turn at the bellows. Chibs suspected he had double counted half of his pumps, but he knew the doctor would deny any foul play. "Her hull isn't high enough yet, moving air into her is helping, but it isn't enough, we need to get water out at the same time."

Dr. LeMeux propped himself up on one elbow and looked out over the water while Omibwe heaved another downward stroke on the bellows handle. "There is a bilge aboard her, right? Couldn't we send a few brave hands in to work her bilge?"

Chibs shook his head, "All that schooling and no sense. What's your next bright idea, doctor? I suppose you think we ought to cut something off of her. Don't you? You sick bastard!" Chibs couldn't help but chuckle as Dr. LeMeux looked back at him with a confused expression. Chibs turned inboard and nodded for Omibwe to take a break from the bellows. He wrapped the fingers of his good hand around the handle and began to pump. "If we pump the water out without making a seal over the breach in her hull, we could pump until the end of time without making any progress." He paused to strain at pushing the handle of the bellows down, forcing another rush of air down the hose and into the belly of the Maiden. "The holes in her hull are too far beneath the waterline now. If we could somehow seal them, and pump water out while also pushing air in, I think we could float her high enough."

Omibwe had flopped himself onto a coil of line in the bow of the rowboat and rested quietly while Chibs outlined their current problem. Another stroke against the bellows sent a wheezing rasp of air through the pipe and down into the Maiden. Chibs drew a deep breath that wheezed almost as much as their improvised bellows. Sweat rolled off of his head and neck as he labored the bellows handle up and down, forcing more air into the hold of the Maiden with each compression.

"Chibs?" Omibwe's voice was barely audible over the sound of the wheezing bellows and his own breath.

"Yes Omi?" Chibs replied.

"What if I could cover the holes in her hull?" Omibwe asked, "If I could cover the holes, could we get her to float higher?"

Chibs paused on the bellows, "I suppose we could, young man. But covering the breach in her hull will be quite a task. I'm not sure you could do it by yourself."

Dr. LeMeux interrupted, "Even if we could cover the holes in the hull Omi, there is no way the coverings would be water tight. In order to float her high enough to beach her we have to get more water out than is coming in, and for quite an extended period of time, hours, maybe days."

Chibs shook his head, "It may not be quite so impossible doctor. If Omibwe can dive down there and get planks fixed over each of the breaches, it just might work."

"Planks won't seal out the water trying to come in Chibs-" Dr. LeMeux began to retort in a sneer.

"Not by themselves they won't, doctor, you're right about that. But if we line the planks with waxed canvas, that should hold out the water enough. If we get someone on the bilges pumping water out, while we are pushing air in, it's half mad, but it just might work!" Chibs clamped his pipe back in between his teeth and looked around the row boat. "Everything we'll need is still ashore. Damn the luck!"

Dr. LeMeux sat up higher in the rowboat, "We'll just row the boat in and-"

Chibs shook his head, the doctor was a source of constant frustration, "No, you'll stay and keep pumping air into the Maiden. We can't afford to lose any of the ground we've gained. Omi and I will swim into shore and get what we need."

Dr. LeMeux rose to his feet and shook his finger emphatically, "Absolutely not. You are in no condition to be-"

Chibs turned to face the doctor as pale moonlight descended onto the cove, "I'll be doing whatever needs to be done, doctor. And right now that means I'll be swimming my arse to shore with the young man while you pump your heart out." He paused and gave Omibwe a smile, "If a boy with one leg can dive into the belly of the ship, I think I can manage swimming to shore with a few scratches and a missing hand."

Dr. LeMeux only managed to shake his head in

response. He pulled himself behind the handle of the bellows while Chibs and Omibwe eased over the side of the rowboat and into the cool water of the cove. The feel of the sea lacing over his legs gave Chibs a chill. He pushed away from the rowboat with his legs and used his good arm to loop out ahead of him and draw in a big stoke of water toward his torso. Omibwe followed close behind, pulling at the water with both arms.

"With my missing hand and your missing leg we'll make a swimmer between the two of us." Chibs mused as he pulled another big stroke of seawater into his side. The water kissed his wounds. Chibs cherished the coolness as he pulled himself toward the beach. Starlight gleamed overhead in the inky darkness of the night sky while pale moonlight illuminated the cove and made the soft sands of the beach glow with a ghostly bluish white hue.

"Almost there Chibs." Omibwe encouraged as they swam toward the beach.

Chibs pulled in a deep breath and relished the soft caress of the seawater against his skin. He pulled in another stroke and let his breath go slowly. The water felt warmer around him. Chibs felt the soft embrace of sand reach up and brush against his legs as he kicked toward the shore. With another stroke the sand was rubbing against his back and Chibs planted his feet into the soft, wet sand and stood up out of the cove. The beach was alive with chatter from the crews hauling tension against lines that led out to the Maiden. Damriq ran from where the line crews labored down to the water's edge where Chibs and Omibwe were sloshing through the shin deep water and up onto the damp sand.

"Chibs! We thought you would stay out until the Maiden was far enough into shore." He huffed a deep breath and slapped Omibwe on the shoulder, "You will be glad to see someone that has returned!"

Chibs scrunched his face and swept his eyes across the beach, "The captain?"

Damriq shook his head and gave Omibwe another gentle nudge on his shoulder, "No, not the captain. Although I can't imagine she will be away too much longer. Jilhal and the Spanish girl have come back with a cart loaded full of tools to help with repairs."

Chibs felt a flutter in his chest. His eyes searched the beach all the way up to the tree line for Omibwe's mother. For a moment his thoughts of sealing the holes in the Maiden's hull became a foggy memory, a footnote of importance next to Jilhal. The ghostly glow of moonlight off of the sands shone bright and Chibs found a slender silhouette that could only belong to one woman. She was nearly as tall as he was, and the shadow of a curved sword at her hip brought an uncontrollable smile to his face.

"There she is!" Omibwe exclaimed and stretched out a hand to point to the shadow on the beach.

Chibs stood still for a moment and took in the shape of her, "Aye. There she is."

As the two friends slowly made their way up the beach, Omibwe clinging to Chibs' good arm for balance, the figure began to move closer to them. Slowly at first, but as they drew closer and closer Jilhal's face became more clear.

She dropped to her knees in the sand and extended her arms to take hold of Omibwe while he rushed away from Chibs' arm and toward the embrace of his mother. "My boy!" she exclaimed as they locked into a tight hug, "my baby boy." Chibs stood over the pair of them with a broad smile, watching as Omibwe's mother smothered him in kisses.

Jilhal extended a hand and Chibs reached and took it, pulling her up to her feet. "Only one good hand to hold you with my dear."

Jilhal extended her arms around Chibs neck and pulled him close, "One will be enough." In the moonlight her features seemed to glow and Chibs could not resist her beauty. He held his good arm tight behind her back and kissed her. It was quick at first, a testing jab to see if she would put up her defenses. When Jilhal returned with a kiss of her own Chibs felt as if the entire world had slipped away around them and the center of the universe was him holding the woman he had fallen in love with while they locked in a kiss.

Chapter 9

'North Wind'
26 Apr 1809
17 Degrees 50' N, 74 Degrees 56' W

Shadows stretched along the sunbaked deck boards of the North Wind. The crew was all assembled under the late afternoon sun and their shadows splayed out in front of them as they faced the aft castle where Admiral Torren and a handful of officers stood in a rigid formation of their own. Drums had sounded a steady marching pace until the crew had formed, then they carried a long tattoo until Midshipman Brant stepped forward with a rolled parchment tucked under one arm. The young officer appeared nervous. Admiral Torren waited for him to look over the crew and then to him for approval. The admiral gave him a nod, satisfied with the young man's good sense and diligence.

Midshipman Brant adjusted his hat and cleared

his throat before unrolling the parchment and reading aloud with every bit of volume he could muster. "I shall now read the Articles of War governing the conduct of all men in service to the crown." He paused slightly and took a deep breath before plunging forward to his task. "Article One. All commanders, captains, and officers, in or belonging to any of His Majesty's ships or vessels of war, shall cause the public worship of Almighty God, according to the liturgy of the Church of England established by law, to be solemnly, orderly and reverently performed on their respective ships; and shall take care that prayers and preaching, by the chaplains in holy orders of the respective ships, be performed diligently, and that the Lord's day be observed according to the law."

Admiral Torren watched closely while the young midshipman continued. The faces of crewmen spelled out exactly what he had suspected. A small number of co-conspirators had created this problem, fueled by the lies of one of his prisoners, they had aspired to take the ship for themselves and return to England to turn over their commanders as traitors to the crown. The admiral gritted his teeth at the prospect. *I should return to England and let them have their way. They can march me before the court and watch in horror as the royal guard slaps irons on their wrists and marches them straight to the gallows.* Admiral Torren's eyes landed on Lieutenant Pike. A shave and a meal had done him wonders, though he still looked a fair amount underweight and his face was plagued by scars and scabbed wounds that had still not fully healed. The Admiral had instructed his junior officers to see to it that Lieutenant Pike was cleaned up and outfitted to stand in formation.

"Article Two. All flag officers, and all persons in or belonging to His Majesty's ships or vessels of war, being guilty of profane oaths, cursing, execrations, drunkenness, uncleanness, or other scandalous actions, in derogation of God's honor, and corruption of good manners, shall incur such punishment as a court martial shall think fit to impose, and as the nature and degree of their offense shall deserve." Midshipman Brant continued with as loud a voice as he could muster. "Article Three. If any officer, mariner, soldier, or other person of the fleet, shall give, hold, or entertain intelligence to or with any enemy or rebel, without leave from the king's majesty, or the lord high admiral, or the commissioners for executing the office of lord high admiral, commander in chief, or his commanding officers, every such person so offending, and being thereof convicted by the sentence of a court martial, shall be punished with death."

Admiral Torren watched Lieutenant Pike closely. The man was visibly in pain from the injuries he had sustained being keelhauled. A pang of guilt struck Admiral Torren's gut. If he had only listened to the young officer, all of this mess would have likely been avoided. Instead, half of his contingent of marines were dead and a fair amount of those remaining would soon be hanging by their necks for their mutinous aspirations.

A breeze from the north brought welcome relief from the Caribbean heat, Admiral Torren could feel the cool on the back of his neck where perspiration had started to gather. Midshipman Brant diligently continued rattling out the Articles of War as the crew remained stock still in formation on deck. The fourth article outlined communications with the enemy, punishable by death. The fifth spelled out the punishment for the activities of spies against the crown, which was death. Article six and seven warned officers and sailors against stealing money, papers or goods seized as part of a prize taken or taken from the enemy directly. The penalty for those infractions, death.

Admiral Torren had heard the Articles of War read out on ship so many times in the course of his career that he could rattle them off almost strictly from memory. The crimes varied from article to article, but the vast majority of the punishments prescribed for each crime was the death of the offender. The admiral looked over each of the six mutineers who had survived the attempt. They had been stripped of their uniform coats and shackled in irons at the wrist. All six men were in front of the quarter deck, facing the aft castle where Admiral Torren and his officers stood. Four marines and two junior officers, a lieutenant and a midshipman, were all on their knees listening while the articles were read off before their summary court martial was to be commenced. It was a forgone conclusion. All six men were active party to the mutiny, and all six men would be hung by their necks until dead. Admiral Torren wrought no pleasure from the business of rendering their judgment or ordering their punishment, but the royal navy was held together by discipline like a ship was held together by timbers and line. Order must stand above all else, otherwise the whole of the organization would be for naught. Ships would go out to sea only to be ravaged by their own crews, taken for whatever ill gains they could be used to plunder away from law abiding seafarers and likely sold off at the nearest shipyard afterward.

"Article ten. Every flag officer, captain and commander in the fleet, who, upon signal or order of fight, or sight of any ship or ships which it may be his duty to engage, or who, upon likelihood of engagement, shall not make the necessary preparations for fight, and shall not in his own person, and according to his place, encourage the inferior officers and men to fight courageously, shall suffer death, or such other punishment, as from the nature and degree of the offense a court martial shall deem him to deserve; and if any person in the fleet shall treacherously or cowardly yield or cry for quarter, every person so offending, and being convicted thereof by the sentence of a court martial, shall suffer death."

Admiral Torren recalled a summary court

martial he attended years ago dealing with a lieutenant who had his below decks in the hold during an engagement. Many sailors believed that to go below decks and hide below the waterline of the ship would render a man safe from the hazards of combat. For a time, the notion is correct. But if a ship is engaged in battle and sustains serious damage, the worst place to be is below the waterline. A man could be trapped deep inside the hold, pinned beneath a falling timber, burned alive or drowned. The admiral almost shivered as he considered the possibilities. *Not me. I will face my death with cutlass and pistol in hand and courage in my heart. A good death at sea. One they will talk of in London around their evening brandies.*

Midshipman Brant continued. He read off article eleven, promising the punishment of death for disobeying orders during battle. Article twelve outlined death as the punishment from an early retreat from combat. Article thirteen threatened death to any member of the service that did not make pursuit of an enemy once sighted. The fourteenth dealt with discouraging others from completing their service to the crown. Article fifteen and sixteen enunciated various types of desertion. The punishment prescribed for which was death. Article seventeen and eighteen dealt with the conduct of convoys carrying goods and properties of the crown and the illicit receiving of goods from enemies of the crown respectively. The punishment listed for both offenses was death.

"Article nineteen. Mutiny, sedition and treason. If any person in or belonging to the fleet shall make or endeavor to make any mutinous assembly upon any pretense whatsoever, every person offending herein, and being convicted thereof by the sentence of the court martial, shall suffer death. And if any person in or belonging to the fleet shall utter any words of sedition or mutiny, he shall suffer death, or such other punishment as a court martial shall deem him to deserve, and if any officer, mariner, or soldier on or belonging to the fleet, shall behave himself with contempt to his superior officer, being in the execution of his office, he shall be punished according to the nature of his offense by the judgment of a court martial." Midshipman Brant paused and looked over the assembled crew before proceeding to the next article. Admiral Torren had given him instruction to stop at article twenty so they may carry out the court martial after reading the pertinent articles without unnecessary delay. "Article twenty. Concealing or abiding with a mutinous party. If any person in the fleet shall conceal any traitorous or mutinous practice or design, being convicted thereof by the sentence of a court martial, he shall suffer death, or any other punishment as a court martial shall think fit, and if any person, in or belonging to the fleet, shall conceal any traitorous or mutinous words spoken by any, to the prejudice of His Majesty or government, or any words, practice, or design, tending to the hindrance of the service, and shall not forthwith reveal the same to the commanding officer, or being present at any mutiny or sedition, shall not use his utmost endeavors to suppress the same, he shall be punished as a court martial shall think he deserves." The midshipman stopped and rolled his parchment up. He looked to Admiral Torren.

The Admiral could feel every eye on deck gravitate toward him. He looked over the faces of his crew. There was an air of sober reality hanging over North Wind's deck. Every sailor and officer knew what was coming. Even the younger lads who were making their first voyage at sea had heard tales of the swift and final actions that followed an attempted mutiny. Admiral Torren stood in silence looking over the failed mutineers as they all kneeled on the weather deck. Their heads hung, weighed by shame or remorse, their eyes remained fixed on the deck boards where they were kneeling. All but one of them. Midshipman Summers knelt next to Lieutenant Grath, second from the right as Admiral Torren looked down on the rank formation of kneeling traitors. His eyes met with the admiral's. For a long moment they shared eye contact, the admiral narrowed his eyes in a half squint as if he were searching the young officer's soul for some redeeming quality. Midshipman Summers looked up through pleading wide eyes. His cheeks were stained by tears. Admiral Torren swallowed hard and tapped his cane twice onto the wooden deck by his feet. The midshipman could be no more than fifteen or sixteen years old. *A boy. A child who ought to be at home with his family. But, a traitor nonetheless.*

"You all know the punishment for treason." Admiral Torren raised his voice over the sound of North Wind's hull sliding through the Caribbean waves. "And you all know the punishment for mutiny." He paused for a long moment and looked over the faces of his crew on deck. "Not only is mutiny an attack on a ship's commander, and by extension an attack on our monarch himself. It is an attack on all of you lads who have remained loyal in your service to our king and our country." A gust of wind flapped the front of his dress coat, but the admiral paid no mind to the distraction. "We are here in the Caribbean to restore the king's peace and bring order out of lawlessness. Under my command, there will never be tolerance for an act of mutiny. Be you of any rank, no matter. The punishment remains the same." Admiral Torren broke from his stance on the aft castle and walked to the stairs leading down to the weather deck where the crew was assembled just behind the row of mutineers. "I find all of you here guilty of mutinous actions aboard a ship of his majesty's navy while at sea. In concert with an enemy of the crown you did attempt to overthrow you appointed chain of command by force and thereby requisition for yourselves a ship of war in service to the crown. According to the articles of war, and by the power placed in me by the faith and appointment from the king and parliament, I hereby sentence you all to hang by the neck until dead. You will receive no honors and you will be buried without ceremony at sea. It is a fate better than you deserve." Admiral Torren's gaze locked with Midshipman Summers. "May God almighty have mercy on your souls."

Pirate Cove
27 Apr 1809

Diving the hose down into the belly of the Drowned Maiden had been easy. Omibwe had made it inside with the end of the hose on the first attempt. Retrieving the hose had been simple. Omibwe was excited to see that the pocket of air had grown to more than twice the size it had been the first time he had made his way into the bowels of the ship. He easily slipped the hose out of the breach where he had originally threaded it in between the shattered timbers. He had found another path to move the hose in. The end didn't quite make it to where the air pocket was, but Chibs had assured him that wouldn't matter. "The bubbles will find their way to the air pocket lad, rest assured, the air we pump in will still do every bit as much good."

The challenge came when Omibwe had to repair the breaches in the hull. His first voyage down had been with a plank wrapped in waxed canvas tucked beneath one arm and a hammer and some nails tucked into his waistline. The wrapped timber fought him for every inch as he tried to dive down toward the deepest of the holes in the Maiden's hull. After kicking and whipping his leg and clawing with his hands for every bit of purchase to move deeper Omibwe had finally relented and floated back to the surface. He blew seawater from his nostrils and wiped at his face at the side of the rowboat while Chibs and Dr. LeMeux took turns pumping on the bellows. The doctor looked beyond exhausted, but Omibwe knew that it didn't take much for Dr. LeMeux to tire.

"It won't work." Omibwe spat out some seawater and pushed the wrapped plank up onto the side of the rowboat, "The plank fights me the whole way down."

Chibs pulled his pipe out from its perch in the side of his mouth, "It's got to work, lad. We won't rescue the ship if it doesn't."

Omibwe clamped his hands onto the side of the rowboat and held onto the edge with a tight grip. "I can't make it down deep enough to seal the lowest hole. I am the strongest diver here. If I can't make it nobody else will either."

Chibs rubbed at his forehead with a furious intensity. Omibwe knew he was growing frustrated with each of their attempts to bring the Maiden into shore fizzling out. Dawn was breaking over the cove, they had another twenty-four-hour shot to lift the ship higher into shore before the tide would come back into her fullest state. To make matters worse, Chibs had told Omibwe that with the full moon beginning to wane away, each high tide would be just shy of the one before it. All of their challenges had seemed to combine against them. Each time Chibs had made a salted comment about "We'll show her," or "She may not want to set back to sail now, but mark my words, she doesn't know what's good for her." Omibwe could tell that the captain's extended absence was beginning to weigh on him as well. Chibs had been high strung after Damriq had shown up with a dozen new hands in tow and told a tale of Captain Lilith setting off with half of their new recruits and a lust for blood in her eye. But now that Omibwe's mother and Emilia had returned, Chibs seemed to be in a constant state of near panic. He hadn't taken to raising his voice to Omibwe, yet. But Chibs had turned all manner of verbal abuse against Dr. LeMeux, even more so than he usually did. And Omibwe had noticed the nervous looks Chibs would cast out toward the narrow opening of the cove. It was almost as if his old sailor friend was scared.

"What if we tied the boards up in a sack with a big stone in it?" Chibs offered, "Then it would all sink down and you could dive freely, fetch what you need and come for air in between fastening planks." Dr. LeMeux raised a finger to give the conversation pause and opened his mouth to object. Chibs balled a fist and shook it on front of the doctor's face, "I think we have had enough naysaying input from you for a lifetime doctor.

Pump the damned bellows and let the sailing men do our work!"

Omibwe felt as if his sails had been filled with the strongest westerly to have ever graced the Caribbean. Chibs had spoken of him not only as a sailor, but a sailing man. His chest swelled. Omibwe could feel his shoulders broaden even as he thought of the compliment. He gave Dr. LeMeux a quick glance before looking back at Chibs, "I think that will work Chibs.

The salty old sailor nodded with a big grin, "That's the way lad! Never give up. We'll get this old broad into shore and have her patched up in no time. You watch, the Caribbean has never seen terrors like a ship coming back from the dead. We'll be the talk of every tavern from Nassau to Barbados. Hell, I'll bet even the Spaniards of Maracaibo will be telling tales of the pirate ship that just won't stay sunk!"

Omibwe imagined scores of ships fleeing from the Maiden in fear as Captain Lilith stood high on the prow with her sword in hand. He looked up at Chibs in the soft light of dawn, "Sink the planks to me and I will do the rest Chibs."

"Alright lad, alright. That will do." He looked around inside the rowboat and fetched up a piece of canvas and a small cannon ball, "These ought to suffice. Just give me a few minutes to thread some line through this and make it into a sack. You'll have to be sure not to let them all float out at once, we only have the one cannon ball and I don't want to listen to the doctor whine if he has to row us back into shore to fetch a stone."

Dr. LeMeux rolled his eyes and pushed hard on the bellows handle.

Chibs turned inboard and began working with furious intensity to thread a small line through some holes in a piece of canvas sailcloth. Omibwe watched from the water's surface as the old sailor hoisted a nine-pound cannon shot into the hastily made bag. He stuffed the wrapped planks in and cinched the bag shut. "Alright lad, watch yourself while I swing this bugger out." Chibs reeled the bag back to wind up a good toss. Omibwe pulled himself close to the rowboat as it swayed under the force of Chibs swinging the bag back and forth. He watched as Chibs gave the bag a final swing and launched it into the air with the cannon ball leading the way inside of the rough canvas bag. The bag splashed into the water and sent a small plume flying as the cannonball dragged the canvas and its contents down to the depths of the cove. Chibs had managed to hurl the bag of planks just a few yards shy of the Maiden's hull.

"There you are lad! A bag of boards, sent straight to the depths just as you requested!" Chibs exclaimed with a satisfied grin shining through his grizzly beard.

Omibwe pushed off from the rowboat and swam toward the spot in the cove where the bag had splashed down. Dawn had painted the sky into streaks of gold and pink and the calm, still water of the cove looked like a crystalline reflection of the heavens above as it bent and waved with the ripples of the bag's impact. When he reached the spot the bag had entered the water, Omibwe took a few short rapid breaths followed by one long slow one. He dove beneath the surface and pulled his way deeper and deeper until he could see the canvas bag resting on the sandy bottom of the cove. The cannon ball weighed the bag down perfectly while the wrapped planks still fought against the depths holding the top of the crudely fabricated piece suspended in the water. Omibwe made his way to the bottom and hastily untied the opening. He slid one of the planks out of the bag and tucked it beneath his arm. Under the crushing weight of the cove, he quickly tied the bag opening shut again before pushing off to make his way toward the lowest breach in the Maiden's hull. There was much more room between the hull and the sandy bottom than when he had last seen it. Omibwe wasted no time in pressing the plank up against the Maiden's hull, he held it steady with one hand while pulling the hammer and a nail from his waistband. He held the first nail against the wrapped plank and sent it home with a few taps. After the first nail was sunk into the wood Omibwe had a much easier time as he didn't have to hold the plank steady to keep it from floating away from where he needed it. He drove three more nails into the plank before he could no longer ignore the burning hunger in his lungs for clean air. Looking toward the surface, Omibwe decided it would be quicker to move into the gap of air inside of the Maiden's hull. He swam upward to the next highest breach in the hull and wriggled in through the opening. Inside of the hold was dark, with only a small trickle of the light from above filtering it's way past the cove's surface. When Omibwe's face finally broke the surface inside of the air pocket, he was delighted to feel just how much it had grown. The gun carriage where he had perched himself on his first voyage down into the belly of the ship was now completely exposed. He had to climb completely out of the water in order to hoist himself onto the gun carriage. Omibwe rested his back along the cold iron of the cannon and breathed in a lungful of damp air. The air pocket was so dark he could barely make out anything around him.

The air was dark and dense. Omibwe felt a chill enter his spine through the cold iron of the cannon he rested on as bubbles rose to the surface from the hose that Dr. LeMeux and Chibs were painstakingly pumping air through. As his breathing rate slowed and the hunger for new air dissipated from his lungs, Omibwe slipped himself off of the cannon carriage and lowered his body back into the water. Streams of bubbles fluttered up from the hose and made a fizzing gurgle noise as they broke and delivered little puffs of air into the growing chamber of buoyancy. Omibwe repeated his dive ritual by taking a few short sharp breaths before one long slow one and submerging himself back into the water of the cove. He had two more planks to secure on the lowest hole before it would be sealed. The next hole higher would prove to be more difficult. It was a longer swim between his bag of boards on the sandy bottom and where he needed to fix them over the breach. Omibwe tried to contemplate how many trips he could make back and forth before he would need to return for air. As he pulled himself through the broken timbers and out into the cove he put the thought of the next hole out of his mind. He still had two more planks to fix in place before that would be a problem. He would deal with those troubles when it was time.

'North Wind'
27 Apr 1809
17 Degrees 48' N, 75 Degrees 07' W

Admiral Torren's cabin was roasting hot. Will stood at attention before the embellished dark wooden desk while Admiral Torren sat in his padded chair staring at him through stony eyes. *This is worse than his chambers in the admiralty,* Will thought to himself, *how is he not sweating?* The admiral looked over Will in silence for the better part of two minutes before finally rising to his feet.

"It would seem, in all of my experience at sea and all of my years of command, that I have finally come across something for which I have no landmark to set my bearings by." Admiral Torren's face remained stony and unchanging as he spoke. "For the life of me, I still cannot understand how things in the Caribbean have devolved into such absolute anarchy. I am utterly at a loss." Admiral Torren turned and faced the fantail window array, "The prisoner you accused of murdering Admiral Sharpe has demonstrated himself to be wholly without honor and therefore, I cannot trust that his account of the events in Kingston is true." The admiral paused and gave Will a look over his shoulder before returning his gaze out to the blue gray swells of the ocean. "The narrative he used to lead my crew to mutiny is also disturbing. I have found that an effective lie is oft not far from the truth. With that in mind, as I think over your sworn recollection of the events, it doesn't seem so farfetched after all."

Will could feel sweat gathering at the collar of the uniform coat he was wearing. The wounds on his back ached, the cuts on his belly burned, he longed for fresh air. He was at a loss for words when Admiral Torren turned back to face him. Unsure if he was about to be clapped back into irons and led below or restored to his place in the Royal Navy.

"Taking up with a crew of pirates. That's a serious charge lad." The admiral shook his head and folded his hands behind his back. "According to your account, you were mutinied on by the crew of the Endurance. The crew aboard H.M.S Valor mutinied against Captain Grimes, and you had no choice but to join with a crew of pirates in order to stop this American rogue."

Will nodded, "The pirates came upon us during the mutiny sir. Their attack was not to our aid, but it benefited us all the same."

Admiral Torren turned and faced Will, "Yes, you've told me as much already. What I don't understand is how you could have thought taking up arms with the pirates against your countrymen, mutineers or not, was in the benefit of the Royal Navy. And how did you go from that, to escorting a pirate right to the chambers of a royal governor? It's madness."

Will nodded again, he swallowed hard, sensing his next words could determine his fate. "There were many departures from conventional wisdom and practice on my path admiral. What I do have to say for myself is this, the American and Governor Alton were conspiring together to smuggle slaves in direct violation of the parliamentary abolition of the slave trade. They conspired together to both use the Caribbean fleet to further their endeavor and when Admiral Sharpe grew suspicious of their illicit activities they murdered him and fired on the fleet from the guns in Fort Charles." Will drew a breath and tried to straighten his posture, "My actions were unorthodox, extreme even. But I never betrayed the cause of our service sir. The enemy was, and is, this American and whoever he is in league with."

Admiral Torren pursed his lips and settled into

the padded chair behind his desk. Will tried to determine how the admiral was weighing his statement, but the man's stony features were unchanged. "Never in my life would I have thought I would say this." His voice trailed away for a moment before he looked Will directly in the eye, "Perhaps these pirates were fighting toward a common interest with the crown."

Will met the admiral's stare and for a moment he couldn't decide if he had blundered into a trap, "Sir, respectfully, the pirates enemies may be our enemies. But their goals do not align with our own. They were brigands and thieves and must have been dealt with as such." Will watched as Admiral Torren's eyes softened.

"Right you are lad. They were not our allies. They may prove useful in our current situation, but, in the end, the result must always be the same. We are on one side, they are on the other." The admiral nodded with satisfaction at Will and gestured toward his battered cabin door, "You have swayed me. Though I never thought I would see the day, Mr. Pike, I hereby restore you to your rank as a lieutenant in the Royal Navy. I expect you will conduct yourself as such from this day henceforth and deliver the King's justice to the enemies of the crown and assist me in returning law and order to the empire's holdings in the Caribbean." Admiral Torren gestured toward a map on his desk, "Our first order of business is Kingston. We will make port there and restore order to the town. We may need to retake Fort Charles, which will prove challenging with the small remainder of our marine contingent. But it must be done. Once the fort and town are firmly back under our control, we will seize and commandeer any ships remaining in harbor for the purpose of hunting down any remaining slave smugglers or pirates and bringing them to justice. We will press every man in Kingston if that is what it takes. Our nation will rule the waves in the Caribbean, no matter the cost."

Will could not believe his ears. The course of his career, his life, had just been altered again. The keelhauling, the flogging, weeks spent in a cramped, wet cell imagining his last moments being on the gallows of Kingston. The mutiny. The horrible fight that had ensued afterward. All of it had led to the restoration of his rank and his honor. The heat of the cabin didn't seem so sweltering in that moment. Will felt his perspiration running down the back of his neck and an odd coolness wrapping itself around his shoulders. His eyes blurred as tears began to pool above his lower eyelids.

"I expect that our fight is not over. Not by a long shot. Whoever has orchestrated this smuggling operation isn't likely to quit after a setback. I would assume there is quite a lot of money involved in the affair." Admiral Torren leaned back in his padded chair and shifted his legs. Will could see that the admiral's disposition had grown tense, almost as if he were in pain but determined not to show it. "What we need, before we blunder into something, is answers. We need an accurate fix on our enemy and the magnitude of the problem we are dealing with."

Will felt a chill in his spine. Did the admiral think he knew something about this conspiracy? "I have told you everything I know sir. If there was more information, I would gladly tell it."

The admiral grimaced and held up a finger to silence Will, "I don't doubt it, son. But there is more to be learned from the American we still hold on board." He winced harder and leaned forward into his desk.

"Are you quite alright sir?" Will asked as the admiral tilted his head down.

Admiral Torren shook his head, "No, lad. I am in excruciating pain. Gout, in my legs and feet. The price I pay for not dying in battle in my youth." After a moment of silence, the admiral seemed to regain some of his composure. "The American. We will have him up here and I will question him. I want you here when I do."

Will nodded, "Yes, sir."

"After we question him. He will be executed for the murder of Admiral Elliot Sharpe and his plot to overtake this ship by setting the crew to mutiny." Admiral Torren lifted a brow and looked at Will from the upper corner of his eye, "I imagine you will find some small comfort in seeing justice done."

Will clenched his hands behind his back, images of Admiral Sharpe's body collapsing after the American fired his pistol. "Justice." He paused for a moment, "It will be very gratifying to see Mr.Sladen meet his end, sir. But I'm not sure I could call hanging him justice. He shot Admiral Sharpe in the chest and let him die in my arms. He ordered his men occupying Fort Charles to open fire on the fleet in harbor and sent scores of sailors to their deaths. Mr. Sladen must die, sir, he is too dangerous to be left alive. But to call it justice is an affront to the souls of our shipmates."

Admiral Torren nodded at Will's response. He shifted in his chair and offered Will a pained grin, "After we have sufficiently questioned him, he will be executed. I said nothing of hanging him." Admiral Torren reached up onto his desk for a cup and took a drink, "I can promise you one thing, lad. When we are done questioning him, you will find that justice is served, he will beg us for death before the end."

'Batard De Mur'
28 Apr 1809
18 Degrees 49' N, 73 Degrees 38' W

She had been sighted just before sunset, in the failing light of the day a glimpse of white sail on the horizon was easy to miss. But Captain Laurent Fontaine had been standing his own sort of watch while he pondered the circumstances which had led to his current station in life. Peering out over the stretches of hazy blue Caribbean waters, he had spotted the sails on the northern horizon. At first, the captain said nothing. He wanted to see how long it would take his lookouts aloft to notice the spot of fluttering white canvas on the edge of visible sea. After a while it became apparent that he alone had noticed the ship and none of his lookouts would catch the sight of her until they were far too close.

Red sails pose a curious problem for a pirate. Normally, a pirate ship looks about like any other merchant ship out at sea. With white canvas sails a pirate vessel can sail near other ships and ports without causing much of a panic if they so choose. They can bide their time and investigate a crew or a port from close range before deciding if they want to engage them or not. On any other pirate ship, the captain would either order a course to be set to close with the unknown ship, or he would match their course and sail until the ships drew near enough to shout a message in between them. At the last possible moment, the captain would order his crew to fly their colors. Once the black banner waved in the wind over a ship, there could be no doubts about their intentions. If that banner happened to be red, they would know they were dealing with a particular pirate. Captain Laurent Fontaine and the Batard De Mur had become the substance of merchant sailor's nightmares. Laurent made it a point to leave one of his victims alive after every engagement. He would shove the unfortunate soul overboard close enough to the nearest port of harbor to ensure their tales were told. In addition, Laurent had developed the gruesome custom of drawing blood every time he boarded a vessel, whether it be to plunder away a ship's cargoes or not. Every time he boarded a vessel from his own, someone would die. The crimson sails that flew over the decks of Batard De Mur had grown to be something of near legend status. For Captain Fontaine and his crew, there was no hiding their intentions until the last moment. Ships would either fire or flee at first sighting. Any crew that faced them was either a hardened group of sailors aboard a military vessel or crew of merchant sailors that had not spent enough time in the Caribbean to have heard the tales of the bloodthirsty crew that sports crimson canvas.

The white spot of canvas was taking a fuller shape, Captain Fontaine looked up toward his man in the crow's nest to see if he had any inkling of it at all. The pirate was facing out toward the beach off of Batard De Mur's starboard side. Captain Fontaine clenched his jaw in frustration, but his anger quickly tempered when the lookout shifted in his seat and caught notice of the sails off to the north.

"Sail on the horizon. Double mast! Can't make out colors yet, sir."

I've been looking on the sail for the better part of an

hour, Laurent thought. "Aye, maintain course. Let's see what they are made of." A glance over his shoulder reminded him that LeFouet was still trailing far behind him, watching his every move. *Let them watch, there isn't a damn thing they can do.* Laurent looked back to the whites sail on the northern horizon.

"Captain! She's turning! Looks like she means to close with us!" the lookout called down.

Laurent smiled to himself and let his hand rest on the pommel of his sword. An idea began to form in the edges of his mind. *The privateer pays me to find the girl pirate, he said nothing about taking other prey.* Laurent's smile spread across his bearded face, *we will see what Captain Callais is made of as well.* If the ship off his larboard rail held course, they would be drawing near in the dead of night. With a full moon in the night sky it would be almost like a daylight engagement. Laurent looked back at LeFouet and judged the gap between her and the Batard De Mur. If Captain Callais were to run up every scrap of sail he had and hold the wind just right, he could close the gap to cannon range before dawn.

The last light of day faded from the heavens and gave way to a blanket of brilliant stars. The moon's illustrious glow hadn't touched the sea's surface, and wouldn't for several hours. Batard De Mur continued sailing on her course, carefully navigating the notorious channels between rocky shoals, reefs and sand bars off the western coast of

Haiti. It wasn't the first time Captain Fontaine had set his ship through the treacherous quagmire in darkness, he had used these shallows to evade both the British and the French navies in the past. Port-Au-Prince lie hours off of their bow and a finger of land extending from Haiti just a few hundred yards off of their starboard side. Whoever the mystery ship they had spotted may be, their course to intercept Batard De Mur would run them right into the same minefield of reefs and shallows that Captain Fontaine was expertly negotiating. If the ship's captain was adept at handling his vessel, and knowledgeable of the dangerous waters he was forging into, Captain Fontaine would see his sails at dawn. But, there was one thing he was absolutely sure of, Captain Callais would run LeFouet aground before dawn broke over the eastern horizon. Captain Fontaine gripped the pommel of his sword and peered out into the darkness behind Batard De Mur's stern, a slow smile spread across his face as he pictured the despair in Captain Callais eyes when dawn found LeFouet stuck on a reef or shoal and his red sails were spotted on the horizon.

Chapter 10

Pirate Cove
27 Apr 1809

"She's rising!" Chibs shouted toward the shoreline with his good hand cupped around the side of his face, "Haul on those lines for your lives! Let's bring her ashore!"

The hulking mass of the Drowned Maiden had risen almost four feet in the last half hour while Dr. LeMeux and Chibs took turns laboring over their improvised bellows and a group of three men including the broad shouldered Damriq toiled at the bilge pump. Water was moving out, air was moving in, and Omibwe's plank seals were holding the cove at bay. Chibs imagined that after a few more hours of pumping the Maiden's stern would rise, making her far easier to run ashore. The ship groaned in protest, her timbers creaked and trembled under the strain of the varying forces being applied. On shore, the line crews were fighting for every inch of movement they could gain. As the ship slowly rose further and further from the deep the lines became easier to pull. After a few hours, and with a rising tide, the Drowned Maiden's keel finally rested high in the sandy shallows. With a final haul against the thick ropes, both line crews lodged the hull of the ship onto the shoreline and let out a collective breath. All that could be done for the moment was accomplished. Both men and women who had been pulling against the burgeoning weight of the ship were relieved of their duties as the ship finally came to a rest. Some collapsed. Others marveled over their collective accomplishment.

Chibs helped Dr. LeMeux pull the small rowboat up onto the dry sands of the beach. The tide was on its way out. As exhausted as he was, Chibs knew there was much to be done during the low tide hours. This first span of time could only accomplish one thing, draining the remaining water from her hull. By Chibs estimate, the tide would drop low enough to expose the entire belly of the ship. He only needed to open a breach and drain what they could before the tide came back in.

With an early morning sun giving light to the cove, Chibs set about his work. The doctor, Omibwe and Damriq were all exhausted beyond help. They had gathered on the beach and laid in the sand while the tide slipped away. Chibs started by removing the planks Omibwe had attached to the Maiden's hull. Seawater came rushing out in a torrent at first, but as the water level inside the ship dropped lower a steady stream trickled down the side of the hull. He looked into the breach he had exposed, when the water drained out and was level with the bottom of the hole it would still be waist deep inside the Maiden's lowest hold. A lot of that could be pumped out with the bilges and some elbow grease. With a piece of hemp rope, he measured the length of the broken timbers and put knots at his measurements. He took another thin line and did the same at the Maiden's shattered rudder. Next, Chibs moved further into shore and untied the pulleys he had set for the line crews to drag the Maiden up to the beach. He moved both lines to a stand of trees with trunks thick enough to bear the force he needed and retied his set at the new angle.

The tide had moved out considerably by noon and the exhausted members of the Maiden's crew were beginning to move again. Chibs organized a crew of the largest men in the group to pull the line on its new angle perpendicular to the ship.

"We need to tip her as far on her side as we can get her. Once we drain as much of the sea out of her belly as we can, we can start to rebuild her hull." Chis said as he threaded the heavy rope leading to the Maiden's main mast through the pulley. "Once they hull is repaired, we'll have to find new timbers for masts. The for'ard mast is ruined, we'll have to replace that one entirely. The main still looks to be in good enough shape to salvage her lowest section, but we'll have to replace the sections above that one though." He could see the work piling up in front of him.

There were mast sections that needed replacing. He would need to find stout hardwood trees with trunks that were thick and true and straight. Most of the starboard railing had been battered away by cannon fire and falling spars and masts. He would need timbers for that as well. The cannons seemed to be in decent shape, Omibwe said he had found two that were damaged by the incoming gunfire. The remaining cannons would need to be cleaned and oiled. Powder was another concern. Once the cannons were cleaned out and ready to fire, they would be worthless without a stock of dry powder. It was a possibility that some of the powder remaining in kegs had kept dry, but Chibs doubted that much of their gunpowder had remained untouched after being submerged for over a week. The powder would need to be opened, all of it, any of the powder that had gotten wet would need to be laid out to dry. That process could take days. Aside from the lines Chibs had Omibwe strip from the Maiden to assist in her resurrection, many of her lines had been severed in the onslaught from the Royal Navy. Lines would need to be brought out from the Maiden's hold. If there were lines that could not be salvaged, they would have to splice together the ropes they had to make do.

Chibs drew a deep breath and held it for a long moment. The work that lay before them seemed almost insurmountable. An impossibly long list of things could go wrong at any given point and foil his plans. But, he had already managed to bring the Maiden up from the depths of the cove and wrangle her into shore. If his rag tag crew of half-starved sailors and runaway slaves could achieve that, they could do anything.

Omibwe hobbled his way close to Chibs. He bore part of his weight on a crooked stick of driftwood with each step through the white sands of the beach. "What do we do next, Chibs?" he asked as he tottered through the sand.

Chibs held his hand over his brow to shield his eyes from the sun, "The next step is to drain what we can from her belly. We'll have to have a crew work the bilges to pump out the rest."

Jilhal followed Omibwe across the sandy beach and put her arm around her son, "What can we do?"

Chibs ran his hand over his beard and squinted as the glare of the sun invaded his eyes. "You helped Emilia bring those tools. See if she can find us trees that will work for suitable timber. We need to replace timbers in the hull, the decks, masts, spars, yard and railing."

Jilhal motioned toward the shipwrecks out on the reef near the mouth of the cove, "Could we salvage timbers from those?"

Chibs narrowed his eyes and looked out to the opening of the cove. With the tide flowing out, there would be a window of opportunity during low tide to salvage what they could before the currents grew too strong. The Valor's wreckage lingered next to the hulk of another navy ship he didn't know the name of. Both ships were in tatters, their hulls had been pounded by the Maiden's own gun batteries. But there were useful timber and deck boards on both and the Valor still had deck guns exposed. It would be a lot of work, but it would surely be a quicker source of sound timbers than crawling through the rain forest. "That is a bold plan Jilhal," Chibs smiled as he looked at her. The angles of her cheekbones seemed to rise as she smiled back, "We'll need as much line as we can get. Our rowboat is too small to carry the timbers we'll need. We can salvage what's salvageable and lash it together. Then we will tow it in to shore."

Omibwe scrunched his nose and followed Chibs' stare out toward the opening of the cove. "Chibs?" he asked.

Chibs shifted his gaze to the young man, "Yes lad?"

"We could tow some of it in, but, with the pulley and lines, couldn't we drag out a few of the smaller lines and have the crew haul them in by hand also?" Omibwe hobbled a few more steps and pointed to the pulley Chibs had rigged to the stand of trees.

Chibs looked over the expanse of cove separating them from the narrow mouth that led out to the Caribbean. "I'll be damned. That's a shot better than I could come up with!" He nudged Omibwe on the shoulder the elbow of his stubbed arm. "If I'm not careful, the captain will have you as quartermaster when she returns!"

'North Wind'
27 Apr 1809
17 Degrees 49' N, 76 Degrees 28' W

The southern coast of Jamaica stretched out alongside North Wind's starboard rail. Rolling hills of green offset by rocky shores rose away from the blue Caribbean as a gentle breeze from the north filled the canvas above Admiral Torren's flagship. Sharp squawks from gulls punctuated the steady sound of waves breaking along the wooden hull while Admiral Torren stood on the bow, taking in the sea air and mulling over what would await him in Kingston. The last reports he had heard indicated that mercenaries had taken the fort and killed what had remained of the garrison. Bedlam, lawlessness and anarchy. The words continued to rattle through the admiral's thoughts. Re-establishing the rule of law wasn't even the first battle he would have to fight. If what Lieutenant Pike had told him was true, the hulks of three sunken Royal Navy ships would be choking off access to the harbor. To gain access to the town, he would have to anchor well away from the port and approach over land. Tactically speaking, it was the only practical approach. But the notion of crossing overland to Kingston turned the old sailor's stomach. Not only would he be leaving the strength of his firepower behind, he would be walking into an unknown situation that could very well become an ambush. *No. We will not be crossing overland. The sea is where our power lies,* the admiral thought to himself. There were too many unknowns, too many variables. The approach to the harbor would be dangerous enough for a big ship like North Wind, they would sail in as far as possible and then launch the longboats under the cover of her batteries. *If they decide to open fire with the fort guns, they won't go unanswered.* Even still, with the detachment of marines whittled down to a fraction of his full strength, the plan was not without its faults. More information was needed, and Admiral Torren knew exactly where he would start.

The admiral turned to Lieutenant Thatcher, "Summon Lieutenant Pike, and have the American prisoner brought on deck, under arms."

"Aye, sir." Lieutenant Thatcher rendered a snappy salute and turned to his task.

The admiral let his gaze drift out over the starboard quarter and fall onto the Jamaican shore as it slipped by. The breeze from the north was growing stronger, North Wind was sailing along broad reach, powered by her namesake. Admiral Torren basked in the sunlight on the bow and savored every breath of the sea air he could fill his lungs with. It was a rare afternoon when the pain that wracked his legs was not near unbearable, he intended to take full advantage.

"You summoned sir?" Lieutenant Pike reported as the admiral was scanning coastline through a collapsing telescope.

Admiral Torren continued to stare through the instrument, "I have sent for the prisoner as well. We shall make Kingston on the morrow, and we need to know what we are up against."

"Agreed sir." Lieutenant Pike replied with an ache in his voice. He was still plagued by the injuries sustained when the admiral had him run beneath the hull.

"We will interrogate the American. I mean to pull every bit of useful information we can from him. When that is done, you shall administer the king's justice and execute him as a murderer." Admiral Torren collapsed his telescope and faced Lieutenant Pike. The young officer's face was healing, albeit slowly. Admiral Torren could only imagine the daily pain he was going through, changing bandages on his abdomen wounds, applying the salve the ship's surgeon had given him for his arms and legs. "This will require a certain amount of constitution on your part, son. But, it must be done. You must not balk. He must understand that we will not relent until he gives us every single detail we wish to hear."

Lieutenant Pike's face remained unchanged, "Yes sir."

As the admiral finished speaking a pair of armed sailors escorted Tim Sladen to the bow. He was bound in iron shackles, blindfolded with a piece of black cloth and gagged with a thick piece of hemp rope. Lieutenant Thatcher followed the prisoner and his escorts, "As you ordered, sir. The American prisoner."

Admiral Torren nodded curtly and motioned for the sailors to remove Tim's blindfold and gag, "Very well, I'll have you lads stand by." He turned to Lieutenant Thatcher, "Order the watch to run a line under keel. From stem to stern, smartly."

"Aye sir." Lieutenant Thatcher hesitated for a heartbeat before departing to relay his orders.

Admiral Torren tapped his cane onto the wooden deck, "Run a damned line under the keel, son. Or you will be next!"

"Yes sir, straight away sir." Lieutenant Thatcher fumbled his feet for a moment before stepping off to his task.

The admiral looked over Tim for a long moment before raising the end of his cane and pressing it to the American's chest. "I have some questions for you, Mr.Sladen. It is in your best interest to be forthcoming, the alternative will be, unpleasant."

Tim looked up at the admiral and stole a glance over to Lieutenant Pike, "You Brits are all the same. You think you own the damned world, but the world is changing. You won't get a thing out of me, I promise you that."

Admiral Torren shook his head, he waved his cane in front of the Americans face before letting the tip prod down onto the deck with a resounding thud. "I'll have it out of you, one way or another. If I must take a pound of flesh to do so, so be it."

Lieutenant Pike took a grip of the prisoner's shoulder and led him to the base of the bowsprit. A spray from the waves misted over the starboard rail bringing with it the salty smell of the water that slapped onto the side of North Wind.

"The overthrow of Governor Alton in Kingston was not a pirate raid. It was your band of mercenaries. How many are there?" Admiral Torren's voice was driven and pointed, he narrowed his eyes and looked over the side of Tim Sladen's face.

"I do not know," Tim answered, "It has been months since I was in Kingston."

Admiral Torren shook his head and gave Lieutenant Pike a crisp nod. The lieutenant fished a line that had been run through the rigging overhead and beneath North Wind's hull. The lieutenant attached the line to the chain binding Tim's wrists together.

"That will not suffice. I understand you may not know how many men currently hold the town, if any. What I want to know is how many did you have when you took Kingston? How many in Fort Charles? How many at the governor's mansion?" Admiral Torren leaned in close to the American prisoner, "You saw what the lieutenant here looked like after only two trips under the keel. You need to understand something, if you don't tell me the information that I need to know, I will run you under until my entire crew is sapped of their strength and can no longer haul on the line, or, until the last ounce of life has bled out of you into the sea. Now speak."

Tim Sladen's eyes shot wide as the admiral withdrew from his shoulder, "I entered Kingston with two dozen men. We took the fort from within, without bloodshed, due to my familiarity with Governor Alton and the soldiers there."

Admiral Torren tapped his cane on the deck and narrowed his eyes against the wind, "And?"

"Then I took half of them to the governor's mansion, we took everything of value to compensate ourselves for a lost shipment he had promised to protect."

Admiral Torren could feel goosebumps rising on the back of his neck, he fought away an angry tremble that was threatening his hand. "Governor Alton had agreed to allow you safe passage for your smuggling operation?"

Tim nodded, "Yes."

Admiral Torren tapped his cane onto the deck. He repeated the motion, each tap getting harder and harder as he continued. "So the lieutenant has spoken honestly this entire time. And you encouraged the mutiny aboard H.M.S Valor in the same manner that you did aboard North Wind."

Tim shook his head, "I was left afloat after my own ship had been blown to bits by the pirates. They had already mutinied against their captain when they rescued me."

Admiral Torren gave a look to Lieutenant pike to confirm, the lieutenant nodded and spoke low into the admiral's ear, "Lieutenant Cobb."

The Admiral nodded and looked back at his American prisoner, "So you had the crew mutiny against the second lieutenant, who had led the mutiny against Captain Grimes. Did Lieutenant Cobb meet his end in your mutiny?"

Tim's eyes fell to the water rushing against the bow below him, "Yes. The crew strung him up by his neck."

"I suppose I ought to thank you for whittling a traitor out of our midst, but you murdered Admiral Sharpe, that I cannot forgive." Admiral Torren motioned to the line crew standing ready behind him, they began to haul on the line attached to Tim's shackles until he was suspended with his feet inches above the deck. The admiral turned to Lieutenant Pike, "Run him under."

Tim writhed against his restraints, "Wait! Wait! There is more, I can tell you more, just spare me this cruelty, please, I beg you."

Admiral Torren held his hand out to pause the line crew, "Tell me what you would say."

"The Order extends beyond the Caribbean, beyond the Americas. The masters of Europe are involved, from the very highest level of society." Tim panted to fill his lungs with air against the tension of his arms being held high over his head. "There are lords in Britain involved. Napoleon and the French, Spanish nobles, even the Church is involved. You have to understand, once I became involved with these people everything got out of control."

Admiral Torren paused for a moment and let what the American had just said sink in. "Do you know these British lords? Their names?"

"No." Tim choked out his answer like breath had been stolen from his lungs. Admiral Torren began to wave his hand toward the line crew, but held it as Tim began to speak again. "Wait! I do know that one of them is the Lord Admiral of the navy. I don't know his name, only that Governor Alton referred to him once when we were discussing our plans for keeping our cargoes from being interfered with. He is in league with them."

"In league with who?" Admiral Torren pressed.

"The British lords who control the East India Trading Company, Napoleon and the French, the church, all of them. The Order." Tim let a gasp escape and sucked in another labored breath.

Admiral Torren ignored his prisoner's rasping breaths and turned toward Lieutenant Pike, "That is where this originates. I should have known the French had their fingers in it. It only makes sense. Napoleon encourages treason against the crown, he uses our own parliamentary actions against us and reaps profits while doing so. Using the East India Company to stuff his pockets. The bastards sailing for the company wouldn't even know they were aiding the enemy." He turned back toward Tim and looked up at his strained face. "Does The

Order have French military power here in the Caribbean?"

Tim drew a ragged breath, his voice was choked by the pressure of his shoulders on his throat, "I don't know, I used men hired from America."

Admiral Torren turned back toward Lieutenant Pike, "If the French have become aware that this operation is now compromised, they may have moved more sea power into theater. We must make all haste for Kingston, in the state it is currently in, we could lose it to the French, and the western Caribbean along with it."

'North Wind'
27 Apr 1809
17 Degrees 49' N, 76 Degrees 28' W

"What do you want me to do with the prisoner, sir?" Will asked after Admiral Torren had come to his realization of the possibility of an increased threat from the French in the Caribbean.

"Hang him, shoot him, dump him overboard. It makes no difference to me. He is a criminal unworthy of the food it would take to keep him alive to stand a trial." Admiral Torren dismissed the question with a wave of his cane.

Will could see that the admiral had shifted his focus onto a larger scale of problems. He looked up at Tim, who was still hanging from his wrists, suspended above the bow of North Wind as the Jamaican breeze propelled her along toward

Kingston.

"He could prove to be useful, sir. He may still know more about this group, The Order." Will suggested with a hand extended toward the line holding Tim's wrists. "We can learn nothing from him once he is dead."

Admiral Torren scowled and tapped his cane on the deck with three hard thumps, "He has already murdered one flag officer of the Royal Navy. He sacked Kingston, and caused a mutiny on two warships. How much longer do you want to keep him alive son? The fact that he is still drawing breath is a threat."

Will squinted his eyes and gave Tim a hard look, taking in the sight of him stretched out. He was in pain. Not nearly the same pain that Will had endured, but there was no denying his discomfort. "I agree, sir. But he may still be of use." Will took a deep breath and turned back toward the admiral, "Nobody wants to see this man meet his end more than I. But, for now, it may be in our best interest to keep him alive. He may have more information, about the French or the corrupted East India officials."

Admiral Torren furrowed his brow beneath his hat and tipped his head forward until his chin was nearly touching the front of his uniform coat, "So be it. We will spare him this day. But, if he instigates any further trouble, with the crew or otherwise, it will be a pistol shot to the head and a swift shove overboard. Do I make myself clear?"

"Yes sir." Will replied, while signaling the line crew to lower Tim back down to the deck.

The American gasped in a lungful of breath when the pressure was relieved from his arms, "Thank you," he croaked as he collapsed onto the wooden deck boards.

Will curled his upper lip for a second, "Do not thank me. This is only a reprieve. You will meet justice before this ordeal is over, and I promise, it will be a fitting end for you."

Admiral Torren stepped close to the crumpled American prisoner, "The slightest hint of trouble from you, and I will see to fulfilling that. Personally. Admiral Sharpe was one of my oldest and dearest friends. Every breath you draw is another you do not deserve. Remember that."

Tim coughed and attempted to hold out his hands toward the admiral in a feeble gesture of surrender, "I won't resist. I promise."

Admiral Torren plucked his cane off of the deck and snapped his hand around the middle, he looked back at Will, "See to it the prisoner is returned to his cell. This ship is yours, inform me when we have sighted Kingston, it shouldn't be much after dawn tomorrow."

Will nodded his assent and rendered a salute as the Admiral left to make his way toward his cabin with Lieutenant Thatcher hot on his heels. He looked back down at Tim as he writhed on the deck with a storm of conflict in his guts. Will gestured to the sailors that had escorted the prisoner on deck,

"Take him below and see him back into his cell." He watched as the sailors jostled Tim back to his feet and kept his gaze locked onto the American as he was escorted off the weather deck. The pain in his ribs and back flared. His wounds were healing, slowly and stubbornly, but the consistent cleaning and application of fresh bandages had done wonders. His hands were still a mess of scabbed cuts and abrasions, as well as his face and neck. The uniform coat he wore rubbed the wounds on his neck and irritated them with each movement. The pain was aggravating, but Will endured it. He was thankful beyond measure to be restored to the good graces of Admiral Torren. The uniform coat, while uncomfortable, reminded him of the vindication he had received, the honor that was restored.

The wind blowing off of Jamaica's coast continued to fill North Wind's sails as she pressed her way westward along the coastline. Will watched the green hills and forests slip by as gulls squawked and cawed overhead. The smell of the sea, the salt and freshness on the air, the sun on his shoulders, it was all a far cry from the cramped and miserable conditions he had endured for the last few weeks. The scene around him was beautiful. The sea ranged from bluish gray close by North Wind's hull to deep sapphire blue closer toward the shore. The foliage of Jamaica was as green as Will had ever seen as it fluttered in the wind. In places, the rocky shores were replaced by beaches of sand so whitened by the sun that it almost hurt his eyes to look on them for more than a moment. Will inhaled deep as a mist of seawater splashed and gently caressed his scarred and scabbed face. Further astern, a leadsman called out his reading which was promptly repeated and recorded by a midshipman near the helm. Bells pealed with the hour, whistles followed orders being relayed on deck, the waves slapped against North Wind's hull and ropes creaked and groaned as the massive warship pushed her way along the coastline. Will savored every moment, every sound, every smell. This was the life he loved, before everything had become so complicated. The simplicity of wind and sails, procedure and order, structure. In his heart he wrestled with the fate of the American, Tim Sladen. Will knew that the prisoner could likely prove to be of further use, but the image of Admiral Sharpe collapsing in a cloud of gun smoke while that sickening grin spread across Tim's face just would not leave him. *I could go below deck right now and run him right through with my saber and the admiral would not utter a word about it.* Will pondered the idea for a moment. It would be a savage scene in Tim's cell filled with half rotten damp straw and a waste bucket overflowing with urine and excrement. Will imagined him laying on the deck, blood pooling into the wet timbers as it poured for a belly wound Will had just inflicted. The thought brought an excited feeling into his chest while at the same time giving him a queasy unrest in his belly. His fingers ached to grasp the handle of his sword and storm below deck to dispatch justice to Admiral Sharpe's murderer. The man who had orchestrated a trap and sunk the majority of the Royal Navy's Caribbean fleet. The images of that day still hung in his mind. Admiral Sharpe collapsing after the shot was fired. The blood that soaked through his uniform coat. The hellfire that ensued afterward in front of the governor's mansion and the mad withdrawal they made through town only to come under fire from Fort Charles. Will could still hear the screams of sailors echoing through his mind, the image of H.M.S Hunter as she caught fire, the way Bayonet had begun to list over after receiving a volley from the fort guns.

"Did you hear that, sir?" A voice snapped Will back into his present surroundings. His hand was clamped painfully tight around the handle of his sword, it ached as he pried his fingers loose and turned to see who was addressing him. Midshipman Brant rested both hands on the starboard rail and leaned forward with an intent stare toward the Jamaican shore. "I thought I heard gunfire, sir. Small arms, nothing that would threaten us. Did you hear it?"

Will shook his head and rubbed his eyes with his aching sword hand, "No, actually, no I didn't hear anything."

Almost as if on cue to make Will question his sanity a distant pop floated into his ears, carried on the breeze.

"There it is again!" Midshipman Brant remarked, "I heard a couple of them. What do you suppose it could be sir?"

Will scoured the coastline through narrowed eyes, the hills were growing steeper and the sun was settling lower on the horizon. "We are drawing closer to Kingston. I imagine it could be the same brigands that sacked the town. Or, perhaps it is a group of locals fighting to restore the king's peace to the island. We will get to the bottom of it when we make port."

"Suppose it is the men who attacked you and the admiral, sir? What do you think our odds?" Midshipman Brant's face looked toward Will with the sober expression of a young man who had just witnessed one of the most savage fights imaginable.

Will forced a smile, "We still have a fair share of our marine contingent, and my guess is that the people of Kingston will likely aid us in the fight, should we have to retake the fort as well as the town. I wouldn't bet against us, were I a gambling man."

"Are you a gambler, sir?" Midshipman Brant asked with a smile.

Will chuckled, smiling back as far as the scabbed wounds on his face would allow, "I am an officer of a warship in his majesty's naval service. I have to be."

Both men looked out to the coast as the sun set and the sounds of more gunshots floated in on the evening breeze. Will could feel a tightening in his stomach with every lone shot and each volley of many. There was a fight occurring somewhere out of his sight, and judging by the sound of it, a very lopsided affair at that.

'Havana's Mistress'
28 Apr 1809
19 Degrees 35' N, 73 Degrees 01' W

Dawn bloomed across the eastern skies over the shadowy silhouette of the Haitian island. Oranges and pink streaked high into the heavens where birds were taking flight in their search for an early morning meal. The wind that carried Havana's Mistress had an edge of cool to it as mist from the waves rode its wispy fingers up over the ships rail and settled on Lilith's skin. She watched the coastline closely. Tall rocky bluffs jutted up from the water's edge ahead of Havana's Mistress. Lilith didn't want to miss the opening of the cove. The ragged bandage that covered her wounded eye had been replaced by a cloth of fine red silk one of her crew had looted from Tortuga. The wound she had sustained in the fighting still pained her, but it was better since Renly had cauterized it. While her new ship plodded through the swells along the coastline, Lilith's thoughts centered around Chibs. Had he been able to drag the Maiden from her watery grave? Had Jilhal and Emilia managed to return from their mission of retrieving the tools they needed? Had any of the men and women they had freed made their way to the cove? Would they join her when she set sail?

Lilith scoured the bluffs as the pink hues of dawn played across the rocky surfaces. She pondered what her next move would be. *If Chibs has raised the ship, we will be legend in the Caribbean.* Lilith imagined the talk that would circulate in the pubs of towns like St. Kitts and Barbados. She pictured merchantmen whispering among themselves of a ship that refused to die. She pictured navy men aboard warships trading stories of the time they had encountered the Drowned Maiden, the ship and crew that was blown away in a hail of cannon fire only to return from the depths to resume her reign of terror. Lilith smiled at the thought until she recalled the ship that had put the Maiden under the waves. It was the biggest ship she had ever seen, she'd had more than twice the gun count of the Maiden just on one side. A ship like that would command fear and awe wherever it went. Her broadsides could lay waste to just about anything that floated. Lilith remembered the scheme Chibs and Omibwe had devised to sink a navy ship that had been pursuing the Maiden. It had been a large ship, but not nearly as big as the one that had come about outside of the cove and unleashed the hellfire that had sunk the Maiden.

Lilith heard Renly's voice explaining to some of her new crew how to secure a line, "Loop it back on itself like this, and then cinch her tight. The pressure on the line will keep it secure as long as you do it properly, otherwise it will fall loose." Lilith turned and watched him as he demonstrated securing the line.

"Renly," Lilith called back to get his attention.

"Yes captain!" Renly replied as he finished tightening the line against itself on the rail.

Lilith leaned against the foremast and narrowed her gaze at the one who had at one time been in the service of the Royal Marines. "That navy ship that opened fire on us in the cove, had you ever seen a ship that big?"

Renly stepped toward the bow with a sobered look, "She was a massive beast, either a first or second-rate ship of the line. I have seen plenty that big, but not this far from England. Usually they sail in armada to mass their firepower with other vessels. Given that she was all the way out in the Caribbean, my guess is that she is being used as a flagship for some admiral or other."

Lilith plucked a finger at the wood grain of the rail, "How many men would crew a ship that large?"

Renly cocked his head and winced as he answered, "It varies really. But with a full complement, six hundred men, maybe more."

Lilith's eye opened wide, she felt a hot streak across her forehead, "Six hundred men?"

"At least, captain." Renly answered with a nod.

Lilith let her gaze wander back out over the dawn painted cliffs as they slipped alongside the ship, growing higher and higher as Havana's Mistress continued eastward. She folder her hands and leaned her weight onto her elbows on the ship's railing, "What would it take to sink a ship like that?"

"Two or three ships of equal size and firepower captain. Are you really considering going after her? After what she did to the Maiden? We barely escaped with our lives, and lost many more than survived." Renly relied with a concerned tone, "Meeting a ship like that in the open, it's just not within our grasp."

Lilith drew a slow breath, she had an idea for what she wanted. She wanted to watch the behemoth tear apart as the seas swallowed her. She wanted the survivors to spread the word about the ship they had destroyed that had risen from the grave. She wanted to scorch the fear of the Drowned Maiden into every seafaring man in the world. "If her magazine caught fire? That would spell her doom. Wouldn't it?"

"Plain as day captain. The problem is getting close enough to her to penetrate her hull without being blown all to pieces. It's no easy task." Renly stroked the stubble that lined his jaw, "And landing a shot into her magazine will be close to impossible, it will be centrally located in the ship, just for that reason. That's a lot of timbers to break through. It may even be below the water line, in which case, we would be better off trying to light her hull ablaze."

Lilith had let her gaze drop to the rolling wash of seawater that frothed in front of Havana's Mistress as her hull pushed its way forward. The white that capped along the top crest of blue gray water surged with each pitch of the deck. "Where do you think her commander would have set course for, after our engagement?"

Renly leaned back on one heel and craned his neck to look upward as if he were inspecting the rigging overhead. "Hard to say, captain. There's no shortage of British ports and colonies in the Caribbean. But given the state of things, with what happened to the fleet and the governor of Jamaica, I would say he probably set his sails for Kingston."

Lilith let her hands come to rest on the pommel of her cutlass. She imagined the giant warship anchored at harbor beneath the protection of a towering fort and sheltered by a series of jagged reefs. "She would be protected in the harbor at Kingston, would she not?"

Renly nodded at his captain's shoulder and leaned against the rail next to her, "It would be suicide to attack her there."

Lilith let her gaze trace over the tops of the cliffs looming to the north of Havana's Mistress. The air was sweet with the smell of the sea and traces of the fragrant flowers and fruits of the island. She caught a faint wisp of smoke smell on the breeze. Havana's Mistress was not a warship by any stretch of the imagination, her gun deck was mostly stuffed with excess cargo that did not fit in the hold below and what guns she did have were much smaller than those the Maiden had. She wasn't particularly fast, nor agile, Havana's Mistress had been built with the strict intention of hauling trade goods from one port to another. Lilith pondered the possibilities in her mind. Perhaps luring the big warship out to sea, to draw her away from the supporting fire of the fort. Lilith pictured Havana's Mistress collapsing beneath a furious hail of cannon fire. It would be a repeat of the Drowned Maiden, out manned, out matched, out gunned. If the Maiden were in fighting shape, she could maneuver the more agile frigate around the big warship's fields of fire, but only with a favorable wind. Attempt after attempt ran through Lilith's mind. They all ended in the same frustrating conclusion, with her ships ablaze and blown full of holes. An assault on the ship at harbor was suicide. Luring her out to sea offered a slim chance of success, but any crew she had manning Havana's Mistress would be cannon fodder, and the chances of success still would be slim. It was a price Lilith wasn't willing to pay. Attacking the great warship seemed to be out of her reach.

Renly's voice cut through Lilith's thoughts, "Captain, any engagement ship to ship with her would be folly, in my mind. But if you are determined to see her to the bottom, there are other ways."

Lilith raised a brow and looked at Renly, "Go

on."

"You have the right idea. Setting her magazine aflame would surely be the death stroke to a ship that large. But, engaging her in a battle at sea or at anchor would be playing right to her strengths. We need to find a weakness and exploit it." Renly looked over his shoulder at the crew he had been training on the deck of Havana's Mistress. "They outnumber us. They have us outgunned. And even with the Maiden, we couldn't hope to maneuver around them quick enough to inflict fatal damage before they blew us to pieces." He drew a deep breath and scrunched his face as he continued, "The guns of Fort Charles cover the entirety of the harbor. She has big guns too, and a furnace with which to heat their cannon shot. That gives them the capability to fire red hot cannon balls at an enemy ship, not blasting a hole in their hull, but setting her timbers to burn once the shot has lodged in them. The fort is at a high elevation from the harbor as well, not only making it easier for them to range and fire but also making it nearly impossible for an attacking ship to return effective fire."

Lilith furrowed her brow and let her eye fall toward the deck at her feet, "I'm beginning to think it may be a fool's errand."

"Oh it is." Renly interrupted, "But not an impossible one." He gestured toward the shores of Haiti, "The problem that warship's commander will have, once he makes anchor in Kingston, is that he will have to restore the peace and secure the town. By now I am sure the mercenaries that attacked Lieutenant Pike and out crew have either fled or dug themselves in. Either way, it will take a significant number of the warship's crew to secure the fort and restore the town."

"Leaving her in the harbor, with most of her crew ashore." Lilith observed, "But she would still be protected by the guns of the fort, wouldn't she?"

Renly smiled at Lilith and nodded his head, "She would. And there lies her weakness."

Lilith wrinkled her nose as she tried to imagine what Renly could be thinking. He had just described how foolish it would be to attack the warship in harbor. "I don't follow Renly, you just said the warship was beyond our reach when she is in the harbor."

"No, captain. I said it would be folly to attack her from our ships." Renly smiled and cocked his head at an angle, "But at anchor, under the protection of the fort, and with much of her crew ashore in Kingston, she will likely be at half watch or even less. Sailing a ship into the harbor would be the last act of a madman, or woman. But, a more subtle approach would likely go unnoticed until it was too late."

Lilith's ears perked and her mind raced at the possibility Renly suggested, "Like a sneak attack?"

Renly smiled ever broader, "Yes captain, a clandestine attack is what we would call it."

The smile that spread across Lilith's face was

uncontrollable. The cliffs rising from the rocky shores gave way to a narrow inlet. The cove was in sight. Between the jutting rises of rock, Lilith felt her breath seize in her chest as she scanned the waters inside the cove for the hulk of the Maiden that had been jutting out of the surface where she had last seen it. As Havana's Mistress moved further past the opening of the cove she came into Lilith's sight. Her hull was dark and sleek except for a few places where new timbers had replaced the shattered remains of old ones. She was beached high in the sandy shore, with lines trailing away from her masts.

Renly called over his shoulder to the helm of Havana's Mistress, "Come about larboard!"

Lilith could see the figures of her crew walking along the beach and on the Maiden's decks. Havana's Mistress angled her way into the cove and past the wrecks of the ships Lilith had laid to waist on the reef. The hulks of the wreckage looked like they had been picked clean of everything that could be used. *Clever bastards used everything they could get their hands on.* As she sailed her way further into the cove, Lilith spotted a pair of long wooden trunks that had been prepared to replace sections of mast. She turned and looked at Renly, "They did it! They brought her back!"

Renly returned the captain's smile and set a foot up on the gunwale, "Aye, captain! Wonders never cease, they brought her back from the dead!"

PART THREE
"SEA BASTARD"

Chapter 11

'Batard De Mur
28 Apr 1809
18 Degrees 49' N, 73 Degrees 38' W

A shower of sparks mixed with acrid gun smoke flew out of the cannons bore. The first shot broke through the silence of night like the opening thunder crack of a storm. Captain Fontaine leered through the haze of cannon smoke and moonlight at the ship that had spent the last few hours closing distance on Batard De Mur. Silvery moonlight glistened on the water's surface and sparkled like a million dark gems over the ripples and waves separating the two vessels. Voices cut through the night as Batard De Mur's first shot laced through one of the trailing vessel's sails.

Pirate hunters. Whatever the nationality of the vessel off of his stern, there could be no misinterpreting now. Batard De Mur would be exchanging no pleasantries at sea, with anyone. Captain Fontaine's ears perked up as the voices came in again. He recognized a few words. They were speaking French. He wondered if they were in league with Captain Callais somehow. *This entire scheme to find the girl pirate could be a trap. They could be luring me into shallow waters to surround me with an armada and finally rid themselves of the crew who would not comply.* Captain Fontaine examined the moonlit shores for a long moment before looking back at the vessel he had just fired a shot at. *They'll learn soon enough.* He traded his glances between the shoreline and the ship behind him several more times, judging their speed relative to his and trying to get a feel for how nimble they were. The Haitian coast stretched along to the south, now running east to west as far as he could see. These were treacherous waters for anyone unaccustomed to the dangers that lay hidden beneath the surface. Most law-abiding trade vessels avoided these shores. Occasionally a smuggler could be found navigating his way through the quagmire of reefs and shoals as they ferried their illicit cargoes between Port-Au-Prince and whatever destination the captain had in mind. Fishermen avoided these waters, though their crafts were mostly small enough that the obstacles beneath the surface were of no threat to them, these waters had a history of dangers that sailed on the surface. Captain Fontaine had charts of this shore more accurate than any man alive. Over years he had painstakingly recorded measurements along this stretch of coast while prowling for any vessel unfortunate enough to come across his path.

A shout drifted in across the sea gap and Captain Fontaine narrowed his eye at the vessel off of his stern. A group of men were at the bow making ready one of their chaser cannons.

"Helm, hard a-larboard. She's making ready to fire back, let's give them a taste of our guns."

Batard De Mur cut a sharp turn with agile precision as the pursuing vessel fired a clumsy shot. The cannon ball whistled harmlessly past, missing Batard De Mur entirely and slicing into the night air as she came about to bear her guns down on the hapless attackers. Captain Fontaine gripped the pommel of his cutlass and waited for his batteries to come into line with the ship. Moonlight traced over her sails, illuminating her in a soft silvery glow. The breeze was gentle but steady and Batard De Mur made her maneuver with grace and precision. As the bow of his target presented itself to his cannons Captain Fontaine drew the cutlass lashed to his waist, he held the blade up in the air and swung it downward the moment he was satisfied with his angle toward the other ship. Almost as one the cannons erupted into a thunder roll of fire that spewed smoke and flashed bright light into the air. *They won't have us quietly. I'll fire every shot and every grain of powder. I'll swing my blade until my arms give out. They took everything from me, I won't give them anything else.* The barrage of shot found its mark, filling the moonlit night with the sounds of shattering timbers, snapping lines and tearing canvas. Without a word of command, Captain Fontaine's crew was already preparing to fire their guns again. Shouts from below deck mingled in the night with screams from the enemy vessel. The first salvo had already yielded serious damage to the pursuing vessel. A few shots fired from the deck of the wounded ship, muskets and swivel gun fire cracked through the air and bit into Batard De Mur's deck and hull. It was a pathetic gesture that Captain Fontaine intended to repay with another full broadside.

"Guns ready captain!" the shout came from below deck.

Captain Fontaine drew a quick breath and replied, "Fire!"

A series of flashes erupted from the side of Batard De Mur, sending a volley of cannon shot whistling into the already wounded ship. Captain Fontaine squeezed the grip of his sword and drove it in front of him, stabbing at the thick night air in the direction of the enemy ship. "Prepare to board!"

A raucous cheer rose from the deck of Batard De Mur as her crew began to arm themselves. Clouds of smoke drifted over the water from the ship they had fired on and cut the moonlight down to a silvery haze. Captain Fontaine's crew tossed grapple hooks as the two vessels drew closer and began pulling them tight. The deck of the wounded ship was a chaotic mess of wounded men crawling to escape the coming onslaught and sailors either struggling to fight a fire that had broken out or arming themselves to repel the imminent attack. Light from the fire washed upward and flashed across Captain Fontaine's face. He smiled as he saw the bedlam already taking place aboard the ship. *I ought to leave one alive to drift into the mainland and spread the news.* Screams echoed from the wounded. Threats and insults were exchanged as the two ships were hauled in close to each other. Pistols and muskets fired, a wooden gangplank dropped across the gap between ships. The sounds of battle rang out through the night and filled Captain Fontaine's ears. Swords collided. Pistols fired. Men screamed out in anger or in pain. Chaos consumed the deck of the ship they had boarded. Captain Fontaine crossed the gang plank with a sword in one hand and a loaded pistol in the other. He wasted no time in firing the pistol at the nearest enemy crewman he found and swung his sword at another. The fight was short lived. Within the first few minutes of boarding the enemy vessel Captain Fontaine and the crew of the Batard De Mur managed to kill or subdue all the resisting sailors on deck.

"Enough!" A voice shouted over the havoc that consumed the ship, "Enough of this! I yield! The ship is yours!"

A hush fell over both crews. Captain Fontaine smiled and looked toward the source of the voice.

The ship's captain stood near the helm. He held a sword in one hand and a length of chain in the other. Captain Fontaine raised his blade and pointed it toward the surrendering captain, "Do you think I want this rotten tub?"

The captain's face twisted in a shocked expression of confusion, "You turned to board us! Why else?"

"You saw our red sails. You turned to and closed with us. Surely you know who I am, who we are."

"We are searching for a pirate crew."

"And you have found one."

The surrendering captain shook his head, "You are not the crew or vessel we set out in search of."

Captain Fontaine lifted a brow and lowered his sword point as he stepped closer to the surrendering captain, "You are searching for the girl?"

"Aye. The girl pirate and her crew sail on a frigate named 'The Drowned Maiden'. We set sail under contract to find them and return with proof of her death and the ship as a prize." The captain's words came uneasy, his hesitation mounting as Fontaine drew closer. "She has interrupted valuable trade lines and drawn a hefty price on her head."

Captain Fontaine's ears perked as he heard the mention of a bounty, "And how much is offered for the girl's death?"

The surrendering captain swallowed hard and drew a ragged breath, "Enough to make a whole crew rich."

Captain Fontaine scrunched his nose and narrowed his eye at the surrendering man, "I was offered similar terms."

The captain's face eased for a moment. A smile began to spread across his mouth, "Then we should join together. There is no need for us to squabble." His face tightened when Captain Fontaine did not share his expression.

"No, captain. I don't think we will be joining our cause with yours." Captain Fontaine turned and made a motion towards his men with one hand. The crew of The Batard De Mur resumed the slaughter, hacking down sailors who had lowered their weapons in surrender. "I think I would rather keep the girl as a prize for myself." Captain Fontaine plunged his saber into the man's belly and sunk it all the way to the hilt. The surrendering captain's eyes widened in shock and pain, he looked at Captain Fontaine with a pleading expression, opening his mouth to form words that wouldn't come. "Shhhhh." Captain Fontaine urged, "Just let go. When you see your masters in the afterlife, you can tell them I am taking back what the order has robbed me of. All of it."

Pirate Cove
28 Apr 1809

Her sails fluttered as she made her way into the cove. From his place on the white sandy shore Chibs watched as the two masted brigantine edged past the mouth of the cove and turned inward, sailing past the reef and what was left of the shipwrecks it had devoured. She was standing high on the prow when he first saw her, a red silk sash had replaced the cloth bandage covering her wounded eye, but there was no mistaking Captain Lilith. Voices rose from the beach as her ship crept further into the cove, "Lilith! Captain Lilith! The captain is back!" Chibs could not control his smile as the crew he had been laboring with dropped their lines and tools and rushed to the water's edge to greet their chosen commander. She was the picture of triumph, leaning out from the bowsprit with a stay line in hand. Chibs felt a rush of pride as he looked on her. He remembered the night they had dragged her out of the water, choking and hacking and gagging after she had drowned in the Port-Au-Prince harbor. The first fencing lesson Trina had given her after she tossed a cutlass into the girl's hand. Now she was sailing into the cove on a ship she had taken, to a crew she had gathered and rescuing him.

Chibs looked up the beach to find young Omibwe struggling through the soft sands toward the water's edge. Jilhal followed close behind him, with a score of the new crewmen at her back. The Maiden wasn't seaworthy quite yet, but with a fresh boost from the reappearance of their captain, the crew would want to have her ready as quickly as possible. Lilith wouldn't want to linger here for very long. The navy ship that had opened fire on the Maiden could be prowling anywhere in the Caribbean, and she would want to settle the score. As he thought of it, Chibs felt the joy of seeing Lilith return leave him, he knew he would have to convince her away from tracking down the massive warship. Even with two vessels at her command, the behemoth was out of their grasp. She was far heavier, manned by six to eight hundred men, and had more than twice as many guns that would all be much larger than the nine and twelve-pound cannons sported by the Maiden.

The brigantine's sails slacked and Lilith spotted Chibs on the beach.

"What do you think of our new ship?" she called out from the bow.

Chibs smiled across the gap of water that separated them, "She's a fine ship, Captain."

"She will see better use from us than her former masters." Lilith replied as she dropped to the deck of the brig. "She doesn't have much in the way of gunnery, and she is slow and cumbersome, but her hold is full of all manner of goods. Powder, food, ale, there's even some tobacco aboard."

Chibs smiled at the thought, he could use a proper meal. The fish Omibwe caught and the fruits they found around the cove had been barely sufficient to keep everyone fed. And it had been weeks since Chibs had been able to fill his pipe and enjoy the rich smoothness of a smoke. His mouth watered at the prospect, "That sounds amazing Cap'n."

Chibs watched as the crew aboard Lilith's newly acquired brig lowered a small rowboat over the side and she launched ashore with a few of her new hands. There were faces he didn't recognize. He marveled at how the young woman had gone from a drowned fish, sputtering and coughing seawater on the deck of Captain James ship, to commanding as much fear and respect as the old captain ever had. The crew ashore gathered at water's edge, awaiting their captain. Chibs could feel as much anticipation from them as he felt while Lilith's band aboard her small boat rowed her into the beach. As the boat's keel rubbed into the soft sands she was inundated by the crew, men and women, new and old. Chibs stood by at the back of the crowd and waited for Lilith to disperse the supplies she had on the rowboat. A crate of hard bread, a cask of salted beef and a small barrel of fresh water were unloaded and handed into the waiting hands of the men and women surrounding her.

"You had me worried captain." Chibs called over the din of the crew as they hauled off their fresh supplies.

Lilith gave him a smile, "You know better than to

worry over me Chibs. I can take care of myself."

Chibs let his good hand come to rest on the pommel of his sword, "I didn't say I was worried about you. I worried you would tear off across the Caribbean without me."

Lilith chuckled and winced; Chibs noticed her hand drift toward a spot on her hip. She was wearing different clothes than when they had last parted, and her gait favored her right side more than usual. "Tortuga won't soon forget us. We managed to free the slaves held at a boiling house just outside of town. I hadn't intended on fighting the town garrison, but it sort of turned out that way."

Chibs frowned as Lilith held her side while she spoke, he asked, "Are you hurt?"

She nodded, "A bayonet caught me in my side. Renly fixed me up as good as he could have, but it still pains me. Is Doctor LeMeux still with us? Or have you run him off?"

Chibs couldn't help but smile, "No, Cap'n. He is still here with us. You might be safe having him look at it, I don't think he would try to cut off your hip."

Lilith grimaced at Chibs jest, "Let's hope not."

Chibs reached out his arm and wrapped it around her shoulders, "For his sake."

The two walked up the white sandy strip towards the Drowned Maiden, Lilith remained quiet for a long moment until they were both close enough to reach out and touch the wooden hull.

"How did you do it Chibs? I thought she was lost to us."

Chibs beamed with pride, "It wasn't all me." He motioned toward Omibwe, who was helping the crew unload more supplies out of the rowboat. "Our young helmsman there is quite the diver. Without him, I'm afraid the Maiden would have been lost to us forever." Chibs reached out and rubbed his hand on the Maiden's hull, "She's not quite seaworthy yet. We have several days of hard work still ahead of us, masts must be tipped into place, yards secured and lines re-rigged. But I imagine with the extra help and a good meal in their bellies, we can have her ready in three days."

Lilith squinted her eye, "The rudder?"

Chibs nodded, "Already seen to Cap'n. We couldn't have done it if it weren't for the tools that Jilhal and Emilia brought us."

"And what about her guns?" Lilith asked, reaching up and rubbing a hand along the hull herself.

"Two of ours were ruined beyond repair in the fight. The rest are being cleaned up and ready for action." Chibs informed her, "Jilhal suggested salvaging the deck cannons off of the wrecks stuck on the reef. We managed to secure three of her guns, nine pounders. They're in fair condition, considering they have been sitting unattended for quite a while. Guns we have, dry powder is another matter entirely. We set out quite a bit to dry, though I'm not sure it will still be as potent as before."

"There is powder aboard the ship we took from Tortuga, several barrels of it in fact, though it is loose. We will have to sew it in bags." Lilith replied while walking along the length of the Maiden with her hand on the hull. "We will take them both to sea, Chibs. We'll need them both for the fight to come."

Chibs heart sank into his stomach, "Are you meaning to go after her? That behemoth from the Royal Navy?"

Lilith turned back to Chibs with a steely look in her remaining eye, "I am."

For a moment, Chibs couldn't find the words to use. A breeze floated into the cove off of the Caribbean, tousling Lilith's curly hair and the silky red sash covering her maimed eye. She seemed dead set on exacting her price from the Royal Navy. Chibs knew the Maiden stood little to no chance against the vastly superior vessel. In open water the Maiden would be blown down by her guns. The Maiden and her crew may prolong the inevitable by maneuvering around the massive ship and trying to fire on them from angles outside of their fields of fire. But the end result would be the same as it had in the cove. As soon as the Maiden came under the view of their guns they would be bombarded in a furious hell storm of heavy flying shot. In close quarters would be just as catastrophic, if they managed to surprise the bigger ship and get the first volley in, the crew of the big line ship would without a doubt recover quickly and return their fire tenfold. Every scenario Chibs could concoct in his mind ended with the same result, the Drowned Maiden plunging beneath the surface after being shattered by cannon fire.

"Cap'n, I don't know how to say this..." Chibs began to speak.

Lilith interrupted, "You think it is a fool's errand?"

Relief washed over Chibs like a wave from the tide stretching up on the sandy beach, "I do."

Lilith pursed her lips for a second and then shook her head, "I won't just slink away Chibs. They came because they know what we are doing. They came because we have liberated. They can't allow us to continue, but we must."

"Cap'n, we can outrun them, even out of favor with the wind The Maiden is still faster." Chibs contended with a streak of hope in his voice, "The slave ships, the plantations, we can still hit them. We just have to be smarter than they are. I know we can do it, James did it for months."

Lilith's expression ran cold, "And where is James now?"

Chibs couldn't argue with her, she refused to be swayed. He looked up at the hull of the Maiden, it seemed like all of his work in bringing her back from the dead would be for one last suicidal voyage. "Do you mean to join him? That is what lies ahead for us if we meet that ship in battle Cap'n. She has too many guns. Too many men."

Lilith withdrew her hand from the hull of the Maiden and let it rest on the pommel of her sword, "I never said anything about meeting her in battle."

Chibs fought to understand, "I'm confused, deary. I asked if you meant to go after them."

"You did," Lilith replied, "And I do. But I have no intention of meeting them ship to ship. We have done that once, and lost."

"But you mean to attack her all the same?" Chibs pushed to see if she had a plan in mind.

"I do. I mean to watch that ship burn while her crew races to abandon her to the depths, just as she did to us." Lilith answered with a spark in her eye and a cold edge on her voice, "Tell me, Chibs, where do you think that ship would be most vulnerable."

Chibs scratched the back of his head, trying to understand where Lilith had her course set, "I'm not sure Cap'n. Were she at anchor with crew ashore, that would be one thing. I suppose in tight quarters around certain reefs, but a ship like that will have seasoned commanders and navigators, I don't think running them aground would work."

Lilith shook her head and smiled, "You're still thinking like a sailor, Chibs. Think like a damned pirate. When would a ship with all of those guns, and all of those men, be vulnerable to an attack?"

Exasperated, and struggling for an answer, Chibs relented, "I'm not sure Cap'n. It's hard to say."

Lilith beamed a clever smile, "When she doesn't see us coming."

'North Wind'
29 Apr 1809
17 Degrees 55' N, 76 Degrees 44' W

"Twenty fathoms, bottom of white sand." The leadsman called back toward the helm through the darkness that had enveloped North Wind. He had kept his voice low, just as the recording officer did in return. Moonlight lit the way for North Wind as she crept along the Jamaican coast, a monster prowling off the shore under the pale glow. Less than a mile the green hills and forests of Jamaica appeared as black as ink as they rose from the white strip of beach that lined the island against the briny gray sea.

Lieutenant Pike had ordered all bells, whistles and loud calls on deck to cease as the sun had dipped below the horizon. He had also ordered all lamps to be put out as they ran along the coast in darkness. With the moon in the late stages of her waxing phase, it was an astute decision in Admiral Torren's mind though the admiral had kept his praise quiet for the time being. Light from the moon allowed North Wind to continue to navigate Jamaica's southern coast and was sufficient to allow the crew to see what they were doing on deck. Lamp light would only serve to make North Wind easier to spot from shore. Kingston lay ahead of them, just over the western horizon by the admiral's reckoning. He had made the calculations himself the preceding late afternoon. His plan was to approach the harbor and launch a landing party while North Wind was still outside the reach of Fort Charles. If the landing party was fired on, he would know for a certainty that the fort remained in enemy hands. If they made it into the harbor, he would send a following party to help ascertain the disposition of the town and secure Fort Charles and its guns. Then in the light of day the admiral would order North Wind to ease her way into the harbor. After that, the real work would commence.

Admiral Torren came on deck for the second time during the night, conducting his habitual brisk walk around perimeter of the ship while observing the crew and officers. He stopped for a moment on the bow and took in the sight of the Jamaican coast. He had spent much of his career facing unknowns from engagements at the Virginia Capes and the Nile to the constant cat and mouse games along France's northern and western coasts. Admiral Torren was familiar with sailing into unknowns, but this time he felt a razor edge of caution where once a bold determination existed. The possibility of arriving in Kingston to find a French garrison occupying Fort Charles was real enough, especially given his new discovery of the close ties between Napoleon and the effort to smuggle slaves. Or, they may come to Kingston and find a force of Americans. Perhaps the townsfolk had beaten back the mercenaries that took Fort Charles and fired on the Caribbean fleet. Or, perhaps they had slunk off into the Jamaican countryside and would remain a constant threat while Admiral Torren and North Wind tried to reestablish law and order. Even if they landed and found no armed opposition, his hold on Kingston would be tenuous until reinforcements could be secured and transported to Jamaica.

"Eighteen fathoms, white sand and broken coral." The leadsman's voice announced, drawing the admiral's mind back to their task of navigating to Kingston under the cover of darkness.

"Helm, come over a point larboard." Lieutenant Pike's order hung above the deck as North Wind made a minor course adjustment.

Admiral Torren had been concerned that the time Pike had spent as a prisoner aboard the ship would degrade their confidence in him. It seemed the opposite, the lieutenant's orders were followed just as swiftly as if they had come from the mouth of the admiral himself. In fact, the lieutenant seemed to share a camaraderie with some of the sailors that even the officers who had been aboard North Wind when she set out from England lacked. His judgment seemed well enough, though the admiral had only witnessed him navigating minor sail changes and small course corrections. The truer test would come when it was time to make landfall.

Kingston lay just beyond the horizon, and Admiral Torren knew who he would send into shore in the first vessel. Lieutenant Thatcher was too inept to command a fleet of bath toys, much less a landing contingent. Midshipman Brant was enthusiastic and loyal, but again, too inexperienced to trust with such a critical matter. If the officer he sent ashore did not make headway immediately, any enemy forces would mount their defenses and the task would become nearly impossible. Lieutenant Pike was an experienced enough officer to handle such a task. In addition to command experience, he held another quality that Admiral Torren deemed necessary for this specific task. He was completely expendable. If the fort should open fire and obliterate the longboat, the admiral would simply devise a new plan and push on.

Wind popped in the canvas sails over the admiral's head. He looked up just in time to catch the sails flutter again before Lieutenant Pike issued an order to have them adjusted. Admiral Torren grinned in the shadow of his hat brim in the moonlight. He was pleased with how his flagship was being handled. North Wind was a gargantuan ship, but Lieutenant Pike had her clipping along as if she were a frigate. The crew were in high spirits, everything considered, and even the admiral caught himself grinning from time to time as he made his rounds on deck. The warmth of the Caribbean had done little to quell his aching joints and throbbing feet. He found little solace outside of hammering laps around the hard wooden deck and casting scowls out to sea as if they were full broadsides aimed at some invisible enemy. Admiral Torren woke every morning in pain and surrendered to the evenings in much the same condition. *Still preferable to listening to that entitled nitwit Admiral Becker. I'll take the discomfort if the sea comes with it.*

"Twenty-two fathoms, sir. Sandy bottom." The leadsman called again in a soft voice.

Lieutenant Pike responded immediately, "Helm, hold your course there. Kingston should be off our starboard flank within a few hours." He turned to Midshipman Brant, "See the men to quarters. Silently. We need all batteries at the ready and marines in the tops. Have a detachment stood up to accompany me ashore when we get closer. We'll need to launch while North Wind is still outside of cannon range."

"Aye, sir. Do you have anyone particular in mind for your landing party?" the fresh-faced midshipman asked.

Admiral Torren braced himself to hear what he knew was coming next, the young officer was hopping mad to see some action. "If I could, lieutenant. It could prove to be a valuable experience for me."

Lieutenant Pike's gaze wandered the deck before landing on Admiral Torren, "Sir, would you have any objections to the midshipman joining the first wave ashore?"

The admiral came to a stop on deck and turned to face both officers. Conflict arose within him. He had grown rather fond of the young midshipman and saw a bright future for him in the King's Navy, and while he did not want to see the young officer blown to smithereens should Fort Charles be manned by some enemy force, he could not abide keeping the young man out of the fray for safety's sake. "I harbor no objections, so long as the young man understands exactly what he is about to partake in." The admiral turned and faced Midshipman Brant, offering a half grimace, "The first boat to make for shore will be facing some perilous danger should Fort Charles be occupied by a hostile force. When the boat is spotted, if it is spotted, the fort will open fire on it with its heavy guns and all manner of small arms. Should that happen, there will be no survivors. If the boat should somehow make it through the harbor and make landfall, they will be facing a complete unknown. It could be the Americans or French occupying the town, or perhaps even rebel slaves or bandits. There will be precious few of ours ashore to hold ground until reinforcements arrive and the best-case scenario for them is an extended fight involving heavy casualties." The admiral took a breath and paused, taking measure if his words were swaying the young officer. They were not. "Even if the fort is unoccupied, and there is no hostile force holding Kingston, both unlikely, we face the high likelihood of a hostile reception. It is almost guaranteed you will see combat face to face."

Midshipman Brant looked eager as ever, "Whatever we face, sir, I wish to accompany Lieutenant Pike and the landing party ashore."

Admiral Torren felt a swell of pride rising in his chest. He recalled a situation involving Midshipman Brant's father almost two decades prior, he had been similarly resolved. "Very well, midshipman. You shall accompany the first boat ashore. Be sure to draw weapons and ammunition from the master at arms."

Pirate Cove
29 Apr 1809

Lilith loved many things about sailing on the open water of the seas. The smell of the salty brine, the freshness of the air. There were plenty of smells aboard ship. Some were not as pleasant as others. The cramped space where dozens of men lived in Caribbean heat was not a pleasant smell. But the smell of the timber that surrounded her cabin was. The earthy richness of wood mixed with Chibs lingering pipe smoke had a way of instantly making her feel at home no matter what scene lay outside her cabin. The briny smell of the sea as it splashed against the Maiden's hull while she was at full sail and making headway gave her a feeling of freedom and wanderlust. The fresh air that swept in on the breeze when there was no land anywhere in sight gave Lilith a thirst to press onward, constantly seeking the horizon. The sounds of the water rushing past the Maiden's hull while her crew called out to each other and made sail adjustments brought her a joy she couldn't quite fit into words. The Maiden was her home. She was the only true home Lilith had ever known. Lilith had no fondness in her heart for the plantation she had grown up on. It had been a place of torment, somewhere she had dreamed of escaping and never returning to. The Maiden was somewhere she longed to be. Lilith felt like the ship was a part of her, somewhere she belonged with people who both loved and respected her.

That day in the cove, beneath the driving rain and storm clouds, her home had been ripped away from her. Lilith had watched helplessly as the hulking navy ship had relentlessly fired volley after volley, pummeling her ship into a slow surrender to the depths. Lilith had gone inland and found new crewmen and women to join her rag tag family, and while she had been gone Chibs had managed to give her back the home that she loved. Her hull had been restored from a combination of timbers rescued from the wreckage of two navy ships lodged on the reef guarding the mouth of the cove. Her masts had sections and yards replace by freshly felled trees from the Haitian forest that nestled the inside of the cove. Lines had been restrung, canvas had been mended, and the rudder had been repaired. Lilith looked onto her ship as the tide that would bear the Maiden up off of the sandy shore edged its way into the cove gently surrounding the wooden hull.

Lilith sat near the water's edge under a painted evening sky, sand cradled her feet and her bottom as she ran an oiled cloth over her cutlass. The sword felt heavy in her hands, its weight reminded her of the responsibility she carried. The men and women rescued by the Maiden had not left one slave master just to have them replaced by another. They had desired freedom from their tormentors. A say in their own destinies. Chibs voice drifted across the sand and washing tide. He was tirelessly working to prepare the Maiden for her next voyage.

A warm breeze flowed in from the Caribbean and caressed Lilith's face. It tugged at her blouse and tousled her hair. The setting sun stretched shadows from the trees lining the cove's beaches across the water like the first chilly fingers of night were taking hold of the Maiden. Soon, she would be loaded with all of the goods needed for her voyage and Lilith knew that before the night was out she must win the crew to her plan. It was a risk. The majority of the men and women she would have aboard the Maiden were not there to witness the overwhelming power of the big navy ship. They had no personal stake in avenging the lives lost that day. The crew members who were with her would be hesitant to tempt fate again. Lilith's plan was risky. She could be caught out in the open on the journey. A ship-to-ship confrontation with the huge line vessel was a death sentence for the Maiden and every soul aboard. If the navy were able to bring their guns to bear on them, the Maiden would be blown apart out in the open sea where there would be no chance of rescuing her. But as long as they prowled the Caribbean, the Maiden would be under her looming threat. Lilith preferred to keep the rest of the world on edge, not the other way around. She walked through her plan in her mind and tried to imagine it from every angle. There were flaws, for sure, but nothing was without risk, especially for a pirate. A cheer rose from the deck of the Maiden and the crewmen who surrounded her hull.

Lilith pulled herself up onto her feet and brushed away sand that had clung to her legs and trousers. Under the last failing light of day, with a pinkish glow giving way to deep purples and the star spotted blackness of night, the Maiden had finally managed to float up off of the sandy beach. The Maiden would be setting sail soon enough and her crew would want to know what their course would be. Lilith knew if she couldn't convince a majority of them to favor her plan she would lose what crew she had. Chibs had already let his feelings on the matter be known, but Lilith knew that if she set sail to face down the entire British Navy, he would remain at her side. Renly was for the plan, they had already discussed the matter in depth on their trip over from Tortuga. Damriq, Jilhal, Omibwe, Dr.

LeMeux and at least forty others would need convincing. It would be a hard sell, to persuade men and women to face down one of the largest warships to ever prowl the oceans. Some of the crew she would try to convince had watched the deadly barrage of the massive line ship firsthand, the others had heard the tale. Lilith wasn't sure which group would be tougher to convince.

A fire had been lit on shore while Chibs and the rest of the crew were anchoring the Maiden in deeper water towards the center of the cove. Lilith watched while the pirates who had surrounded the Maiden's hull gravitated to the orange and yellow glow of the flames. Soon the small fire was piled high with wood and flames reached higher and higher into the dark night. Dancing shadows played along the trees and the water inside the cove silhouetting the gathered group like the iron fingers of a brazier on the deck of some giant ship. Casks of rum and wine had been brought ashore from the hold of the Havana's Mistress and soon drinks were being passed around and held high as the crew toasted the successful resurrection. Lilith stood on the outside of the gathering as a half-moon rose higher in the night sky. She took in the cool air and the crisp sound of waves rolling up onto the soft sand shores.

"Here's to Chibs! He never gave up on her, even when she was beyond the grasp of lesser men! And all with only one hand! Chibs!" Renly held a mug high and toasted the quartermaster. A roar of agreement filled the space of the cove, echoing off of the tall trees and ringing between the rock faces of the entrance.

Dr. LeMeux held his drink up and appeared to wait for a lull in the shouts so he could raise his own toast. The crew grew louder for a moment until Chibs stepped close to the fire and lifted his drink. Firelight played across Chibs' face highlighting the gray streaks in his beard.

"I've got something to say." Chibs gave Lilith a look and raised his cup toward her, "Here's to Lilith. The captain who has led us against such a number of foes I have lost count. She is brave, she is beautiful, she is smart, but more than anything, she is fierce." He lowered his cup for a second and winked one eye, "Cap'n, I'd follow you anywhere, I'd face the whole Royal Navy if you asked me to."

"To Captain Lilith!" Another shout echoed from the perimeter of the crew. Shouts arose and drinks were lifted.

Lilith smiled at the gesture and walked through the group toward the roaring fire's side, "Everything I have done, I have done for you!" Her voice was loud and strong, and a hush settled over the crew. Someone handed a mug filled with spiced rum and Lilith snatched the drink and upended it, consuming the warm liquid in a long deep drink. When the mug was empty, she wiped the corner of her mouth with her forearm and turned to face the gathered crew. "We have regained our ship!" A cheer ensued and Lilith held up a hand to quiet the uproar. "But our fight is not over! The ship who sunk her in the first place is still out there!" The hush that fell over the crew was telling. Lilith could feel their enthusiasm fade like the heat of day retreating with the sun as it slipped below the western horizon. Flickering firelight danced over the sandy beach and washed over the faces of her crew as Lilith turned and looked them over, examining each one as if she was peering into their hearts with her one good eye. "As long as the Maiden lives, they will never stop hunting her." She paused, letting her gaze fall onto Chibs, "And while the ship that sank her still floats, her name will mean nothing. She will be just another rogue ship, brought low by the mighty Royal Navy and all their guns. But that is not what we are. We are not some band of cowards who are going to slink off into hiding! I say we find her! We find her and we put her on the bottom of the sea just as she did to us!"

A voice called out from the crew circled around her, "How? They out gunned us already!"

Lilith nodded her head and pointed to the crewman who had called out, "Yes. That they did. They outgunned us. They caught us unaware and unable to defend ourselves. But, that is the very weakness I propose we use against them!"

Chibs face was long, Lilith could see he didn't want to say anything, but felt he must, "Cap'n, even if we catch them off guard, as soon as she brings her guns to bear on the Maiden, it will be the same result as last time." His voice was low, as if he did not want the whole crew to hear him disagree with her.

Lilith smiled at the enduring loyalty Chibs had for her. Even when he disagreed, he didn't want to display it to the entire crew. "Aye, it would be the same result. I agree. But I am not proposing to sail the Maiden out and face the Navy in battle. I had something a little more subtle in mind."

"How will we even find them? They could be anywhere!" one of the crew asked as the fire flared ans sent a spew of sparks into the night sky.

Lilith let her hand rest on the pommel of her sword, "Renly believes they would have headed for Kingston. When he was still serving aboard a navy ship there was a battle there. He believes the big line ship would have gone there next."

"Who is to say they are still there?" Dr. LeMeux raised his voice, "We could go to find this ship and be caught by surprise on the way there!"

Lilith nodded and smiled at the French doctor, "That is why we must be very careful. I have a plan, a plan that will see that ship straight to the bottom of the sea and leave ours intact. But I won't force anything upon you all. I have won many of you your freedom, but you owe me nothing. If you wish to depart, do so. If you would stay, I promise you will live to see that ship sent to the deep and you will bring freedom to many more just like yourselves."

The cheer that arose was so loud Lilith could feel

it shake the sands beneath her feet. The night air had a chill to it, but Lilith could feel a warmth radiating through her as the crew sounded out in solidarity. She would have her vengeance, the Maiden would sail again, and her enemies would soon tremble at the sound of her name.

Chapter 12

Kingston Harbor
29 Apr 1809

The night was still warm, uncomfortably so for Lieutenant William Pike as he sat in the front of the longboat listening to their oars slip into the water and churn their boats forward. The ominous placement of Fort Charles towered over the harbor. Every few minutes the lieutenant would trace his eyes over the parapets, watching for any sign of alarm. His small group of sailors and marines would be completely exposed should some enemy force decide to open fire on them from the fort. Moonlight gave a silver glow to the harbor's surface and the same pale light washed over the side of Fort Charles facing Kingston and cast a long shadow that stretched down toward the landing party like a dark claw waiting to wrap its icy fingers around them when they drew too close. Sweat collected on Lieutenant Pike's brow under the still air of the night. The warmth seemed to intensify as the boats came closer and closer to the shore. The lieutenant thought of the first time he had accompanied a landing party ashore in Kingston, he silently prayed that this sortie would go very differently. Admiral Torren had expressed how confident he was in their chances of success. He had heaped praise upon the sailors and marines who were undertaking the endeavor and promised their efforts would not go unrewarded. Lieutenant Pike knew the rousing words, he had heard them before. They were much the same as the ones Admiral Sharpe had spoken.

As the two longboats rowed their way through the harbor, Lieutenant Pike could see where the hulks of the sunken ships had come to rest. H.M.S Hunter and H.M.S Bayonet had collapsed into hulks of seawater-soaked timbers and masts with lines and shredded canvas hanging from their protruding yards and masts like the last sinew and tendons hanging from the rotten corpses of some long dead creature. The air was still and the harbor was quiet. Lieutenant Pike could hear his own breathing as the rowboats continued past the wrecked ship hulks. Kingston was ahead, a still and shadowy collection of dark buildings laying just beyond a swath of sandy beach.

Lieutenant Pike looked at Midshipman Brant and gave him an affirming nod, "Make ready lad. If there is a fight to be had, it will likely come as we first make landfall. Once we are all ashore it will be much more difficult for them to defend against advance."

"Aye, sir." Midshipman Brant replied.

"See to it the rest are prepared for a fight as well. If we are engaged on landing, we must prevail."

Midshipman Brant turned to pass the lieutenant's orders on to the rest of the landing party. For a long moment, Lieutenant Pike let his gaze wander out to the glimmering silvery water where the Hunter and Bayonet hulks jutted upward like desperate hands reaching for rescue. As he looked over the glimmering moonlit waters at the jagged remains of the ships Lieutenant Pike could hear the echoes of the cannons thundering out through time. The smoke that poured from both vessels. The futile screams and cries of pain as their crews were mercilessly hammered by the elevated guns from the fort rang through his ears. He shook his head and tried to refocus on his present tasking, Admiral Torren had instructed him to bypass the town and make for Fort Charles immediately. Once inside the fort, Lieutenant Pike was to secure the walls and guns. Once the fort was secure, the lieutenant would signal out to North Wind and Admiral Torren would have her sail into the safety of the harbor. Beneath the guns of Fort Charles, North Wind would be safe from any attempted engagement from the sea. The admiral could then send more sailors and marines ashore and they would begin patrolling the Jamaican countryside to ensure Kingston remained safe from further assaults.

The longboats slid onto the soft sands of the

shoreline and Lieutenant Pike disembarked amid a flurry of sailors and marines scrambling their way onto the beach. Kingston remained dark and quiet, only the smell of wood smoke indicated that anyone inhabited the town. Soft moonlight made the beach glow under its radiance as the landing party gathered together to prepare to move inland toward Fort Charles.

"Form up! Form up!" a marine encouraged the group to make ready, "Hold your weapons at the ready! We're not there yet!"

Lieutenant Pike drew his sword and flexed his fingers around the handle. The injuries he had sustained had mostly healed, though his ribs and back still pained him. To get to Fort Charles, they would have to cross through part of Kingston. The buildings that lay between them were all dark and closely huddled together. It was the perfect place for an ambush. Most of the buildings were two stories, with windows elevated over the street and narrow pathways in between structures that were obscured by shadow. Lieutenant Pike took in a deep breath and looked over his formation of marines and sailors all holding rifles at the ready. "We move for Fort Charles, no matter what happens, keep moving towards the fort."

The group departed in a column formation leaving the sands of the beach and crossing onto stone cobbled streets. Lamps were dark, and the moonlight cast ominous shadows across their path. The town was quiet and still. Lieutenant Pike wondered if the inhabitants had all fled for somewhere safer. The Jamaican countryside was known to have bandits, without a strong garrison manning the fort, Kingston would have become an easy target for them and her townspeople would have suffered for it.

The column wound its way between shops and houses through the dense part of town that led uphill toward Fort Charles. The ramparts stood high above them looking down on the town. In the paleness of the moonlight, Lieutenant Pike thought he could make our several forms on the side of the fort's wall facing the town. It was difficult to make out exactly what the shapes were, whether it was damage to the fort's wall or something that had been hung against the side he couldn't tell. A barking dog caused the column to halt for a moment. One of the marines leveled his rifle at the creature but was halted by another.

"No shots unless we are fired on damn you!" the marine snarled at the rest of the column, "Keep your shots until we need them!"

The hill steepened leading toward the entrance of Fort Charles and the column pushed forward past buildings that were growing further and further apart as they wound their way around the part of Kingston that hugged the harbor. Eerie silence encircled them and even the thick humid air seemed to muffle the sounds of the men pushing their way uphill. Sweat collected on Lieutenant Pike's brow and neck, the night was warm and lacking the typical ocean breeze he was used to. He remembered the last time he had marched with a group of marines through Kingston, it had been folly to go directly to the governor's mansion, this time they were headed for Fort Charles. With the guns of the fort under their control they would be able to secure the harbor and easily take control of the town. With the fort manned and the harbor secure their next task would be to clear the wreckage so ships could safely traverse in and out of Kingston. Trade would resume, and troops could be brought in to relieve the admiral's contingent ashore.

"The gate is open! Fort Charles is abandoned!" A marine from the front of the column announced as they approached the fort.

Lieutenant Pike sped his pace and passed toward the front of the column of troops. He shifted his gaze nervously between the road ahead and the walls of Fort Charles. There was still the possibility of an ambush. Cobbled streets had given way to dirt roads and Lieutenant Pike lengthened his strides to speed himself to the front of the column. Trees hugged the sides of the road and choked away the moonlight, allowing only small scraps and streaks to shine through broad leaves that appeared almost black in the night. The fort entrance stood ahead of him, its thick wooden gate doors rested ajar.

"Push in. Secure the walls and the guns first. Go!" Lieutenant Pike ordered with an edge of tension in his voice. They were at their objective, but the day was not won just yet. The marines that surrounded him broke into a run and filed into the fort. Lieutenant Pike followed with his sword at the ready in one hand and a pistol in the other. As he passed through the open threshold and into the fort his breath left him. Moonlight poured over the walls of the inner courtyard illuminating a grisly scene of slaughter in its pale glow. The stench was awful. It filled his nose and stung his throat with the sour rotten smell of decomposing flesh. Inside of the fort's walls, the courtyard was littered with the bodies of fallen soldiers. The wooden structures that had housed the garrison were nothing more than burned heaps of what they had once been. Charred beams protruded toward the sky like arms reaching for rescue. Sailors and marines filed along the tops of the walls and hurried for the gun batteries while Lieutenant Pike looked at the remains of a soldier near the front gate. His red uniform coat was stained with blood in the front. The face of the dead man was sunken and hollow, rot had begun to take the body, he had been dead for quite some time.

"The walls and guns are secure, sir." Midshipman Brant reported over Lieutenant Pike's shoulder.

The lieutenant stood from where he had been examining the dead man and looked around the inside of the fort. "We will need to remove the dead. Have a party formed to begin digging graves, so we may dispose of them with honor."

"Aye sir. And what of the men hung from the wall? Do you want that we should cut them down?" the midshipman asked.

"Men hanging from the wall?" Lieutenant Pike frowned with confusion.

"Yes sir. I wasn't sure what it was when we were approaching, but from the looks of it, they are soldiers from the garrison. Their corpses are hung from the ramparts of the west wall."

Lieutenant Pike clenched his jaw and nodded, "Yes, lad. Have them cut down and buried with the rest."

"How could this have happened sir? It appears there were more than enough soldiers here to hold the fort against an assault." Midshipman Brant pressed inquisitively.

Lieutenant Pike grimaced at the thought, "Without reinforcement from the fleet, cut off from the rest of Britain's power. Likely the gate was breeched. I would assume that the assault came from within at first. Someone they trusted."

"A traitor sir? From within their own ranks?" Midshipman Brant turned and gave a disgusted look over the inside of the fort.

"Not within their ranks, lad. Above their ranks. Governor Alton betrayed these men, he betrayed us all, though these poor souls seem to have paid the worst price for it."

Resurrecting the Maiden

'Le Fouet'
29 Apr 1809
18 Degrees 49' N, 73 Degrees 44' W

Captain Callais fumed as fingers of dawn began to break over the distant horizon. Alongside his ship, the soft sandy coastline of Haiti stretched out past the visible distance. LeFouet had followed their newly hired mercenary into these waters only to realize far too late that they were riddled with shallow sand bars and reefs. The first encounter with the bottom had been a minor annoyance, Captain Callais had felt the hull slipping along sand and mixed rock. Without heeding the warning of the sea, he had ordered LeFouet to continue following Batard De Mur after the sun had faded out of the sky. It wasn't long after that LeFouet became hopelessly lodged on a shoal of sand and gravel. The impact had thrown most of the crew on deck off of their feet. In the commotion an oil lamp had toppled and shattered setting a fire on deck. Luckily enough, the crew had managed to extinguish the flames before the damage became too severe, though there was a significant area of the deck near the bow that was charred from the incident.

Columns of light stretched into a pinkish red sky while the crew of LeFouet tried increasingly desperate measures to free their ship from the clutches of the sandbar. Captain Callais paced the deck, from bowsprit to stern, chastising every hand that dared cross his path. The ship was stuck, all that was left was for him to accept that as a fact. Shouts echoed through the crisp morning air as the sailors aboard failed at another attempt to free the vessel. They had gently lowered their anchor down into a small wooden rowboat and pulled it as far away from the ship as possible before tossing the weighty hook overboard. Using the capstan, the crew had tried to use the force of hauling in the anchor to free the ship from its sandy captivity to no avail. Another attempt was made with sails rigged to catch the feeble breeze that blew out of the north only to render the same results.

Every failed attempt brought Captain Callais deeper into rage. He cursed the folly mission he had been sent on. He cursed the predicament it put him in. He cursed the ship, the crew, even the sea itself. The winds weren't nearly strong enough to aid them with freeing the ship. The tide was at its highest point. LeFouet was hopelessly stuck. Captain Callais ended his tirade of pacing and curses at the bow. Whispers of cool breeze brushed against his cheek as the sun began to peak over the horizon and light LeFouet's top sails and masts with her first direct rays of the morning. He clenched his jaw and flared his nostrils. The pirate had intended for this. He had laid a cunning trap and led LeFouet directly into it. The realization crept into his spine and wrapped icy fingers of rage and fear around Captain Callais' ribs. How could he have been so foolish? His thirst to prove himself at sea had led him to drink from a poisoned cup. A cup handed to him by a one-eyed French pirate.

"Sails on the horizon!" An alarmed shout came high up in LeFouet's rigging, "Red sails!"

Captain Callais closed his eyes and inhaled sharply through his nose. He knew what was coming next. He knew what Captain Fontaine had in store for him and there wasn't a damn thing to be done about it. In a matter of hours those red sails would carry the pirates within range of their cannons while he watched. Captain Callais opened his eyes and let them adjust to the bright dawn on the eastern horizon. A set of red sails billowed over the black silhouette of a ship beating its way closer to them by the minute. LeFouet's cannons would be of little use, with her hull lodged into the sand bar she could not be maneuvered, and the pirates would be smart enough not to linger in the field of fire they did cover. Captain Callais stood frozen for a moment that seemed to drag on for hours. The crew had come to a halt. Silence enveloped the deck of LeFouet while their impending doom pitched and swayed in the gentle swells and breeze along the Haitian coast.

"Captain! The pirates approach!" a voice interrupted Captain Callais as he was pondering what his final moments would entail, "What are your orders? Should we abandon ship?"

Fiery red rage crawled up Captain Callais spine and clenched his jaw even tighter, "The next man who suggests surrender to me will feel my sword in his belly! Run out the guns and make ready to fight!"

As if the vessel of pirates had heard his order, a shot sounded from the chase cannons mounted on her bow. The low thump was followed by a sharp whistling sound that grew in intensity until men on the deck of Le Foeut covered their ears at the shrill noise. Captain Callais looked high aloft and watched one of his sails shudder violently as a heavy shot passed through it.

The morning mist still hung low over the surface of the Caribbean as menacing red sails drew closer and closer. Captain Callais could only watch with a growing sense of doom as the pirate vessel came within effective cannon range.

"Be ready on the guns! We'll only have one chance at her when she passes our field of fire!"

The red sails fluttered in the morning breeze and the pirate ship made a hard turn in front of LeFouet. Captain Callais heart dropped into his stomach as the exposed flank of the pirate vessel revealed a row of open gun ports with the ugly snouts of cannons protruding from them. They had turned close enough off of LeFouet's bow that Captain Callais could see the faces of the enemy crew when the cry echoed into the morning crispness.

"Fire!"

A flurry of thunderclaps sounded sending iron projectiles shooting through LeFouet's bow and foremast. The deck of LeFouet trembled under

Captain Callais feet. He could feel structural timbers snapping below deck as cannonballs blasted their way through the innards of his ship. Stay lines snapped and recoiled in violent arcs just over the deck. Jagged shards of wooden shrapnel splintered away from LeFouet's railing and deck peppered the air finding its way into the vulnerable flesh of his crew. Captain Callais stumbled from his feet and fell to the deck, his cheek and chin felt the bite of coarse grain as LeFouet began to sing her death song. The splintering crack of the foremast met Captain Callais ears, he lifted his head just in time to watch the towering structure lean far over the starboard rail and tip into the sea. Screams followed. Captain Callais struggled to lift himself off of the deck of his ship. His arms didn't want to obey, his legs felt like they were made of pudding. LeFouet was already listing to one side. Smoke poured out of her gun ports and wafted from the open weather hatch on her main deck. As he drew his legs under him, Captain Callais shifted his focus to the waters out in front of LeFouet. His 1tormentor had circled his ship and was coming back around for another volley. Her red sails gleamed in rising sunlight like the foreboding shadow of a reaper that had been stalking him and was finally ready to come for its dark harvest.

Captain Callais walked toward the bow of his ship on shaky legs. All around him a scene of misery and chaos was unfolding. It was just as he had imagined. The red sails flapped for a second into the breeze as the pirate captain ordered his ship to come about for another pass at LeFouet's bow. Captain Callais reached the bowsprit. He held his hands out and placed them on the shattered railing. He closed his eyes and inhaled the mixture of smoke and sea air. He had sealed his own fate the day he had succumbed to the promise of riches from the lucrative slave trade. Captain Fontaine may be the one ordering the cannons to fire, but Captain Callais knew that when the souls under his command perished, it would be tallied on his account in the afterlife.

The last volley fired from beneath those crimson sails and tore into LeFouet. Splintering wood filled the air like shards of durable glass. Captain Callais was lifted from his feet by the force of the impact, dozens of wooden shards penetrated his chest and belly. He landed somewhere near the mainmast, as far as he could tell. With LeFouet groaning beneath him from the mass of seawater flowing into her belly, Captain Callais looked up into the morning sky as his blood soaked the deck planking around him. There was nowhere for LeFouet to go, she could not sink into the sea as she was still lodged onto the sandbar. The onslaught had damaged her beyond any reasonable hope for repair. He wasn't even sure how many of his crew still survived. Still, defiance filled the captain's blood as he watched smoke swirl over the deck of his ship. Pain wracked his chest and shoulders and stung his belly as he tried to pull himself up to his feet.

Gripping a hanging stay line, Captain Callais managed to fight his way up and stood near the intact mainmast. The scene that met his eyes was grisly. Dead crewmen scattered the deck between broken and buckled hardwood planks. Flames licked up from LeFouet's sides while smoke poured out of every opening in the deck. Captain Callais looked down at chest and belly, four large shards of wood had stabbed their way into his flesh. One protruded from just beneath his collar bone on his right side, another just a few inches lower in his ribs. The other two shards of wood were lodged in his lower belly on either side of his naval area just above his waist. Blood poured from the lower wounds with every movement the captain made, he knew it would bring his death. Every breath of air was a struggle through pain and the mix of smoke that choked his throat and stung his eyes. Another cannon shot sounded and Captain Callais looked up through the haze and flames to find red sails drawing close off LeFouet's starboard side. They were a couple hundred feet away, but close enough that Captain Callais could see the menacing faces of the crew lined up on one side of the vessel. Jeers and shouts of torment floated on the air in between ships like they were another volley of cannon fire. One face in particular stood out to the captain, this one remained stone still with nothing but a broad sickening smile spread beneath a black leather eye patch.

'Drowned Maiden'
3 May 1809
19 Degrees 28' N, 73 Degrees 33' W

The smooth richness of tobacco smoke flooded in through Chibs mouth and nose as he lit his pipe. It was a joy he had been deprived of when the Maiden had been sunk, but now that she was back above the surface, and with the supplies Captain Lilith had brought from Tortuga, Chibs could finally enjoy the familiar earthy flavors he craved. Dawn was breaking, and a northern breeze had ferried the Maiden and her new consort, the Havana's Mistress, out of their cove and into the swells of the Caribbean.

Early morning on deck was Chibs favorite time of day. Except in the case of foul weather, the winds were normally steady in the early hours and they usually held a bit of a chill that Chibs liked to take in before the Caribbean sun rose high and began baking everything in sight under its relentless rays. In close to land, birds were usually most active in the morning hours as well, Chibs like to watch as gulls and cranes made swooping passes over the water's surface in search of a morning meal. Sunrise was just as spectacular an event as sunset in the Caribbean. The early morning rays would reach into the sky and chase away the dark tones of night, drowning out the stars light one by one as the sky lightened from inky blackness, to violets and pinks and oranges until blue hues overpowered everything above. The salty brine of the sea mixed with fresh cool air from the breeze and the occasional puff of smoke from his pipe all lingered in the air above the deck of the Maiden and gave Chibs a sense of satisfaction he couldn't quite fit into words.

Omibwe was dutifully standing his post at the helm of the vessel. Chibs had noticed the young man took to it as if he had never left. Even on one leg, the boy managed to skillfully manipulate the ship.

"It is going to be a glorious day at sea my friend." Chibs offered with a nod, pipe smoke spilling from his nose while he spoke.

"I'm just happy she is above water again," Omibwe replied between looking aloft and giving the ship's wheel a small adjustment. "I was afraid I would never get to sail her again."

Chibs nodded and pulled his pipe away from his mouth with his one good hand, "So was I, Omi. But, I have to tell you, we all have you to thank for the Maiden coming back to us. If it weren't for you and your diving skills, and all the damned courage you showed us, I'm afraid the Maiden would still be half underwater in that cove."

"Maybe I should quartermaster now!" Omibwe grinned from ear to ear as he spoke.

Chibs chuckled and nodded his head, "Maybe you ought to be. You'd certainly do us a fine job, laddy."

Omibwe shook his head, "Not while you are

with us, Chibs. I couldn't do what you do. I don't know all of your sailor tricks."

Chibs smiled even broader and held his pipe stem up at the young man, "I do have my tricks, but you can learn the same way I have. It's not so hard once you learn the basics. You already know just about everything I do about manning the helm. I could teach you a few knots and some tricks to reefing sail in high winds. Most of what a man knows, he learns through doing."

Omibwe smiled and looked down at the void where his missing leg should have been, "I'm afraid I can only do so much."

Chibs winced and pulled himself in closer to the young man, "Hogwash. I watched you dive further underwater than most men I know with two legs would ever dare to. You can do whatever you set yourself to. Don't sell yourself short on account of missing some pieces." Chibs held up his stumped arm, "I myself am missing a digit or two!"

The smile that spread across Omibwe's face lit a joy inside of Chibs and he gave a satisfied puff of his pipe, enjoying the rich smoke as Omibwe's chest puffed out with pride.

"Just the two I was hoping to find." Lilith's voice interrupted from over Chibs' shoulder, "I have something to discuss with you both, and I was hoping to catch you both at the same time."

Chibs pulled a long drag of smoke from his pipe and squinted his eyes. Lilith seemed hesitant, like she was about to deliver news she didn't want to, or ask something she knew they would both wouldn't like. "Here we are cap'n, let's hear it."

Lilith paused for a long moment and looked out over the side of the Drowned Maiden. Hesitation played out on her face, though Chibs could tell she was fighting against it. "My plan to sink the navy ship will surely be the death of one of our vessels. After your all of your labor to bring the Maiden back from beyond the grave, I cannot bring myself to risk the ship again."

"Ships are meant for sailing, cap'n. A pirate ship most of all. If we refuse to risk her, we might as well beach the vessel to preserve her hull." Chibs jeered with a snort of pipe smoke, unsure of what she was getting at.

Lilith smiled at the jest, "What I have in mind is more than a chancy sail into a strong storm. The vessel I enter Kingston's harbor in will be destroyed. Thankfully, we have Havana's Mistress to use for such a task."

Chibs pulled his pipe from his mouth with his hand and wiped at the corner of his brow with his forearm, "Beggin your pardon cap'n, but what exactly is it you have planned? Sailing into the harbor with the Maiden is suicide, Havana's Mistress won't fare any better."

"I intend to sail a vessel into the harbor and blow that ship straight to the bottom of the sea, though we won't be sailing in and trading broadsides with her. I know that much." Lilith shot Chibs a look back over her shoulder with her hand on the pommel of her sword, her one good eye seemed to glisten in the morning sun, "I will take Havana's Mistress into the harbor, with a crew of my choosing, to take on this task. But I won't risk either of you. You are to stay aboard the Maiden and keep her safely out of range from the fort and any navy ships we may encounter."

Chibs felt his chest tighten as the words met his ears. He nearly fumbled his pipe in shock. Shock was soon replaced by a wave of anger and he felt as if he would snap the wooden stem off between his fingers. "Cap'n, you can't... Surely you don't expect me to sit idle while you risk your life?"

Lilith turned and faced Chibs and Omibwe, "I do Chibs. I need you and Omi to stay on the Maiden and keep her out of reach of the fort guns and any other ships that may be in the harbor while I take the Mistress in and sink the warship."

Chibs shook his head, he couldn't believe what he was hearing, "It's not right cap'n. I won't watch you sail into a sure death."

Lilith paused a moment and gave Chibs a soft look, the corners of her mouth almost threatened a smile. "I appreciate the concern Chibs. But, I have a plan. We won't be sailing toward a sure death. There is a plan, but for it to work you must keep the Maiden safely out of reach from any of the threats in the harbor."

Chibs folded his arms against his chest and clamped his pipe in between his teeth, he drew short puffs of smoke while his mind raced to work out what Captain Lilith could be planning. "There are plenty on board who could make sure the Maiden stays out of harm's way."

Lilith's reply came quick and flat, "None that I trust half as much as you."

"Dr. LeMeux..." Chibs began to interrupt.

"Don't even start to imply that I trust that man with my ship Chibs." Lilith cut back with an edge rising in her voice.

"Cap'n, I only mean to say that there are others who could keep the Maiden safe and away from the harbor."

Lilith paused, her face hardened for a moment as if her patience was beginning to wane, "None that I would trust with the ship, Chibs. Like I said, I need you to do this for me."

'H.M.S North Wind'
29 Apr 1809
Kingston Harbor

Fort Charles stood in darkness, towering over the rest of Kingston and the harbor. Admiral Torren had watched from the deck of North Wind as the longboats were lowered down to the water well out of cannon range. The crews had made their way ashore under the admiral's watchful eye.

"A tea sir?" Lieutenant Thatcher had offered while the admiral held his vigil on deck, "Something to eat while you wait?"

Admiral Torren shook his head without

removing his eyes from the guns of Fort Charles, "No. No tea. I will eat once we have secured the fort and not a moment before." Admiral Torren tamped the end of his cane on the wooden deck beneath his feet, "Arrange for another landing party to be ready, once the fort is secure, we cannot dally about wasting time. I want at least another twelve men ready to depart with orders to secure the governor's mansion. With the fort and the mansion secured we can begin to restore some semblance of law and order to Kingston."

Lieutenant Thatcher paused for a moment, "Will you be accompanying the next party ashore sir?"

"I will. Once we are sure the harbor is safe we will bring North Wind in. With her batteries, and those of the fort, Kingston will be an impenetrable target for any brigands or Frenchmen who may have plans of taking her."

"That she will, sir." Lieutenant Thatcher replied before turning to relay the admiral's orders.

Hours passed through the night while a fog gathered. Admiral Torren kept a watchful eye on the fort and over the darkened building tops of Kingston. Light from the moon had illuminated the shoreline and given everything a ghostlike silvery glow. As the rowboats disappeared from sight the admiral's nerves began to itch. His legs twitched in pain, tingling at first until pangs of pain started shooting from his feet up his ankles and into his knees. He shifted his weight at first, trying to lessen the impact on one foot and then the other while he waited for the prearranged signal that Fort Charles had been secured. The deck of the North Wind was uncharacteristically quiet. Her sails were all reefed, the canvas only showed in tight bundles along each spar in between the tied lines securing each portion of the sail. What crew remained on deck had joined the admiral in his silent vigil, from their places near the helm or up on the aft castle. Some had climbed far aloft and were watching as the contingent of troops led by Lieutenant Pike made their way through the harbor before disappearing into darkness. No calls floated over the deck of North Wind. No matter how many hours tolled by, her bell did not peal. Admiral Torren had ordered complete silence on deck, nothing more than a conversational tone was permitted while the landing party made their way through Kingston's harbor. When the longboats had disappeared and no shots were heard the tension on deck gradually began to diffuse. Admiral Torren continued his watch however, anxiously awaiting the signal he had instructed Lieutenant Pike to give once the fort had been secured.

Long minutes stretched into hours. The moon glistened off of the sea and shone on the harbor. Admiral Torren could see evidence of the ships that been fired on from the fort. Dark fingers of timber stretched out of the sea with ragged lines and canvas hanging off of them. He wondered how many souls had perished at the hands of his American prisoner who even now drew breath in a cell within the confines of North Wind. The thought added to Admiral Torren's inner torment. He had wanted to hang the American from the yard and be done with it. Somehow, Lieutenant Pike had the idea that the American could be of some use to their cause. While Admiral Torren seriously doubted these notions, he was learning that in the current state of affairs it was best to heed the advice of Lieutenant Pike. The young officer had been through hell and back, some of it by the admiral's own hand.

No shots had been heard from Kingston, only an occasional cool breeze swept over the Jamaican shoreline and rustled the trees and a few unlatched shutters. For all Admiral Torren could tell, the city was empty. The harbor looked to be halfway impassable due to the wreckage that lay under the surface just beneath Fort Charles. With a cringe, he tried to imagine what the barrage from the fort must have been like. In his days as a young officer he had come under the fire of an elevated fort along the coast of Spain. It had been for only a short duration, but the ship he was serving on had sustained serious damage and lost so many sailors and officers that they were only able to crew half of the guns on one battery at a time. The voyage back to England had been a somber affair, and the commanding officer floundered the rest of his career at the bottom of various bottles of spirits. The event marked for Admiral Torren just how deadly a small error of judgment could be. There were no shortage of cautionary tales in the Royal Navy. Sailors were often told, "One hand for the ship, and one for yourself." This was due to the number of top men who had fallen from their lofty posts and perished by either coming to an abrupt stop on the hard wooden decks below or by landing into storm tossed waters when it was too hazardous for a ship to make a turn and attempt a rescue. Officers were drilled daily about how critical their accuracy of calculation was when doing navigation. More than one ship of the Royal Navy had spent weeks dithering about the open sea in search of coastline while her crew slowly starved or died of thirst. A small error in reckoning could land a crew along a hostile shoreline or cause them to miss an important landmark sighting. In the confusion that followed, officers would often compare their navigational calculations, this would inevitably lead to disagreements and further strife aboard a ship. More than one mutiny had been a direct result of poor navigation.

Admiral Torren pondered the causes of his own mutiny while he scanned his eyes over the shadows of Kingston. The American had played his part, surely. But there were other issues, something underlying, that caused the men who had risen against him to doubt the honor of their commander. It had been a bloody affair, keelhauling Lieutenant Pike, but at the time he had seen no other alternative. On some levels, the admiral still questioned Lieutenant Pike's loyalty to this girl pirate. Would the young officer have turned on him if forced to choose between his loyalty to crown and country? The admiral shook his head at the notion. Young William Pike had dutifully accepted the harrowing task of leading a party ashore in what could have very well become a suicide mission.

The walls of the fort remained dark, like a looming omen they towered above Kingston, making all of the other buildings look tiny by comparison. There hadn't been a single shot. Admiral Torren poured over the possibilities in his mind. The landing party could be held at gunpoint right where they made landfall. They may have been taken by surprise somewhere in the city. Even as the admiral stood on his painfully swollen ankles they could be being marched toward the fort with their hands held high in surrender. Again, the admiral shook off the notion. A shot would have been fired. The men he had sent ashore were all armed, and not likely to surrender without a fight. But it had been hours, if they had met resistance, he should have heard gunfire. *Where are you, Pike?* The possibilities rolled through Admiral Torren's mind like a never-ending tide. The fort could be held by anyone, bandits, the American mercenaries, the French. North Wind was safely out of range from Fort Charles gun batteries, but she was also too far away to be of any assistance should the landing party fall prey to a waiting ambush. *We should have made landfall elsewhere and gone overland to Kingston, you damned old fool. Now they are held captive by some hostile force and there is nothing to be done about it.*

Just as Admiral Torren was beginning to come to grips with the possibility that he had lost two dozen of his remaining men to a silent capture by some unknown enemy force, a light appeared from the ramparts of Fort Charles. For a moment the orange glow of a torch flickered and sent light dancing on the wall of the fort. Admiral Torren could see the glimmer reflecting off of the water below as the torch bearer, presumably Lieutenant Pike, waved the orb of flame back and forth several times. The torch was then used to light another and the same gesture was repeated.

They've done it. The fort is ours! A smile spread across the admiral's face, for a moment the pain throbbing through his ankles and into his knees seemed to lessen. Lieutenant Pike had recaptured the fort. The most treacherous obstacle was now firmly in the admiral's grasp. If any foe should come prowling, he would have the upper hand. There was still much to do, but they would do it under the security of the batteries of Fort Charles. Securing the governor's mansion would be next on his priority list and clearing the harbor of wreckage soon after that. Once he had done that, the admiral planned to commandeer any vessel he could so they may start patrolling the Caribbean coastline. With a secure base of operations and his knowledge of the smuggling activities he would finally be able to put this shadowy enemy on its heels and drive them back.

"The fort is alight, sir," Lieutenant Thatcher interrupted the admiral's thoughts, "Would you like for me to send the next party ashore?"

Admiral Torren faced the young officer and nodded, "I will accompany the next wave. Bring my sword belt and pistol, lad."

Chapter 13

Fort Charles
5 May 1809

Sunrise fell over Kingston revealing all that the darkness of night had hidden away. The town was in shambles. Shops and businesses had been looted, homes had been burned and the sparse population that was left seemed hesitant to make themselves seen. Lt. Pike had risen with the breaking of day as sunlight washed over the walls of the newly occupied Fort Charles. As he looked down onto the winding streets and crowded buildings of Kingston from the ramparts of Fort Charles Lt. Pike remembered the frenzied dash he had made through those narrow pathways on the day Admiral Sharpe had been killed. He could almost hear the gunfire again. Sunlight kissed the waters of the harbor, illuminating them and sending a million hues of blue and green cascading from the surface to the depths. Lieutenant Pike looked over the crystalline colors and remembered the onslaught coming down from the fort as the crews of the Hunter and the Bayonet squandered helplessly as cannon fire rained down on them. The evacuation from Kingston had been sheer panic and reaction. One ambush after another until both H.M.S Valor and H.M.S Endurance had made their way out of the reach of the fort batteries.

Things were different now. This time the fort was in their control. The harbor was guarded by both the batteries of H.M.S North Wind and the guns of Fort Charles. Lieutenant Pike had two dozen men with which to reestablish law and order to the town and launch a new offensive against the slave smuggling order which had brought so much chaos and destruction to the colony of Jamaica. Admiral Torren had made landfall during the night and promptly made his way to the gates of Fort Charles. He had spent much of the early morning hours inspecting the condition of the fort guns and sending small patrols into the town to look for any signs of an enemy force. All they had discovered were a few townsfolk, some livestock animals that were loose and roaming the streets and the damage inflicted by raids from bandits. Without the fort garrison, Kingston had been laid bare by outlaws from the Jamaican inland. The damage had been plain enough to see even in the dark of night, but now that the sun had shown its face it was all the more apparent. Work details had been organized to address the dead bodies of their countrymen left inside of Fort Charles. The officer who had been hung from the wall of the fort had been removed and a mule and cart were being loaded with the deceased to ferry them outside of the fort for dignified burials. There was weeks' worth of labor before the crew of North Wind, and the townspeople of Kingston.

The two officers met on the ramparts overlooking Kingston as the light of day displayed a scene of wanton destruction below.

"Well executed, Lieutenant. The fort is secure. We will surely have Kingston back in good order, in due time of course." Admiral Torren looked out over the town, his eyes drifted upward towards the sea horizon as he spoke. "We must resume sea patrols as promptly as possible."

"Yes sir." Lieutenant Pike replied, watching the admiral's face as he stared out over the decimated buildings of Kingston. There were a few small vessels in the harbor, none suitable for combat should he meet with some enemy force, but there was a sloop he could use to reconnoiter the southern coast of Jamaica and determine if there were any sea threats in the immediate vicinity. The lieutenant began to silently piece together who he would as a crew to man the small vessel.

"I will give you the command of North Wind for the task of searching out and engaging any sea threat in our immediate vicinity." The admiral's words came suddenly, like a bolt of lightning had split the clear morning sky and struck Lieutenant

Pike directly in the chest.

"North Wind sir?" Lieutenant Pike struggled for words for a moment, "We would need to sail her with a skeleton crew, so that repairs and land patrols may be made here in Kingston."

Admiral Torren nodded and turned to Lieutenant Pike with a half-smile on his face, "Are you trying to talk me out of handing you the command Lieutenant?"

Lieutenant Pike shook his head, "No, sir. Absolutely not. But with the crew we would need to sail her, wouldn't it be more effective to make our patrol with a smaller vessel?"

Admiral Torren nodded brusquely and tamped the tip of his cane on the stone ramparts beneath their feet, "It is a calculated risk, lad. It does leave the harbor a little less protected, but I believe that manning the fort and her guns is adequate for the time being. We must determine the sea threat. Without dominance of the waves lad, we might as well be France."

Lieutenant Pike looked down to where North Wind sat in Kingston's harbor, the first light of day was illuminating the water around her and a bank of mist was retreating from the edges of her hull. "It would be a great honor for me admiral. I won't let you down."

Admiral Torren nodded and tapped his cane again, "You most certainly won't lad, of that I am certain. We will discuss crewing later today, for now, make whatever preparations you can. You won't be able to supply her for more than a couple of weeks at sea for now, I'm sure provisions here in Kingston will be stretched. But I believe we will be able to send you with enough manpower to sail her and man one of her gun decks on both sides. Should you come into contact with an enemy force, it will be crucial for you to exercise good judgment and superior tactics. I know she will be in capable hands, given the instruction you have received. Leave enough men ashore for us to continue our mission of securing the town and the surrounding countryside."

"Very well, sir." Lieutenant Pike replied, "I will see to it that preparations begin immediately."

'Drowned Maiden'
12 May 1809
17 Degrees 40' N, 76 Degrees 26' W

"Sail ho!" Jilhal's alarm could be heard on deck as she called down from high in the Maiden's rigging. There was an edge in her voice. A sense of urgency almost creeping on panic. Lilith knew the minute she heard her friend calling down from above that something wasn't right, there was something different about this sighting. Lilith left her place on the bow to see where Jilhal was pointing off of the starboard quarter of the Maiden's stern. At first, only crystal blue sky and blue gray waters met her eyes. After a few moments, Lilith spotted the spec far away on the horizon. Lightning hit her veins as the shape began to take form.

"Chibs!" Lilith called out for her quartermaster.

"Aye, cap'n. What is it?" Chibs replied while trailing a breath of pipe smoke over his shoulder. He hurried along the starboard side, squinting in the direction his captain was looking.

"Sails on the horizon, Chibs. But they don't look like any sails I have ever seen." Lilith extended a hand up to shield her eyes from the harsh sun. "Is it my eyes? They look red."

Chibs pace slowed as he drew close to where Lilith stood, she could see his squinting eyes slack open as he recognized the sails on the horizon. Lilith watched while Chibs quick pace devolved into slow steps that finally stopped a few feet away from where she stood. His eyes were locked onto the red sails on the horizon, his jaw slacked and he fetched the pipe from between his teeth with his one remaining hand.

"Crimson death." Chibs muttered as the heel of his hand rested along the starboard rail, smoke still drifted from the stem of his wooden pipe. Without any warning Chibs turned toward the helm and then looked high aloft, "Run up the tops and gallants! Come about with the wind to our backs and hurry!"

For a heartbeat it seemed as if everyone aboard was confused. The sailors on deck hesitated as Chibs' voice carried across the deck and into the rigging. The quartermaster looked back out over the sea and paused for a moment before turning aloft and shouting, "Well, what are your waiting for? A blade at your throats? Keep lolly gagging and we will get just that! Unfurl those damned tops and gallants, come about with the wind and tighten those sheets! Make ready the stunsels!"

The crew snapped into action after the quartermaster's scolding. The Drowned Maiden turned with the wind at her stern and picked up speed as her remaining canvas was unfurled and filled with wind. Lilith looked over Chibs as the crew scrambled to heed his orders. His face had reddened a shade darker than its normal ruddy hue. He seemed disheveled, irritated almost, but in a way that belied an underlying sense of fear rather than anger.

"Chibs, what is it? Why are we running?" Lilith called toward the quartermaster as he purposefully strode toward the helm. Her hands rested on the pommel of her cutlass as she spoke, her words came with a breathless gasp of confusion and fear.

"The crimson death, cap'n. A ship I had thought left these waters years ago." Chibs stopped at the helm and looked aloft, inspecting the sails as they unfurled. "We could coax a little more speed if we held her at a bit of an angle to the wind, lad. Keep them taught." Chibs said to Omibwe, he placed his hand on the ship's wheel and helped the young African man adjust the ship's course over to the starboard quarter by a point. Chibs nodded with satisfaction before looking over his shoulder for the red sails on the horizon, "That should do. But, we need to rig the stunsels if we can hope to outrun her."

A streak of anger ran through Lilith's veins, she could feel her muscles tense, her heartbeat quickened by the minute as Chibs continued his tirade on deck while leaving her guessing why he was in such a state. "Chibs! Answer me! Why should we fear this ship with red sails? Why shouldn't we turn to and run out the guns?"

Chibs turned to face Lilith. His eyes were wide like she had never seen before, his face was drawn in a tight expression, like he had seen a ghost. "There's only one ship I know of that flies red sails cap'n. She's been around since my days of sailing for the company, but I have never crossed paths with her until now. Hell, I'd started to believe she wasn't even real, just a story that sailors told."

Lilith's blood tinged cold as she recognized genuine fear in her stalwart quartermaster's eyes. Lilith had never seen him like this, "Who is it?"

Chibs shook his head and struggled to fish his pipe out of his vest with his one good hand, "From what I've heard, she's captained by a failed French merchantman who turned pirate. When I sailed with the company, she was the bane of both the French and British navies in the Caribbean. I've never laid eyes on her sails myself, but I know her reputation. It is said that her captain has sunk a dozen ships from both the French and the British, evaded American pirate hunters and even managed to take an East India Company ship as a prize. He flies red sails and a red flag and gives no quarter to anyone who crosses his path. Cap'n we cannot face her in open seas."

Lilith nodded as Chibs spoke, trying to understand what made this pirate captain so fearsome that Chibs would react this way. "Perhaps the tales you have heard are embellished, Chibs. Sailors have been known to exaggerate these sorts of things, I'm sure we have been the talk of every port from Nassau to Barbados and back at one point or another. What makes you think that the tales are true?"

Chibs furrowed his bushy eyebrows into a deep frown and puffed at his pipe with growing intensity, "Any captain who is so bold as to announce his presence by flying colored sails is a different sort, cap'n. We can hoist our colors and announce our presence to the world at any time, true. But to fly sails of red is boldly telling the entire world exactly who they are and inviting anyone who would chance fate to come and take a try." Chibs let a furious puff of smoke roll out of his mouth as he spoke, "It's not a ship I would cross swords with if I could help it."

Chapter 14

Kingston Harbor
6 May 1809

Crisp, cool morning air carried the peal of North Wind's deck bell across Kingston's harbor and met Lieutenant Pike's ears as the longboat carried him out to his new command. It was a temporary assignment with the North Wind's true captain left in Nassau, but William Pike would be able to list command of a line ship on his accomplishments. He had gone from a traitor, captive in the brig of the gargantuan ship, to holding command over her. It was a legitimate command, ordered by a fleet admiral. Streaks of gold and pink streaked the early morning sky as the longboat's oars slid in and out of the calm harbor waters. North Wind sat still and calm on the almost glassy seawater, a behemoth of warfare. Will marveled at her silhouette against the rising dawn. Her masts stretched toward the sky like towering spears that looked like they could almost pierce the clouds. Her hull rose high out of the water, a floating fortress with all the firepower of one. She was the picture of Britain's power at sea, an extension of the might of the empire. Will traced his fingers over the collar of his uniform coat. This was what he had wanted his entire life. His career had been brought back from what many would consider irredeemable circumstances. It was a miracle things had happened the way they did. Will looked over Midshipman Brant. The hopeful young officer had again begged Admiral Torren to let him accompany Lieutenant Pike on what he viewed as an opportunity for action. The landing in Kingston had proved to be a somewhat dull affair, without a shot being fired in anger. Will knew the eagerness to prove himself that the midshipman felt, at one point in his life Will had felt the same.

As North Wind grew larger and larger in front of them, Will could feel a sense excitement building in his chest. High in the rigging, sailors scurried up and down rat lines as the watch changed with the tolling of the deck bell. The familiar sounds of the ship reverberated over the calm water and brought a wry grin to Will's face. Returning to the ship was like coming home. Soon enough they would be underway with full sails and rocking deck. Will would plot out their course and give his orders to the sailing master before making rounds to inspect the crew for combat readiness.

Like a wave, the thought of inspecting and

training the crew to conduct rapid reloads and coordinated fires washed Will into a flood of memories. Thoughts of instructing the crew of escaped slaves how to reload, how to time their fires for an effective raking pass and how to range a target overcame his mind. He tried to shake them away. They were a distant memory of a crew he had once known and a captain who had once betrayed him. Will had watched as the volleys of fire had impacted the Drowned Maiden's hull, masts and rigging. He had seen her sails torn to shred and the yards topple over into the water. In his mind he could see how she had listed over, a doomed vessel clinging onto the last remaining buoyancy as it slipped from her hull and out into the cove. The Drowned Maiden had succumbed to the sea. Will wondered for a moment if any of the crew had survived. The ship had certainly been close enough to shore for any survivors to escape and make it to land. That raised another question. If there were survivors, what had become of them?

"Ready to board, sir?" the question rocked Will out of his thoughts and into the present. Midshipman Brant gestured toward a plank and rope ladder that would lead them up onto North Wind's deck.

Will nodded at the young officer and clapped a hand on his shoulder, "I certainly am, lad. Onward we go."

Will made his way up the planks of the shaky ladder until he found the formidable deck of the massive line ship beneath his feet. He wasted no time.

"Officer of the watch. Report." Will called across the deck to summon a junior officer. He was greeted by a seasoned looking sailor wearing a midshipman uniform.

The midshipman rendered his customary salute, "Midshipman Allen reporting as ordered, sir."

Will gave the salted looking sailor a once over, "Kind of old for midshipman rate, aren't you?"

The sailor nodded his head and rubbed a hand across his whisker stubbled jaw, "Aye. I am. Admiral Torren himself promoted me after the mutiny. Shorthanded as far as officers go I guess."

Will nodded, "So it would seem." He gave the deck a quick scan and let his gaze land back onto Midshipman Allen, "Weigh anchor and unfurl the mains and tops, fore and aft. Come about close reach and take us out of the harbor."

Midshipman Allen snapped another salute and replied through a set of stained teeth, "Aye, sir. Weigh anchor, mains and tops and come about close reach."

Will nodded, "That will be all for now."

A group of sailors began working the capstan while others let the main and topsails fly. In short order North Wind was making the burgeoning turn on her way out of Kingston's harbor. After a few fluttering pops the sheets were tightened and North Wind began to build speed. Sailors scurried along yards and climbed the rigging shouting and repeating commands. Will walked the deck, taking in the familiar sounds and smells. The salted air tingled in his nose. The spray of the sea felt cool on his skin. Will took in a deep breath. It was like being home.

'Batard De Mur'
12 May 1809
17 Degrees 40' N, 76 Degrees 26' W

Two sets of white sails danced on the horizon. Captain Fontaine had watched them for the better part of the morning from the bow of Batard De Mur as she closed the gap with the distant vessels. At one point, as the afternoon wore on and the winds grew warmer and warmer, the vessels seemed to have spotted his red sails. Both ships altered course slightly and ran out every bit of sail they could fly. It brought a wry smile to the corners of the pirate captain's mouth. He loved the cat and mouse game of engaging a vessel at distance. The red sails that flew above Batard De Mur's decks left little to imagine about his intentions. He would give no quarter to any vessel that crossed his path. In the recesses of his mind, he only hoped that the two fleeing ships were vessels commissioned by the order. If that turned out to be the case, he would take particular joy in seeing every member of the crew bleed their last out onto the deck of their ship before setting them afire and letting them drift the Caribbean.

Captain Fontaine knew the coast of Jamaica lay just over the northern horizon. The occasional sighting of birds in the air confirmed this. The two vessels seemed to be sailing in concert with one another. Judging by their sails, one of them was a larger ship, possibly a frigate. Captain Fontaine was used to ships fleeing the sight of his sails. He fed off of it. The pursuit thrilled him. It could be a matter of hours or as long as a few days, but the end result was always the same. He would catch them. Batard De Mur would hunt them down and get inside of cannon range. After a few ranging shots he would target their masts and rudder. If that didn't draw a white flag he would continue to close the gap. Usually, after a few rounds found their mark in a ship's hull, the crew would give up on the merits of running. Then it would either be a fight or an outright surrender. A ship as large as the one he was looking at wouldn't be raising any white flags. Captain Fontaine knew it in his bones, they would turn and fight. He relished it, savored the thought of crossing swords with an adversary worthy of putting up a decent fight. It had been quite some time since he had run afoul of a crew that could match Batard De Mur in either seamanship or close combat. Perhaps this one would.

As sure as the sun streaking its way through the western sky, Batard De Mur made steady progress closing the gap against the fleeing ships. Captain Fontaine remained steadfast in his place on the bow, watching for any sign of either vessel turning to engage. As far as he could tell, they were making every effort to keep out of the range of his guns. Every available sail flew from the masts. They had even run out their stunsels. The grizzled pirate captain gritted his teeth and watched the seas for any sign of discarded cargo. Sometimes in a panic crews would jettison heavy cargoes in hopes of speeding their vessel. Neither of these had.

Warm winds filled Batard De Mur's crimson sails as she pitched and rocked her way through the Caribbean in pursuit of the fleeing ships. Captain Fontaine ordered his crew to ready the guns as they began to approach firing range. Through the distance, the pirate captain could make out some detail as the sun began to sink low in the sky. One of the ships sported fully rigged sails while her deck bristled with the ugly snouts of cannons. Captain Fontaine extended his telescope and began to scour the figures of the ships for any detail he could spy.

To the right and slightly closer, sailed a brigantine of approximate size to his own Batard De Mur. Her decks seemed to be scarcely manned. Captain Fontaine strained his eye to focus on the name painted across the ship's fantail, Havana's Mistress. He'd never heard of her before, though there were thousands of ships that sailed these waters. The ship that sailed to the left and slightly further in the distance was of more concern to him. It was without a doubt a frigate, British made by the look of her. Her deck was teeming with activity as sailors made constant adjustments to her rigging and sails. It appeared that they were preparing for a fight. The captain looked over the ship's fantail and tried to distinguish the vessel's name. Sunlight glinted and sparkled on the rippling surface of the sea as the wind blew over its surface. Captain Fontaine focused on the stern of the larger vessel through the glare until the ship's name came into clear view. A tinge of adrenaline touched his veins as he read the name silently. Drowned Maiden. Under his breath, so quiet that none around would hear, he uttered a curse.

It was the infamous vessel, captained by the escaped slave girl. The very same that the order had wanted him to track down. She was legend in every port pub and tavern from the Americas all the way to Europe and beyond. The girl had managed to put a stranglehold on the illicit transatlantic slave trade. Many coin purses had become considerably lighter since she had begun her reign of terror. In someplace deep within himself, Captain Fontaine admired the reputation of the young woman. He had heard tales in a smuggler's roost of how she managed to sink not one but two warships of the British Royal Navy. She had evaded a fleet sent all the way from England with the express mission of sending her vessel to the briny depths. The rumors told it she was sunk with all hands off of the Haitian coast. Captain Fontaine grinned beneath his hat as he continued to peer through the telescope. The rumors were wrong. As he continued to examine the stern of the larger vessel he saw her. She climbed onto the railing with a stay line in one hand and the handle of a cutlass in the other. Her white blouse ruffled in the breeze as she stared back across the sea gap. Captain Fontaine studied her for a minute through the foggy focus of the telescope. The girl captain held her sword up in his direction and turned her head inward toward her crew. Just as quickly as she raised the blade, she dropped it low in a hacking motion. Two puffs of cannon smoke appeared from the stern railing.

"She's set up some chase guns, has she?" Captain Fontaine uttered under his breath, "A lively one this girl is."

The whistling of incoming shot shrieked through the air. Captain Fontaine hardly paid it any mind until the cannon shot impacted the sea surface and sent a pair of plumes high into the air. "Still a little out of range my dear. Don't waste your shot so frivolously."

A chorus of shouts rose from the deck of Batard De Mur as the mist of seawater that had been rocketed into the air fell back to the surface. Captain Fontaine grinned to himself and turned over his shoulder, "It's the girl and her band of runaways! Who is ready for a scrap?"

Another chorus of shouts erupted, louder than the one before.

"Arm yourselves and ready the chase guns! We'll

have them on their heels by sundown!"

The shouts and cheers intensified as Captain Fontaine turned back toward the Drowned Maiden. He raised his telescope to his eye and looked back at the infamous ship as his own continued to gain on her. He watched as a pair of her crew raised their black banner over the stern. He had heard of the skull with its twisted horns and the canted trident, the broken chain that crossed the bottom of the field. This was definitely the crew he had heard of.

The distance closed. Captain Fontaine could make out individual faces through his telescope. He was well inside of cannon range by now, though the girl captain's crew had not fired another shot.

"Chase guns are ready captain!" a voice reported from over Fontaine's shoulder.

Captain Fontaine continued looking through his telescope, "Aye, stand by at the ready."

The Maiden had abstained from firing on Batard De Mur, even though they were well within cannon range. Something was off. Her gun ports were open, her guns were run out, but she hadn't come about to open fire. Captain Fontaine scoured the deck for any sign of activity. He found nothing but the girl captain standing tall and proud on the stern rail of her ship, sword in hand.

"Is she inviting us closer?" Fontaine pondered to himself in a whisper so low only he could hear it. "What is this madness?"

The captain peered through his telescope again, bringing its focus onto the girl captain. They were near enough now her could see her clearly. She leaned back and turned her head inward toward the deck of her ship. A pair of her crewmen stood nearby. Captain Fontaine could see clearly that one of them, a seasoned sailor by the look of him, appeared to be missing a hand. The other man reached a hand over the stern rail and pointed directly at Batard De Mur. He was a taller fellow with dark hair. Something seemed familiar about him. Captain Fontaine locked his focus onto the taller man. There was something about the hand gestures he made. Something Captain Fontaine couldn't quite pin down. It felt like a distant memory, a sense of remembering without quite being able to place what he was thinking of. The tall man reached both hands up behind his head and rubbed the back of his neck while shaking his head in frustration.

A cold streak shocked the captain's blood. Even through the heat of the Caribbean sun he could feel goosebumps rising on the back of his arms, his neck and his legs. For a moment he lowered the telescope. He couldn't believe what he saw. It couldn't be. He raised the telescope back up and caught the tall man as he stepped into direct sunlight. Captain Fontaine gritted his jaw together and fought back a rush of emotion as he whispered to himself, "Philip LeMeux."

'Drowned Maiden'
12 May 1809
17 Degrees 40' N, 76 Degrees 26' W

A hot wind gusted as Lilith watched the crimson sails grow larger on the horizon. Hour by hour the ship flying blood red canvas slowly gained against Drowned Maiden while Chibs and the crew tried desperately to coax every bit of speed from their ship. Every sail adjustment, every small course correction to grab just a little more of the wind failed. The ship which had raised so much alarm with Chibs would overtake them before nightfall. Lilith knew there were few options left. There wasn't enough powder in the Maiden's magazine to rig a barrel the way they had done before. They were caught in the open sea, without a coastline to seek cover and hide or a reef to run the enemy afoul. The last remaining choice in Lilith's mind was to turn and fight. She had the size advantage with the Maiden. The ship with red sails appeared to be a brigantine, so the Maiden's gun count would typically be double what a brig would carry. Together with the Havana's Mistress, surely they would be able to overcome this enemy.

"Chibs!" Lilith called over her shoulder as she stepped high onto the stern railing.

"Aye cap'n?" Chibs replied while making his way toward the stern, trails of pipe smoke drifting along behind him.

Lilith paused for a moment, taking in the sight of

the approaching red sails. "Make ready to turn and fire."

Chibs pulled the pipe stem from out of his mouth. "Cap'n, we don't want a fight with her. She's death to all who have crossed her path."

Lilith drew her Saber and held it high above her shoulder. "So are we. Chase guns, make ready to fire!"

"Cap'n we just got her off the bottom-" Chibs began to make his protest.

Lilith watched as the chase gun crews made the final preparations to their cannons. When the shot had been loaded and the pans primed she slashed her cutlass downward in a chopping motion and cried out, "Fire!"

Two thunderous reports belched clouds of acrid smoke into the wind. The cannons recoiled with vicious force as their shots screamed through the late afternoon and splashed into the surface of the sea. Lilith squinted and made a mental calculation of the distance. She turned to where Chibs was standing on the deck with his pipe in hand.

"They will be in range in less than half a turn if the wind holds. If we continue this folly of trying to run we will spell out our own doom. She will pick away at us with her chase guns, maybe even get lucky and hit our rudder. Have the batteries make ready and run the guns out. When they get close we can turn and fire on them. Perhaps if we make our turn quick enough we can score some raking fire hits on her as we pass and be able to come about with the wind in our favor."

Chibs stood stone still for a moment, clasping the bowl of his pipe in hand and squinting out at the gleaming sunlight on the sea surface. Slowly, he began to nod, a smile spread across his bearded face as he returned the pipe to his mouth. "Aye cap'n. That just might do!" Chibs turned inboard and started to bark out commands, "Run these stunsels in! They won't do for a tight turn and the cap'n is going to want us laid alongside pistol range for a passing volley!" He turned skyward and pointed with the stem of his pipe, "You there! Quit your lolly gagging and heave to that line! Can't you see they're already on us?"

Lilith smiled and turned back to look over the sea astern of the Maiden. The figure of a man wearing a large hat appeared below the crimson sails. He was standing just to the side of the bowsprit. Lilith narrowed her eye and flexed a tight grip on her cutlass.

"Beg pardon Captain Lilith, but are you sure of the intentions of this vessel? The talk Chibs has heard may very well just be that. Pub talk. Tavern blabbering without any shred of truth or credibility behind them."

Lilith broke her gaze away from the approaching ship to find Dr. LeMeux gazing up at her with a sincere grimace of concern.

"If I were to believe all the talk I heard from sailors, I would never have boarded a vessel bound for the Caribbean in the first place. Well, after the tales I heard in Brest, with leviathans and krakens and such, I might not have ever boarded a ship at all." The doctor rattled on while Lilith turned her attention back to her pursuer.

"You would have been better off for it doctor." Lilith tried to hide her disdain for the Frenchman as she replied, "As it stands, the Caribbean has not been good to you. First you were taken by slavers and now you are forced to live among pirates. How unlucky for you."

Dr. LeMeux wasted no time in replying, "My journey has not gone as expected, true. But, I would not account that it has been misfortune that has me in my current standings." He took a deep breath and continued, "Had I not been pressed by that company crew I would not have met Omibwe. I would have never been forced to summon the courage that it took to lead a mutiny against those awful slavers. If we had not crossed paths with you at sea, we would likely have died of thirst out on the open sea."

Lilith grew tired of the doctor's rambling. "Doctor, does this have a point? If you didn't notice, I am a little occupied."

Dr. LeMeux raised his hand back and rubbed at the back of his head, something Lilith had noticed he made a habit of when he was growing frustrated or fearful. "Captain Lilith, what if this happens to be another chance encounter of fate? They haven't fired their guns. Even after you have fired yours, their guns remain silent. Will you turn on them and open fire out of fear?"

Lilith turned her narrowed eye away from the pursuing ship and gave a hard look down to the doctor. "What would you have me do? Turn to and let them fire first?"

"Perhaps," Dr. LeMeux replied, "they will not fire at all."

Lilith hardened her look at the doctor. "Perhaps we turn toward them and hold our fire. What then? Am I supposed to trust that they will not send a volley against us, split our hull open and send us down to the depths. We are too far from shore for anyone to survive if that happens."

"They may not be hostile, captain." Dr. LeMeux gave Lilith a pleading look, "But a sure way to make sure they are, is to open fire."

Lilith gritted her teeth and looked over the closing sea gap between the Maiden and the pursuing ship with its crimson red sails. Chibs was convinced they were being chased down by enemy so dreadful that he wanted to run. The doctor proposed that they turned toward the ship and hold their fire. Lilith pondered her options, which were quickly becoming fewer and fewer as the pursuing ship drew near. If she waited too long to make her turn, the pursuing ship would be able to maneuver as well and may retain their upwind advantage. If she turned too soon, she may force an engagement that Dr. LeMeux was convinced may not be inevitable. Lilith flexed her grasp on her cutlass. She turned to begin issuing orders to the

Maiden's crew when a thunderous roll of cannon shots exploded out from the pursuing ship's batteries. Every member of the Maiden's crew paused to take in the shocking sight as cannon smoke rolled away from the crimson sailed ship and curled in the sea breeze. The ship had just fired all of their guns out in a harmless arc over the Caribbean.

Chibs hurried his way through a web of rigging and crew to get to his captain's side. Lilith exchanged a confused look with him before the two of them both looked out over the sea gap and took in the sight of the crimson sails slacking to let their hold on the wind go.

"What in blazes are they doing?" Chibs uttered through a wisp of pipe smoke. "What madness is this?"

Dr. LeMeux beamed with a smile and leaned against the stern rail where Lilith stood. "They are calling for a parlay."

Lilith shot a glance at the French doctor and then one at Chibs. "It's a trap. It must be."

Chibs swayed his pipe from one side of his mouth to the other. "I hate to admit it cap'n, but the Frenchman is right. They've discharged their guns. Whatever their intentions. It would seem they wish to lead with words. If we turned to now, they won't have time to reload and make ready to fire."

Lilith took stock of what the doctor and her quartermaster had to say. She didn't want to risk leaving her ship vulnerable to a trap. But Chibs agreeing with Dr. LeMeux was significant. Too significant to disregard. She tightened her grip on her cutlass handle. "Hard a larboard! Gun crews stay ready! Lay us up alongside her in range of pistol shot and prepare to repel borders." Lilith turned to Chibs, her hand flexing on the grip of her sword. "If you two are wrong, God help us."

Chibs puffed a lungful of pipe smoke into the sea breeze and let his hand fall to his own sword, "If we are wrong, cap'n, I will be the first to draw my blade and defend her."

Chapter 15

'Batard De Mur'
12 May 1809
17 Degrees 40' N, 76 Degrees 26' W

A line of sweat formed around Captain Fontaine's collar. The warm wind was carrying a thick humidity and a front of burly dark clouds from the north. They were in for a storm when the sun went down, if not before.

The ship he had pursued through most of the day had fired two lonely rounds from their chase guns on the stern. But since their shots had splashed into the Caribbean there had been no following fire. Even when Batard De Mur was well within range, her guns remained silent. Captain Fontaine ground his teeth. Could it be? After all this time? When he had last seen Philip, his boyhood friend had seen him off before his long journey to the Caribbean. Captain Fontaine took in a deep breath and let his mind slip from the muggy sea air whipping at his face. He remembered Philip's face as it had been that day. His friend had wanted to join him on his adventure across the ocean, but Philip's father had other designs.

Laurent and Philip had been fast friends since early boyhood. Philip, the son of a doctor, belonged to a family of well-known scholars who had descended from a storied line of French nobility. His name preceded him in every room he had ever walked into. Laurent however, was the son of a common man with a common name. His father had provided a humble living as a carpenter. The pairing of the two young boys had been a constant source of frustration and disdain to Philip's father who believed the association to be an embarrassment. When the two young men grew closer as time went by, young Philip's father continued to discourage the friendship. When it became apparent that the two boys would be impossible to separate, Philip's father devised and implemented a plan with the help of a wealthy merchant fleet owner. Laurent was offered a position on a trading ship sailing for the Americas, an attractive offer to a young man from humble beginnings. On the very day the merchant ship was set to sail, Philip would be departing Brest for a very different endeavor, he would attend a prestigious school in Paris. In this fashion, the two young men had been effectively separated.

Their parting on the docks in Brest had been a torturous one. Philip said his goodbyes with a carriage waiting to usher him off to fulfill his father's wishes. Laurent had slipped away from his new crew just long enough for a few parting words before the shouts of an angry mate floated their way up the pier. In those parting moments, the two friends had agreed that they would someday reunite in the Caribbean. Laurent as a merchant sailor, hopefully owning his own ship by then. Philip, as a schooled physician. The two of them would then sail the world, Laurent as a captain and Philip as the ship's doctor. Their plans had fallen apart. First when Philip did not arrive in the Caribbean when his correspondence had said, and next when Laurent's encounter with the Order had altered his course through life so severely.

A gust of muggy wind fluttered the sails of the Drowned Maiden and snapped Captain Fontaine back to his senses. The ship was coming around for a tight turn with her gun ports open and rows of ugly cannon snouts protruding from her sides. Adrenaline laced his veins. She was coming about to fire.

"Fire all guns! Both sides!" Captain Fontaine cried out in alarm.

A sailor on deck shriveled his face, "But Captain, we haven't lined up with her yet."

Captain Fontaine seethed with anger. With a lightning fast draw he pulled his cutlass from its place on his belt and rammed the point toward his inquisitive crewman. "I gave an order. Now do it!"

A chorus of voices carried from the deck of

Batard De Mur, "fire the guns!"

The cannons erupted in a volley of roaring reports and thick clouds of smoke sending their projectiles out over the open sea to splash down harmlessly.

"Loose those sheets and spill the wind lads! Hold your fire and stay those blades!"

The inquisitive sailor took a stride toward Captain Fontaine. "Captain, have you gone mad? We are within striking distance of our prey!"

A flash of rage crossed Captain Fontaine. His vision seemed to sharpen, his fingers tingled as a hit of adrenaline soaked through his bloodstream. The cutlass in his hand came up with a flick of his wrist and a flash of sunlight glinted off of the blade. Captain Fontaine drove the point home into his challenger's midsection, just below his breastbone. The pirate grunted a little and let a guttural gasp of air loose. Captain Fontaine held the man close, he examined the pirates eyes as the last sparks of life faded behind a sheen death. He whispered to the dying man before wrenching his blade free and letting his victim collapse to the deck, "My ship. My crew. My orders, mate."

Captain Fontaine let his gaze wander over the faces of his remaining crew. A mixture of shock and fear painted their expressions. Wide eyes and slack jaws. "Loose the damn sheets and spill the wind! Don't make me repeat myself again!"

Resurrecting the Maiden

'Drowned Maiden'
12 May 1809
17 Degrees 40' N, 76 Degrees 26' W

A change in the wind came as the Drowned Maiden made a tight turn to face the ship flying crimson sails. It wasn't a change in direction but temperature. Lilith could feel it as she made her way along the larboard side, the muggy heat chilled giving rise to goosebumps along her arms and neck. Even though the temperature shift was a telling sign of incoming foul weather, she dared not avert her gaze from the decks of the ship that had been pursuing her. The slightest sign of provocation, the smallest hint of a trap could not be missed. If this ship with its red sails did have hostile intentions, she must not hesitate. She would order the batteries to open fire and keep her sails taut and full of wind. With any luck, they would score a hit against one of their adversary's masts and leave them helpless to maneuver. With Havana's Mistress turning right behind her, the two ships would be able to make a single pass and leave the pursuer dead in the water if it became necessary.

The decks of the ship with red sails were calm. Not a soul had moved once they spilled the wind from their sails. It was as if the crew were paralyzed, frozen in place like they were held by some nefarious spell. Lilith paced her way along the Maiden's battered rail as the winds grew colder all around her. She had hardly noticed the dark clouds that had gathered along the northern horizon and were creeping their way southward along her western flank. All Lilith could see was the decks of the ship with red sails.

"You there!" Chibs shouted across the sea gap as the Maiden completed her turn, "State your intentions!"

Lilith looked over the stern of the vessel. A blood-red flag flapped with the breeze displaying a pair of crossed swords in the center of its red field flanked on one side by an hourglass and on the other by three skulls. A chill ran up her spine. She scanned the deck as two ship's bowsprits passed each other. The opposing crew had gathered at the larboard rail of their ship, eyes locked onto her and her crew. The man she had seen earlier removed his large hat revealing his face from out of the shadow it had cast. He wore a black patch over one eye and sported a large mustache and goatee as black as coal.

"State your intentions or we'll send you to the depths!" Chibs shouted again from the Maiden's bow.

The man with the eye patch looked over his own crew and then cupped a hand next to his mouth to reply to Chibs, "We had intended to make you our prey!"

Lilith's blood tinged with a cold shock of adrenaline. Her mouth went dry and her hand tensed around the grip of her cutlass. She pulled the blade high, breathing in through her nose in preparation to give the command that would send a volley of cannon fire into the flanks of the opposing ship.

The man with the eye patch waved his arms open wide, the large-brimmed hat in his hand flurried in the growing intensity of the wind. "You have someone aboard that I recognize. A dear friend of mine." The man paused for a long moment before continuing, "Philip! Where are you? I know it was you I saw, come out and greet your old friend."

Lilith looked over the deck of the Maiden, searching for the French doctor while her heartbeat against her ribs so hard she thought it might pound its way right out of her chest.

Dr. LeMeux pressed his way through the crew that had crowded against the larboard rail of the Maiden. "Who are you?" He shouted, "How do you know my name?"

Lilith found herself passing her gaze between the man with the eye patch and her ship's doctor, until she saw a streak of recognition paint its way across Dr. LeMeux's face.

"Laurent?" the doctor paused for a moment and then shouted louder, "Is that you? How could it be?"

The man with the eye patch made a broad gesture with his hat before replacing it onto his head. The hat brim flopped in the wind which was now whipping at the surface of the sea and making white caps along the tops of choppy waves. "It is."

Dr. LeMeux leaned his torso over the rail, "What happened to you my friend? You came to the Caribbean to be a merchant sailor!"

Laurent cupped his hand around the side of his mouth and yelled back, "And you were to come and be my ship's doctor! It seems you have found another crew to sail with!"

Lilith narrowed her one good eye and watched the doctor form his response. He looked at Lilith and Chibs and then called back to his friend, "It seems fate has directed me to where I am now. These are good people Laurent, they mean you no harm as long as you are mutually agreeable to such terms!"

Laurent hoisted himself onto the rail of his ship with a stay line in one hand, "I was sent by the Order to kill the girl captain and send the ship you sail on to the bottom!" He lowered his head as a sprinkling of rain began. "But the Order can piss off! I came to the Caribbean to sail a lawful merchant ship, and they have made a criminal of me."

Lilith breathed a sigh of relief. She felt the weight of tension lift from her shoulders. There would be no fight between the vessels.

Dr. LeMeux climbed onto the larboard rail and clung to a stay line with both hands, something he had never done before. "Laurent, my friend, sail with us! Help us bring justice to these crooks!"

Laurent held his saber up as a bolt of lightning

tore across the darkening sky. "I am not interested in justice, only revenge!"

Lilith smiled as she heard the sentiment. The Maiden, it seemed, had found an ally.

"Captain!" Jilhal's voice carried down through the rigging and the wind, "Ship on the horizon to the north! A ship with big sails and she's headed our way!"

'H.M.S North Wind'
12 May 1809
17 Degrees 43' N, 76 Degrees 25' W

North Wind's canvas was taut as the rains came whipping behind her. Full sails and full stores had propelled the ship and her crew along on their hunt for any hostile that posed a threat to British supremacy of the waves. Lieutenant William Pike kept a close watch on the helm, especially with the rising foul weather. Having completed a circuit of the coasts of Jamaica , his next course would take him south toward common lanes of sail traffic where he suspected pirates may be lurking in search of prey. After a week of near insufferably hot weather the storm was welcome relief for North Wind's crew. Sailors gathered on deck and took in the rain, letting raindrops fall on their bare chests and faces and dribble down their sun burned arms and legs. The winds were strong but manageable and Will had ordered full sails to take advantage of the speed boon. The crew's spirits seemed high with the refreshing wind and rain only adding to their morale. It seemed even the occasional split of lightning across the sky wouldn't damper their attitudes.

Pacing his way toward the bow, Will grinned at the Sailors enjoying their respite from the brutal Caribbean sun. Rain dripped on his shoulders and off of the brim of his hat while the spray of the sea intensified. The decks were slick with the rain as he plodded his way past rat lines and ropes coiled into neat formations. A memory struck him of a walk he had taken on the deck of H.M.S Valor with Captain Grimes. Will fought a rush of emotion as he thought of his former commander and the way he had perished. He fought it until his very last. North Wind's deck did not heave and pitch as much as the Valor had. She was a considerably bigger ship. But the seas were rising. Will looked high into the rigging and judged that the masts and stays would hold the force exerted on them just fine. The extra speed would hurry North Wind on her way south, where he hoped to find something he could engage with and report back to the admiral.

Amidships, the leadsman was working his line and reporting to the watch officer. "Eleven knots!" he shouted as the wind picked up a little more strength. Will smiled and looked aloft again. The sheets were taut, and the canvas was full with little dribbles of rain pouring off of the corners of each sail. He traced his eyes along the stay lines and up the masts where top men worked their way across spars in preparation to make any sail adjustments he may require. Lookouts posted high above the deck were diligently focused on the surrounding horizons. It was almost dream like. Something he had fantasized about for years. To be in command of a ship of the line with a first-rate crew on a mission to search out an enemy vessel. Will drew in a deep breath of the sea air and continued his walk forward to the bow.

"Sail ho! Southern horizon, two points off the starboard bow!" the lookouts voice barely carried through the driving wind and rain.

A moment elapsed and Will tried to focus his eyes through the haze of foul weather. He could see waves, but no sails.

"Another set of sails! She appears to be sailing with the first vessel!" the lookout cried down.

An edge of alarm bit at Will's nerves. He felt the scars on his back and ribs tighten as another gust of rain-soaked wind heaved against him. He was blind to the scene that the lookout sighted. A hundred questions rattled through his brain. Who could it be? Were they hostile? Is there more than two? What class of ship did they look to be? Are they flying any colors? His eyes scanned the waves in front of North Wind, as if by looking harder He could pry focus through the rising and falling seas and determine the answers to his questions himself.

In between rolling waves, Will caught a glimpse of the spotted sails. It was hard to see through the haze of rainfall and windblown seas, but a pair of ships were sailing north by northwest. Another edge bit into Will's nerves. He felt the scar tissue on his back grow hot even as he was being soaked through by chilled rains. One of the ships was large enough to be a frigate. He turned skyward to call up to North Wind's lookouts.

"What class of ship be they?" Will asked in a hoarse shout.

A moment elapsed as the lookouts studied the distant vessels. In between driving gusts of wind, the forward lookout called down, "One is a frigate, I believe. Three masts." He stopped for a moment and studied the horizon again before calling back, "The other looks to be a brigantine. Two masts."

Will faced outboard and tried to catch another look in between the rising waves. He looked back up to the rigging and called to his lookouts, "Are they flying colors?"

The lookouts all studied the horizon with intense stares as North Wind's decks began to shift and sway more heavily with the growing seas. Will held his breath as he waited for the answer. Rain drops stung his face as the wind drove them at a hard angle. He squinted against the driving wind and watched while the forward lookout's face drooped in an expression of shock and fear. The lookout looped his arm around a line high up on the foremast and used both hands to cup around the sides of his mouth.

"Lieutenant! They are flying black flags, sir!" the

lookout shouted before turning back to look at the horizon for a moment. After a long pause, he looked back down toward the deck and shouted again. "And there's another ship! Three ships! The third one is flying red sails and a red flag!"

Will's blood turned as cold as the rain driving against the soaked deck boards beneath his feet. He turned outboard for a moment. Three ships. All hostile. North Wind had the weather gauge, and the advantage of firepower. But he was only manned to run two batteries at a a time. The massive line ship wouldn't be able to outmaneuver a frigate. And if she was sailing in concert with two other ships, their combined manpower might be enough to overwhelm his crew should they be boarded. His stomach tied in knots. The scars on his back and ribs grew hotter, almost as if the wounds had been reopened. He had put to sea in hopes of finding an engagement that would keep him in Admiral Torren's good graces. A three on one battle was not exactly what he had in mind. If North Wind survived this encounter, it would only be by her superior class and the sharpness of his wits. A black flag was foreboding enough, but any vessel brazen enough to fly a red banner would certainly not hesitate to engage, regardless of the size of his ship.

"Master at arms!" Will called back across North Wind's deck, "Beat to quarters!"

In moments a drummer began rattling away tattoo as the crew frenzied to get to their assigned battle quarters. The wooden clunk of gun ports opening echoed off of the waves below North Wind and met Will's ears on deck. He withdrew a collapsing telescope from his coat and extended the instrument. As a North Wind crested a wave, he held the telescope to his eye. It took only a fraction of a second for him to find focus. He could make out the brigantine plainly, it was the closest vessel to North Wind, sailing about four cable lengths off of the larger ship's starboard rail. The biggest of the three ships was a frigate, or at one time had been. Will marveled at the look of her for a moment. She was ragged. Her hull looked to have been recently repaired with timbers that mismatched the discoloration of the others. Her sails appeared to be mended in several places, some of the large patches were so discolored it looked like they had been stained by smoke.

Will withdrew the instrument from his eye as another wave obscured his line of sight. He flexed his jaw and silently cursed his luck. *I go looking for a hostile ship and find myself facing three, damn the luck.* He thought of his late commander for a moment. Captain Grimes had once faced down three enemy vessels aboard H.M.S Valor. If he could do it, so could Will.

With a sharp turn, Will moved toward the quarterdeck with his telescope in hand. "Helm, come about two points starboard and make your heading for the last sighting of those ships!"

"Aye, aye sir!" The helmsman barked back

through the blustering wind.

Will turned toward his Master at arms and tipped his chin skyward toward the rigging, "Sergeant, as many sharpshooters in the tops as you can muster, smartly."

"Aye aye, sir!" the marine sergeant snapped to and began directing his men to their stations.

Will made his way behind the helm and stood at the starboard rail as North Wind was about to crest another wave. Behind him a flurry of activity continued as the crew made ready for battle. He extended his telescope and peered through it in the direction of the enemy sails as they came into view. They were closer this time. Much closer than Will had anticipated. All three vessels were continuing their course north by northwest. His present course would intercept them amidships and allow him to turn hard a larboard, opening his starboard battery to a full broadside that, with any luck, would field effective fire over two of the three vessels.

He scoured the ships for anything he could use. Any sign of weakness. The ship with red sails trailed the largest of the three about two cable lengths off of her larboard stern. Will found her banner and studied it for a moment.

"Lieutenant Brant!" he shouted over his shoulder, "Go below and find the log of known pirate flags. See if you can find record of a flag on a red field with two crossed sabers in the middle flanked by an hourglass and what looks like to be three skulls."

"Aye, sir!" Lieutenant Brant gave Will a sharp nod as he turned to and hurried off the deck to complete his task.

As Lieutenant Brant shuffled away, an experienced looking sailor passed close to him, almost butting his shoulder into the young officer.

"Red flag you say?" the sailor asked as he leaned forward and looked over the railing next to Will.

Will frowned in bewilderment at the seasoned sailor's conduct. "Yes. It appears to be so."

The sailor turned his eyes back toward Will in a hard gaze and wrinkled his brows into a deep frown, "Crossed swords with an hourglass and skulls? You don't need to look that up in a book. That is the Bastard of the Sea, the French red terror. I've heard her captain is a cannibal and she is crewed by a tribe of freed slaves and savage natives from the depths of the rainforests!"

Will frowned at the old sailor for a a moment, unsure whether to listen to the man or have him locked away in a cell so he couldn't spread a frenzy amongst the crew. "Go on." He said.

"She's the terror of every lawful merchantman sailing these waters. I've heard she's been at large longer than the Teach and Vane in their day. That's a hard crew to be lining up against, sir. And there are three of them!"

Will shifted his gaze from the fearful sailor to the other crewmen on deck. Memories of how quickly the sentiment of a crew could turn came to him. He braced one hand against the ship's wooden railing.

"She may be a red terror, but we are on the finest ship in the Royal Navy! And this is the finest crew I could hope to go into battle next to. We will close with them and demand their surrender. If they do not strike their colors, we will open fire and send all three ships down to the depths." He looked about to find all eyes on deck were locked on him. "Do we not have the wind in our favor? Do we not have a considerable firepower advantage? Steel yourselves men! We are not turning from this fight!"

With that, Will looked over starboard rail and saw that his line of sight with the ships was open again after a wave subsided behind North Wind. The ships were drawing close to cannon range. He turned toward the midshipman standing watch and shouted through the driving wind and rain, "Gun one, maximum elevation, fire when ready. Let's get their range, shall we?"

"Lieutenant! They are coming about!" One of the lookouts cried down from the rigging, "And their gun ports are open!"

Will turned back outboard to find the waves parted between North Wind and her foes. Just as the lookout had said, they were turning to, with all gun ports open. The heavy winds would give their ships a natural list, artificially increasing the elevation of their guns. *Damn the luck, I didn't see that coming either. The weather gauge is on my side, and they turn it against me.* Will opened his telescope and examined the largest of the three ships. She was indeed a frigate. Her hull was marred and pocked by action, with fresh timbers replacing what was undoubtedly the scars of a recent battle. One by one, her gun ports erupted with gray clouds of cannon smoke as her battery fired.

Will turned and screamed, "Cover! Take cover!" He dove to the rain-soaked deck as cannon shot whistled through the air with a piercing shrill howl. Overhead, one of North Wind's sails shuttered as a shot punched through the canvas. A stay line snapped and whipped violently through the air striking one of the top men. The force of the impact sent him falling of off the yard he had been perched on to the deck where he landed with a stomach turning thump. Will remained sprawled on the deck for only a moment before he sprang back to his feet. He leaned against the starboard rail and returned his telescope to his eye. The battle marked frigate kept her heading steady. Her guns were surely reloading.

"Starboard battery, prepare to fire!" Will barked over one shoulder.

Lieutenant Brant relayed the order below deck before turning back toward Will. "Sir, we haven't ranged them yet."

Will searched over the deck of the frigate, looking for signs that the ship would make a course correction. Without removing the telescope from his eye he replied to the younger officer, "We will overwhelm them with firepower. Have the larboard crew ready the starboard battery and the lower gun deck."

Will traced over the frigate, watching for signs of the next volley they would fire. Near the enemy's stern he caught a glimpse of something that twisted his stomach into knots.

"It cannot be." He said to himself.

"Sir?" Lieutenant Brant asked.

"I watched them sink in that cove. It cannot be them."

Through the haze of rain and wind and sea spray. Through the distance that separated them, he spied their banner. A skull with twisted horns on a black field, a canted trident and a shattered chain running across the bottom. Will let his telescope drop from his eye. *Damn the luck. But, how?* The gun ports of the Drowned Maiden erupted with bright flashes and clouds of smoke once again.

Thank you for reading this installment of
Treachery and Triumph
Be on the lookout for the next titles in the series.

Find my other book series, sign up for newsletter announcements including special releases and giveaways.
Just scan the QR code below.

Follow along on Facebook and Instagram for cover reveals and special announcements.

If you enjoyed this title, please be sure to leave a review on Amazon or Goodreads.

Made in the USA
Columbia, SC
24 January 2025